GHOUL GIRL

ALSO BY ELIZABETH K. KING

THE HORRIFIC FAIRY TALES SERIES
Rotting Beauty
Beast By Day
The Little Sea Monster
Seven Hexes
Ghoul Girl

Don't Go Into the Woods (novella)

GHOUL GIRL

HORRIFIC FAIRY TALES BOOK 5

ELIZABETH K. KING

GHOUL GIRL

Published in the United States by Elizabeth King. For inquiries, please visit the author's website: www.elizabethkking.com

Cover Art by Miblart.

Map by Saumya Singh (@Saumyasvision/Inkarnate).

The text for this book was set in EB Garamond.

ISBN 979-8-9987153-3-4 (hardcover)

ISBN 979-8-9987153-4-1 (paperback)

ISBN 979-8-9987153-2-7 (ebook)

First Edition, April 2026.

For anyone who's ever believed they only have one destiny.

You don't.

Contents

Author's Note

As this is the fifth book in the series, the story contains references to characters, places, events, and elements from the previous four books. In the back of this book, you will find a glossary that may be helpful if you are having trouble remembering some of these elements.

The glossary is spoiler-free for *Ghoul Girl*. It is intended that you can reference it from the very first chapter of this book without being spoiled for anything later in the story. However, it will contain spoilers for the first four books: *Rotting Beauty*, *Beast By Day*, *The Little Sea Monster*, and *Seven Hexes*.

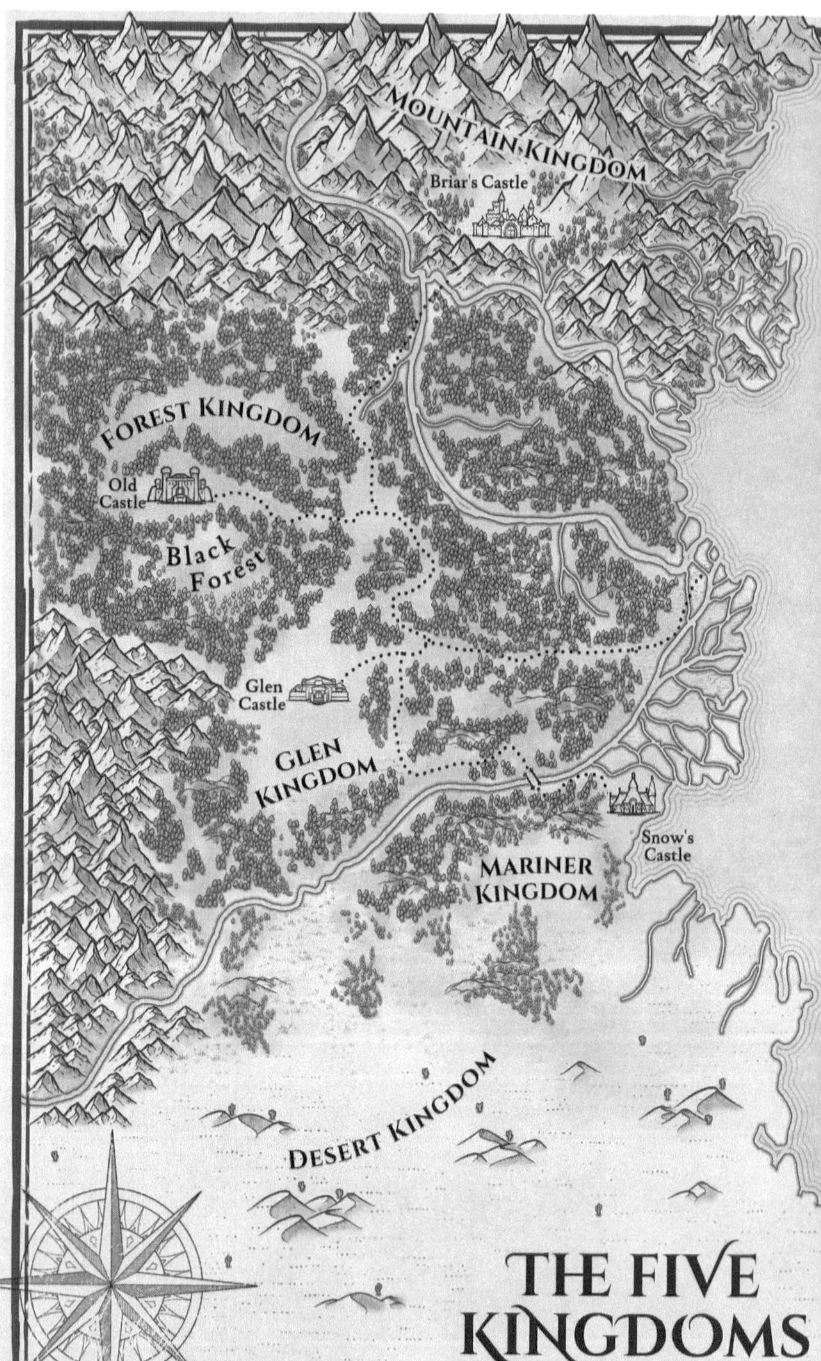

MOUNTAIN KINGDOM
Briar's Castle
FOREST KINGDOM
Old Castle
Black Forest
Glen Castle
GLEN KINGDOM
MARINER KINGDOM
Snow's Castle
DESERT KINGDOM
THE FIVE KINGDOMS

PROLOGUE

THE PRINCESS RAN THROUGH the dark forest, trees rising around her like silent, forbidding sentries. Tangles of bramble snagged at her ankles, and low-hanging branches sliced through her skin. But she didn't slow down. She didn't stop. Because if she did, it would mean the end for her.

It would mean being devoured. It would mean annihilation.

So she ran and didn't stop running.

The moon was fat overhead, bursting with luminous brilliance. The princess cursed that misfortune. She should have fled days ago under the cover of a darker night, but she would have had too far to run. She knew—had always known—that she wouldn't get far. She wasn't fast enough, strong enough, or clever enough to make it on her own. That had been drilled into her for her entire existence.

Her only chance was to reach Glen City before anyone caught up to her. That was the other reason she couldn't run before today: she didn't know how to get to Glen City. She didn't know how to read a map or use a compass or...whatever else people did to figure out how to get somewhere. But this morning, she'd overheard some of the servants in her delegation talking, saying they should reach the city tomorrow. Which meant a smaller traveling party—say, one girl on her own—could probably reach it sooner. It took only a little sleuthing on her part to discover the way forward was a straight route down the main road they were traveling. She stayed off the road now for better cover, but she kept it in sight, stopping now and then to check she was going in the right direction.

Catching herself around a stout oak tree, the princess stopped and heaved a breath. Her chest burned, her legs throbbed, and her stomach roiled. She was going to be sick, she thought. She'd never run so fast and so far in her entire life.

The darkness was suffocating, a manifestation of her fear. It wasn't the dark itself that scared her—it was what lurked in the dark. What might hide in the shadows, just out of sight.

A light wind blew through the forest, something creaking overhead. The princess jumped, but it was only a nearby tree, its spindly limbs swaying in the breeze. Heart thumping wildly, the princess staggered away, pushing off from her tree. Its rough bark scraped her palm, leaving the skin raw.

She pushed through the trees more carefully now, looking for the road. It shouldn't be far, unless she'd veered off in the wrong direction. Her thick, frazzled hair caught on a thorny bush, and she cursed, wincing as she pulled it free. She'd changed into practical clothing before sneaking away from her retinue, but she hadn't thought to tie her hair back. So stupid.

Everyone was right about her. She was an idiot.

But you don't have to get far, she reminded herself. *Just to Glen City. Then the king and his son will help you.* Or so she hoped. Not only had she never met King Victor or his son, the crown prince, but she knew very little about them. Still, she wasn't coming to the king empty-handed. She was going to warn him. There was danger coming to the Glen Kingdom, and King Victor had no idea. Surely he would be grateful for the information the princess had. Grateful enough to help her, to protect her. Or perhaps he would be so angry, he would throw her in a dungeon. That was just as likely.

But the king was her only chance at safety. She had nowhere else to turn.

The wooded land rose sharply just ahead. The princess forced her legs to move faster, breaking into a jog as she crested the hill. She stumbled again, tripping over the jut of a stone half-buried beneath the earth, barely catching herself as she lurched forward.

Right out onto the road.

The princess gulped. She hadn't realized the road was *this* close. It was as though she'd stepped through a hole in the world, from one realm into another, tangled woodland suddenly becoming paved road. She was so startled, she nearly darted back into a cluster of prickly bushes.

But a noise caught her attention. A sort of *clop-thud-clop-thud*, loud and clear in the darkness. The princess flinched, instinctively ducking her head, trying to make herself small. Trying to blend into the shadows. But then she realized what the sound was.

A horse and carriage. Or something like it. And it was just ahead of her on the road.

The princess hesitated. It was probably wiser to stick to the woods, to stay on her own. But her exhausted legs quivered uncontrollably, and her chest and throat felt like they were on fire. If she continued on foot, she might never make it to the city.

She made the decision in a split-second. Then she hurried down the road.

As she grew closer to the vehicle, she made out its shape in the darkness by the glimmer of two lanterns, the bright lights bobbing back and forth with each step of the horse. It was not a carriage but a small cart, carrying a load. As she jogged after the cart, the princess called, "Wait! You there! Cart driver! Wait! Wait!"

The cart jangled to a halt, the loud huff of a horse audible in the near-darkness. Relief flooded through the princess so strongly that it gave her a jolt of energy, and she picked up her pace, dashing forward to make up the distance. The cart was not large, its bed filled with wooden crates. At the very back of the cart, legs swinging off the edge, perched a boy. The cart's two lanterns were hung on poles up front, so the boy was cast in shadow, his features obscured. The princess eyed him warily as she circled the cart, coming to the front where a driver sat, loosely holding the reins of a single horse.

The driver did not climb down from his seat, but he peered at the princess, his expression kind. "Are you all right there, 1—miss?" he asked, changing his word at the last minute. He'd probably taken her for a boy instead of a lady. He certainly wouldn't recognize her for a princess, garbed as she was, in rumpled brown breeches and a simple, baggy white shirt.

The driver cast a puzzled look down the road. "Where've you come from? Is something wrong? Do you need help?"

The princess licked her lips. "I'm all right." She tried to make her squeaking voice sound calm and assured. "I just—I wondered whether—I might have a ride? Are you going to Glen City?"

"That I am." The driver smiled, and she tried to smile back. "It's not much further up the road here, but I don't blame you wanting a ride so late at night. Have you got a name?"

"I'm—Lena. My name is Lena."

"Well, Miss Lena, hop into the back with the lad there. Won't be the most comfortable seat, but as I say, we've not got far to go."

The princess—Lena, now—managed another, less tremulous smile. "Thank you," she said and was very proud her voice didn't shake. She walked to the back of the cart, trying not to feel apprehensive of this boy she was to sit with. There was nothing particularly menacing about him, aside from the fact that she couldn't see him very well. Now, as she struggled to climb into the cart bed, the boy said nothing, nor did he make any move to help her. She managed to hoist herself into the cart none-too-gracefully, nearly sprawling into the stacked crates.

"All right back there?" the driver called cheerfully. "Ready to go?"

Lena cleared her throat. "Ready."

A moment later, the horse started up again, and the cart jolted down the road. Flushing, Lena righted herself beside the boy, her legs dangling off the cart next to his. Running her fingers through her matted hair, Lena eyed the boy sidelong. Now that her eyes had adjusted to the dim light, she could see him better. Though the brim of his cap still obscured his face.

"Hello," Lena ventured, wondering if the boy would ignore her outright.

The boy gave a start before turning to look at her, and Lena wondered if he'd been asleep all this time. Or perhaps he was just shy. "Hello," he said. "Going to the city too?"

"If you mean Glen City, then yes."

The boy shrugged. "No other cities 'round these parts."

Lena felt her flush return. "I'm sorry. I'm not very familiar with—with this part of the country." She'd nearly said, *"with this kingdom,"* but that answer would invite questions about what kingdom she was from. And she didn't want to answer those questions.

The boy looked at her more directly. Taking her in. His gaze was frank but not leering or improper. "Farm girl?"

Lena forced a smile. "How did you guess?"

The boy answered with another shrug.

"And you?" Lena followed up. It was only polite, and besides, the conversation kept her nerves at bay. Kept her from staring into the dark woods, kept her from jumping at every shadow. "What supplies are you and your—erm—master bringing to the city?" She stumbled over the word *master*, wondering if it was the right term. She really had no idea how hierarchy worked among the lower classes, in any kingdom.

Lena thought the look the boy shifted her way was resentful. Perhaps she had used the wrong word. But he only said, "Perishable goods, mostly. From our orchard. Apples, pears, plums. Some jam too."

Lena tried to look as though she found this information interesting. She was casting around for a follow-up question—what was there to ask after when it came to jam, anyway?—but before she could think of anything, there was a terrible *clank!* The cart gave a violent lurch, and Lena gasped, flinging out a hand to keep herself from pitching off the cart. "What was that?"

The boy, who had also managed to keep his seat, peered around. "Jammed axle, it looks like."

"You two all right back there?" the driver called.

"Yes." Lena half-slipped, half-jumped off the cart. "What happened?"

The driver smoothed a hand down the horse's neck, patting it gently. Trying to calm it, Lena guessed, for the horse was wild-eyed, stamping its hooves and whinnying softly. "Not sure," said the driver. "Some damage to the wheel, sounded like." He smiled at her, the lantern light slanting down across his face. "You sure you're all right? And the boy?"

"I'm fine." Lena turned to look for the boy. Coming around the back of the cart, she asked, "You're all right, aren't—"

She broke off.

The boy was gone.

Perplexed, Lena stared at the empty cart bed. Well, all the crates were still there. But not the boy. Lena glanced left and right, into the woods, back down the road, but there was no one.

The boy was just gone.

Lena swallowed. A nasty feeling grew in the pit of her stomach. Turning back to the driver, she said, "Erm—he's gone."

"Sorry?" the driver called. He had left the horse and now bent beside the cast-iron wheel, fiddling with it. His stout form cast a long, lumpy shadow behind him in the stretch of light pouring from the twin lanterns. "What's that?"

"He's gone." Lena pitched her voice a little louder. "Your boy. He just—"

"My boy?" The driver straightened with a quizzical frown. "You mean the boy riding back there with you? He's not my boy. Just another young 'un needing a lift into the city."

Lena's mouth went dry. "He doesn't work for you?" The disquiet inside her grew into a yawning pit of alarm. "But—"

She didn't get a chance to finish.

A pair of snakelike arms materialized from the shadow behind the driver, wrapped themselves around his neck, and twisted. There was a sickening snap, and the driver fell to the road in a lifeless heap. His neck was wound about at an impossible angle, skin sagging from chin to collarbone like it was made of rubber.

Lena screamed.

The shadow grinned at her. White teeth in the darkness, bodiless and maniacal. "Hello, princess."

Lena spun and ran, plunging into the forest.

She tore through the woods. There was no thought in her head, not a single one. There was only mindless, instinctual fear, like that of a rabbit fleeing a wolf. Her boot skidded over a mossy stone, and she tripped, her ankle twisting, but she didn't even feel the pain as she staggered to her feet and kept running. She had to get away, had to keep moving—

Something tackled her from the side, a solid, heavy weight. She crashed to the forest floor face-first. Pain registered as a hard, knobby root made contact with her forehead, its pitted surface catching the corner of her eye. But again, fear surmounted the pain, driving it out. Lena scrabbled blindly against the ground, but that heavy weight pinned her down. Then it flipped her over, and Lena found herself staring into a face.

It was the face of the boy, the one who had ridden in the cart beside her.

The boy straddled her ribcage, putting so much pressure on her chest, she could barely breathe. He grasped her by the wrists. "Dear, sweet princess. Did you really think you could escape us?"

"I—I'm—to be the r-ruler," Lena whimpered, barely getting the words out, "of the Desert King—Kingdom—s-so you had better—let me go—"

"The ruler of the Desert Kingdom!" The boy threw back his head and let out a howl of laughter. "Is that what you think? Still, after *this?*" He leered down at her. "Not anymore, dear princess. You chose a new fate when you decided to run tonight. And I get the pleasure of delivering that fate to you."

The boy's grip tightened. Lena tried to scream, but she couldn't make a sound. The boy lowered his head towards her.

Then the pain came, and it was suddenly, searingly brighter than anything the princess had felt before. Pain she couldn't ignore, pain her fear couldn't drive out. They were one now, her fear and her pain, mingling together.

She screamed and didn't stop screaming.

1

DOUBLE

GEMMA WAS ALMOST HALFWAY home when she heard the scream. It was a thin, distant sound, distant enough that, had Gemma been someone else—someone living a different kind of life—she might have decided she'd just imagined it.

But Gemma was a hunter and a tracker. Gemma was a soldier. Gemma served a prince who regularly went out looking for monsters. Gemma knew a scream when she heard one, no matter how distant it was.

She stopped in her tracks, staring ahead into a line of peeling hickory trees and dark, verdant pines. She was making her way along a winding dirt path that led out of Glen City proper and back to the castle. It was not the most direct route, but it was the shortest. It led through a stretch of dense woodland—a large copse, really, not a proper forest—that most people would avoid this late at night.

But Gemma had lived in the woods for most of her life, until a couple of years ago, when she'd joined the ranks of the Glen Kingdom Royal Army. And she still felt more at home among the trees than anywhere more "civilized." She wasn't afraid of the woods at night. There wasn't much to be afraid of. Wolves were native to these woods, but this close to the city, they were rare. And bears were unheard of in these lowlands.

Which was why Gemma was so startled to hear that scream. Narrowing her eyes, she rotated on the spot. The scream hadn't come from the copse she was headed into but from the vast woods to the east. The *real* woods.

Gemma let out a long, low breath, going loose and alert at the same time. Relaxing her body, letting go of distracting worries or irrelevant tension. Honing in on what she could hear. Listening for another sound, another scream.

She didn't hear another scream. Instead, she heard the barest *scrape* against the pebbly path behind her.

Gemma released another breath, silent and controlled. Then she drew her pistol and spun.

"Whoa." The young man on the path before her raised his hands. But there was no alarm on his scarred face. "I would say, 'Don't shoot,' but you really can't, can you?"

Gemma repressed a flinch. "Klaus," she growled.

"I'm just saying." Klaus—fellow soldier and fellow woodsman—lowered his arms. "Why even carry that thing? You should be reaching for your knife."

Gemma seethed. Because Klaus was right. It was still her instinct to reach for a firearm, though her hunting knife was the better bet. That had been the way of things, ever since an evil witch had caused a bleed in her brain that had damaged the sight in her right eye.

"What are you doing out here?" Klaus asked. "You left the tavern twenty minutes ago. I thought you'd be back at the barracks by now."

Gemma holstered her pistol. She and Klaus had both been at the same tavern with a number of their fellow guardsmen. Gemma left before most of them because she had an early shift tomorrow. "I heard something in the woods. Someone screamed."

"Are you sure?"

"I'm half-blind, Klaus, not deaf."

"Oh, come on." Klaus stepped forward, coming abreast of her. Despite his flippant tone, Gemma knew he was as alert as she was. His gaze was sharp. "You aren't half-blind. More like three-eighths blind, probably."

Gemma bit her lip, turning so Klaus couldn't see her face. It was true she hadn't completely lost the sight in her right eye; it had only been damaged. For weeks, she'd seen the world through a gauzy gray film bleaching everything of color, shadows crowding her vision and turning everything blurry, indistinct. Things like walking down the block or navigating a crowded room had become difficult, let alone shooting a target with any accuracy.

What Klaus didn't know—what no one knew—was that Gemma's sight had gradually improved over the last few weeks. In fact, at her last appointment in the barracks infirmary, her physician had assured her that her physical exam indicated her sight was just fine. She should be fully recovered, or very nearly.

But Gemma didn't trust this assessment. Which was why she hadn't told anyone.

So she said to Klaus, "That's why drawing my pistol was the right move. Because even with only five-eighths of my sight, I surely could hit you at five paces."

"But a kill shot? You'd hit me maybe."

"Maybe I don't want to kill you," Gemma said lightly. "Maybe I just want you screaming and bleeding."

"Ah, Gemma. That you want me at all touches my heart."

Before Gemma could retort, another scream broke the night. Klaus and Gemma both went silent. This scream was different than the one Gemma had heard before. It went on and on, echoing through the night, a raw, wretched, animalistic shriek of pain and terror.

When it finally stopped, Klaus swore. "That sounded like—"

"Someone being tortured," Gemma said.

"Yes." Klaus exhaled. "Check it out?"

"I think we'd better."

They left the path, crossing the scrubby field that separated the city's outskirts from the forest to the east. The main road from the city diverged a few miles into the woods, forming three separate routes that led south through the Glen Kingdom, east to the coast, and north through the thickest woods to the Mountain Kingdom beyond. In other words, it was a well-traveled route; even at this time of night, it was not unheard of for travelers and merchants to make their way into Glen City down the road.

"That delegation from the Desert Kingdom," Klaus said, as they approached the tree line at the edge of the forest, "they weren't arriving yet, were they?"

"No. Prince Garrett said they aren't expected to arrive for another couple of days." Still, Gemma thought, there was no telling how close they were. If they had made better time than expected. Which was one of the reasons they needed to investigate this disturbance. King Victor wouldn't be pleased if something attacked this foreign princess less than a league outside the city.

Klaus chuckled softly. "And how did Garrett sound when he mentioned this?"

"How do you think?" Gemma cast him a wry glance as they started into the woods, the foliage engulfing them as the treetops closed over their heads. "Everyone's on edge over this princess's visit. Even Prince Garrett."

"That's because he knows his father's trying to set him up with this princess."

"How do *you* know that?"

"Everyone knows it. I wonder Briar isn't getting testy too."

"She knows better." Briar, a Mountain Kingdom princess who'd left her homeland and taken up residence in Glen Castle, was the love of Garrett's life. "She knows Prince Garrett would never go for it, no matter what his father wants. Garrett would sooner run off with her and leave his title behind than marry someone else."

"And that doesn't bother you?" Klaus asked.

Gemma paused. It was a fair question. She was sure Klaus wasn't bothered about it. Not that he wasn't loyal to Garrett—but, well. Klaus had been a guard for less than a year. Before that, he'd served Prince Garrett's exiled brother, and before *that*, he'd lived on his own. A woodsman, like Gemma and her father. Gemma was sure it wouldn't trouble Klaus much to go back to that life.

For Gemma, that wasn't such an easy choice. Prince Garrett had handpicked her for his guard; she was more loyal to him than she had been to anything in her life. If he abandoned his title and ran off somewhere with Princess Briar...

Well. There was a time where she simply would have followed him wherever he went. She knew many other guardsmen would do the same. Now, though, after her injury…

She couldn't help but wonder if there was still a place for her at Prince Garrett's side.

They entered the forest at a northeast angle and reached the road quickly, emerging from beneath the forest canopy. The road was smoothly paved here and continued that way towards the east, though the northern and southern routes were older, rougher paths. Klaus lifted his rifle and clicked on the light attached to it, mounted below the barrel. The light was a recent addition, thanks to Princess Briar's inventive genius. "You know," Klaus said, sweeping the tiny bright light across the road, "I can check this out on my own. You can go back to the castle or into town. Get reinforcements."

"Do you think we need reinforcements?" Gemma asked coolly.

"Kind of hard to say, since we don't know who was screaming or why. I'm just saying, you could at least fetch a lantern or something."

"I'm fine, Klaus. I grew up out here, same as you."

"It's just." Klaus lowered his rifle as he turned towards her. Beneath his jagged scars—angry red slashes marking him from hairline to jawline—his pale face shone in the darkness. "I think we'd do better to split up here."

Gemma looked at him. His expression was carefully blank, no trace of concern there. Though they were soldiers in the same company, they could not have looked more different. They wore the same navy-blue uniform coat, but where Gemma's was neatly pressed, brass buttons gleaming, Klaus's was rumpled and unbuttoned, revealing his plain vest and the thin scarf wrapped around his neck to ward off the cold. His boots were scuffed, his leather belt worn, and a day's worth of stubble covered his chin.

Still, he was a good soldier, though Gemma would never tell him so. And right now, Gemma knew he was concerned about her, though he would never tell her so.

"So let's split up," she said. "No need to have a teary goodbye about it."

Klaus rolled his eyes. "Fine. You stick to the road, keep heading east. I'll scope out the woods over here." He tossed a nod towards the north side of the road.

They parted ways, Klaus vanishing into the trees. Gemma started up the road, sweeping her gaze from left to right. Despite what her physician said, Gemma was sure, from time to time, that hazy shadows still encroached on her vision. But out here, in the black of night, it didn't matter. That was one advantage Gemma had—growing up in the wilderness, her father had taught her how to maneuver in the dark. It wasn't that she could see in the dark better than any other person, but she knew how to use other senses to augment her sight, how to discern common shapes, sounds, and smells. And most importantly, how to relax and become comfortable in the darkness, as comfortable as anyone else was in the bright light of day.

Once she'd gone a couple hundred paces up the road, Gemma stopped and scanned her surroundings. One of her hands rested on her holstered pistol, and the other she flexed constantly. This was to keep her hand warm, keep the blood moving, so her fingers wouldn't stiffen in the cold. It was really, really cold. Far colder than it had any right to be. The spring equinox was two weeks away, and yet the chill of winter persisted. Just this morning, Gemma had woken to an icy sheen of frost coating the windows in the barracks.

The road was still and dark. The woods were quiet too. Gemma cocked her head to listen, not just for another scream but for anyone on the road. Clopping hoofbeats, squeaky carriage wheels, the scuff of booted footsteps. She scanned the skies through the treetops, looking for smoke, signs of campfires. But she saw nothing. Heard nothing. Smelled nothing. Nothing out of the ordinary.

Gemma watched her breath mist the air before her. Contemplated her next move. Klaus told her to stay on the road. But there was nothing to find here. And she wasn't going to stand around waiting for him. He said he'd search the north end of the woods.

So Gemma turned right, heading south through the trees.

She tread even more carefully over the forest floor, wary of roots sticking up from the earth and slick patches of dead leaves. Still, though the trees in these woods were aged and tall, most of their branches were bare, the weather too cold for any spring growth. And the moon overhead hung full and high in the sky, shedding light through the gaps in the trees. Enough light that Gemma could make out distinct shapes in the darkness.

She didn't have to go far before she heard it. Not another scream, but a faint mewling sound, like a wounded animal. It was a sound that made everything inside Gemma go still. Hand tightening on her holstered pistol, Gemma followed the noise until she came around a cluster of misshapen oak trees, their knobby limbs entwined together. Her chest was tight as she rounded the trees, as she prepared herself for what she might find. A mauled fox or badger, perhaps.

But it was not a fox or a badger.

It was something much bigger.

At first, that was all Gemma could see. That it was big. Her gaze caught on something white in the darkness, and as she ventured closer, she wondered if it was a wolf, perhaps a wolf with pale fur...

She reached the dying creature and stood over it. It was not a wolf.

It was a girl.

For a moment, all Gemma could do was stare. It was a *girl*, a young woman, garbed in a baggy white shirt. That was the paleness she'd seen, lit by the sheen of the moon. The girl's face was pale too, absolutely bloodless, and as Gemma fell to her knees, she realized that was because all the girl's blood was outside of her, staining the neck of her shirt.

The girl was still alive, but not, Gemma thought, for much longer. As her training kicked in, she assessed the damage clinically, though with a sinking feeling. Blood oozed from jagged wounds in the poor girl's neck and shoulder, drenching her collar and matting her dark hair. Gemma placed a hand over the worst of the wounds to staunch the bleeding, but she knew it was too late. The girl's flesh was shredded; even just in the time it would take Gemma to find Klaus, the girl would be dead.

Gemma met the girl's gaze. Her dark eyes were wide and fearful, her lips moving soundlessly as her body heaved. "It's all right," Gemma told her. Just for something to say. "It's going to be..." Gemma trailed off. She'd reached for the girl's hand only to realize there was nothing to hold. Her eyes traveled down the length of the girl's arm.

It ended in a bloody stump. As though something had chewed her hand off.

Gemma caught her breath.

And when she looked into the girl's face again, the girl was dead.

Gemma stared, the shock and ugliness of the moment making her strangely numb. Then she released her breath, a sting of regret piercing the numbness. She cursed quietly, rocking back on her heels. The shock and regret remained, but Gemma didn't sit too long in either emotion, ever the consummate professional. Questions flooded her mind. Who was this girl? What was she doing out here, all alone? And most importantly, what had done this to her? She supposed a wolf might have, a very desperate, hungry wolf. It certainly was not usual behavior.

One thing she was sure of. She'd found the source of all that screaming.

"Gemma? Gemma, can you hear me?"

Gemma cursed again. Klaus, calling for her from the road, by the sound of it. Gemma rose to her feet, strangely loathe to leave this girl, even though she was dead. Gemma cast a quick, searching glance around—something had attacked this girl after all, something that might still be here...

"Gemma!"

Swallowing hard, Gemma turned away.

When she reached the road, she didn't immediately see Klaus. The road looked empty. Then— "Gemma," said a voice, and Gemma turned to see Klaus emerge from the trees on the north side of the road. "I thought I told you to stay here." His tone was faintly aggrieved.

"Because I follow your orders," Gemma said, a little testier than she intended. She knew Klaus well enough to understand that if he sounded peeved with her, it was because he'd been worried. But she, too, was out of sorts, unnerved by what she'd discovered in the woods. She didn't have it in her to cater to his feelings right now. "What's happened? Did you find anything?"

Klaus gave a tense nod. "I thought I saw—something—a shadow in the trees." He shook his head. "Probably just a wolf. And then—"

Something moved in the woods behind Klaus. Bramble quivered, shadows shifted.

And a figure emerged from the darkness. A figure in white.

Gemma's hand went for her pistol, though she stopped short of drawing it. Something must have shown on her face, something alarming, because Klaus raised his arms, half-blocking the figure behind him. "Gemma. It's all right." He made a vague gesture. "This is...Princess Solena. Of the Desert Kingdom."

Gemma was sure she must have misheard him. "She's *who?*" What, by the Gift, was the Desert Kingdom princess doing out here at this hour, and with no one from her delegation anywhere in sight?

"Princess Solena." This time it was the figure herself who spoke. The princess. "Of the Desert Kingdom. I can speak for myself." Garbed in a long cream-colored gown, she looked like a wraith ghosting out from the trees. But as the princess stepped out from behind Klaus, Gemma saw she was a solid person, no ghost at all.

Except...

Gemma stared at the girl, and her stomach dropped. It was a horrid, plummeting sensation that swooped through her, leaving her unsteady and nauseous. Her hand instinctively tightened on the butt of her pistol.

Because as the young lady emerged from the gloom of the woods—as this *princess* joined them on the road—Gemma got a clear look at her beneath the light of the full moon.

It was the girl. The girl she'd found in the woods.

The dead, bloodstained, mangled girl she'd left in the woods.

Only, it couldn't be her. Gemma felt slightly dazed, her mind hazy like her damaged eye. Her gaze dropped to the princess's arm. It couldn't be her because she had both her hands. And she wasn't bleeding. There was no blood or dirt spotting her muslin gown.

Idiot, Gemma chided herself. It couldn't be her because this girl wasn't dead.

"Is there anyone else out here with you?" Gemma asked. More abruptly than was really proper for a guard addressing royalty. "Was there anyone else?"

Princess Solena looked quite peeved. "No. It's only me. And I will thank you not to—"

"Are you sure?" Gemma demanded.

Solena looked appalled at her temerity, daring to interrupt her. "Of course I'm sure. I think I would know if—"

But Gemma didn't hear anything else she said. Seized with sudden dread, she turned her back on the princess and ran, plunging into the trees.

She needed to get back to the girl she'd left. The dead girl.

"Gemma!" Klaus called after her. "Gemma, wait!"

But Gemma did not wait. She tore through the woods, back the way she'd come, uncharacteristically heedless of the noise she made crashing through the brush. It wasn't long before she was forced to slow her pace; it was too dark, too dense, and even in her agitated state, Gemma realized she was going to trip if she kept running. Moving at a crawling jog, she picked her way through the undergrowth, ducking and dodging prickly branches. Then—as she approached the spot where she'd left the dead girl—she slowed even further, coming to a halt.

But there was no dead girl.

The bloody corpse was gone.

Gemma inhaled, the cold night air burning her throat. Her eyes darted in every direction. Blinking, trying to dispel any film clouding her vision, she stood and stared, focusing on that specific spot where she'd left the dead girl. It was the same spot, she knew it was.

But there was nothing there. Only broken twigs and clumps of dead leaves.

As though the girl had never been there.

As though Gemma had imagined her.

Gemma dropped to her knees, just as she had before. Beside the dying girl. Cold mud dampened her trousers. She bent close to the ground, searching for anything, any sign that the girl had been there. Drops of blood, or a scrap of clothing caught on the brush. But there was nothing. The ground *was* disturbed, as though something had been through it, but that could have been anything.

Gemma's hand closed around a clod of soiled leaves, lifting them to her face. Looking for some clue. Even if, somehow, the girl's body had been moved—in the few minutes Gemma had been gone—there would be some trace of her here. There would have to be. There had been so much blood.

But Gemma found no blood on the leaves clutched between her fingers. Only mud. Trembling, Gemma opened her fist, letting the leaves fall back to the ground. The dying girl's bloodless, terrified face swam to the forefront of her mind, mouth gaping, eyes bulging. Gemma *had* seen her.

Hadn't she?

2

SURROGATE

GRYPHON LEANED HIS SHOULDER into the cold stone wall, hiding his nerves beneath a veneer of impatience. The alley where he waited was dark and smelled of burnt bread, thrown out from the tavern inside. Around the corner, a burst of cheerful talk and laughter sounded into the night as the tavern door opened. A handful of figures, indistinct silhouettes in the darkness, appeared at the end of the alley. Gryphon squinted, but he couldn't make out any details, couldn't make out their identities. It was too dark.

But—if he focused on his breathing, if he reached, carefully, for that storm inside him...

He called to the beast.

Only a little. His gums and nailbeds throbbed with pressure as his claws and fangs threatened to emerge. His skin itched, fur ready to sprout all over his body, and even his bones seemed to vibrate as they prepared to crack.

That didn't happen. But his eyesight *sharpened*.

The figures at the mouth of the alley came into focus. A man and three women. As he watched, two of the women broke away, vanishing down the main street with the man in tow. Leaving the last woman behind. Standing there. Facing him.

Gryphon knew her.

Isabelle stepped into the alley. Using the beast's night vision, Gryphon could make out more than just the burgundy traveling suit she wore. He could parse out the differentiating shades of her hair, rich chestnut brown spiraling into night-sky black. When she reached him, smiling, he let the storm go, releasing the beast. His vision returned to normal.

"Well?" he asked gruffly.

Isabelle looked amused. "He's arrived. You can go in."

Still more nervous than he liked, Gryphon tugged at the makeshift hood he'd attached to his overcoat. "I don't like this. It's far too public a meeting place. Anyone could see me here."

"Not anyone who's going to recognize you." Isabelle smoothed a reassuring hand down his chest. "Keep your hood up if it makes you feel better."

"Oh, yes, I'll just keep my hood up the entire time I'm talking to him," Gryphon grumbled. "That won't seem dodgy at all. I mean, a man concealing his face might not seem strange in a less reputable establishment, but of course, he had to choose this high-end pub."

"He chose this place because it has private booths in the back," Isabelle informed him, "which is where he's waiting. So hood or not, no one is going to see you once you're in there." She smiled again. "Just try to relax, Gryphon."

"Easy for you to say. You're not exiled from this entire kingdom. By the king. Who happens to be your father."

"Fair enough," Isabelle conceded.

"Are you sure you won't come in as well?"

"I'm going to visit with Briar. Apparently, she's in a dress shop two streets over."

"What dress shops are still open at this hour?"

"For a princess? All of them, I would imagine. Now. Are you going to stand out here all night, or are you going inside to see your brother?"

If the alley was as dark as the blackest night, the tavern's interior was as bright as midday. Gryphon had to blink a few times when he entered, allowing his eyes to adjust. Globe-like gear bulbs set in brass fixtures on the walls gleamed with white light, ringing the entire tavern. Gryphon yanked his hood so far forward that he could barely see, then made his way to the back where the private booths were set apart from the rest of the tavern, and from each other, with decorative floor-to-ceiling panels. As he stepped past the first panel, he pushed the hood back from his head—and was promptly tackled.

"*Oof*," he grunted.

"Gryphon!" his attacker exclaimed. Only, it wasn't an attacker. It was his brother, Garrett.

Who was hugging him.

Thankfully, it did not last long. As Garrett stepped back, Gryphon glowered. "What was that?"

Garrett had the grace to look a bit shamefaced, but it did not change him much. His green eyes sparkled, his fair face lit with that damned exuberance he never seemed to lose. "You're looking well." He gestured for Gryphon to join him in the first private booth, a long, varnished table with cushioned benches on either side.

"Oh, I suppose," Gryphon scoffed as he slid into the booth. "Given that I'm little more than a vagabond these days." He gestured towards Garrett, indicating his fine clothes—a posh black suit and a bronze-colored waistcoat, richer garb than Gryphon had seen him in the last time they'd met. "I'm not living in the lap of luxury, like yourself."

"Don't you live with Isabelle?" Garrett asked mildly. "In her big old manor?"

"*Old* is right."

"A manor that I procured for her—"

"So am I supposed to thank you?"

Garrett grinned. "Do you really miss it? Being a prince?"

Truthfully, Gryphon didn't. He had wondered—worried—that the bundle of nerves he'd been carrying inside him, ever since they'd stepped foot into the city, had been something more. That it had been that horrible yearning, his old deep-seated resentment for what he had lost. But now that he was here, safe—more or less—with his brother, the nerves were gone. There was no yearning, no resentment. The life he'd lived here was gone, and he didn't want it back. Not even a little.

"So what was so urgent?" Gryphon demanded, fiddling with the top clasp of his overcoat. It was stifling in here, a crackling fire in an enormous stone fireplace suffusing the booths with heat. "Your telegram said I needed to come at once."

"Well," Garrett said unnecessarily. In contrast to the overly bright main room, the gear-bulb fixtures back here were shaded, casting warm slashes of light over Garrett's face. He smiled his usual pleasant smile, but there was something weird about it, something forced. "Sure you don't want to order something first?" He gestured towards his own mug on the table between them.

"Garrett, I assume you asked me here for something important, not just for a friendly chat over a drink. So what is this all about?" Gryphon prodded. "Some new beast threatening the kingdom?"

"Funny you should mention beasts." Garrett drew his mug towards him and lifted it to his lips. "Since the last time I saw you, you were one."

It was true. The last time Gryphon had seen his brother, a year ago, was in an abandoned castle in the old Forest Kingdom, where he, Gryphon, had taken up residence. In point of fact, the last time they had seen each other was at the bonfire where those stupid villagers had tried to burn Gryphon at the stake. Gryphon had escaped that fate when he'd transformed into the beast, and Garrett had faced him down to keep him from slaughtering all the villagers.

Gryphon didn't remember that encounter. But though he never would have admitted it out loud, he was glad that some part of him, deep down, had recognized Garrett, even as the beast. And not killed him.

He would never admit it. But he loved his stupid, cheerful, annoying little brother.

"Yes, well." Gryphon flexed a hand. "I've got that under control now." *Mostly.*

"And Isabelle's all right, too? Not any more—ah—beastly than before?"

"Her beast form isn't like mine, if that's what you mean." Gryphon leaned back, shifting his long legs to the side so he could stretch them out without knocking into Garrett. His "little" brother was nearly as tall as he was. "It's only a partial form. Isabelle's fine. I'm fine. And you're fine, from the look of it, and your corpse princess, presumably, is fine—"

"She'll probably live forever, for all we know. Did you know she died and came back to life once?"

"We're all fine." Gryphon's tone went stony. "So why am I here, Garrett?"

"Well." Garrett took another long sip from his mug. "Look, Gryphon. The reason I asked you here—well, there's no beast or anything threatening the kingdom. But someone *is* coming here. Arriving any day now."

"Who?"

"A princess. From the Desert Kingdom."

"I didn't know the Desert Kingdom had any more princesses. Didn't they all die in some plague?" Years ago, from what Gryphon recalled. He'd only been a child. He didn't know much more than that. The Desert Kingdom was a long way from here, and it was twice the size of the Glen Kingdom. News from that part of the world was scarce.

"Evidently, one of the princesses survived," Garrett told him. "And they've kept her quite sheltered all these years, as she's the only one left to inherit the Desert throne. She's been sequestered in some keep on the far side of the kingdom."

"And she's traveled all the way here now because..."

"Well, I don't know whose idea it was—I mean, perhaps her people reached out first. But Father invited her to come and stay. For the spring season."

Suspicion arched through Gryphon. "Courting season."

"You noticed."

"I remember." Every spring or summer since Gryphon had turned eight, his father had invited some princess or young lady to stay at the castle. Hoping to make a match—a political match, of course, not a romantic one. "So Father is still trying to set you up with someone else." Someone besides Princess Briar.

"Yes." With a long-suffering expression, Garrett gazed out the window to the side of their booth. It was paned with frosted glass to ensure privacy, making the black night outside even more unfathomable. "He's so stubborn."

"I thought I told you to tell him to go to hell."

Garrett barked a laugh. "I did. Well, not in those words. And he seemed to drop it for a little while, but now..." He leaned forward, clasping his hands together over the gleaming tabletop. "He's not come right out and said he wants me to court this princess—I can't remember her name, Serena or Selana or something like that—but he's made enough pointed comments. And it's all so stupid. He *likes* Briar, Gryphon. His only hang-up is that she can't have children, and he's still obsessed with the idea of a blood-born heir."

"Medieval. Does he even know what century this is?"

"That's what I tell him!" Garrett rubbed a hand over his face. "But he won't listen."

"You could just adopt some orphan off the street," Gryphon said with a straight face. "That's basically what he did with you."

To Gryphon's disappointment, his brother did not react to this barb. He barely seemed to hear it. "Right. Yes. Exactly. Thank you." Garrett tipped him a nod. "The point is, I'm done putting up with it. I'm done making Briar put up with it. She says she doesn't care, and, well, she knows I'm not leaving her for anything. But we went through a bit of a rough patch over the holidays, and I'm just done. And so is Briar."

"So what are you going to do?"

Garrett fiddled with the bottom edge of his waistcoat. "We're leaving. Briar and I are leaving."

Gryphon gaped. "You're what?"

"Leaving."

"You're giving up your title?"

"Oh. No, I'm not going that far. We're just taking a little holiday. Far, far away from Glen City. And we're not coming back until after this princess has gone home. But I wouldn't give up my title." Garrett eyed Gryphon in a way that made Gryphon nervous. "Unless you want it back."

"You know I don't," Gryphon retorted. "Anyway, I don't have much of a say in that, do I? I've been disinherited and exiled."

"Yes, but if you weren't—"

"I still wouldn't want it."

Garrett wrapped both of his hands around his mug, staring into its contents. "I thought you might say that. And it's fine, really. But don't you think you and Father should talk? Sort things out between you? I mean, you should be able to step foot in the city. Come here and visit from time to time."

Gryphon gave a hollow laugh. He still remembered the look on his father's face when he'd caught him standing over Garrett's bed with a knife in the middle of the night. "I don't think that's going to happen."

"It could." There was something almost pleading in Garrett's tone. "I've spoken to him, you know. About you. I told him what really happened, that you weren't trying to kill me. And

Father—well, you know how stubborn he is—but I know he regrets it, Gryphon. Exiling you. I think he'd be willing to talk."

Gryphon pinched the bridge of his nose. It was a lot to take in, a lot to think about. His father maybe, *maybe*, willing to talk to him? Even if that was true, Gryphon wasn't sure he wanted that. Unless his father was going to outright apologize, Gryphon wasn't really interested in anything he had to say. And he had a hard time believing his father would ever apologize for anything.

Gryphon dropped his hand from his face. "What does this have to do with you and your princess leaving town?"

"Ah. Yes." Garrett pasted a winsome smile on his face. A smile that made Gryphon more nervous than ever. "You see, Father is going to be furious when he finds out Briar and I have left."

"You're not telling him you're going?"

"Well, I've arranged everything with Magan, you know, his steward, and I've left a note for Father. But no, I'm not telling him. And he's going to be especially furious that Princess—er, whatever her name is—has come all this way with no prince to court her."

Gryphon was bemused. "And?"

Garrett only smiled that awful smile.

Then it dawned on Gryphon. "Oh. Oh, absolutely not. You must be mad!"

"Gryphon—"

"In case you've forgotten, I'm in love with someone else too!"

"You don't really have to court her," Garrett said earnestly. "Just, you know. Pretend. It won't go anywhere. It can't. Father would never seriously consider a betrothal between you and the princess, not like he would with me."

"You're right, he bloody well wouldn't consider it," Gryphon shot back, "since I'm not a prince anymore! Garrett, even if Father is willing to talk to me, that doesn't mean he's going to give me my title back. I don't even want it back. And—" He tried to tame the desperate note in his voice. "Did it occur to you that being part of your little scheme might turn Father against me even more?"

"He won't know you're part of it. He'll think I've duped you too—"

"I feel duped."

"—and when you step in for me, you'll be helping Father, see? And, well, he won't have any choice but to lift your exile."

"Unless he beheads me instead."

"He would never do that."

Gryphon snorted. "Because I'm his son?"

"Because he's too concerned about saving face for this Desert princess," Garrett said with aplomb. "Oh. And because you're his son."

The way Garrett tacked that on was, Gryphon thought, not overly reassuring. "Look, Garrett—"

"I came to save you," Garrett said quietly. "When the were-wolves took you, I came to save you."

Gryphon broke off. It hung there between them.

"One of my men died trying to save you," Garrett added.

"Falcon." Gryphon closed his eyes against the twinge of pain in his chest. "I haven't forgotten." Garrett had left his soldier Falcon to guard Gryphon in his castle, while he had gone to rescue Isabelle from the were-wolves. Only, the wolves had come to the castle instead—and Falcon had died trying to save Gryphon.

Gryphon opened his eyes and found his brother watching him closely, a beseeching look on his face. Gryphon let out an explosive sigh. "And this is really how you want me to pay off that debt?"

"Yes." Garrett's tone was more than firm. It was fierce. "Father needs to learn, once and for all, that *I* get to choose who I want to marry, even if that's Briar. And he needs to forgive you, since you hardly did anything that warrants forgiveness anyway. So. We do this and kill two birds with one stone. Figuratively speaking, of course."

"Of course." Gryphon leaned back, rubbing two fingers between his eyes. He felt a headache coming on, pounding between his temples.

Garrett left a short while later, assuring Gryphon that the private booth had been booked for the entire evening, so he could stay as long as he liked. But Gryphon was not alone for long before Isabelle returned, laden with two large shopping bags. She slid into the booth across from Gryphon, a broad smile lighting up her face. "So? How did it go? Garrett's all right, I hope?"

Gryphon didn't answer. He slouched glumly in his seat, staring out the frosted window. By the dim glow of the shaded gear bulbs, his faint, distorted reflection stared back at him.

Stars and stones, was he really going to entertain this madness?

"Well?" Isabelle prompted. "What did Garrett want?"

"The princess didn't tell you?"

"Briar? No. She was very mysterious. So what was it?"

"You won't believe it," Gryphon told her. "You just won't believe it."

3

GUARDED

GEMMA LET THE DOOR to the offices in the barracks swing shut behind her as she stepped out into the cold, crisp day. The long, paved stretch of the parade grounds lay before her, a courtyard enclosed by square barracks buildings on three sides and imposing iron gates on the fourth. The sun wasn't high enough yet to peek over the buildings, but the morning was already bright. Too bright. Gemma rubbed the heels of her palms into her eyes. She needed more sleep, but she wouldn't get it anytime soon.

It was the morning after she and Klaus had discovered Princess Solena out in the woods. Gemma hadn't gotten back to the castle until near midnight and not gotten to bed until a while after that, since she'd had to report everything to Kinsley, her supervising officer. Luckily, her early shift had been moved until later this morning, but she'd still had to get up for a briefing with Kinsley and some of the other soldiers. Now, as she dropped her hands from her face, she took in a deep breath, willing herself awake. The cold air felt good, somehow. Bracing.

"Gemma—hey, Gemma." The door to the offices creaked open behind her, and Gemma recognized Spencer's hesitant voice. "Are you all right?"

Gemma paused before turning to face him. Wondering why he was asking that. "Yes," she answered in her usual monotone. "I'm fine."

Spencer shifted his weight, his beanpole frame adding to his awkwardness. Spencer was a fellow guard and one of Gemma's closest friends. "Look...I know how you feel." Spencer rubbed a hand behind his neck. "But it's nothing personal. It's not even a real mission. I mean, yes, all right, this is Prince Garrett we're talking about, so I've no doubt he'll happen upon a band of trolls or flesh-eating monsters because, well, he just attracts them somehow. But there's no real danger attached to this trip. It's a holiday. They just want to get away while this Desert Kingdom princess is here."

Gemma stared at him. Kinsley had just broken the news that Garrett and Briar were leaving—had already left, as of a couple of hours ago. They'd taken off before dawn so as to get out of the city unnoticed. As Gemma had predicted, Garrett had no intention of humoring his father and pretending to court this foreign princess. What Gemma had not anticipated was his leaving entirely, before the princess even arrived—and leaving his half-brother, Gryphon, in his place. Unbeknownst to the king.

And Gemma was not among the guards who would be accompanying Garrett and Briar. She was to stay and help Kinsley do damage control. Gemma had to admit she was not looking forward to that. No matter how Garrett had "arranged" things, there was sure to be drama to unfold and hell to pay when the king realized Garrett had left his exiled brother in his place. And there was nothing Gemma detested more than drama.

But as Gemma stood there facing Spencer, listening to him console her, she realized he thought she was upset about more than just that. He thought she was upset Prince Garrett had not chosen her to accompany him. He thought she was taking this decision to leave her behind personally.

Because of her injury. Because of her damaged sight.

It wasn't so strange of Spencer to assume that, she supposed. But truthfully, she didn't mind being excluded from Garrett and Briar's venture. In fact, there was a teeny, tiny part of her—a shameful part of her—that was secretly relieved.

But Spencer had misread her. "They're not taking Kinsley either, Gemma. Nor Klaus, even."

Gemma grimaced. "Who the hell would take Klaus with them on a holiday? Assuming they want to relax and enjoy themselves, I mean."

"Exactly." Spencer's tone was eager to agree. "My point is, wherever Briar and Garrett are going, they obviously don't anticipate needing a tracker, much less a..."

Gemma felt an uncomfortable churning in her gut. "A sharpshooter."

He was right, of course. If, for some reason, a sharpshooter was needed, they could have taken Kinsley. Hell, it was unusual for Kinsley not to accompany Briar anywhere, so either Kinsley had opted out for personal reasons, or Garrett and Briar really were not anticipating danger of any kind. And no reason they should.

Still. Anything could happen. And Gemma felt sick at the thought of what she would do if it did, if Prince Garrett *had* elected to take her on this trip. What if her particular skills were called upon, and she couldn't get the job done? What if, it turned out, they did need a sharpshooter? Yes, the barracks physicians claimed Gemma was doing much better now. Her physical exams looked fine, they said. At her last appointment, she had been given the go-ahead to pick up a rifle again and try a long-distance shot.

But she hadn't picked up a rifle yet.

It was stupid. The fact was, even if her sight was never fully restored—even if the damage was permanent—she could still be a sharpshooter again. Some snipers learned to shoot with one eye closed; she could do the same. It would take a lot of time, a lot of retraining, but. She could do it.

So why did the thought of even touching a rifle fill her with dread?

She didn't know if Prince Garrett had excluded her from this trip because of her injury. He certainly wouldn't have done so because he thought her useless. But he might have done it out of pity. And Gemma didn't like the idea of being pitied. In fact, she loathed it. Especially if it was coming from Prince Garrett. But even so, she didn't mind staying behind, whatever the reason. She preferred to just work her rotations here in the castle. Keep her head down. Stay out of anything important.

Because Gemma didn't trust her own eyes. The physician couldn't know for sure that her sight was restored. Only she could. And she was far from sure. Especially after what happened last night.

Gemma sighed. "Well. It is what it is. Anyway, we haven't got time to stand around here. The Desert Kingdom delegation arrives later this morning." *Assuming everything went all right last night.*

After discovering Princess Solena out in the woods, Gemma had returned to the city to report what had happened. But Klaus had agreed to accompany the princess back to her delegation. And—just to make sure there wasn't more trouble—Klaus was going to remain with the delegation until they arrived at the castle. Gemma had initially balked at that idea, but in the end, she'd realized it was a good thing. Because she was hoping Klaus could snoop around a bit and investigate this princess.

"I doubt I'll get a chance to talk with her," Klaus had said when she'd brought this up, before they'd parted ways last night.

"I don't know," Gemma replied. "She seems to like you. For some reason." Indeed, the princess heaped fulsome praise upon Klaus for volunteering to accompany her back to her people.

"Perhaps she was charmed by my winning personality," Klaus drawled. "Or she just thinks I'm handsome."

Gemma rolled her eyes. She knew Klaus's mock-vanity was an attempt to mask his self-deprecation. He was under the impression that his scars made him hideous, which was ridiculous. Klaus *was* handsome in a rugged sort of way. Not that she would ever tell him that.

"Well, while you're busy flirting with the princess," Gemma had told him, "see if you can find out why she ran away from her retinue last night."

Gemma hadn't told him what she really wanted to know. What really disturbed her. That Princess Solena was the spitting image of the corpse she'd discovered in the woods. The corpse that had completely disappeared.

Now, Gemma left the barracks and headed into town. She was technically off duty until the delegation arrived, but Kinsley wanted to speak with her privately, down in the city, at one of the local taverns frequented by the guard. It was clear he wanted to discuss something work-related with her—something he didn't want overheard.

She arrived at the tavern before he did and squinted at her dim surroundings. Only scarce patches of pallid daylight came in through the few windows to punctuate the murky room. Kinsley had chosen their meeting place well, Gemma thought, as she took a seat at the rustic bar. It was the sort of establishment where no one would be surprised to find her sitting by herself—and where no one would bother her if she was. Especially this early in the day. Indeed, the wobbly square tables and hard-backed wooden chairs were almost empty.

She wasn't alone long before Kinsley appeared, sliding onto the stool next to her. "Buy me a drink?" he asked.

Gemma eyed him sidelong. "Isn't it a bit early for that?"

"What are you drinking, then?"

Gemma inhaled the warm steam wafting out from her mug. Its dark, heady scent seemed to fill her, sparking her senses. "Coffee."

"Well, I wouldn't say no to a chocolate."

Gemma shot him another look. "I'm pretty sure you make more money than I do now."

"The perks of being a personal bodyguard."

"I wouldn't know." Despite her quip, Gemma raised a hand to signal to the bartender. "Though I suppose I will now."

Kinsley placed his order for a hot chocolate, then rotated on his stool to face her more fully. He was dressed like a civilian in a smart tan coat and neatly pressed shirt. His shock of black hair looked freshly washed and so dark it was almost blue, in contrast to his pale face. "It wasn't my decision, you know. That you stay behind to keep an eye on Prince Gryphon." He cast an idle glance over the near-empty tavern. "You might have noticed I'm staying behind as well."

"I had noticed." Gemma took a careful sip of her coffee, still piping hot. "Which is a little weird."

"It's further proof they don't anticipate needing a sharp-shooter." Kinsley's tone was noncommittal.

Gemma traced a finger around the metal rim of her mug. "It's just. You said it yourself. You're Princess Briar's bodyguard. Doesn't that mean you're supposed to go everywhere she does?"

Kinsley did not answer right away. His chocolate arrived, and he took a long, slow sip, holding the mug close to his face. Obscuring his expression. "The truth is, neither Gryphon nor Briar really need bodyguards. Considering what they are. Considering what they can do."

"Still. You and Princess Briar are quite close. Even if she doesn't need you as her guard, I'm surprised you were left behind."

"Well," Kinsley said delicately, "Briar and Prince Garrett have had a tough time this last year. This trip—while meant to send a message to King Victor—is also for them." He lifted an eyebrow. "It's romantic in nature, I mean."

"And, what? You'd be in the way?"

"Briar says I'm an old maid."

"You are."

Kinsley smiled, taking another sip of his chocolate.

Gemma followed suit, taking a deeper gulp of her coffee. Then she set her mug down, wiped her mouth, and said, "Look, you just said it. Gryphon doesn't need a bodyguard. So the fact that Prince Garrett left us to guard him..."

"Well, I think Garrett thought you—and Spencer and Roy—a good choice to stay with Gryphon because you're the few who already know him. You know him quite well, I understand. Since you were the one who helped Isabelle track him down last spring."

Gemma shifted uncertainly. It was true she'd spent a good month with Isabelle, tracking Gryphon when he'd been trapped in his beast form. She wouldn't say she knew Gryphon *quite well*, though. It wasn't like Gryphon was more comfortable with her than he was with the others. He knew she was a good tracker, she supposed. And he knew she'd failed to protect him at his castle.

He knew she'd let Falcon get killed. He'd been present for that.

"But also..." Kinsley went on. "Look, I told you it wasn't my decision, that you stay here. But I don't know that it was Prince Garrett's either. I assumed so, but then I found out the king asked after you."

"The king?" Gemma felt the stirrings of panic. "King Victor asked about me? Why? He doesn't even know me." And what had he heard about her? That she'd been damaged? That she couldn't shoot anymore? That she wasn't valuable enough to serve in his army—

"Of course he knows you, Gemma." Kinsley's tone was calm. He didn't sound as though he was about to tell her she was being fired. "You might have been handpicked by Prince Garrett, but the king knows all the royal guard. Especially one as talented as you."

As talented as you once were, said a nasty little voice in Gemma's head. Aloud, she said, "But King Victor doesn't even know Gryphon will be here."

"No, but he knows this princess from the Desert Kingdom will be here," Kinsley said. "The princess has her own guard, of course, but the king is expected to provide an escort as well. As a courtesy. And the king specifically wants you guarding the princess."

"Why?"

"I believe he thinks your particular skills might be useful."

My particular skills. Which no longer included sharpshooting. Still, Gemma thought grudgingly, at least Kinsley felt she still had valuable skills. But this wasn't quite adding up. "So are we expecting some kind of attack on Princess Solena? Assassination attempts? What?"

"Oh, no." Kinsley eyed Gemma cannily. "I don't think anyone anticipates any threat to the princess. Rather, she could be a threat herself."

Gemma found herself intrigued against her will. "What kind of threat?"

Kinsley shrugged. "It could be nothing. But we know very little about the Desert Kingdom these days. In fact, everyone thought all the Desert princesses had died in that plague they suffered several years ago. Now quite suddenly, we hear one survived and has been sequestered away all this time."

And already acting strangely, running away from her retinue. If that was really what had happened. Gemma ran a finger over a deep groove in the countertop, trying to conceal how these implications made her feel. She'd begun to accept that her mind—or rather, her damaged eye—had been playing tricks on her last night. Perhaps she had seen a mangled girl. Perhaps—as Klaus had suggested, when she'd told him what she'd seen—that girl's body had been dragged off by some animal. But it couldn't have been Princess Solena. That was what she'd told herself. She must have imagined that.

But if there really was something wrong with this princess, some reason to suspect her of false intentions...then maybe not. Maybe there was some other explanation.

What, she didn't know.

"It could be nothing," Kinsley said. "But King Victor is no fool. He might be considering an alliance with this princess, but he wants to thoroughly vet her first. And given your skills at tracking and discretion, he feels you're well-suited to keeping an eye on her."

"So I'm meant to be a spy," Gemma deduced, "acting as a bodyguard."

"That about sums it up."

Gemma gave a slow nod.

Kinsley slapped a few coins on the bar as he came to his feet. "I hope I put your mind at ease."

"About what?" Gemma asked swiftly.

Kinsley spared her a knowing smile. "I suggest you finish your coffee quickly. The princess will be arriving soon, and you'll be expected at the welcome."

Indeed, by the time Gemma made it back to the barracks, word had arrived that the Desert Kingdom delegation had been spotted coming into the city. Gemma joined several other soldiers in quickly dressing in uniform best before heading into the throne hall, where they would await the arrival of Princess Solena.

The throne hall was an opulent room, one of the most opulent in the castle. The ceiling was adorned with embellished panels and bordered in thick, gilded crown molding. Three separate chandeliers hung from the ceiling, each set with two tiers of delicately wrought crystal casings for bulbs, creating a bright, glittering effect over the hall. Heavy brocade curtains framed the towering oaken doors at the entrance, as well as behind the throne itself—an intricately carved, heavily gilded chair upholstered with rich velvet cushions, set atop a dais at the back of the room. The hardwood floor was covered in a broad, plush rug, and a few receiving benches and chairs lined the walls. But aside from that sparse furniture, the bulk of the room remained empty—except when a large crowd gathered for some significant event, like they did today.

The hall was packed with people today, filled with soldiers and servants in their simple navy-blue uniforms, and lords and ladies of the court, bedecked in much more ostentatious garb. Gemma wormed her way through the crowd to join a small contingent of guards that would serve as Solena's escort once she arrived. They arrayed themselves to the left of the throne, right beside the dais.

King Victor arrived within short order, garbed in formal morning attire, including a heavily decorated tailcoat. As he ascended the throne's dais, an excited ripple spread throughout the hall, everyone looking from the king to the entrance.

But it was another ten minutes before the delegation arrived. An advisor to the Desert Kingdom throne made a few remarks, expressing formal greetings from one kingdom to another, etc. Then, with much fanfare—a lot of flowery titles and the ringing blast of a trumpet—Princess Solena was announced, and she entered the hall.

She was a young woman, of an age with Prince Garrett, Gemma guessed, perhaps a year or two younger. Gemma watched her approach with little emotion, but as the princess stopped short of the dais and offered the king a deep curtsy, a sense of unease crept through Gemma, her muscles tensing. The princess looked different here in the brightly lit hall, garbed in a resplendent gown, her dark hair brushed and styled. So different from the bedraggled young woman she'd encountered last night.

So different from the mauled, bloodied, dead girl she'd left in the woods last night.

And yet...though she was so different now, so polished and regal...a small, sure voice whispered inside Gemma's head.

This is the girl I saw.

King Victor welcomed the princess, which took some time. In Gemma's experience, the exchanging of pleasantries between lords and ladies always took some time. She tuned out the words but remained alert, surveying the room. A number of the princess's guards, servants, and attendants lingered near the entrance at the front of the hall. Some of the nobles among the party—advisors and attending ladies, Gemma guessed—were dressed as splendidly as the other nobles here in the hall, but the servants and soldiers, she noted, all wore uniforms in the Desert Kingdom's royal colors: bright crimson and radiant gold. Among that sea of red and gold, standing out in navy blue, Gemma found Klaus's scarred face.

Klaus. *Klaus.* With everything that had gone on this morning, she realized one thing had completely slipped her mind: Klaus and his history with Gryphon.

His very complicated, very troubled history with Gryphon.

Klaus had served Gryphon when the exiled prince lived in the Black Forest. More than that—from what Gemma had gathered—they had been close friends. But they'd had quite the falling-out when Gryphon discovered Klaus had betrayed him. And while there had been extenuating circumstances surrounding that betrayal, Klaus had left Gryphon's service and never returned. That was the reason Klaus had come to work for Prince Garrett—so he wouldn't have to see Gryphon again.

But now Gryphon was here.

Before Gemma could even imagine how to warn Klaus, the king concluded his pleasantries with Princess Solena and turned to introduce his son. The king's herald announced the arrival of the crown prince with just as much fanfare as Princess Solena had received—a long list of titles recited, trumpets blowing clear, resounding notes. All eyes turned to the left of the dais, to the wide, paneled door there, set into the wall.

The door boomed open.

And Prince Gryphon stepped out into the hall.

4

NEGOTIATION

G RYPHON KNEW HE NEVER should have trusted Garrett. Because as soon as he stepped foot into the throne room, his father turned a shade of purple that told Gryphon he most certainly did not regret exiling him. Still, Gryphon reflected, as he followed the king down a narrow stone corridor, at least his father hadn't ordered his execution yet. That had to be a good sign.

At the end of the corridor was a dark, winding stone stairwell, leading up through a tower. Gryphon watched his father as the king started up the stairs. Then he glanced at one of the guards beside him. The king had six guards ringing him, and Gryphon didn't think any of them were Garrett's people. He certainly didn't recognize any of them. As he ascended the stairs behind his father, Gryphon wondered idly if he was being led to a dungeon.

But as they neared the top of the tower, Gryphon recognized where they were. It was the scent that did it—fine leather and stale smoke and ash. Of course. His father's study. He had nearly forgotten it. Strange, considering how often he'd been brought there to endure a scolding. Just like now, he supposed.

The tower was cold when they entered, that stale smoke scent lingering from a long-dead fire. His father made no move to light another, nor did he order anyone to do so. The king strode with swift, purposeful steps, every movement like a sharp blade. "Sit," he ordered, coming behind his gleaming mahogany desk.

The moment could have been taken straight from the past, it was all so familiar. The shadowy room, lit by only a few gear-bulb lamps. Heavily carpeted marble floors beneath Gryphon's feet, and a high, vaulted ceiling above his head. He felt dizzy with *deja vu*. It was not a pleasant feeling. It made him a little queasy. Still, he thought it best not to argue and plopped down, quite indolently, into the chair opposite his father's desk.

The heavy oaken door to the study *boomed* shut with a note of finality. Gryphon managed not to flinch at the sound, nor at the soldiers moving in to surround him.

You are not caged, he reminded himself. No one could cage him anymore.

He looked up at his father and found it more difficult than he liked. The king cut an imposing figure, though not, Gryphon thought, so imposing as he had been when Gryphon was a child. King Victor was a tall man, though not quite so tall as Gryphon. He was powerfully built, the set of his shoulders broad, but he was not so broad and well-muscled as Gryphon. Gryphon had grown since he'd been here last, thanks in no small part to his beastly curse.

But the king was not looking at him. His iron-gray head was bowed, his eyes on his desk, where he busied himself with some papers and parchment, neatly stacking it all before pushing it off to one corner. With a start, Gryphon realized his father did not want to look at him either. Because he was so angry? Because he hated Gryphon that much?

Surely not out of any shame at having banished him. Never.

Finally, his father cleared his throat, gripped the back of his chair, and looked at Gryphon. Meeting his gaze.

Gryphon slouched in his chair.

The corners of the king's mouth turned down, showing his displeasure.

Gryphon slouched a little more, trying to get comfortable. He was not deliberately antagonizing his father. Not *really*. Actually, he was trying to ease his own anxiety. Trying to remind himself that he was not the boy who had been exiled from this castle six years ago. His father could not hurt him. Literally. No one could.

He had the beast for protection now.

And more importantly, he was no longer a prince. So he could do what he liked. Slouch as much as he wanted to.

Either his father also realized this, or it just wasn't a battle worth fighting to him, because he didn't demand that Gryphon sit up straight. He settled for a stern frown instead and barked, "What, by all the stars in the sky, are you doing here?"

Gryphon cultivated an innocent expression. "Didn't Garrett tell you?"

King Victor's frown deepened. "What does he have to do with this? No, don't bother." His father cut him off with a flick of his hand. "I've sent for him. *He's* the crown prince, after all. He can explain why the hell he wasn't in that throne room and why you—"

"He's not here," Gryphon interrupted.

Before the king could respond, there was a sharp rap on the thick wooden door. At a look from King Victor, the guard nearest the door left formation to open it. A servant stepped inside.

"Well?" the king snapped.

"Ah—" The servant quavered. "Your Majesty, it would appear Prince Garrett—ah—isn't here. Nor Princess Briar."

The king leveled a flinty look at this servant. With half a glance for Gryphon, he commanded, "Keep him here," to the guards, then swept from the tower, the door slamming shut with another resounding boom.

Gryphon glanced up at the guard closest to him and bared his teeth in something like a smile. The guard quickly averted his gaze.

Gryphon's smile widened. *Keep him here*, indeed.

It was several minutes before the king returned, several minutes that Gryphon and the soldiers passed in complete silence. The king's ringing footsteps announced his return, echoing up the stone stairwell before the door burst open again and King Victor stormed inside. There was a murderous look in his eyes. "Explain," the king said curtly as he strode behind his desk to face Gryphon.

"Explain what?"

"You said Garrett wasn't here. So. Where is he? What have you done with him?"

Gryphon returned these questions with an expression full of scorn. "I haven't done anything to him. We're friends now, or hasn't he told you?"

"You—"

"And even if I did want to hurt him or get rid of him or whatever ridiculous notion you have, don't you think that monster of a princess he's so mad about would have stopped me?"

"Don't you dare insult Princess Briar," his father retorted.

"That's rich."

"Excuse me?"

"Don't you understand?" Gryphon gripped the leather arms of his chair, allowing some of his own hostility to come through. "Garrett and Briar have run off together so Garrett doesn't have to go through this charade of courting another princess."

"Garrett wouldn't do that," his father snarled.

"Oh, really? Even though he's already told you he won't marry someone else?"

"So I suppose this was all your idea!"

"Of course it wasn't."

"And I'm supposed to believe that? It was only after Garrett's hunting excursion last spring—when he found *you*—that he told me he was going to marry Princess Briar, no matter what I thought. And I'm supposed to believe you didn't put that notion into his head?"

"Well, that's not—" Gryphon blustered. "The notion was already in his head. I...may have encouraged it."

"Why am I not surprised?" the king raged. "Before he reconciled with you, Garrett was always an obedient son. A dutiful prince. He did what he was told, what he had to do, for the kingdom—"

"Victor, Garrett is his own man. I didn't tell him to do this. I didn't want him to do this. But his mind was made up."

The guard on his right shifted, the heel of his regulation boot squeaking over a bare spot on the floor. "You shouldn't address the king so informally."

"Well, I'm certainly not going to call him *Father*."

The king waved a dismissive hand at the guard, waving the man to silence and expressing his utter disregard for what Gryphon called him at the same time. "You say you didn't have anything to do with this. Why, then, are you here? I seem to recall exiling you from this kingdom on pain of death."

"You know, I seem to recall that too."

His father slapped a hand down on his desk. "Don't play games with me, Gryphon. I announced the crown prince's arrival back in the throne room, and there you stood. I don't care what Garrett's done or where he's gone. If you think, for one minute, that I will name you my heir again—"

"I don't," Gryphon coldly. "Even if you offered, I don't want that."

"And what do you want?"

"Honestly? I'd be happy to leave this castle and never come back." The ire in Gryphon rose with every word. "I'm not here because I want to be. I came because Garrett asked. I *stayed* because he asked. I owe him a debt. So I agreed to this for him."

"Agreed to what exactly?"

"To staying in his place. Entertaining this bloody princess in his place. Just while he's gone. I'm not usurping his title. He'll be back. But for now, he asked me to stay."

For once, his father didn't snap at him. For a long, long moment—one that seemed to stretch for an eternity—King Victor only stared at him, a vein pulsing at his temple. Then he pulled back his chair and practically collapsed into it.

Gryphon remained silent while his father leaned back, rested his elbows on the ornately carved arms of his chair, and rubbed a hand over his wrinkled forehead. Then he said, "Even if you are not crown prince—you are no longer a prince of any kind, Gryphon." He didn't sound angry anymore, only tired. "You're not supposed to step foot in this kingdom. So how exactly did Garrett think you might court Princess Solena in his place?"

Gryphon straightened. Only because his back was starting to ache. He felt, rather than saw, all the guards shift around him as he moved. Gryphon stifled the urge to roll his eyes at them and said, "Look. I've already told you, this wasn't my idea." He eyed the guard on his left. "You can try and chop off my head, but you won't get very far, I promise you that."

"Is that a threat?" the king asked dryly.

"No. A fact." Gryphon turned his gaze back on his father. "But I will leave. Tell me to go, and I will. I'll be out of your kingdom by dusk, and I won't come back. But...Garrett said you were willing to talk."

There was a pause.

"If he was wrong, just say so," Gryphon added, more hastily than he intended, "and I'll go. But if he wasn't wrong..." Gryphon shook his head. "I meant it when I said I don't want my title back. I don't want to be your heir again. But you're the one who stripped me of all that. I could be a prince again, in name. All you have to do is say the word."

His father dropped his hand from his face. The look he turned on Gryphon was scrutinizing. "And you truly don't care either way?"

"I don't. I have my own life now. One I'm content with."

"I should send you from this city," King Victor muttered, "with a score of soldiers to see you out. And send another score to bring Garrett back. In fact, I am going to send people to bring him back."

The king had not mentioned, Gryphon noticed, chopping his head off as a viable option. Taking this as a positive sign, Gryphon said, "You do that. But in the meantime, you have this Desert princess here in your court. What exactly are you going to tell her that won't insult her?"

Victor leveled another hard look at him.

Gryphon held up a placating hand. "I'm just saying."

"I don't like being manipulated."

"Well, nor do I, but here I am."

"Oh, you've been manipulated, have you?"

"He called in a life-saving debt," Gryphon muttered. "What was I supposed to say?"

"Everyone knows you were banished!" the king burst out.

"Well, just say you've un-banished me." Gryphon clasped his hands together. "Look, let's not, as you said, play games. You banished me to save face with the Mariner king, and he's dead now, thanks to that witch he married. Which might be funny if it weren't so tragic."

"His death *was* tragic."

"I meant the fact that you banished me for running around with a witch, when it turned out he was doing the same thing. That's what's tragic."

"He didn't know she was a witch!"

"More fool him," Gryphon said bluntly, "since, from what I hear, she was incredibly evil. At least my witch was only looking out for the kingdom. And helped Garrett out recently, from what I hear."

The king glowered.

"Anyway," Gryphon went on, "the Mariner Kingdom has too much to worry about now to be concerned with what I've been up to. And the Desert Kingdom is so far off, they probably never heard I was banished to begin with. So just make something up."

His father continued to glare at him. Gryphon stared back, remorseless.

"Fine," his father said. "*Fine*. I'll go along with this for the time being. But this does not mean I'm capitulating to your brother's ridiculous stunt! I will have him back here in a fortnight, mark my words. And as soon as he's back, you can leave and return to this new life of yours you're so happy with."

Gryphon rather doubted his father would have Garrett back by the end of the month, let alone within the fortnight. But all he said was, "Fine by me."

"I will announce your return." King Victor sounded as though he spoke through gritted teeth. "I will lift your exile. We'll say evidence has come to light that you were bewitched. And perhaps we'll say you saved Garrett's life in the old Forest Kingdom last year. Yes...we'll say you saved his life from that beast he went after."

Gryphon nearly choked on that.

"Yes," his father mused, more to himself than to Gryphon. "There were a lot of rumors about *something* happening out there, but since it was all in the middle of nowhere, no one really knew the truth. So it can be whatever we need it to be. As for Garrett's absence, I'll explain he had to leave suddenly to take care of some danger up north...yes...something in the

Mountain Kingdom. That will explain Briar's going as well." And just when Gryphon thought his father had forgotten he was there, King Victor turned another glare on him. "And as for you—you will entertain Princess Solena. You will behave with all the grace and dignity the station of a prince demands. Because I can still chop off your head if I want to, Gryphon. Make no mistake about that."

Gryphon didn't try to correct this misapprehension. He only said, "I'll do it. Don't worry."

"I am going to worry." King Victor's chair scraped dully over the rug as he pushed it back and rose to his feet. His expression suggested he was getting a very strong headache. "I am going to worry until Garrett is back here where he belongs, and *you* are gone."

Gryphon swallowed, his throat tight. Garrett had suggested his father was willing to talk about what had happened between them. He had suggested his father might regret banishing him to begin with.

It didn't sound like that was true.

Gryphon rolled his shoulders back. *It doesn't matter*, he reminded himself. It didn't matter what his father thought of him. Not anymore.

Not ever again.

He was shown to new quarters. He was told a new wardrobe would be outfitted for him, and his meals for the day brought up. He was told, for now, to stay put. He would be formally introduced to the princess on the morrow, he was told. Until then, he wasn't to wander the castle, let alone leave the grounds. The six guards who escorted him remained outside his door, as though to emphasize all of this.

Luckily, Gryphon had other means of going to and from his quarters, so long as he waited until the evening when it had grown dark. All it took was a small summoning of the beast, enough to grow his claws and enhance his strength.

Then he leapt through his window, launching himself down to the next window ledge below him. He caught himself deftly on that ledge, using his claws to grip the stone exterior, then continued from there, springing from one ledge to the next until he reached the ground.

From there, it was no trouble to sneak away in the vast shadow of the castle, creep across the grounds, scale the outer wall, and set out into the surrounding land. He didn't go into Glen City. He stuck to the small wood that dotted the land around the castle, up to the outskirts of town, and from there, into the wilds beyond. The land sloped gently upwards along his path, taking him out of the low valley that cradled the city, until he found himself in another wooded area that ran along the base of the rugged hills to the east.

Within that wooded area was his destination: a small cottage nestled within a grove of thick alder trees. It was a secluded spot, sheltered from passersby and their prying eyes.

He called out when he entered the cottage, but no one answered. The place was empty and cold, the ashy scent of the last fire lingering in the air. Beneath the smoke was a second, more appealing fragrance—Isabelle's scent, her flowery soap laid over her skin to create a perfume that was uniquely her. Gryphon stood in the sparsely furnished room and felt the ache of loneliness gnawing at him. It was an old feeling, unwelcome but familiar, and for a moment, he let that feeling in, wrapping him tight in its embrace.

But only for a moment. Then he shook it off. Still, a part of him wanted nothing more than to *run*. Tear out of the cottage, vanish into the thick of the trees, and transform fully into the beast. When the beast took over, the world was...more, somehow. Crisper, clearer, more vibrant. The strength and agility of his body, the intensity of his physical senses dampened everything else—thought, feeling, all those pesky human things. Even now that he'd learned some measure of control, it was still like that. And Gryphon craved it right now. He wanted to give in, let the beast take control, and run into the night. Escape everything.

But he knew that was a bad idea. He smiled wryly, remembering his father's plan to explain that Gryphon had saved Garrett from a vicious beast. He supposed it wouldn't do for that same beast to be seen roaming the woods less than five leagues from Glen City.

So instead, Gryphon lowered himself into the large, cushy armchair in the sitting room, leaned back, and let his eyes fall shut. He was exhausted. He'd spent most of the day in his new room at the castle, pacing back and forth, trying to ignore the restless energy building inside him, trying (and failing) to relax. He couldn't see how he was ever going to relax in that place. So for now—while he had the chance—he shut his eyes and dozed.

When the door clicked open about an hour later, he came awake at once, tense and alert. But it wasn't anyone he wasn't expecting.

"I see you didn't get your head chopped off," said Isabelle, as she removed her traveling coat and slung it over the back of a chair at the table. Beneath the coat, she wore a pleated, deep-violet dress that complemented her rich-brown skin and hugged her willowy form in all the places Gryphon loved most.

"And where have you been?" Gryphon asked.

"Well, it took me a while to get the horse back here."

"Horse?"

"Yes. I bought one." Isabelle's tone was absent as she pulled pins from her hair, her thick curls falling free around her shoulders.

"Why?"

"I'll tell you," Isabelle said, coming towards him, "if you tell me how you kept from getting your head chopped off." She perched beside him on the wide arm of his chair. "The contingent from the Desert Kingdom rode through the city this morning. So. Unless you got cold feet and crept from the castle before anyone was the wiser, I take it you met with your father?"

"I met with him." Gryphon took Isabelle by her waist. "And I told him he'd have a time of it if he tried to chop my head off."

"Well. I can't say I blame you. And?"

"And I convinced him to let me stay. Keep this princess busy while she's here. He still intends to send soldiers after Garrett, but I doubt he'll find him."

"So do I," Isabelle murmured. "Well. That's that, I suppose."

Gryphon gazed up at her, full of warm appreciation. This feeling, unlike the loneliness, was a pleasant one. One of the things he loved so much about Isabelle was that she never prodded him to talk, to tell her how he was feeling, to pick apart every little detail. This was because, probably, her mind was always half-somewhere else, pondering over some tome she'd read earlier. But Gryphon didn't mind. "It won't be so bad, I suppose," he said, "with you here. I'm sure I can get away from time to time."

Isabelle looked down at him and smoothed a hand over his hair. "I'm not so sure that's a good idea."

"What? Why not?"

"Because as much as I would love to steal you away from time to time, it could jeopardize Garrett's plan."

Gryphon stared at her, stung. "I didn't realize we cared about Garrett's plan." Much.

"Well, we don't really. But Gryphon—look, I know you don't care about making things right with your father. I know what he did to you, and I don't blame you, I really don't. But that doesn't mean this is a bad idea, reconciling with him. It could be good for you. For us." She cocked her head to one side. "I mean, for one thing, it would be nice if we didn't always have to creep through the Glen Kingdom. It is sort of in the middle of every place else."

"I don't think there's much chance of a true reconciliation, Isabelle." Gryphon tried to sound indifferent, but there was a hollow ring to his words that bespoke his bitterness.

"Well, there's even less if anyone finds you here with me. And anyway. There is that horse."

"What about the horse?"

"Well, you asked why I bought it."

"And?"

"I think I might have a lead," she said in a rush. "On the witch who cursed you."

Gryphon's stomach flipped. She meant the witch who'd cast the original curse on his ancestors some two hundred years ago. He caught Isabelle's hand in one of his own. "You're not going after this witch alone."

"Of course not. It's not really a lead, anyway. More a lead on a lead. And I'll swing by the manor and pick up Ellery and Stefan first. We're more than capable of taking care of ourselves. We'll be fine."

"So you're leaving *me* here alone?" Gryphon asked. The thought was more worrisome than he let on.

"You won't be alone either. You'll have Garrett's guards."

Gryphon tightened his grip on her waist. "I'd rather have you."

Isabelle's breath hitched in her throat. She laid a hand upon his chest. "Well, you could have me," she murmured, "one last time before you go."

5

SKELETAL

GEMMA WAS NOT PERMITTED to accompany Gryphon—Prince Gryphon?—as he was escorted out of the throne hall. No one from Prince Garrett's company was. She fervently hoped this wasn't because they were escorting him down to the dungeons. But even if they were, there was nothing she could do about it. Prince Garrett might have wanted her to keep an eye on his brother, but when she was given direct orders, there was only so much she could do. After all, she worked under a chain of command.

Instead she was instructed—along with two other soldiers—to accompany Princess Solena to her guest quarters. Gemma felt fairly superfluous as she strode down the wallpapered corridors, trailing Magan, the royal valet. That was not just because of the princess's own guards but because of the countless servants, ladies, lords, and advisors who also accompanied them, following the princess.

When they reached Princess Solena's chambers, most of those attendants fell away, off to find their own quarters for the duration of their stay. Gemma stationed herself outside in the corridor with Roy and Gallia, the other two soldiers who'd accompanied the princess here. But no sooner had she taken up her position by the door than a servant stuck their head outside. She was a petite young woman with fine yellow hair, dressed in a maid's uniform—a simple, high-necked black dress. "The princess requests you," she said, gesturing to Gemma.

Gemma was nonplussed. "Just me?"

The young maid looked her over with a lofty expression and gave a sniff. "Yes. Hurry."

Gemma looked at Roy and Gallia. Roy shrugged. Gallia's returning stare was unsympathetic.

Holding in a sigh, Gemma stepped inside.

The quarters provided for Princess Solena were some of the grandest in the castle. This front room was a receiving parlor, adorned with only the most extravagant furnishings: gleaming rosewood tables and chests, inlaid with painted designs, decoratively embroidered cushions and soft wool throw blankets, peppering upholstered armchairs. But Gemma's gaze did not linger on the lushness of her surroundings. It lingered on the possible exits, the doors and windows, the curtains and wardrobes where someone might hide. It lingered on the people—servants, soldiers, and ladies—the number of them, where and how they stood, how they were dressed, what they were doing. Their mannerisms. Their facial expressions.

She wasn't primarily here to guard the princess. But she couldn't turn off her training.

Turning to the petite maid who'd led her inside, Gemma introduced herself. "My name is Gemma. And you are...?" She found it prudent to familiarize herself with every servant or guard she might come in contact with while on a job.

The maid didn't seem to feel the same. "My name is Tashi," she said with another haughty look. "But it's the princess you should be trying to win over, not me." She waggled her fingers impatiently, indicating Gemma step forward to greet the princess.

Princess Solena had already made herself comfortable in the parlor. She faced Gemma from a long chaise, where she lounged on several plush satin pillows. Even in the woods, in the darkness, Gemma had noticed that the princess was beautiful. Here, that was even more evident. Her rich-brown hair was so dark that it was almost black, half of it elaborately piled and pinned atop her head, the other half spilling over one shoulder in perfect waves. Wide, expressive eyes were the highlight of her oval-shaped face, and her plump, pouty lips were a deep rose. Not a single blemish marred her tan-brown skin, and when the princess raised a hand to beckon the maid, Gemma saw her nails were perfectly manicured and lacquered a dark crimson.

Tashi hurried forward with a porcelain tray laden with grapes, cheese, and some kind of tea, placing it on a small table at the end of the chaise. Princess Solena dismissed the maid with an imperious nod, eyeing the proffered food as though it were a prisoner awaiting her sentencing. She plucked a grape from its stem and rolled it distastefully between her fingers. Then she looked up, her gaze alighting on Gemma. "You!" She didn't sound angry, exactly, but it was the kind of tone to make one snap to attention. Gemma would have done so had she not already stood that way, straight and alert. "You were the other one out on the road last night. Gemma?"

Gemma concealed her surprise that the princess remembered her name. "Yes, Your Highness."

"Where's the other one?" Princess Solena spoke with a sulky air. "Klaus."

"I imagine he's returned to the barracks, Your Highness." Given that he'd just arrived from the same journey the princess had, and probably had as little sleep as Gemma. But she imagined this Solena would never have considered that a soldier might need as much rest as she herself did.

Princess Solena sulked some more. Apparently, she really had taken to Klaus. Gemma half-expected her to send for him, but all the princess said was, "Very well. You will do."

"I beg your pardon, Princess," Gemma said politely. "Do for what?"

"To answer my questions!" Solena plopped her grape into her mouth. She chewed and swallowed, then fixed Gemma with an accusatory look. "I spent all my way here learning what I could about Prince Garrett. Only to arrive and find I had the wrong prince!"

Behind her back, Gemma clenched her clasped hands. She stayed silent, her expression betraying nothing. Waiting for an actual question.

"Who is this Prince Gryphon?" Solena demanded. Another maid—this one tall and gangly, with dark hair—approached meekly with a damp towel, but the princess shot her a look of daggers. The poor maid cringed, retreating quickly. "I've never even heard of him."

"Prince Gryphon is Prince Garrett's elder brother," Gemma answered.

Solena's perfectly shaped eyebrow shot up. "His *elder* brother? But I thought Garrett was the crown prince."

Gemma considered her words. She would have to tread carefully here. For all she knew, Gryphon was being scheduled for execution as they spoke. Or—if Prince Garrett's plan succeeded—he was working out a deal with the king to stand in for Garrett during the princess's visit. But Gemma had no idea what the outcome might be. Even if King Victor agreed to the deal, that didn't mean he would reinstate Gryphon as his heir. Hedging her words, she said, "I don't know, Your Highness."

"You don't know? You serve the royal family, and you don't know which prince is the heir to the throne?"

"My job is to protect the royal family, Your Highness," Gemma said cautiously. "Matters of inheritance are none of my business."

"Unless those matters become a threat."

Gemma dipped her head, hiding her surprise again. This princess might be more astute than she appeared. "Yes, Your Highness."

"So where is Prince Garrett? Won't he be here at all?"

"I'm not sure, Your Highness," Gemma evaded.

Luckily, the princess did not linger on Prince Garrett, pivoting to his brother instead. "So what about Prince Gryphon? Why have I never heard of him?"

Gemma kept her expression impassive. "He's been away for some time, Your Highness. On matters of state, I believe. Of the highest importance," she added, hoping the princess would infer Gryphon had been seeing to some secret task for the king or something.

She was in luck again. The princess did not press the issue of Gryphon's recent whereabouts. Instead, she tapped her mouth, looking thoughtful. "Hmm. So what is he like? Or don't you know?" Her mouth twisted viciously on that last word, as though it was meant to be a dig.

"I have spent some time guarding Prince Gryphon," Gemma replied. That was no lie. She had guarded Gryphon back in the old Forest Kingdom, in his ruin of a castle. The night Falcon died.

"So what is he like?" Princess Solena repeated. "Klaus told me Prince Garrett is friendly. That everyone likes him. Is Prince Gryphon the same?"

Gemma might have had a hard time controlling her expression at that, were she not so practiced in doing so. Gryphon, anything like Prince Garrett? Gryphon, friendly and likeable? No, she didn't think anyone would describe Gryphon that way. Not even Isabelle, and she was in love with him.

"Prince Gryphon is more reserved than his brother, Your Highness." Gemma maintained a neutral tone. "But not in an unfriendly way." *Definitely in an unfriendly way.* Gemma didn't begrudge him that; she was a bit similar. But she couldn't say that to the princess. "He's..." Curse it, how to describe Gryphon? He wasn't a bad person. She thought, from what she'd seen of him, that he might be quite sensitive. But it probably wouldn't do to call a prince "sensitive." She didn't think Gryphon would thank her for that. Recalling the workshop she'd glimpsed back in the castle in the Forest Kingdom, she settled on, "He's an artist."

"An artist?"

"Yes, he...paints."

"He paints." Solena sounded decidedly unimpressed.

"And sculpts. Sculptures." Gemma struggled to remember what she'd seen in the tower Gryphon had used as a workshop. But not being an artist herself, she didn't really know much about it. Gemma didn't pay attention to anything that didn't interest her or didn't involve her job.

"Hmm." Solena's expression became intrigued. Perhaps she liked the idea of an artistically inclined prince. "Well. That's something, I suppose." She gave Gemma a critical, sweeping look. Then she waved a hand. "You can go."

Gemma didn't need to be told twice. She bowed, then backed out of the room as quickly as she could. Gallia and Roy awaited her in the corridor, looking expectant. Gemma glanced at the two guards on either side of the door—Solena's guards—and jerked her head at her companions. They all three retreated down the corridor, keeping the princess's quarters in sight. Attendants still bustled in and out, so the door remained open.

Gallia flipped her long yellow braid over her shoulder. "What did she want?"

"She wanted to know about Gryphon," Gemma replied.

Roy's eyes widened. "What did you say?"

"As little as I could. For all I know, Gryphon's down in the dungeons right now."

But Gryphon was not in a dungeon. Within the hour, another set of Glen soldiers came to relieve them. Klaus was one of them, and so was Spencer. Klaus idled near the doorway while Spencer came down the corridor to let them know they were free to go. He also told them they'd had word: Gryphon had been reinstated as prince, though not as the heir. He would be living in the castle accordingly and had been escorted to new rooms.

"The king wants to talk to all of us first thing tomorrow," Spencer added. "I suspect to make sure we know the party line."

"All of us being who?" Gemma asked.

"Prince Garrett's company. I suppose we'll be in charge of guarding Gryphon and Princess Solena. Since some of us already know Gryphon."

"I don't," Gallia said.

Spencer turned owlish eyes on her, looking uncertain. As though he wasn't sure if she was joking or not. "That's...why I said 'some' of us."

Gemma, Roy, and Gallia departed, heading back to the barracks. As they passed Princess Solena's open door, Gemma locked eyes with Klaus, still idling in the corridor there. She opened her mouth to speak, but before she could, Klaus snapped, "A warning might have been nice."

Gemma blinked. "What?"

"About Gryphon." Klaus cast a discreet glance behind him as though to make sure no one was listening.

"I'm sorry." Gemma was aware she didn't sound all that sorry. She *was* sorry he would have to deal with Gryphon, but it was hardly Gemma's fault he was here.

"I guess no one remembered he and I aren't exactly friends anymore," Klaus added caustically. "Or more likely, no one cares."

"What did you want me to do? Turn around and come warn you as soon as I got back here?" Gemma hadn't even known about Gryphon's arrival until this morning.

"Might've been nice."

"Grow up, Klaus. We're soldiers. Sometimes we have to do things we don't like. Deal with people we don't like. This is your problem. So don't take it out on me."

Gemma stalked away down the corridor. But she could feel his glare on her the whole way.

———◦———

When Gemma arrived at the barracks, she was informed she was off duty until the evening. She took the time to eat a solid meal, have a quick bath, and grab a few hours of much-needed sleep. At dusk, she prepared to head back to the castle. Time to return to the princess.

Full dark had fallen when Gemma left the barracks. Wispy gray clouds drifted lazily across the night sky, shrouding much of its light, but by the time she found herself on the upper floors of the castle, climbing what must have been her fifth staircase, the moon had showed itself, its gibbous form sending glowing beams through the windows overhead.

Gemma finally mounted her last step—the princess had been given quarters high in the east wing, about as far from the barracks as one could get—and headed down the corridor. Her surroundings suddenly darkened, and for a moment, she feared it was her damaged sight, shadows encroaching upon her vision. But then Gemma realized the lights themselves had dimmed. The brass-plated light fixtures on the walls, gear bulbs cupped in frosted glass shades, usually gave off a bright gleam, but for some reason, they had been lowered, throwing broad swathes of shadow over the floor.

Gemma locked eyes with Spencer as she approached the princess's rooms. "What happened to the lights?"

"The princess requested they be lowered," Spencer said. "Apparently, she has very sensitive eyes. Says she's prone to headaches."

Gemma frowned, looking questioningly at the door to Solena's quarters. It was shut.

"I know." Spencer lifted his eyes heavenward. "But we asked if we could raise them once the door was shut. She said no."

Figures. "I think it's a security risk."

"So do I, but you'll have to take that up with her. Or we could appeal to the king about it."

"Might be something to mention tomorrow at this meeting with him."

Spencer departed then. Gemma looked for Klaus, but apparently, he'd been relieved earlier. It was only her and Gallia now, who'd also returned for the late shift. Well, her, Gallia, and Princess Solena's own guards. Two of them, garbed in their red and gold, flanking the door to Solena's room.

After thinking it over, Gemma went up to the door. "I'll be heading Princess Solena's armed escort while she's here," she said to the guards. "I'm to present myself to her now. If she's not already abed, that is." She hadn't actually been given such orders, but, remembering Kinsley's instruction to keep a close eye on the princess, she figured checking on her now—getting a look around her rooms while there was less activity than before—might be a good idea.

If the guards found anything strange about this, they didn't say so. Indeed, they showed very little expression and said nothing as one of them lifted a hand to rap on the door. They didn't even give her a nod of acknowledgement.

The door was opened promptly by Tashi, the petite handmaiden who Gemma had met earlier. The guard who'd knocked repeated what Gemma had said—nearly word for word—and Tashi opened the door wider, gesturing for Gemma to come in. The maid also stayed silent as she shut the door, though her expression was faintly disapproving.

Inside, the parlor was just as dim as the corridor. Only two lamps were lit, shaded in multicolored glass, each in opposite corners of the room. The only other light came from a faintly flickering candle in the corner, which the handmaiden gestured towards. Gemma realized the princess was in that corner. Solena sat on an upholstered stool, facing a long mirror framed in gold gilding. Despite its sumptuous frame, the mirror looked old, the glass a bit smudged. A tall, lissome lady-in-waiting stood behind the princess, brushing Solena's long dark hair. When Gemma approached, the lady stopped brushing and turned, giving Gemma a flat, unfriendly look. As though Gemma had interrupted an important state meeting rather than a nightly bedtime routine.

"It's all right, Kova," Princess Solena said in a languid tone.

The lady, Kova, dropped a quick curtsy and retreated, leaving Gemma and the princess alone.

"Well, come on then." Princess Solena's voice seemed lower and huskier in the darkness. But still tinged with that haughty impatience Gemma was already becoming accustomed to. "You're here to present yourself?"

Gemma quickened her pace, closing the distance between her and Solena. The princess did not turn to face her, remaining seated, gazing into the mirror. As Gemma stepped up behind her, slightly to Solena's right, she glanced into the mirror herself.

A skeletal visage gazed back at her in place of Solena's reflection.

Gemma caught her breath. In the feeble light of the candle, the princess's face in the mirror was that of a hideous corpse. As though her flesh had been peeled back, revealing the bare skull beneath—an upturned nub of nasal cavities where her nose should have been, a toothy grimace where her lips should have been. Her cheeks were sunken in, her eyes hooded and dark.

For a second—a single frozen second—those hooded eyes locked on Gemma, the skeletal wraith meeting her gaze in the mirror. Then the princess whipped around to face her.

And she was...the princess. Just the same beautiful princess Gemma had seen before.

No bony corpse. No skeletal creature. Just the princess.

"Oh, it's you, is it?" Princess Solena flicked her gaze up and down, scanning Gemma. "Is something wrong? Why do you look like that?"

Gemma realized her jaw hung open. Clamping her lips shut, she inhaled deeply through her nose. *It was just the shadows,* she told herself, *just the shadows making her look...making her reflection...* "It's nothing, Your Highness." Gemma clasped her hands behind her back, trying to calm herself.

"So? You'll be heading my escort while I'm here?" Solena prompted.

Right. That's why she was here. "Yes, Your Highness. I'll head your guard for the duration of your stay. Please let me know if there are any problems we can see to or anything you need of us. We take your safety very seriously."

Princess Solena studied her a moment longer. Her face had gone curiously blank, all traces of the puffed-up princess gone. Then—quite suddenly—she flashed a smile at Gemma. It was a creepy smile, something of the uncanny about it, as though the gesture didn't come naturally to her. Indeed, it rather reminded Gemma of the skeletal rictus she'd glimpsed—she *thought* she'd glimpsed—just a moment ago.

A chill glided down Gemma's spine.

"I'm sure I'll be perfectly safe while I'm here," Solena said with that twisted little smile. "Now if that's all, I'm quite tired."

Gemma bowed low. When she straightened, the princess was already on her feet, sweeping out of the parlor into the next room. But Gemma stood there, staring after her. It wasn't until Tashi returned with a beckoning gesture that Gemma turned away, following the handmaiden out into the corridor.

6

COMBATIVE

K LAUS STEPPED INTO THE mess hall about an hour before dawn and found it practically deserted, the long rows of wooden tables and benches mostly unoccupied. That suited him just fine. He didn't want company. After filling a plate with cold herring and a large hunk of bread, he found a spot at the end of one of the tables and sat to eat.

He was about halfway through his breakfast when a shadow fell across the table, and someone stepped over the bench on his right. The table shifted and squeaked, the sound rebounding off the wooden-beam ceiling. Klaus looked up, a nasty jibe forming on his lips, but it died when he saw who'd taken the seat beside him.

"Morning," said Kinsley. He didn't seem to have noticed Klaus's ill expression. In fact, he wasn't looking at Klaus at all, his attention on the steaming cup of tea that accompanied his breakfast. His blue eyes were a little bleary, his black hair a little tousled.

"Morning," Klaus said sourly. Klaus did not want company, but if someone had to sit with him, Kinsley was probably the only person he could stand. Klaus did not like people in general. Most people were annoying. Even Prince Garrett could be a little too cheerful sometimes. But Kinsley was pretty difficult not to like. Everyone liked Kinsley.

Klaus eyed Kinsley sidelong as the soldier tucked into his breakfast. His fare was more varied than Klaus's plate. In addition to the tinned herring, he had tomato and mushrooms on his plate, plus a bowl of porridge and jam for his bread. Despite this, Kinsley did not approach his breakfast with much enthusiasm; he picked at his porridge, taking it in slowly.

"Didn't sleep well?" Klaus asked.

Kinsley gave a noncommittal grunt. "Not really."

They continued eating in silence. Kinsley seemed to perk up the more he ate, his food quickly vanishing from his plate. Soon only his mushrooms and tomato were left, and still, he had not said another word. Klaus watched as Kinsley used his fork to carefully spear a tomato slice and a mushroom each, eating them together.

"So," Klaus said.

"Hmm?"

"Was there something you wanted to say to me?"

Kinsley chewed, swallowed, and said, "Like what?"

"Oh, come on. Let's just get it out in the open."

Kinsley lowered his fork. Then he said, "Look. I didn't know what was going to happen any sooner than anyone else. There was no time to warn you about him. But I promise you won't be put on any of his guard details."

It was a moment before Klaus realized they were talking about Gryphon. "Right."

"I know there's bad blood between the two of you—"

"Do you?" Klaus could not repress the acerbic note in his voice.

The look Kinsley gave him was a cool one. But when he spoke, his tone remained mild. "I wasn't there, in the Black Forest. I don't know every detail, but I know enough—"

"Gryphon hates me," Klaus said. "He thinks I betrayed him."

Kinsley gave him another cool look.

"All right," Klaus amended, "I did betray him. But. Not as badly as he thought. Anyway, it wasn't just him. I was duped too. Even worse than he was," he added in a mutter.

That last bit was more for himself than for Kinsley, though a quick glance at the officer made it clear he'd heard him. Kinsley furrowed his brow as he speared another mushroom with his fork. "Yes. Well." His voice went quiet. "I know a little something about that."

That's right, Klaus thought. *You do.* In fact, Kinsley—more than anyone else Klaus knew—could relate to the betrayal he'd been through with Viveca. Kinsley knew what it was to realize the person you loved was a liar. To realize the person you loved was only using you to further their own agenda.

Klaus's stomach gave a nasty tug. And how many days had it been since he'd last thought of Viveca? The woman he'd loved. The woman who'd used him. The woman who was now dead.

He resisted the urge to actually count the days. He had done that for a long time. He'd count the days he managed to go without thinking of her. Only, when he started, it wasn't days. It was hours. Sometimes minutes. Eventually, he'd forced himself to break that habit. It only kept her in his mind. And Klaus knew she didn't really deserve a space there. Deep down, he knew that.

"Look." Kinsley's fork *clinked* against his plate as he scraped up the last bit of tomato. "It'll be fine. All right? I think Prince Gryphon—you should try to remember to call him 'Prince' now—"

Klaus snorted. It took enough to remember to call Garrett 'Prince.' He certainly wasn't going to bother with Gryphon.

"I think Prince Gryphon is rather more concerned about keeping his father from chopping his head off—and this Desert princess as well—"

"Is there a concern *she* might chop his head off?" Klaus asked with a straight face.

"—to worry much about your presence here."

Klaus tore off a piece of his bread. "All I'm saying is," he grumbled, "if we run into each other, I don't know what he'll do."

"Well, there's a good chance you won't see each other," Kinsley said bracingly. He stood with his empty plate and bowl and went to stack them on the table near the kitchen. The mess hall was more crowded now, the sounds of chattering soldiers and clattering silverware filling the air. After exchanging hellos with a few people, Kinsley returned, pulling his cup of tea close to him. Which was good, because Klaus wasn't done.

"Anyway," Klaus said as Kinsley lowered himself onto the bench, "I wasn't talking about Gryphon, Kinsley. I was talking about Gemma."

Kinsley looked surprised. "What about her?"

"Come on." Klaus tapped his boot against the leg of the table, jiggling it a bit. "You can be straight with me."

"I still don't know what you're talking about."

"Why the hell did Garrett—Prince Garrett—leave her behind, Kinsley? He takes her along on almost every venture of his—"

"This isn't a venture." Kinsley calmly sipped at his tea. "It's a holiday."

"—and now that she's been injured, he leaves her behind? You know she thinks Garrett doesn't value her anymore, right? You know she's worried they're going to kick her out of the guard."

"I don't think she thinks that at all."

"Shows what you know."

"Klaus, I've already spoken to Gemma about this." Kinsley gave him a level look over his cup of tea. "I've been straight about it—with her. Because it's her business. So if you want to know more, you need to talk to her about it."

Klaus pulled a face. He didn't want to talk to her about it. They had an understanding, the two of them. They didn't talk about things like that. But lately...well, lately that had been a lot harder for Klaus. Keeping his concerns to himself. Keeping his concerns about *Gemma* to himself.

Because he was concerned for her. He was worried about her. He had been almost constantly, ever since that witch had nearly killed her in the southern wood.

And that was something he didn't want to dwell on, much less talk about. With anyone.

Aloud, he said, "I don't think Gemma's going to talk to me." Recalling their encounter outside the princess's quarters yesterday, he added, "I might have snapped at her. Unfairly."

"So, nothing new, then."

Klaus tore off another piece of bread, stuffing it into his mouth. He and Kinsley sat in silence for a few more minutes,

Klaus finishing off his bread and Kinsley sipping at his tea. The mess hall was considerably more crowded now, soldiers filling up the tables as they gobbled down their breakfast. Some of the latecomers simply grabbed a piece of bread and a mug of hot tea before trickling back out of the hall.

Klaus looked at Kinsley. He looked a lot better than he had when he'd first sat down. His breakfast had brightened his face, putting some color into his pale cheeks. Still. Kinsley was not one to stay out late drinking or carousing at a time like this, with newcomers in the castle and guard details to arrange. Which begged the question...what had kept him up so late?

"I notice you didn't go either," Klaus said.

"Go where?"

"With Garrett and Briar, of course."

"Ah. I noticed that too."

"And the reason for that is..."

Kinsley was quiet for a moment. Then he said, "Also something I discussed with Gemma."

"Meaning you won't discuss it with me."

"I wasn't needed, Klaus. That's why I didn't go."

When it became clear Kinsley wasn't going to say anything else, Klaus pushed his empty plate away and leaned back. Beneath the table, he stretched his legs out, crossing them at the ankle. "So that's it, then? There's no other reason you stayed behind? You don't have other plans?"

Kinsley frowned at him. "What are you implying?"

"Well, you obviously haven't slept well."

"And...?"

"I just thought maybe you'd gone out last night—maybe to meet someone privately?" Klaus suggested. "A certain witch?"

Kinsley stared at him for a long moment. Several different emotions flickered through his eyes, too quickly for Klaus to identify them. Then—as the mess hall began to empty once again—Kinsley put his cup down on the table and said, "Let me get this straight. You think I stayed behind deliberately so that I could, what? Sneak out to meet Castel during my off hours?"

"I'm just saying." Klaus raised his hands. "I know something about secrets trysts, Kinsley."

"You don't know as much as you think." Kinsley's tone became downright frosty.

"I wouldn't blame you, you know. I mean, he did help us out in the southern woods a few months ago, when we were up against that coven and their demon—"

"Klaus." Kinsley's tone held a warning note.

"Can you honestly say you haven't seen him since you left the Mariner Kingdom last summer? Can you tell me that?"

The Mariner Kingdom was where Kinsley had met Castel, a morally ambiguous witch with mysterious intentions. Castel had lied to Kinsley about who and what he was, and about why he'd become involved with Kinsley in the first place. And yet—when Kinsley had been irrevocably injured, his brain damaged—Castel had healed him. Even though it had cost him.

That was why Kinsley understood what Klaus had gone through with Viveca.

Now Kinsley went quiet for a long moment, in response to Klaus's question. Then he said, "No. I can't say that."

"So you are seeing him again."

"No. I'm not." But there was the slightest pause before Kinsley answered. Maybe it wasn't an outright lie, Klaus thought, but there was something Kinsley wasn't telling him. And perhaps

Kinsley caught the look on Klaus's face because he added more firmly, "And I certainly would not have begged off an assignment from Princess Briar so I could stay behind to see him." Kinsley rubbed at the bridge of his nose. "Besides. It doesn't matter where I am. If I stay here, if I go." A soft, bitter note entered his voice. "He's in my head."

Klaus sat very still. Those words struck a nerve. Those words twisted like a knife.

Viveca was dead and gone, but she was in his head too.

"You want to know the truth?" Kinsley said. "Yes, Castel is the reason I didn't sleep last night." He gripped his teacup a little too tightly. "I have this recurring dream. I've had it since last summer. Since he healed me." He lifted his gaze, and his eyes were haunted. "I'm lost in a maze. In this dream. I'm lost in a tangled, overgrown maze. And it's getting dark, as though night is falling. I start running, but no matter what I do, I can't find a way out." He clenched his hand one last time around his cup, then released it, pushing it away. "And then I turn a corner. And there he is. Castel. Standing there. Waiting for me. And then...I wake up."

Klaus waited a beat to make sure Kinsley was done. Then he said, "Doesn't sound so bad."

"Maybe not. But the feeling it leaves me with..."

"What feeling?"

Kinsley looked at him. "The kind of feeling that keeps me awake the rest of the night." He cleared his throat. "Anyway. I'm sure you can relate. I'm sure you have nightmares."

"I do," Klaus admitted, rising to his feet. "But our situations weren't the same, Kinsley."

"Oh?" Kinsley glanced up. "How so?"

"Castel never tried to kill you," Klaus said bluntly. "In fact, he saved your life." Picking up his plate, he added, "Come on. We're going to be late for the meeting with the king."

⚬

Later that afternoon, Klaus made his way to the training grounds outside the barracks. He'd been given the entire day off, on account of his traveling back with Princess Solena and her retinue. So after the early meeting with the king, he'd gone back to bed for a few hours. Now he was plenty rested and itching to work off some of the frustration he'd built up over the last twenty-four hours.

As soon as he approached the grounds, he spotted Gemma leaning over the low wooden fence surrounding the yard, watching other soldiers fight with practice blades and shoot off arrows. There were no firearms here; the shooting range was on the far side of the grounds, around the back.

As Klaus passed Gemma, he slapped her lightly on the arm and said, "C'mon. Let's go."

The look of surprise that flickered over Gemma's face melted into a flat expression. A very irritated, very familiar flat expression.

"I need a sparring partner," Klaus said, a petulant note in his voice. "Hand-to-hand combat. Come on."

"What?" she asked. "You're done yelling at me, so now you want to beat me up a little?"

"Stars, Gemma, have a little faith in yourself. Maybe you'll beat me up a little."

"Tempting." Her voice went as stony as her face. "Then again, maybe you just think I need to practice hand-to-hand because I'm useless with a gun now."

"We all need to practice hand-to-hand. We're all on bodyguard work for the foreseeable future. So are you coming or what?"

Gemma eyed him a moment longer, her gaze implacable. Then she followed him onto the grounds, removing her coat and rolling the sleeves of her starched shirt up to her elbows.

It was a bright day, but a cold one. The sun's rays had little effect on the chill in the air. Even so, Klaus, too, removed his uniform coat as they entered a side pen, slinging it over the railing. He would warm up soon enough. Gemma sidled up to the display of practice weapons hanging nearby. "Weapons?" she asked.

"Not for me." Klaus rolled a shoulder back, then the other, warming up. "You take whatever you want. If you think you need it."

"It's not about need." Gemma selected a long, slender practice knife, then—rather offhandedly—went back for a second, smaller knife, which she strapped to her hip. She turned back to face Klaus, and Klaus's mouth went dry at the look on her face. She didn't smile, exactly—Gemma almost never smiled—but there was something like one lurking beneath her lips. Tightening her jaw.

Oh, yes. She was going to make him pay for snapping at her.

"Too bad I can't actually stab you with this." She circled towards him, flipping the long knife in her hand.

"You probably could if you tried hard enough." It was true the practice blades were blunted, but. With enough force, even a dull blade could penetrate skin. "And if you get close enough."

"Oh, I'll get close enough."

Klaus swallowed. Getting close to Gemma was something that had been on his mind a lot lately, though not for the reason she was implying. He shrugged, trying to shake away those distracting thoughts. Now was not the time. *Never* was the time. For a lot of reasons.

Still, he found himself watching her now, beneath the pale sky. As she took a step to the left, the sunlight obscured her for a moment, slicing through her, and Klaus experienced an odd moment in which he felt like he was gazing at her reflection through broken glass.

Gazing at Gemma. The one who'd killed Viveca.

Because Klaus had been too spineless to do it himself.

Perhaps Gemma had noticed how distracted Klaus was—though she couldn't possibly know the reason why—because she took advantage of the moment, coming at him to attack, her quick, nimble steps kicking up the sandy dirt coating the ground. She made a wide, overhand swing, the dull tip of the practice blade sinking towards his neck.

It was an obvious move, almost clumsy, and though Gemma was not so practiced with a blade as she was with a rifle, Klaus was sure she knew better than that.

It was a trick.

Klaus ducked low, half-raising his head to keep her in his sight.

Sure enough, she swung for him with her other arm, as fast as lightning. If he'd popped back up like she'd obviously hoped he would, she would have caught him in his face. Instead, Klaus veered away, digging the toe of his boot into the dirt to keep from slipping. Using the momentum he'd already begun to build, he lunged at her, swinging his own closed fist.

Gemma veered back too, but not quickly enough. His swing caught her on the shoulder, his knuckles glancing off her, and she stumbled. More stunned than hurt, Klaus thought.

Gemma shook her head at him. "You'd better not be pulling your punches, Klaus."

"Please. Like I would."

She shook herself again, dancing back to regroup. "So," she said in a casual tone clearly meant to put him at ease. "Princess Solena seems quite taken with you. What did you two talk about on the way here?"

"Garrett, mostly."

"That's all?"

"That's all." Klaus let out a quick breath, loosening his body, tightening his thoughts. He kept his eyes trained on Gemma as she moved in again, shooting forward. She gripped her blade differently this time, jabbing upwards.

Klaus caught her wrist and twisted it back, not enough to seriously hurt her, but enough to force her to slacken her grip. Sure enough, she dropped the blade, but when she snapped her other fist forward and landed a solid punch to his kidney, Klaus lost his grip on her.

Winded, smarting, he managed to get a leg up and knee her squarely in the middle. Just hard enough to knock her off-balance. She stumbled back.

Klaus gritted his teeth. Stones, that punch had *hurt*. He felt bruised on the inside. Gemma seemed unsympathetic; she only glared at him. "You didn't try to find out what she was doing out there in the middle of the night? Why she'd run away?"

"What?" Only then did Klaus remember they'd been talking about the princess. "Oh." He gulped a breath, the cold air a bristle against his throat but a salve to his lungs. "No. I mean, how could I have asked her that? Besides, there really wasn't time."

"Let me guess. Did the princess spend all her time flirting with you?"

"No. Truth be told, she wanted to know about *you* as well as Garrett. So maybe you're the one she wants to flirt with."

"Me?" For a moment, Gemma looked dumbfounded. Klaus took advantage of that rare occurrence and moved in, going on the offensive. As he rushed Gemma, she raised one arm to fend him off and swung for him with the other, her practice blade aiming for his flank.

Klaus dodged the blade, shooting in close. Blocking her swing at the elbow, he caught her around the waist with his other arm. Grunting at the effort, he swept her down onto the ground. There, he tried to pin her, but she was up again quickly, using his grip on her to leverage herself into a crouch.

"I don't think the princess is interested in me." Gemma rose to her full height. Her words were breathless, showing her exertion. "Unless her form of flirting is to treat people like they're incompetent."

Klaus only half-listened, tracking Gemma's movements. Tracking her knife. She wasn't holding it anymore, he realized, and he dropped his gaze, spotting it on the ground between them. It was only for a second that he looked away—but it was long enough.

Gemma snapped a kick at him, her boot catching him in the middle. Klaus staggered back, and it was only then he remembered the second blade, the one Gemma had strapped to her hip before they started. She wielded it now, driving the smaller knife towards him with an overhand swing.

Caught off guard, Klaus barely recovered in time, crossing his hands at the wrist to block the blow. He trembled at the effort of holding her back, keeping the tip of that dull blade from crashing into his neck.

"Then again," Gemma panted, "maybe the princess does flirt like that. She seems strange enough."

"It's not—so strange," Klaus managed to reply. Damn it, he couldn't fend her off, his strained muscles quavering uncontrollably. "Sometimes—"

He couldn't push her back. So he stopped trying. He let his arms slacken and sank to the left, turning his head aside—out of the reach of her blade. Caught off by her own momentum, Gemma staggered forward. Klaus ducked beneath her wildly swinging arms and caught her around the middle again.

Then he flipped her onto the ground.

"Sometimes," Klaus finished, stepping clear of her, "there's a thin line between love and hate."

He took a second to recover, then leaned over Gemma, checking she was all right. She lay on her back, breathing hard, wisps of dark hair wild around her flushed face. But she was conscious and, judging by the look she gave him, unhurt. Mostly.

"Yes, well." Gemma ran a hand over her face, pushing those stray hairs out of her eyes. "You'd know. Wouldn't you."

Klaus felt those words harder than any physical blow she could've dealt him. It hung there between them.

Viveca.

Always between them.

That was why Klaus could never think of being close to Gemma. Not in the way he wanted, not in the way he dreamed of. Because he had loved the woman who'd taken Gemma's friend from her. The woman who had killed Falcon.

And then he'd been too much of a coward to end Viveca himself. Leaving Gemma to clean up his mess and save his worthless life.

Whether or not Gemma had meant to wound him so soundly with her words, Klaus didn't know. He couldn't tell by her face. She was as impassive as ever, her voice as toneless as it had been when she'd killed Viveca. When she'd told him, *"You're welcome."* For doing what he couldn't.

"Yes." Klaus strove to make his voice as toneless as hers. But he wasn't sure he succeeded. "I do."

7

TASTED

GEMMA HAD BEEN NERVOUS to see Gryphon—*Prince Gryphon*, as she tried to think of him now. It had been almost a year since she'd last seen him, and she wasn't sure what feelings the sight of him might dredge up. One memory in particular swam to the forefront of her mind when she thought about Gryphon. One night in particular. The night when she and Falcon had guarded Gryphon in his own castle. She and Falcon had been playing at cards while Gryphon fretted over Isabelle, who was being held captive at the time.

She remembered leaving the room to scout the castle corridors.

She remembered hearing the front doors explode and realizing the castle had been breached.

And she remembered what came after that.

But strangely—when she saw Gryphon again, the day after sparring with Klaus—she didn't think of that awful night. She didn't think of Falcon, even.

All she could think was—the very last time she saw Gryphon—he'd been naked.

She had completely forgotten about that. The very last time she'd seen Gryphon had been after she'd helped Isabelle track him down. He'd gotten trapped in his beast form and wandered far from his old castle. Isabelle begged Gemma to help her track him down, and Gemma had agreed. The two of them had ranged far to the north of the Black Forest, into the foothills of the northern mountains. When they finally found Gryphon—when Gemma tracked the beast to a rocky glade and spotted him dozing near a winding stream—Isabelle had gone down to him alone, whispering to Gemma that she would be perfectly safe, that Gryphon would never harm her.

She'd been right, but Gemma had taken no chances. She'd waited on the higher ground nearby, out of sight within a cluster of boulders, stretched out in a prone pose. Watching Isabelle approach the beast through the scope of her rifle.

So naturally—when the sight of Isabelle prompted Gryphon's change back into a very nude human—Gemma saw it all.

She hadn't seen it *all*. She hadn't been very close, after all, and Isabelle had blocked out much of Gryphon's body with her own. But even still. Gemma had seen Gryphon naked.

And now—as she, Princess Solena, and several other guards and attendants joined the prince out on Glen Castle's grassy eastern lawn—Gemma found she couldn't think of anything else.

She didn't get a chance to speak to Gryphon right away. He was there for Solena, after all, not for her. They had taken dinner together last night—Gemma had not been present for that—and now they were going for an afternoon ride out on the castle's vast grounds. It was a nice day for it, Gemma supposed, a little warmer than it had been. The occasional breeze rippling through the grass was light enough to keep the air balmy, and the sky was a clear blue dome, not a cloud in sight.

Gemma hung back with her fellow soldiers as the princess greeted Prince Gryphon, who, of course, was clothed now, in riding breeches and gleaming black boots, paired with a russet coat that brought out the warm bronze undertones of his deep-brown skin. She was surprised when Solena made a little curtsy—Gemma would have thought the princess too proud to bow to anyone, even someone of her own rank—but then she realized Solena was only showing off her blush-pink dress, asking, by the look of it, what Gryphon thought of it. Or rather, what he thought of *her* in it. Gemma watched Gryphon's face carefully, but if he thought the princess silly or annoying, not a trace of it showed in him. His expression was neutral as he responded to her, his posture reserved but urbane.

But when the princess turned away, looking to the white mare trotting out for her, Gryphon raised his gaze. His eyes quested over the gathered crowd and found Gemma. Now she saw a flicker of surprise cross his face—he was startled to see her, perhaps—and then, ever so slightly, his eyes widened, flicking from Gemma to the princess. As though to say, *Can you believe her?* Or perhaps, *Help me.*

Gemma stifled a laugh. She let a brief smile touch her face, then assumed her dispassionate stare, looking out over the colorful crowd on the lawn. It was quite a party, considering the only two people this outing was meant for were Princess Solena and Gryphon. But Solena had her guards, of course, garbed in red and gold—four of them, which Gemma thought a bit excessive, since she and two other Glen soldiers were here to guard Solena. Prince Gryphon, too, had his contingent of guards, including Spencer, in their navy-blue uniforms. Then there were the servants, dressed in black and white, many from the kitchens, bringing along fare for afternoon tea. And Solena had her attendants as well, three ladies-in-waiting bedecked in pastel tea gowns to match their princess.

But the princess only had eyes for Gryphon. If Solena was still dismayed to court him instead of Prince Garrett, it didn't show. She kept up a steady stream of chatter with Gryphon as the two of them mounted their horses. All of the guards were riding as well, so Gemma mounted her own horse, wincing. Her backside was still sore from her rout with Klaus yesterday. If his goal had been to prove how much she needed to practice hand-to-hand combat, Gemma thought sourly, he had achieved that. Painfully. Which, perhaps, was why she'd been a bit thoughtless and cruel to him, making that comment about love and hate. And him knowing about that.

She hadn't meant to be cruel, but she thought she had been. She'd realized afterwards how he might take her words as a comment on his relationship with Viveca—obviously a touchy subject for him. But she hadn't intended that at all; truthfully, she didn't know what she'd intended. She'd been angry, sore, and a little humiliated, staring up at him from the ground, so she'd said the first retort that came to mind. Well, the first retort after *"Shut up, Klaus."*

But the words were said. She couldn't take them back now. He'd get over it. He always did, and things went right back to normal between them.

Gryphon and Solena started across the grounds, walking their horses leisurely over a field covered in bristly winter grass, heading towards a cultivated thicket nearby. The slow pace was necessary since the servants had to keep up on foot. Gryphon's mounted guards took position at the front of the party, so Gemma fell into place behind them, on the fringes of the group, where she had a clear sight of Solena.

They rode for less than an hour before stopping for tea in a shady spot near the trees. It was late in the afternoon, the descending sun scattering rays of golden light through the wood. Some of the princess's servants erected a small silk tent—in only a few minutes, at that—and Solena, along with two of her ladies, disappeared inside to "freshen up."

While she was gone, the rest of the servants prepared for tea. A fine wool blanket was spread over the grass, a blanket so large that it took four servants to lay it flat. Ten people would have been comfortable on that blanket, much less two. Food was quickly emptied from dozens of baskets, starting with bowls of fruit and boards arrayed with cheese, cured meats, smoked heron, and delicate quail eggs. Silver trays filled with little square sandwiches came next, and then, of course, all the sweets. A whole basket of scones with clotted cream, a plate filled with colorful tea cakes, another with tartlets bursting with fruit fillings. There was even a roast duck, freshly garnished and served with dark gravy.

Gryphon stood by in the shadow of a tall tree, watching all of this as though it were a play put on for his amusement. Though not a particularly interesting play, for he looked quite bored. Gemma took this moment to sidle up beside him, though she said nothing, waiting for him to speak first.

"I didn't expect to see you here," he said.

Gemma blinked.

Gryphon flicked a glance her way. "I assumed you'd be off with Garrett and his princess."

"Oh." To Gemma's horror, a rush of embarrassment swept through her. Which was stupid. Gryphon probably had no idea what had happened to her—that a witch had nearly killed her and injured her eyesight. He was probably not standing there wondering about Gemma's fitness as a soldier, as a sharpshooter.

He doesn't need to wonder, the snide voice inside her head said. *He's seen you shoot. He's seen you miss a target two paces in front of you.*

Ah. There it was.

That horrible night. The shot Gemma had missed. The shot Gemma hadn't taken because she just...froze.

And then, Falcon. Dead.

A terrible wrenching went through Gemma, but she felt it in a detached sort of way. As though she were a spectator to her own pain. This was a trick she'd learned years ago. How to remove herself from the moment, how to step outside herself. She imagined Kinsley knew a similar trick. It was a necessary skill for a sharpshooter.

Gryphon was looking at her, and Gemma realized he was waiting for an explanation. Or at least a response beyond, "Oh."

"I think Prince Garrett wanted Spencer, Roy, and I here," she said, "because you know us. I suppose he thought that might make you more comfortable with all of this."

Gryphon snorted with some of that sullen disdain Gemma was used to from him. "As though anything could make *all of this* comfortable."

Gemma arched an eyebrow. He caught her look and admitted, "Though I suppose it is nice to see some familiar faces around here. Besides the ones who remember me from before I was exiled."

"Had any trouble with that? From anyone, I mean?"

"Not so far. A few startled looks. But no one has said anything within my hearing."

"And you do have very good hearing."

"Yes." Gryphon eyed the servants critically as they rushed to set out a few adornments along the wide blanket—bunches of flowers, pansies and winter jasmine, artfully arranged and tied with white satin ribbon. "I suspect no one will dare say anything now my father has officially reinstated me as prince. But that doesn't mean I don't wonder what they're thinking. About me." He released a quiet sigh. "I can't wait until this is over and I can leave this life. Again."

"You seem well-suited to it," Gemma remarked.

Gryphon cast her a sidelong look. "Are you making fun of me?"

"Of course not. I wouldn't dare. Your Highness."

Gryphon sighed again. "It's honestly a bit upsetting. How easy it all comes back. All the social graces ingrained into me. It's like putting on a very familiar coat. But one that's not really my style. Anymore."

How poetic, she thought. As one of Princess Solena's ladies emerged from the little tent—Gemma recognized her as the sharp-eyed Lady Kova—Gemma said in a low voice, "I don't know if you know. But I'm in charge of the princess's armed escort while she's here. And apparently, I'm meant to keep a very close eye on her—and not just for her sake."

Gryphon's gaze sharpened. "On whose orders?"

"The king's."

"So he doesn't entirely trust this Desert princess." Gryphon's dark eyes turned thoughtful, his gaze flitting to the princess's tent. Its silk flaps rustled in the breeze, though they were bound with a knotted cord. "I've wondered about her myself. I could have sworn all the princesses in the Desert Kingdom died of some plague."

"That's the rumor. Still, if she was the only survivor, it's not too weird they'd want to keep her safe. Keep word of her quiet."

"Perhaps." But Gryphon didn't look convinced.

Gemma wasn't either. She only liked to look at a problem from all sides, consider all the possibilities. But she hadn't stopped wondering what Princess Solena had been doing out in the woods that night, so far from her retinue, all on her own. And she hadn't forgotten what she'd seen—that mangled girl who'd looked so much like Princess Solena.

And then. Two nights ago. In Solena's quarters. What she'd seen in the mirror...

It might have been nothing. It had been dim after all, and the mirror a bit smudged. It could have just been the shadows obscuring her reflection. And it had only been for a second...

Still. Some part of Gemma's brain pushed back at those excuses. *I know what I saw.*

The princess emerged from her little tent then, and Gryphon went to join her as she exclaimed over the food. Gemma watched, torn between amusement at Gryphon's discomfort (even if he did a very good job hiding it) and her own suspicions, gnawing at her as she watched Princess Solena's every move.

They spent close to an hour on tea—not just eating, but lounging on the blanket there. The princess continued chattering, and if Gemma was not mistaken, she caught Gryphon nodding off a few times as he leaned back on one elbow, his long legs stretched before him. But Solena did not seem to notice, and then—as the servants moved in to clear away the tea fare, much of which hadn't been touched—Solena and Gryphon stepped away from the party to take a short stroll, venturing into the thicket. Just in the short time they had spent eating, the light had changed, the golden sun vanishing beyond the trees, painting the northern sky a blend of pale violet and peachy pink. Dusk was not far off.

Two of Solena's guards followed the couple at a distance, and Spencer broke away too, lingering at the tree line. But when Gemma tried to follow, Princess Solena shot her a glare, jerking her head. So Gemma stayed where she was, just out of sight. She felt strangely anxious. She reminded herself what Kinsley had said—that Gryphon hardly needed bodyguards—but something about Solena made her deeply mistrustful. A gust of wind blew past, stronger and colder than the earlier gentle breezes, and Gemma shivered, trying to shake off her discomfiture.

She was both surprised and relieved when, a few minutes later, the princess called for her. "Gemma!" Her strident voice was very near; they hadn't gone far. "Come here!"

Gemma exchanged a glance with Spencer, then ventured into the thicket. It was even darker in here; the trees were mostly yew, their thick, dark boughs deepening the murk of twilight. Gemma spotted Gryphon first, standing with his arms crossed, and she made her way over to him.

The princess knelt on the ground beside a patch of wildflowers, scattered before her in a vivid array of brilliant indigo. In her blush-pink gown, she was like a single lily in the darkness, the only light patch beneath the trees. Solena looked around impatiently as Gemma approached. "Do you have a knife?" She indicated the flowers. "I want to cut some of these."

Gemma glanced, bemused, at Gryphon.

"I don't have one." He raised both hands, then added in a low voice meant for Gemma's ears only, "As though my father would let me carry a blade. Even a ceremonial one."

Deftly, Gemma removed a small paring knife from her waist, turning back to the princess. "I can do that for you, Your Highness," she offered.

"No, no, I want to do it," the princess insisted. She barely looked up, her gaze bent on the wildflowers, cupping their fragile petals. Ready to rip them free of the earth.

Gemma flipped the blade around to offer it to the princess hilt first.

And the princess snatched it out of her hand so quickly and forcefully, the blade sliced right through Gemma's palm.

Gemma sucked in a pained breath, cradling her hand close to her chest. Blood eked out of a thin wound that ran across the top of her palm and onto the base of her index finger.

"Oh, I'm so sorry!" Princess Solena gasped. "Are you all right? So clumsy of me—I'm not used to handling blades."

"It's fine," Gemma muttered. "It's not too deep."

"Here." Gryphon fished about in his coat pockets. "I may not have a blade, but surely I have a handkerchief."

Gemma shot a quick glance at the princess. Solena's face was the picture of innocent concern, but something about her sympathy felt off. Overdone. It was the first time Gemma had seen the princess show any concern for someone of lower rank than herself. But what was more, in the instant Solena had grabbed the blade—in the split second it took her to slice through Gemma's palm—something had flashed across the princess's face. Something malicious.

In that instant, Gemma had been sure the princess had cut her on purpose.

But now that seemed ridiculous. She was growing overly suspicious, Gemma thought, as she inspected her bleeding palm. The princess might be spoiled and petulant, but what reason would she have to deliberately harm Gemma? Lifting her gaze, Gemma snuck another glance at the princess.

Just in time to see Solena lick the blade, still wet with Gemma's blood.

"Here you go," said Gryphon.

Gemma whipped around. Gryphon stood before her, holding out a neatly folded handkerchief. When Gemma didn't take it, he frowned.

"What is it?" he asked.

Gemma turned to the princess again. Solena hummed softly to herself as she used the knife to cut a few wildflowers, gathering them together. Dusk was closer than ever, but the princess didn't seem bothered by the low light. She wasn't looking at Gemma or Gryphon, and there was no sign that she had just—

That she had just—

Gemma turned back to Gryphon. It was clear by the puzzled look on his face that he hadn't seen what she had. But she had not imagined anything this time, she was sure of it. It had happened quickly, but even so—

Princess Solena had just *licked* the blood off that blade. Gemma's blood.

Had she cut Gemma on purpose? But why? So she could...taste her blood?

"Gemma." Gryphon was still proffering his handkerchief. "Are you all right?"

Gemma stared at him a moment longer. Then she took the handkerchief from him, pressing it into the cut on her palm. "Yes," she said, "I'm fine."

8

TRESPASSED

GRYPHON WAS HUNGRY AGAIN. Which was a problem because it was the middle of the night. Just past midnight, according to the steadily ticking clock on the mantelpiece.

This had been happening a lot since he'd been back in the castle. Now that Gryphon could control his turning, he no longer lived a nocturnal lifestyle. But he didn't really keep "normal" hours either. He and Isabelle enjoyed staying up late into the night, Isabelle reading and studying, Gryphon working on his art. Not to mention, they also enjoyed the occasional midnight run through the woods.

Add the additional stress of being back here in the castle, along with the accompanying insomnia, and, well. This was not the first time Gryphon had found himself lying awake in bed, listening to his stomach growl.

He didn't mind fetching a snack from the kitchens. But his father—and by extension, most of the castle guards—didn't like him prowling the castle in the middle of the night. As a result, Gryphon often had to sneak out of his room as he had before: leaping out the window, then from balcony to ledge to balcony, then using side corridors and secret passages to get to the kitchen.

But if he was lucky, he didn't have to do that. After a moment's indecision, Gryphon sat up and quietly rose from his bed, tossing back the silk sheets. He pulled a shirt and coat on over his pajama pants, then padded over the rug-covered floor on bare feet, out into the sitting room. There he stopped, mere inches from the oaken door leading out into the corridor.

He inhaled deeply, scenting the two guards on the other side of the door. They were familiar scents. Both of them.

With relief, Gryphon opened the door.

Out in the corridor, two guards looked up at him. They sat playing cards, using a short stool as a table between them.

Roy and Spencer.

"Erm." Spencer blinked. "Can we help you...Your Highness?"

Gryphon shuddered a little. He tried to control his expression, but he must have failed because Roy said, "I know. It's weird. But we're trying to get in the habit. Don't want to go calling you by your name in front of the wrong person."

"I understand," Gryphon said glumly.

"So, was there something?"

"I'm hungry," Gryphon said.

Spencer and Roy exchanged a look. "I can bring you something?" Spencer offered.

"Don't bother. I'll fetch it myself." Gryphon stepped out into the corridor and shut the door behind him. Belatedly, he realized he was still barefoot. Someone else might have gone back for shoes—part of the route to the kitchen would be over bare stone—but Gryphon didn't much feel the cold like other people did. Or rather, he felt it, but it didn't bother him. Part of that was because of the beast. Part of that was just him.

As he started down the corridor, he could not fail to notice Roy and Spencer jogging after him. "I know you don't need protection," Roy admitted, "but it is our job."

"Of course," Gryphon said, resigned.

"Are you sure this is all right?" Spencer asked. "I'm not sure what the cook will think of you turning up at this hour."

"I've done it before. She's one of the few people in this castle who remembers me and still likes me. For some reason."

"I'm surprised the other guards let you wander the castle at night," Roy said cautiously.

"They don't. I usually sneak out my window."

"Oh. I suppose that works too."

The castle was very different so late at night. Darker, of course, but eerily quiet too. During the daytime, nothing about this castle reminded Gryphon of the abandoned ruin he'd occupied back in the Black Forest. In the daytime, Glen Castle was warm, clean, and bright. Plenty of long, high windows let in plenty of daylight, and the more secluded corridors were lit with gear-bulb fixtures, set into sconces at close intervals. When it was cold out, fires burned in every hearth, and most of the stone floor was covered in rugs to keep the warmth in.

And yet at this late hour, the castle did remind him of that old ruin. It was the still silence echoing into the castle's vast spaces, it was the shadows sweeping the floors and retreating into the corners. There was a reason Gryphon liked to stay up late, even though he didn't need to anymore. The night was primal and quiet in a way that appealed to the beast inside him. The night, and all that was in it, was his domain.

Though sometimes, someone trespassed there.

They had just crossed into the west wing when Gryphon caught the scent. It was a *wrong* scent. That was the first thing that came to mind, the way he registered it: wrong. Out of place, but also wrong in the way it made him feel. All the hair on his arms prickled, standing up straight, and the beast inside him growled. Sensing a predator. Sensing a threat.

Gryphon stopped dead in the middle of the corridor. Spencer muttered half a curse as he nearly ran into him, then mumbled an apology. Gryphon ignored him, raising his head. Trying to pinpoint the scent.

"Something wrong?" Roy asked. Then—perhaps noting Gryphon's posture—he said, "What is it?"

Gryphon turned. He took a few steps back the way they'd come. He reached for the beast again, just enough to enhance his senses. The wrong scent sharpened, coming into focus. It was a foul odor, one that made his stomach turn. It smelled a bit earthy, like dirt, but dirt tinged with something rotten. As though an animal had dug up a fresh grave, ripping soft, decaying flesh off the bones of some carcass.

Without saying a word, Gryphon followed the scent, turning down a dark corridor that led further into the castle. Roy and Spencer followed. Spencer asked, "Where are we going?"

"I'm not sure," Gryphon muttered. "What's back this way?"

"Just more quarters. Mostly empty," said Roy. "Though if we keep going this way and take a left turn, that will take us straight to the king's apartments."

They kept going that way. They took a left turn. Rounding the corner, Gryphon stopped short.

A door down the corridor stood ajar, casting a long shadow across the wall, darkening the patterned wallpaper. It was the door to the king's apartments. Gryphon knew because, well, he'd remembered now that he was here, but he also knew because there were two guards in the corridor outside the open door.

They both lay on the floor, crumpled, unconscious.

In an instant, Roy and Spencer had pistols drawn. "Let us check it out first—" Roy started, but Gryphon was already running down the corridor.

That wrong, rotted scent was coming from inside the king's quarters. Inside his father's quarters.

"Check on the guards," Gryphon ordered Roy. Then he burst into the king's apartments, claws and fangs at the ready, the beast's eyes bright and penetrating in the darkness.

The rooms *were* dark, but Gryphon's enhanced senses zeroed in on his surroundings. Oversized shadows coalesced into solid forms—a long chaise, two thick, cushy armchairs, a low, varnished table. Bookshelves and a huge display cabinet with glass casings lined the walls. This was the king's sitting room, and it was empty, so far as Gryphon could tell.

But that faintly sweet, sickening scent drew him in, pulling him into the rooms beyond the sitting room. Another door stood ajar there, and inside it was even darker, all light fixtures turned down and candles extinguished. Even with the beast's enhanced night vision, it was a few seconds before Gryphon could make out the scene before him.

An enormous four-poster bed, centered along the back wall. Its curtains tied back. A single figure sleeping in the bed—King Victor, Gryphon's father. And another figure standing at the bedside, leaning over the king. A figure garbed in black from head to toe, disguising their identity, concealing their face.

Gryphon let out a deadly snarl, the sound grumbling up from his chest. The figure in black looked up, and Gryphon saw two eyes staring back at him. The whites of those eyes shone brightly in the darkness, practically glowing. They were all that showed from beneath the figure's hood.

If the intruder was startled to see Gryphon—half-man, half-beast—standing in the doorway, they didn't show it. Immediately, the dark figure drew a dagger from behind its back, the long, thin blade glinting as it hovered over the king. Gryphon launched himself forward, but rather than stabbing at King Victor, the attacker threw the dagger with deadly precision at Gryphon. The tip of the blade embedded itself in the fleshy junction just beneath his shoulder, and he grunted, stumbling, slamming into the king's bed.

The hit was enough to rattle the bed and wake the king. "What—" Mumbling, King Victor stirred, pushing himself upright. He blinked several times as he looked from Gryphon—slumped over the foot of the bed—to the intruder, turning to flee.

"Stay there!" Gryphon ordered his father, the words distorted by the elongated fangs jutting from between his lips. He caught a glimpse of astonishment on the king's face before he straightened himself, ready to dash after the intruder.

But there was no intruder. They were gone.

Gryphon gaped, turning left and right, his night vision piercing the shadows. It only took a second for his gaze to snag on the single window, set in the far wall.

It was cracked open, about a hand's span wide.

Gryphon crossed the room in two massive, leaping strides, reached the window, and shoved it open all the way. Leaning out through the window, he took in his surroundings in disbelief.

The window overlooked a narrow stone courtyard directly below the king's apartments, but it was far below, and no balconies or footholds lined the sheer wall on the way down. The night outside was black, a spittle of cold rain coating the air. Gryphon could scarcely make out the terrace below, but he saw no sign of the attacker, no trace of movement or shifting shadows.

He lifted his gaze. The walls encasing the terrace ran straight up on four sides, forming a chute outside the apartments here. But directly across from this floor, one of those walls opened up, curving around to the right. Even still, there were no balconies or ledges there to give someone a foothold.

No one could have escaped this way. There was nowhere to go.

But there was no other way the intruder could have escaped.

"Gryphon!" the king barked. "What is *happening?*"

Gryphon turned away from the window. He raised a hand to shield his eyes as a bright light flared into the room. Too bright. Too bright for the beast's sensitive eyes. As he lowered his hand—his clawed hand, touched with patchy fur—he met his father's gaze. King Victor had climbed out of his bed and lit the gear-bulb lamp there. His face was pale, his eyes wide.

Right, Gryphon thought, a sinking feeling sliding through him. The claws. The teeth. The *eyes*. The glowing, yellow eyes.

When Garrett had returned from the Black Forest last year, he'd told their father about the beast he'd encountered. But he hadn't told their father that Gryphon was the beast.

Now he knew.

Luckily, both of them were spared saying anything, for Roy and Spencer chose that moment to burst into the room, pistols drawn. Spencer turned left and right. "What happened?"

"An intruder," Gryphon snapped. "Here in the king's apartments. The guards outside?"

"They're all right," Roy reported. "Just knocked out, but they should be fine."

"Then find that intruder," Gryphon ordered. "A small figure, dressed in black. Looks like they went out the window, perhaps along the back wall towards the center of the castle. Go!"

Roy and Spencer leapt into action, Roy shouting—rather hilariously, Gryphon thought—"At once, sire!" The two of them dashed out of the room and into the corridor. Gryphon crossed to the door and called after them, "And send some of the king's guards this way!"

The sound of their sprinting footsteps faded quickly. In the silence left in their wake, Gryphon stood in the doorway, his back to his father. He had released the beast, he realized, when Roy and Spencer came in. The claws were gone, and his teeth had shrunk back to normal size. His senses felt dull without the beast. He could barely smell the faint stench left by the intruder.

"Gryphon," King Victor said.

Gryphon turned, facing his father from across the room. The king still looked pale, but the wild expression had gone from his face. Instead, there was a speculative look in his eyes as he took Gryphon in, his gaze almost searching.

Gryphon said, "Someone was here in your room." Probably unnecessarily. He evaded his father's gaze as he strode to the foot of the bed, where something glinted on the floor. Gryphon bent to pick it up.

It was the dagger the attacker had thrown. Gryphon hadn't even noticed the blade slip out of him.

King Victor said, "You're bleeding." Also unnecessarily.

Gryphon glanced at the blood staining his shirt and shrugged. Turning the needle-like dagger in his hand, he examined it closely. He had never seen a blade like this before—

No. That wasn't right. He *had* seen a blade like this before. In the Desert Kingdom.

Suddenly, the sound of pounding footsteps filled the air, growing louder as they neared. Half a dozen soldiers spilled into the room, pistols drawn. They were all the king's personal guard, Gryphon thought, recognizing one or two of them. They took in the scene before them, and the one nearest Gryphon leveled his firearm straight at him.

Gryphon suddenly realized how familiar a scene this was. Here he stood, holding a bloodied dagger, in the quarters of one of his family members. In the middle of the night.

Gryphon held up his other hand in a pose of surrender. "This is *not* what it looks like."

Half an hour later, Gryphon sat in one of the cushy armchairs in his father's sitting room, pressing a small towel against his bleeding shoulder. The guards were still there, though none of them, thankfully, pointed a pistol at Gryphon any longer. King Victor had glimpsed the intruder before they'd disappeared, so he'd vouched for Gryphon and explained what had happened—though, Gryphon noticed, he left out the bit about Gryphon half-turning into a beast.

Gryphon added a little more to the explanation. He, too, left out a few details—such as the scent he'd caught that led him to the king's room—saying instead that he'd seen someone sneaking through the corridors and followed the intruder here.

One of the guards shook his head. "But how did they escape? Anyone jumping out that window should fall to their death!"

"And even if they didn't, they'd have to scale the sheer walls of the castle," another guard added. "That's got to be impossible. Unless they had some kind of climbing gear?"

Gryphon shrugged. He wasn't sure there was an explanation for the intruder's escape—at least, not a natural one.

As the soldiers turned away, discussing possibilities in hushed tones and slipping in and out of the bedchamber to investigate, Gryphon stood up. One of the guards gestured towards the wound in his shoulder. "We can send for a doctor, Your Highness?"

"It's fine," said Gryphon. "Roy can take a look at it when he gets back." Roy was one of the medics in Garrett's company. "I think I'll go and see where they're at, if they found anything—"

A sharp voice interrupted. "No, you will not."

Gryphon looked around as the soldiers fell silent. The king stood in the open doorway to his bedchamber, and in that moment, he seemed to fill it, despite the wool pajamas and dressing robe he wore. King Victor hadn't shouted, but he may as well have. His voice was naturally commanding. Gryphon met his father's gaze, but it was impossible to tell what he was thinking.

The king said, "Give us the room, please. I'd like a word with Prince Gryphon alone."

Gryphon repressed a flinch. *Prince Gryphon.* Well, King Victor could scold him all he liked. *I'm not a boy anymore*, Gryphon thought. Nor had he done anything wrong. Then again, if his father wanted to have words with him, he was quite sure it wasn't about anything he'd done.

It was about what his father had seen.

Neither Gryphon nor his father looked away from each other as the soldiers filed out of the room, shutting the door behind them. In the silence that followed, a cold, creeping tension built within Gryphon. Even though this was not like the last time—even though the king had spoken up for him, assuring the soldiers that Gryphon had not attacked Victor—the scene still felt too familiar. Memories of the last time his father had confronted him, the last time he'd spoken to his father before he was exiled, rose to the surface of his mind.

And yet, the longer Gryphon stood there, facing his father—the longer the silence went on—the less familiar it began to feel. The king's expression still gave nothing away, but Gryphon began to feel that his father wasn't speaking because he *didn't know what to say.* It was uncertainty lurking behind his father's eyes, not judgment. Uncertainty for the son who stood before him.

So Gryphon broke the silence first, leaning his hip into the back of the armchair. "What did you want to talk about?" He wasn't going to make it easy on his father. If the king was on uneven footing, well, good. *Let him see how it feels.*

The look Victor gave him was resentful. As though he knew exactly what Gryphon was thinking. Finally, his father said, "It seems your brother left out a few key points when he returned from the Black Forest last year. For example. He failed to mention that the beast he encountered was *you*."

Gryphon affixed a surprised expression on his face. As if he'd had no idea Garrett had left out such an important detail. Or as if he had no idea what Victor was talking about, though he suspected he would not be fortunate enough to pull that off.

He was right. The king cast him a dark look as he stepped forward, coming into the sitting room. "Don't give me that. I know what I saw in there, Gryphon." He jerked his chin, indicating the bedchamber behind him. "Or are you one of those...were-wolf things Garrett talked about?"

Gryphon dropped his pose of ignorance. He leaned back, slumping down onto the arm of one of the cushioned chairs. "No, I'm not a were-wolf. I am the beast." He cocked his head, considering. "Though that's a bit academic, really. Since we were all descended from the same bloodline and beset by the same curse."

"Bloodline? What are you talking about?"

Gryphon studied his father. He hadn't shown much reaction to Gryphon confirming what he'd suspected. That he could turn into a beast. He only wore a puzzled frown on his face.

"What do you know about my mother's family?" Gryphon asked. His mother had always been a touchy subject, much to Gryphon's dismay. He could never get Victor to talk about her. "Where they came from?"

"Her family? Well, they were from the Black Forest, like my family. Truth be told, she didn't know much about them. They were rumored to come from old nobility, but after the kingdom plunged into ruin, bloodlines were difficult to trace. And just about everyone who migrated here claimed to be from noble stock." Victor shook his head. "What does this have to do with anything? You know as well as I it's just as likely our ancestors were farmers back in the old country, regardless of what my grandfather became." Victor's grandfather was the one who'd led the invasion here and become the new king of the Glen Kingdom. "That's true for your mother's family as well."

"Only apparently, it's not." Gryphon stretched his legs out, crossing one ankle over the other. He still wasn't wearing any shoes. "She never said anything about being descended from the royal line in the Forest Kingdom? From the last king?"

"No." King Victor looked more confused than ever. "As I said, there were rumors. Some of them fairly outlandish. But Alivia always just laughed about it. I don't think she knew where her family came from. What is this about, Gryphon?"

Gryphon studied his father a moment longer. Then he said, "As it turns out, one of those outlandish rumors was true. She *was* descended from the last king of the Forest Kingdom."

He went on to explain what had happened to him in the Black Forest and what he had learned about his ancestors. About the curse that had been put on the last Forest royals—turning them into beasts—and how the curse was tied to the old Forest castle and the royal bloodline. How when Gryphon, unknowingly of that bloodline, walked into that old castle, he'd triggered his family's curse and become a beast himself. How the were-wolf pack he met in the nearby woods were also descendants of the last king, the curse—diluted over generations—turning them into variants of the beast, slightly weaker, smaller, turning less often.

It was a lot to explain. By the time Gryphon got to the end of it, his throat felt dry and scratchy. He fell silent, awaiting his father's reaction.

The king had not moved a muscle the entire time Gryphon spoke. His expression was more unreadable than ever. Then he said, "So. Through you, we have a claim to that kingdom. Through your bloodline."

Gryphon wondered if he'd heard right. "I beg your pardon?"

"The kingdom's just been sitting there for almost two centuries." By the light of the glaring gear-bulb fixtures, Gryphon could see the calculating wheels turning in his father's eyes. "But if you're descended from the last king..."

Gryphon could not believe what he was hearing. "The Black Forest isn't a kingdom anymore, Victor. It's just land."

"Unclaimed land," his father corrected. "People still live there—"

"Yes, but only by their local laws."

"That's exactly my point. But we have a claim to that land."

He was very quick, Gryphon thought despairingly, to use that "we." Clearing his throat, he pointed out, "*I* have a claim to it. If you really want to pursue it, you'd have to seriously reinstate me as prince of the realm." Which Gryphon heartily did not want. This was meant to be a temporary agreement, and his father knew that.

But instead of agreeing, his father cast him another speculative look. Gryphon stifled a groan. "Look. Before you go haring off into the Black Forest, I'd suggest you take care of things at home first. Because in case you've forgotten, someone tried to kill you tonight. And unless Roy and Spencer managed to catch the assassin, we have no idea who. So. Tell me. Who would want you dead, and why?"

9

SHADOWS

G EMMA STALKED THE CORRIDORS of Glen Castle, her watchful gaze seeking out every corner and crevice. She'd been on guard for Princess Solena for most of the evening and left the princess's apartments half an hour ago. Solena had gone to bed early, complaining of a headache, so Gemma had also departed, leaving the guarding of the princess in Gallia's capable hands.

She'd decided to use the last hour of her shift scouting the corridors in the east wing near the princess's quarters, a casual perimeter check. Scouting was one of Gemma's specialties. It was quick, quiet work, and Gemma was quick and quiet, deft at blending into the darkness and encouraging others to overlook her. Scouting here in the castle was a somewhat perfunctory task, since she was unlikely to find any threats or outsiders lurking in here. Still, with guests in the castle, Gemma thought it a good idea, and it left her mind free to wander over...other problems.

Like whether or not her suspicions of Princess Solena were warranted.

After Prince Gryphon's picnic outing with the princess yesterday, Gemma had managed a moment alone with him to ask if he'd seen what she had. He'd been stunned at the idea that Solena might have cut Gemma on purpose, and all so she could taste her blood. (Stunned but not quite as revolted as Gemma had expected. Then again, Gryphon probably hunted down animals when he was the beast, so...) But Gryphon hadn't seen what she had, distracted in his search for a handkerchief, and nor had Spencer, who hadn't seen them at all from where he'd stood outside the trees.

Which left Gemma wondering, yet again, if she had imagined what she'd seen. She'd barely seen it, just out of the corner of her eye. Then again, even after her sight had been damaged, she hadn't had any issues with her peripheral vision—in fact, sometimes it was better than when she looked at something head-on. Still, it had all happened so quickly, and it had been dark under the trees...

Gemma huffed, continuing her sweep down the corridor. Though her current surroundings were bright with gear-bulb fixtures, up ahead, the lights dimmed. Gemma turned the corner into a shadowy part of the castle, where the stone walls were unadorned and hardly lit. Most of the castle was decorated in a modern fashion, but it was a very old castle, and some neglected alcoves and forgotten halls showed it.

This dark corner was familiar to Gemma, near the back of the castle at the edge of the east wing. The cavernous stone landing bore an ancient stairwell in the far corner, one that was probably only used by servants—if anyone used it at all.

She started up the stairs, each of her booted footsteps a mere whisper against the stone. Everything was quiet and still in the dark—a bit sinister maybe. To some people. But Gemma liked the dark. She felt at home in it. Weirdly, that was even more true after her sight was damaged. In the dark, she couldn't see well anyway, so it evened everything out.

The stairwell opened up into a small landing halfway up, then turned into another flight of stairs. Gemma rounded the landing and began her ascent up the second flight, glancing up for a glimpse of the top—

She stopped, going still on the third step. The top of the stairs was awash in shadow. Gemma flicked a glance to the side; there was a window up there that usually gave some light to the stairs, even at night. But it must have been completely overcast tonight because the stairs were so dark, Gemma couldn't even see the window.

That wasn't what made her stop though. She stopped because the darkness above her was *moving*.

She wasn't sure how else to describe it. It was more something she sensed than saw. Shadows shifted over the stairwell, but not like they did when the light that cast them was moving, nor like they did when someone moved through them. No, the shadows themselves seemed to move, slithering over the far edge of the steps. Clinging to the wall, as though trying to remain unseen.

Gemma blinked hard, trying to dispel any blurriness, any film covering her eye. But it wasn't her damaged sight; the shadows were really moving. She watched the undulating darkness descend the steps one at a time, coming nearer. Then the shadows seemed to shiver, stuttering, nearly halting their downward progress. Although Gemma had the sense, with every passing second, that she, too, was being watched—although the thought made her chest tight—she stood frozen, unwilling to take her eyes off the shadows. She felt certain that the moment she did, they would vanish, melting into the stone wall.

The shadows continued their descent, though at a more sedate pace. Almost wary. But they did not stop, even as they began to slip past Gemma, inching down the stairs. Even as Gemma turned slowly, rotating on the spot to keep the darkness in sight. She narrowed her eyes, debating, keeping calm, despite how unsettling this was.

Then she reached out and stepped onto the shadow, as though her boot could pin it to the floor.

That was not what happened. What happened was an icy cold washed over Gemma from the soles of her feet to the top of her head, as though a bucket of frozen river water had been dunked over her in reverse. She jerked her foot back with a gasp.

And from the slithering shadows, a figure materialized. A person. Solid and whole, dressed in black.

For half a second, Gemma was too shocked to move. Even she was not that good at blending into the darkness. Her thoughts congealed in her head, but she didn't need to think. Her training took over. Moving past the impossible, past the fact that a person had been hiding in those shadows, Gemma retreated a step, reaching for a weapon. But she hesitated—hearing Klaus's voice in her head, saying she should reach for her knife and not her pistol—and before she could decide which to grab, the figure in black whipped forward, catching Gemma's arm and yanking it away from her weapons.

Through a hood so dark and big, Gemma could make out no face at all, the figure spoke. "What are you?" The voice that issued from that gaping darkness was guttural, barely human. "Where do you come from?"

Somehow, Gemma found her own voice. "I think you should be answering those questions. Seeing as you're the one concealing your face, stranger."

But the stranger in black didn't answer any questions. Instead she yanked at Gemma again, her gloved fingers digging into the fleshy inside of Gemma's forearm with bruising force. She pulled Gemma in close, close enough that Gemma could make out two eyes on the stranger. Dark eyes. Yet they almost seemed to glow, as though lit from within by some unnatural light.

Then the stranger sucked in so deep a breath, it was startling, alarming. It was a moment before Gemma realized she wasn't just breathing in, but *sniffing*. Scenting Gemma.

"You reek of humanity," the stranger hissed. Her tone was strangely accusatory.

"Sorry," Gemma said shortly.

"But you taste like the grave. Like dirt and worms and decaying flesh, clinging to old bones."

"I...what?"

"Where have you come from?" The stranger's grip tightened even further, squeezing Gemma's bones in a crushing grip, and Gemma winced, trying to twist free. "You're new, aren't you? Newly released from the shadow. What do you serve?"

Gemma shifted ever so slightly, the toe of her boot sliding over the rough stone step. Her free hand inched towards her waist. If she could get a weapon without this intruder noticing— "My name is Gemma," she retorted, more to distract the stranger than for any other reason, "and I am a soldier in the company of Prince Garrett. I serve the royal family and no one else."

Deep within that dark cowl, the stranger's eyes widened. "Don't you even know what you are? Or have you disappeared so completely into those bones?"

The words startled Gemma. She hesitated a moment. But only for a moment.

Then she yanked a knife out from her weapons belt and swiped at the stranger.

The stranger let out a yelp as the blade slashed through her black sleeve, barely making contact. But it was enough that she loosened her hold on Gemma, who wrenched free so forcefully, she nearly lost her balance, one foot slipping off the edge of the stair. Before Gemma could steady herself, the stranger shoved Gemma in the chest, hard enough to send her tumbling down to the landing. Gemma's knee banged into the steps, and her hands slapped hard against the cold stone to keep herself from sprawling on her face. She looked up just in time to see the stranger scramble past her, sprinting down the first flight of steps.

Gemma lurched to her feet. Her already bruised backside throbbed worse than ever, and so did her knee, pulsating with pain. But she ignored this and darted down the stairs, back the way she'd come, in pursuit of the hooded stranger.

By the time she reached the bottom of the steps, wheeling around to search the alcove below, the stranger had vanished. Gemma ran in the only direction there was, around the corner and down the corridor, back into the bright, wallpapered east wing.

She ran right into someone, but it was not the stranger.

It was Klaus.

"What are you doing here?" she asked stupidly, peering around him. Sweeping the long corridor for any sign of the stranger.

"Coming to relieve you, of course." Klaus looked quizzical. "I have next shift, remember? Thought I'd scout the corridors before I started. What are you doing?"

Gemma didn't answer. She barely heard him. "Did you see her come this way?"

"Who? I haven't seen anyone."

"There was someone." Gemma tried to stifle her impatience, gesturing back towards the dark stairwell. "Back there. A stranger. Dressed in black, hooded and masked."

"Like...a burglar?" Klaus sounded dubious.

"I suppose. Like someone up to no good. She grabbed me and said all sorts of weird things. Asking where I came from and who did I serve and—" And. Making strange comments about the way Gemma smelled...and *tasted*.

Thoughts shifted in Gemma's brain, falling into place. Her gaze locked onto Klaus. He stared back at her, his eyes dark and serious beneath his angry red scars.

"Where is Princess Solena?" Gemma demanded.

"I don't know." Klaus sounded exasperated. "Where did you leave her? You were the one on duty, not me. I'd think at this time she'd be in her quarters—Gemma! Where are you going?"

For Gemma took off at a dead run, skirting around Klaus and racing down the brightly lit corridor. She turned three corners, traversing the twists and turns of the east wing until she reached her destination—the door to Princess Solena's quarters. Slowing to a halt, Gemma slumped before a wide-eyed Gallia and two Desert Kingdom guards.

"What's wrong?" Gallia asked.

"The princess." Gemma heaved in a breath and straightened. "Is she in there?"

"Of course. She hasn't gone anywhere."

"Has anyone been in or out since I left?"

"No." Gallia shook her head, her sunny blond braid whipping back and forth behind her. "No one. What's going on?"

"I need to look inside." Shoving between the princess's guards, she banged on the door several times. When one of the guards made as though to stop her, Gemma sent him a glare so fierce, he recoiled. "There was an intruder in the castle. I need to make sure the princess is safe."

"She told you," the guard said. "No one has been in or out."

"I still need to check." She reached up to rap on the door again, but before she could, the door swung open. Gemma bare-ly caught herself from tumbling inside.

"What is it?" asked the handmaiden who opened the door. This was not Tashi, the snobbish handmaid Gemma had met the first day she'd entered these quarters. This was the tall, gangly one with jet-black hair and pale skin. "What's going on?" she asked. "The princess is sleeping—"

"I need to see her." Gemma barged into the room, moving past the handmaiden before anyone could stop her. The lights in the parlor were as low as ever, creating hulking shadows out of the rich furnishings. "Now."

"Pila?" One of Solena's ladies-in-waiting emerged from a side chamber, a look of mingled annoyance and concern on her face. She was a slender but solid young woman, broad of shoulder, with dark-golden hair. "What's going on? The princess isn't to be disturbed until morning, we told you—"

The handmaiden, Pila, dropped a quick curtsy. "Yes, Lady Ilana. I—"

But Lady Ilana had just noticed Gemma. "What are you doing in here?" she demanded. "The princess isn't well. She cannot be disturbed."

"I'm sorry to hear that," Gemma said in as calm a tone as she could muster, "but I have to see her. Now. It's a security matter."

"What could possibly be so—"

"What is all this racket?"

Lady Ilana fell silent. Gemma turned and found Princess Solena standing in the doorway to her bedchamber. She was dressed in a lacy nightgown and a black silk dressing gown, draped around her like a heavy curtain. Her arms were crossed over her chest, her beautiful face a thundercloud.

"I was asleep," she snapped. "And I have a terrible headache, one that is only getting worse with all this noise."

"I'm so sorry, Your Highness," Gemma said. "I can explain."

"Someone had better," Solena said waspishly.

But Gemma didn't explain, not yet. Instead, she strode into the princess's bedchamber. The room was dark, the lights doused, making it difficult to see anything. Still, Gemma could make out the window at the back of the room, muted starlight leaking in through the gauzy curtains. By that faint bit of light, Gemma spotted a gear-bulb fixture on the wall and wound it on. Then she turned to survey the chamber.

The four-poster bed jumped out at her first, its heavy curtains drawn back. The layered bedsheets were rumpled, pillows strewn everywhere. More pillows than any one person could need. Gemma's eyes traveled onto the leatherbound trunk at the foot of the bed, and from there, over the rest of the furniture.

But there was no one else there and nothing out of place. Not that Gemma could immediately see.

She didn't stop there. She circled through the room, looking for anything amiss, checking any possible hiding place. She pulled open the massive ornate wardrobe and flipped through the gowns hanging inside, she knelt to search beneath the bed, her gaze sweeping the dark, dusty floor—

"Are you going to explain to me what is going on?" Solena's cranky voice sounded from behind her. "Or do I need to send for the king?"

"I'm sorry, Your Highness." Gemma rose to her knees as she finished checking beneath the bed. She kept her expression wiped clean. "An intruder was spotted in the castle. I just needed to be sure you were safe in here."

"An intruder?" Solena sounded appalled, but not afraid. Her tone was laden with sarcasm as she asked, "Does this sort of thing happen often in this castle?"

"No, Your Highness. Of course not."

Princess Solena let out a huff, looking tetchy. She tapped an impatient foot as she watched Gemma continue her search, even going so far as to open the princess's trunk.

"Do you really think someone could hide in there?" Solena's tone was so irritated, she practically snarled.

"Just want to be thorough." Gemma shut the trunk—rifling through it would be a step too far; she'd be reprimanded for that—and turned to face the princess.

"Are you satisfied?" Solena asked. "Can I go back to bed now? I'm meant to breakfast with Prince Gryphon tomorrow, and at this rate, I will be far too unwell to meet him."

"I'm sorry, Your Highness." Gemma tilted her head to one side, studying the princess. She had just noticed that Solena really did look unwell. Her face, normally a rich tan, was ashy and colorless. She even looked thinner, her cheekbones sharper, her eyes sunken into their sockets.

Sunken into their sockets...yes. She looked almost skeletal.

Surreptitiously, Gemma swept one last look over the princess. The stranger's words echoed inside her head. *You taste like the grave.*

And in her mind's eye, she saw Princess Solena on her outing with Gryphon, kneeling in the darkness amongst the wildflowers. Licking Gemma's blood off her blade.

But Gallia swore no one had come in or out of these quarters. There was no other entrance Gemma knew of, not even a balcony. No secret passages; Gemma knew most of them. Not to mention, the intruder would have had only a few minutes on Gemma, yet here was Solena, dressed in rumpled nightclothes, her face drawn and tired, as though she had just risen from bed...

That's when Gemma noticed. Something she should have seen when she first came into the room, even before she'd turned on the light. The gauzy curtains covering the window on the wall fluttered lightly.

Stirred by a brisk breeze.

Gemma said, "You shouldn't sleep with the window open, Princess. Not when you're already feeling poorly. It's quite cold out."

"My headaches make me too warm." Princess Solena touched a pained hand to her forehead as she moved towards her bed and pulled back the sheets. "But go ahead and close it, if you must."

Gemma crossed to the window, pulling the curtains aside. The fabric was cold and damp to the touch. The window was set over a long table with drinking glasses and a pitcher of water, so it was a bit awkward to lean over it. But this worked to Gemma's advantage, as it gave her time to glance out before she shut the window.

Outside, the night was dark and cold, gray fog and thick layers of cloud obscuring the sky. Light rain thickened the air. There was no ledge outside the window, nowhere for anyone to stand or grab hold of anything. The castle's exterior was sheer stone.

Impossible for anyone to climb.

Gemma leaned back, shut the window, and latched it. Then she turned around.

Princess Solena stood before her, inches away.

Gemma's heart lurched into her throat.

Solena rolled her eyes. "I'd like a glass of water?"

"Oh. Of course." Gemma turned to pour her a glass. Solena did not move, leaving Gemma little room to maneuver. For some reason—with the princess hovering so close behind her—Gemma felt that same unease she had before. When she'd glimpsed that slithering shadow in the stairwell.

Stomach churning, Gemma turned and handed Solena her glass of water. The princess swept her gaze over Gemma, then raised the glass to her lips. Not until she finished drinking did she retreat, turning her back on Gemma and returning to bed.

Gemma let out a slow, silent breath. She felt so rattled, nearly a full minute passed before she could move. Solena ignored her as she stood there, clutching the table behind her, and by the time Gemma left the room, the princess was already asleep.

10

Hostilities

Klaus figured out where Gemma had rushed off to fairly quickly, and since it was the same place he needed to be, he set off there too—for Princess Solena's quarters. When he got there, he found a perplexed, scowling Gallia out in the corridor (but that was not unusual; Gallia always scowled, or at least, she always scowled at him), and Solena's two Desert Kingdom guards, who refused to let "anyone else" in. So Klaus waited for several long minutes until the door opened, and Gemma emerged from the rooms.

As soon as she stepped into the corridor, Klaus could tell something was wrong.

"What is it?" he asked.

"Nothing." Gemma ran both hands over her thick, braided knot of hair. The braid was not as neat as usual, a few strands escaping its confines, wisping around her face. "The princess is fine. Everything in there is…fine."

But Klaus could see everything was not fine. Or at least, Gemma wasn't. She seemed shaken, her brown eyes troubled, her hands clenching and unclenching down by her sides. He watched her for a moment, then cast a glance at the guards behind him. The two Desert guards had relaxed when Gemma said the princess was all right, but Gallia looked between the two of them, frowning.

Klaus caught Gemma's eye and jerked his chin, indicating she should follow him down the corridor. She did so, still distracted, almost anxious. That was not like her. Gemma was always entirely self-possessed. If she was ever worried, she hid it well.

Once they were out of earshot of everyone else, Klaus stopped, turning to face Gemma. "What's going on?" he asked in a low voice.

"I told you." Gemma cast a glance over her shoulder. Every part of her body was strained, from the set of her jaw to the frame of her shoulders. Fear lurked behind her eyes. *Fear.* Klaus had never seen Gemma afraid. "There was an intruder. I just wanted to check everything out. Make sure the princess was all right."

"Gallia said no one had been in or out."

"I know, but…"

"Anyway, that's not what I meant." Klaus couldn't hide the impatience creeping into his tone. "What's going on with *you?*"

Gemma finally seemed to focus, her gaze latching onto Klaus, going flat. Instantly looking more like herself. "What do you mean?"

Klaus debated for a second. True, there were some things he and Gemma just didn't say to each other. But sometimes—no matter who he was talking to—Klaus knew the best thing was just to be blunt. "You seem rattled."

For a moment, Gemma looked as though she was going to snap at him. But instead she surprised him, relaxing her defensive stance. "I suppose I am."

"Why?" He jerked his head back down the corridor. "Because of Solena?"

"No. It's not her. It was that stranger I ran into. The intruder. She said such weird things, talking about bones and shadows—and..." Gemma's voice actually shook. Her dark eyes became distant and haunted.

"And?" Klaus prompted.

"And the way she appeared. I saw—I *thought* I saw—" Her tone turned edgy, filled with frustration, and she pinched her fingers around her right eye. The seemingly unconscious gesture tugged at Klaus's heart. "But maybe I didn't. Maybe it was all just—" She trailed off again.

"Just what?" Klaus asked in a steady voice.

But Gemma only said, "Nothing. Nothing, it doesn't matter." She dropped her hand to her side, still looking frustrated.

Klaus watched her for another moment. Debating again. Wondering what he should say, wondering if he should press her. She seemed calmer now, but still distracted, still uncertain, rubbing at the bridge of her nose, wiping a hand across her face. She was certainly distracted enough that she didn't snap at Klaus for staring at her.

But before he could say anything else, hurried footsteps sounded down the corridor, alerting them to someone approaching. Klaus spun around, but it was only Spencer. His eyes were a little wider than usual, his dark face slick with sweat, as though he'd run all the way up here. He stumbled to a halt before them.

"Something wrong, Spence?" Klaus drawled.

"Intruder," Spencer panted, "in the castle."

"We know," said Gemma and Klaus.

<hr>

Thirty minutes later, Klaus stood in the dark stone stairwell where Gemma had first encountered the intruder—or possibly, the assassin. He was not alone. Several other guards accompanied him, quietly comparing notes and searching the stairwell for any clues the stranger in black might have left behind. Gemma was not there. The king wanted to debrief her straightaway, no matter that it was the middle of the night, so at his summons, she had gone to his apartments in the west wing. Gallia was still on duty, guarding Princess Solena. Klaus probably should have been too, but he knew no one would question his being here instead.

He was a tracker, after all. And though this work was not exactly tracking, it did require keen eyes.

Evidently, this intruder had first been spotted in the king's own bedchamber. For what reason, no one knew, though the stranger had been armed and taken care to conceal their identity. That didn't add up to anything good. From the king's apartments, the intruder had fled through a window—apparently scaling a wall that should have been unscalable.

This stairwell, deep in the oldest and dustiest reaches of the castle, was not close to the king's apartments. Though if it was true the stranger could walk on walls, then Klaus supposed they—*she*, according to Gemma—could easily have reached this place and entered the castle through a window. Possibly the window at the top of the stairwell. Klaus moved in that direction now, climbing up the stone steps from the middle landing.

The landing at the top of the stairs was like the one at the bottom—a secluded alcove, dark, built from old, roughly cut stone. The corridor it led to eventually brightened, but here, shadows gathered in every corner like wisps of cobweb. The sky outside the smudged, dirty window was blanketed in thick clouds, no moonlight seeping through. Klaus lifted the gear-bulb lantern he'd borrowed from one of the soldiers below and swept it across the floor, stone by stone.

"Makes me wish I had my rifle." Klaus glanced up as Spencer joined him at the top of the stairs, peering into the darkness. "To use the light on it, I mean," he added when Klaus turned a puzzled look on him.

"Oh." That would be useful, though the lights on their rifles were quite small. "Makes you wonder why the princess can't make some of those lights by themselves. Like a gear-powered lantern, but one more focused that you could point with."

"She's tried," said Spencer. "You'd think it would be simpler than attaching it to a firearm, but apparently, it's more difficult. Something to do with the power? Like, in a rifle that's already gear powered, she just has to re-circuit it or something. But on its own, it's more difficult to, er—calibrate it or—"

"You don't actually know what you're talking about, do you?"

"No. I really don't. Have Princess Briar explain it to you sometime."

Klaus didn't see the point in that, since he wouldn't understand the explanation any better from her. He turned his attention back to his survey of the landing. Once he'd swept the floor thoroughly, he raised the lantern, studying every stone built into the wall—

He paused, eyes narrowing. There was something there below the window—which was latched shut, Klaus noticed, as he eased closer. Still, the fact that it opened at all was of interest. And there below the latch, on the stone wall—

A dark splotch. A damp splotch, the wetness gleaming faintly in the lantern's light.

"Blood," Klaus said triumphantly. "Fresh blood."

"I'll let the others know," said Spencer, trotting down the stairs.

Klaus bent closer and lowered the lantern, looking for a trail, but there was none. Only this one spot here, a stain on the stone. So, perhaps the intruder had been wounded, but not so severely that they left a trail. Perhaps they'd staunched the bleeding with a hand and then unthinkingly touched the wall here. Touched it as they came in through the window?

But Klaus couldn't quite fathom that theory. He leaned forward to peer through the glass. The window was set in a flat stone wall. There was no slope of the roof, no eaves or ledges the intruder could have used. Perhaps there was something below this window; he couldn't see far without opening it. Even still...

But according to Spencer and Roy, the intruder had fled through a window that was just as impossible an escape route. Klaus was still perplexed by that. He opened his mouth to call down to Spencer, but before he could, a voice drifted up out of the hum of murmurs below, reaching his ears.

"So this is where she saw the intruder?"

Klaus stiffened. The voice was not particularly loud, not much louder than any other voice down there. Yet Klaus heard it like a bell tolling in his head. A bell tolling for something dreadful, like a funeral. Or an execution.

Slowly, he turned and cast a surreptitious glance below him.

Gryphon stood on the middle landing, his brawny form unmistakable amidst the soldiers. His dark hair was cut much shorter than the last time Klaus had seen him, close to his head instead of curling around his ears. But otherwise, he looked the same. Dressed down in his shirtsleeves and barefoot, if Klaus wasn't mistaken. And seeing him here in this dark, old stairwell...

A chill ran down Klaus's back. It didn't take much to imagine he was stuck in a memory. Stuck in a run-down, abandoned castle in the Black Forest, and not here in Glen City. Still stuck there. The thought awoke a troubling juxtaposition of feeling. His mind didn't know whether to reach for nostalgia or trauma. That life with Gryphon in that cursed castle had certainly been a darker life than the one he lived now. Yet it was a life he had chosen, one he could have walked away from at any time.

The reason he never had stood before him now. On the landing below. Talking with the soldiers.

The sound of his own name startled him, rooting him in the present. "—a fresh bloodstain on the wall up there, Klaus found it—oh—"

Klaus jerked, glancing down the stairwell. Realizing, too late, that he shouldn't have.

Spencer and Gryphon stood just off the bottom step, staring up at him.

Klaus barely held in a flinch. He wanted to look somewhere, anywhere else, but he found his eyes locked on Gryphon's face. And Gryphon's eyes—no longer yellow, Klaus noted, but a more mundane brown—locked on him. His face was blank, but Klaus wasn't fooled. The only reason Gryphon would look at him with so little emotion was because he was working hard to hold it in.

The betrayal. The resentment. The rage.

Klaus felt his features assume an equally blank slate, lines smoothing out, eyes deadening.

"*Oh.*" Spencer, by contrast, lay all his emotions bare. His face was chagrined, his tone horrified by his own mistake. "I forgot—that is—I can show you the bloodstain, Prince Gryphon. Er, Klaus, why don't you—"

"It's fine, Spencer." Klaus managed a deceptively calm tone. He let a little of his mask slip as he turned his gaze on Spencer, and Spencer winced at Klaus's withering look. "We're all professionals here. Aren't we?" He turned back to Gryphon, looking him in the eye.

A challenge.

Gryphon cleared his throat. "Yes, of course." He mounted the steps to the top landing, and Klaus was not proud at how hard he had to work to stand his ground, not to lean back or drop his gaze as Gryphon came closer. Spencer hurried up the steps too. The dark little alcove felt quite crowded with the three of them in it, especially since one of them was Gryphon, broad-shouldered and insanely tall.

"Show me." Gryphon spoke in a clipped tone. The note of command in his voice was so familiar that it was easy for Klaus to respond as he had so many times before. As though nothing had changed between them.

Everything had changed.

"Here." Klaus indicated the splotch beneath the windowsill. "There's no trail, just this one spot."

Gryphon frowned. As he crouched down to inspect the damp spot, Klaus leaned back, giving him room. He wondered what had happened to Gryphon's eyes. He'd heard that Gryphon had gained some measure of control over his curse, that he could assume his beast form whenever he wanted. Did that mean Gryphon's eyesight wasn't as keen in the dark as it had been before? Unless he assumed the beast? That was inconvenient.

"I didn't wound him," Gryphon murmured.

Spencer shifted from one foot to the other. "What?"

"The intruder. When I saw him in the king's room, I didn't wound him."

"Her," said Klaus. "Gemma said it was a 'her.'"

"Was she certain?"

"I dunno. Didn't really press her on it."

Gryphon touched a finger to the dark wetness on the stone. "Are you sure this is blood?"

"Seems to be. Why?"

"It doesn't...smell right." Gryphon rubbed his now-stained index finger against his thumb, inhaling deeply. Scenting it, as Klaus had seen him do many times before. So he still retained some of those beastly senses in human form. "A bit like blood but also...something else. Something wrong. And the color's a bit off." He held up his hand to show Klaus and Spencer.

Klaus leaned in to look, then flicked his gaze up unthinkingly. Looking Gryphon in the eye.

They held each other's gaze for a beat. A beat too long. Then they both looked away, Klaus taking another step back as Gryphon rose to his full height.

"Is this really all right?" Spencer blurted out.

Gryphon and Klaus turned to look at him.

"This, I mean, the two of you—that is—" Spencer wilted under their stares. "Working together—"

Klaus's stare became frosty.

"Why?" Gryphon's tone was cool. "Do we seem not all right?"

"No, not at all! Er, I just—well—I'm going to go back—down there—oh, Roy is waving to me, I'd better..." Spencer's babbling voice trailed off as he hurried down the stairs, fleeing them both.

Leaving the two of them alone at the top of the stairs.

They stood in silence for a moment. Then Klaus said, "It might have happened after she fled."

"What?" Gryphon sounded bemused.

"The intruder," Klaus said tersely. "You said you didn't wound her. She might have sustained some injury during her escape."

"Possible," Gryphon agreed in a neutral tone. He glanced down at his fingers again, still absently rubbing them together. "We should get a sample of that blood or whatever it is. See if someone can analyze it."

"I'll tell Roy."

"Good," Gryphon said. "You found nothing else up here?"

"No. Though I should probably make another sweep."

Gryphon gave a curt nod. Then he turned to go, starting down the steps.

"Is that it?" Klaus called after him.

The words were out of his mouth before he could stop himself. Before he'd even realized they were there. But now he could feel it, simmering in his chest. The heat fueling those words. His own rage and resentment, no longer content to be held at bay.

On the top step, Gryphon turned back. "Was there something else you wanted me to say?"

Resentment flared, burning up the back of Klaus's throat. "It's not about what I want." Inside, he was hot, but the words coming from him were as cold as ice. "It's about what I know *you* want. What I know you want to say. To me." He took a step forward. "You know. That I betrayed you to Viveca." His voice only shook a little when he uttered her name. "That you can never trust me again. That I shouldn't dare stand here and face you after what I did, after getting involved with her and letting her into the castle. That I'm dead to you."

Gryphon stared at him, and for the first time, Klaus glimpsed a flicker of life in his dark eyes. A hint of the anger he knew was there. "I suppose I don't need to say anything then." Gryphon came back up onto the landing, facing Klaus fully. "If you already knew I was going to say all that. I suppose that's why you never came back, is it? Why you ran off with my brother? Because you knew what I was going to say?"

"Yes, and because I knew anything I said wouldn't make a damn difference," Klaus snapped. "That's how it is with you, Gryphon. How it always is. It doesn't matter that I was your friend, it doesn't matter that I served you for how many years. I made a mistake, one mistake, and that's it, right?"

Gryphon's eyes flashed. Klaus felt savagely satisfied but also strangely unnerved. Because there was something so different about the anger in Gryphon's eyes. Or maybe it was just the eyes themselves. They were no longer the yellow eyes of the beast. It should have made Gryphon less frightening, and it did, in a way.

His anger had become so...human.

"Excuse me, Prince Gryphon?" It was Spencer again. The young man stood halfway up the stairs. "Some of the soldiers down here have more details from the king."

Klaus could practically see Gryphon choking on a retort, a muscle working in his jaw. But he simply turned to go, nodding at Spencer.

Then he paused.

When he turned back to Klaus, his eyes were piercingly, startlingly yellow. Beaming like twin bulbs in the murky stairwell.

The eyes of the beast.

Klaus tensed. He tensed even more when Gryphon gave a flick of his hand, and sharp, curved claws emerged, flashing from the beds of his fingernails. Below them, Spencer let out a tiny yelp.

Gryphon raised his clawed hand, stretching his arm out, but not in an attack. He merely held his hand before Klaus and said, "You don't know me as well as you think you do, Klaus. You don't know me anymore. As you can see, I've changed." The claws suddenly retracted, and his eyes faded to brown. "In more ways than one."

He held Klaus's gaze a moment longer. Then he turned and descended the stairs, following Spencer.

Klaus watched him disappear around the corner below. "Yes, well," he muttered to himself, "you're still as melodramatic as ever."

11

EXPOSED

G EMMA DIDN'T GET TO bed until nearly three in the morning following her encounter with the intruder. She was up for hours debriefing with the king. Yet even after Gemma tumbled into bed, eyes dry and aching, body heavy with fatigue, she lay awake for a long time before falling into a fitful sleep.

Her dreams were dark and troubling, formless dangers menacing her mind. Mingled with these dangers were half-buried memories, images and words she hadn't thought of in years. Her father's face floated before her, rippling away as a dark wood closed in around her, as she tore through the trees, pulse racing, footsteps pounding, all of it *thump-thumping* in her ears. Then her father's voice echoed through her sleeping thoughts, his deep baritone a low rumble. *"Never stop moving."* That had been his mantra; he hadn't believed in staying in one place long enough to put down roots.

But then her father's comforting voice faded into the void, replaced by another's. A sibilant, inhuman growl, echoing through the darkness. *Where have you come from? Don't you know what you are?*

You taste like the grave.

With a wrenching gasp, Gemma shot upright in bed.

The sleeping quarters around her were dim, though sunlight strained through the blinds. In the far corner, a shadow shifted, its form obscured by the two-tier metal bunk beds. Gemma's pulse quickened, and she was already reaching for the blade beneath her thin pillow when the shadow said, "Gemma? I didn't wake you, did I?"

Gemma's fingers uncurled beneath her pillow, splaying over the lumpy mattress. It was only Beckett. She was one of the soldiers who shared these sleeping quarters with her. As Beckett stepped around her bunk, her tall form coming into focus, Gemma blinked, trying to clear the sleep from her vision. Was it just her imagination, or did her right eye remain a little blurry?

Beckett frowned at her. Well. She probably looked a mess, Gemma thought. Strands of flyaway hair stuck to her brow. Smoothing a hand over her face, she said, "You didn't wake me."

"I hope not. I know you were up late." Beckett pulled a face. "I've just come off a shift myself. Been up since four this morning."

"What time is it now?"

"Nearly two."

Midafternoon. Gemma would be back on duty in another seven hours. Stifling a groan, she rubbed a hand over her eye and blinked. Once, twice. Three times.

Everything still looked a little blurry.

She squeezed her eyes closed and did not open them, dropping her head into her hands. Images flashed through her mind, images from her dreams, coupled with everything she'd seen over the past few days.

A body in the woods. A dying girl that looked just like Princess Solena.

Solena's reflection in the mirror, her face replaced by that of a skeletal corpse.

The princess kneeling amongst a bed of wildflowers, licking Gemma's blood from the sharp edge of a knife.

The intruder last night, a stranger dressed in black. Appearing out of nowhere, materializing from shadow.

Everything she'd seen. Everything she *thought* she'd seen.

There was good reason to be suspicious of Princess Solena, several good reasons. Word of her coming so suddenly from the Desert Kingdom. Her running away from her retinue, out in the woods, which still had not been explained. Her general sort of...creepiness. But it wasn't anything solid, which was why Gemma had not confided her suspicions to the king last night when she'd been debriefed. She almost had, but. It just wasn't enough.

Especially when she could not trust her own eyes, her own mind. Especially when she might have imagined it all.

Gemma opened her eyes. And what if she hadn't imagined it all? What if everything she'd seen was real? What did it add up to? Something very wrong with the princess, that was for sure. But did it mean Solena was the stranger from last night, the intruder who'd been found in the king's apartments? Did it mean Solena wanted the king dead? But why?

And what about all the things the stranger had said to Gemma? It was possible, Gemma supposed—even likely—that those things meant nothing. That the intruder, Solena, whoever she was, was simply mad. *You taste like the grave. Newly released from the shadow. Have you disappeared so completely into those bones?*

It was all just nonsense, she told herself. Just insane nonsense. But she couldn't let it go.

Fighting off a shiver, Gemma rose and gathered her things, heading for the washroom. She took her time washing up, getting dressed, fixing her hair. Ordering her thoughts. Shaking off her dreams. But as she emerged from her barracks dormitory, she still felt perturbed, not to mention tired.

She needed light. She needed fresh air. She needed a change of scenery

Her stomach growled. She needed food.

As she headed down the parade grounds towards the outer gate, she spotted Klaus across the courtyard, shrugging into his blue uniform coat and squinting up at the scant sunlight filtering from the hazy sky. He always wore that coat, Gemma thought, slowing her pace so he could catch up to her. Rumpled, unbuttoned, but he always wore it, even when he was off duty. For all Gemma knew, it was the only coat he owned.

When she was nearly at the gate, she stopped and turned, looking for him. He walked about ten paces back, eyes fixed on his feet, the tops of his scars the only visible part of his face. He seemed lost in thought.

"Hey," Gemma called.

Klaus glanced up. When his gaze fell on her, his shuttered expression became a full scowl. *What did I do now?* Gemma wondered idly.

Klaus said shortly, "I don't want to talk about it."

Gemma blinked. "All right."

"I mean it. So if that's what you want, you can forget it. Find someone else to hassle."

"Klaus, I truly have no idea what you're talking about." Gemma rubbed an exasperated finger between her eyes. "So..."

"You haven't heard? I ran into Gryphon last night. It went poorly."

"Well, you're alive." Gemma turned back towards the gate, and Klaus fell in beside her. "Can't have gone that poorly."

"I don't want to talk about it."

"Klaus. When have I ever been the kind of person to push you to talk about your feelings—or about anything, really?"

Klaus seemed to consider this, the dark look on his face vanishing. "Well. Right. You don't do that."

"No. I don't." The tall iron gate loomed before her, and she pushed it open, leaving the barracks. Klaus followed her, and the gate fell loosely shut behind them with a *clank.* "I'm hungry. Want to go into town for a drink and a meal?"

"Yes, all right."

They left the castle grounds, taking the shortcut through the wooded land into Glen City. They were silent for a long time as they walked the dirt path through the trees, lofty pines stretching up around them, closing them within a secluded, quiet little world of their own. The silence was amiable, welcome even, for as Gemma had pointed out, she was never much of a talker, and neither was Klaus, when he wasn't taking the piss out of someone. There was a beauty in silence and in stillness, and an appreciation for it was early instilled in people like themselves, who'd grown up beyond the hustle and bustle of city life. They were quiet and calm, breathing in the deep, resinous perfume of the trees.

The silence wasn't broken until they left the copse behind, stepping beneath the open sky, the road into town stretching before them. "Do you remember the first time we met?" Klaus asked.

Gemma raised her eyebrows. He hadn't mentioned Gryphon, but this topic of conversation was rather tangential to him. Because they had met in the Black Forest, back when Klaus still served Gryphon.

"Well?" Klaus prompted.

Gemma said, "Do you mean when I was peeing in the woods, and you spied on me?"

Klaus made a choking noise. "*What?*"

"In the Black Forest. I was with Prince Garrett's party, hunting...the beast." She hesitated briefly over Gryphon's name. "I stepped away from them to relieve myself, and you tried to sneak up on me."

"That's—I—that's not—" Klaus sputtered. Beneath his angry scars, his pale cheeks had turned bright red, a rare occurrence for Klaus. "I didn't *see* anything."

"Of course not. Because I knew you were there and got the jump on you."

"That is not what happened."

"Oh?" Gemma cast a glance his way, enjoying his discomfort and outrage. Klaus was a difficult person to unsettle, so Gemma enjoyed any opportunity to do so. "You let me capture you at gunpoint? Even though it meant risking the life of...the person you were looking for?"

"You can say his name," Klaus said acidly. "He's not a devil."

"Gryphon, then. Even though he nearly got killed for it, you let me capture you?"

"Look," Klaus blustered. The blush was fading from his face. "I had no idea any of you were out there. As you pointed out, I was a bit distracted, trying to get Gryphon back to the castle without being mauled for a second time. So, yes, Gemma, you got the jump on me. For the first and only time in your life."

Gemma kept her smirk to herself.

"Anyway." Klaus's gaze was fixed on the road ahead. The first buildings were coming into sight, the city's oldest outskirts starting at the bottom of this rugged hill. "That was not the moment I was talking about."

"Well, that was when we met."

"Technically, but I was thinking of the first time we exchanged words. Besides 'Don't move or I'll shoot.'"

Gemma humored him. "All right. When was that?"

"That same day, I suppose. Or, that night." Klaus sobered. "After your young friend passed. Evans."

Gemma's heart clenched. Young Evans with his tomato-red hair, reedy voice, and freckly face. He had been on the hunting party as well and taken a bite from a were-wolf early in their venture.

They hadn't known at the time that a were-wolf bite was always fatal. Eventually.

Evans had descended into feverish madness as soon as they'd arrived at Gryphon's castle and died only a few hours later. That was fortunate, according to Klaus and Gryphon. Apparently, the victims sometimes languished in illness and madness for days or weeks before they succumbed to the bite. Gemma considered it fortunate that, thanks to their efforts, there were now far fewer were-wolves in the world.

They rounded a final bend in the road and entered the city, the path beneath their boots turning to cobbled stone. This far out, the streets were nearly empty, save for a few ragged urchins running up and down the block, tossing around a ball. "That night," Klaus continued, as they passed ramshackle apartments and small businesses, "I found you and Spencer in the wine cellar. Drinking a toast to Evans, Spencer said. He went off to bed straightaway, but you stayed down there. Even after I left, you stayed."

"I remember," Gemma said. She hadn't had much to drink. Even then, in those circumstances, she hadn't thought it wise. Not in that unfamiliar castle, not with strangers—including Klaus—prowling around. Supposedly, they'd been guests, but Gemma had taken no chances. "I had the distinct impression you didn't like me roaming the castle on my own. As I recall, you suggested I head up to bed too. More than once."

"Your impression was right." Klaus snorted. "I didn't trust any of you."

"The feeling was mutual." Which was why she'd ignored his suggestion. She wasn't going to stay in an abandoned castle without getting to know every twist and turn, every corridor, inside and out.

"But I just remember—Spencer was a mess. Prince Garrett was a mess. Which was understandable since you'd all lost a friend. But you..." Klaus trailed off.

"I what? I was my usual cold, unfeeling self?"

"No, not cold. I didn't think that at all. You cared about Evans, but you had a job to do. Protect your prince. And nothing was going to get in the way of that." Klaus shoved his hands into his pockets. "You weren't cold. You were unflappable. Like nothing could touch you."

Gemma had nothing to say to that. If she was honest, she was rather pleased at this assessment of her character. She prided herself on her professionalism, on her ability to see a job through without flinching.

Klaus squinted up at the bleached sky. "Which is why I was surprised to see how rattled you were last night. After running into the intruder and talking to the princess." He glanced aside at her. "You're never like that."

The pleased, proud little bubble inside Gemma popped. "Well. Thank you."

"I'm not trying to criticize you, Gemma. I'm just—"

"What? Worried about me?" She did not bother to stifle her sarcasm.

Klaus didn't answer, not at first. His silence stretched on a little too long, the obvious reply becoming more and more evident. Then he said in an irritated tone, "No. Of course not. Wouldn't want *that*, would we?"

He quickened his pace, leaving her to trail after him as they neared their destination, the same tavern where Gemma had met Kinsley a few days ago. Gemma stared after him as he pulled open one of the front doors and disappeared inside. The door fell shut right as Gemma reached it.

Oh, fine then, she thought grumpily. *I'll just eat alone.* She couldn't handle Klaus and his moods right now.

Inside, the tavern was more crowded than Gemma expected. Certainly more crowded than the last time she'd been in here. But it was the last day of the work week, she realized, as she wove her way through the jumble of tables, every one overflowing with patrons. Granted, many people worked the whole week through, Gemma and her fellow soldiers included. But there was still something special about the weekend, something to be celebrated.

Gemma spotted a few of her fellow soldiers dotted around the room, some in their navy-blue uniform, some in plain clothes. It was a little early for copious drinking, but they were still enjoying themselves—playing darts, eating a meal, laughing and chatting, and yes, having a little afternoon drink. Gemma ordered a plate of food at the bar and remained seated there as she dug into it: roasted quail and potatoes. The quail was good if a little overcooked, and the potatoes could have used more seasoning. But it was still better than the food at the barracks.

She did not look for Klaus in the crowd. For all she knew, he'd left. But when she was nearly done with her meal, someone sidled up to her, plopping down onto the stool beside her and asking in an affable tone, "How's the food today?"

Gemma glanced up. It was Roy, dressed as casually as she was, his dark, wiry hair a little more unkempt than it typically was when he was on duty. She hadn't seen Roy lately, probably because he and Spencer were often assigned to guard Gryphon rather than Princess Solena.

"It's all right," Gemma replied. As Roy raised a hand to signal the bartender, she asked, "You were with Prince Gryphon last night, weren't you? You and Spencer. When he found the intruder in the king's rooms?"

Roy nodded.

"Did she—the intruder—say anything?" Gemma kept her tone nonchalant as she speared her last potato with her fork. "Anything strange?"

"Didn't say anything that I heard."

"Hmm." Gemma swallowed her food with a little more force than necessary, her mouth suddenly dry. Stones, she couldn't get Klaus's words out of her head. *I was surprised to see how rattled you were. You're never like that.*

"You heard about this ball?" Roy asked.

"What?" Gemma asked, startled at the change in topic.

"Apparently, the king's hosting a ball next week. In Prince Gryphon's honor." Roy snorted.

A ball. That would be quite an affair. And so soon after finding an intruder in the castle, right in the king's apartments, no less. Then again, maybe that was the point. Maybe King Victor wanted to send a message, put on a show of strength and confidence. Especially with Princess Solena here. Still, security was going to be a nightmare. It wasn't like this was the first ball the king had ever hosted. But given the intruder and the princess—they would have to take more precautions than usual.

"So what's going on with you and Klaus?" Roy asked.

"Me and Klaus?" Gemma shot Roy a suspicious look. But Roy didn't look at her. He was seated backwards on his stool, lounging against the counter, his gaze fixed on something across the room. Gemma followed his gaze to a far corner and spotted Klaus playing at darts with a couple of other soldiers.

"I saw him come in." As the bartender arrived with his food, Roy swiveled back around to tuck in. "Then you came in a few seconds later. You both looked annoyed."

"Well, Klaus is an annoying person," Gemma grumbled. "I don't know what sets him off. You heard he ran into Gryphon last night? They...talked? I think?"

Roy nodded. "I was there."

"What happened?"

"Not sure. Klaus didn't say anything?"

"Just that he didn't want to talk about it."

"Not even with you?"

"No. Why would he want to talk about it with me?"

Roy shrugged as he chewed and swallowed, then set to cutting off another piece of chicken on his plate. "Just, you two spend a lot of time together. Look, Klaus doesn't spend much time with anyone, and he's not exactly friendly, but. He seems comfortable with you."

"Well, we work together a lot. Though now I think of it, he has been kind of weird lately. Just." Gemma tapped restless fingers against the countertop. "I don't know. He gets in these moods out of nowhere."

"Weird, how? I mean, Klaus is weird to begin with, so..."

"I don't know. Like today. He said—" Gemma paused, considering. She didn't want to tell Roy what Klaus had said about her being rattled because then Roy would want to know if she *was* rattled and why. "He was acting worried about me, I suppose. And when I told him to stop, he went off in a huff."

"Hmm." This answering hum from Roy was as vague as her explanation, but Gemma sensed there was something more there. Something Roy wasn't saying. He lifted his mug and gazed at her over its rim. When Gemma frowned at him, he dropped his gaze and his mug, returning to his plate of food.

"All right, what is it?" Gemma demanded.

"What do you mean?"

"There's something you want to say, Roy, so just say it."

"I don't..." Roy swallowed a mouthful of potatoes, then took another long sip from his mug. Buying time, Gemma thought.

Deciding what to say. When he finally spoke, he asked, "How long has Klaus been acting weird like that?"

"I don't know. A while. Maybe..." Gemma kicked the toe of her boot against the counter, casting her mind back. "Since we went south with Prince Garrett, I suppose, to fight that coven of witches. At least."

"Since you got injured."

A knot formed in the pit of Gemma's stomach. Was that it? Was that why Klaus was being weird? Did he think her incapable of doing her job? Did he think her a liability? Or worse...what if it wasn't about her physical abilities, but about how she was mentally? He'd been concerned she was *rattled*, after all.

Did he suspect she was seeing things?

"Gemma?" Roy prompted, cutting into these thoughts.

"He thinks I'm cracked, doesn't he." Gemma's tone was bleak. "He thinks, what? I'm too damaged to do my job?"

"What? Ah—no, Gemma. I don't think he thinks that at all."

"Then what?"

Roy put down his fork. "You really don't know?"

"Know what?" Gemma was startled by his sudden change in tone, by the look that came into his eyes. Half-serious, half-amused. "What are you talking about?"

Roy rubbed a hand behind his neck. "Look, it's not really my place to say..."

"You'd better say something," Gemma said flatly, "before I stab you with my fork."

Roy looked more amused than ever, though he also eyed her fork apprehensively. "Gemma..." Roy hesitated. Then a resolute expression came over his face, and he looked her in the eye. "Gemma. Klaus is in love with you."

<h1 style="text-align:center">12</h1>

<h1 style="text-align:center">IMPOSTER</h1>

G EMMA STARED AT ROY, uncomprehending. "What?"

"Klaus. Is in love. With you."

"That's—no—" Gemma shook her head. *Klaus is in love with you*. The words fell through her like raindrops slipping through the cracks of a shabby roof. Invasive. Unwanted. Disturbing. "Roy. Klaus can't be...in love with me." She could barely say that last part. "That's mad."

"Well, I don't know what to tell you because it's the truth."

"No. That's impossible. It doesn't make sense—"

"Actually, it does." Roy took a sip of his drink, the gesture far too calm and collected for this insane conversation. "It's honestly quite obvious."

"Obvious?" Gemma blinked several times, trying to reconcile the world she was living in with the one Roy was living in. Absurdly, heat flushed through her body, her black coat suddenly far too warm for this crowded tavern. She refused to take it off, ignoring the bead of sweat forming on her back. "Roy. Falcon was *obvious* about his feelings for me. He flirted outrageously with me and tried to get me alone every chance he could. But Klaus? All Klaus does is insult me. Even since I got injured, he insults me. Stones, he insults me *about my injury*. Oh, and that's when he's not beating me up in the practice grounds."

"Look, it's all a bit childish, I grant you. But this is Klaus we're talking about."

Now a cold thrill flushed through Gemma, as though the blood in her veins had turned to ice water. She shifted uncomfortably, cold on the inside, hot on the outside. *Yes, exactly*, she thought. *This is Klaus we're talking about.* "Roy," she said, her voice quiet, "Klaus can't be in love with me."

"Look, Gemma, it's not like he's confessed it to me, but—"

"No." She peered down into her mug, which was still half-full. The thought of taking another sip felt nauseating. "You don't understand. Klaus *can't* be in love with me."

She could feel Roy watching her, clocking him out of the corner of her eye. She didn't dare lift her gaze to check his expression. But his voice was steady when he said, "You mean because of Falcon? And because—it was Viveca who..."

Who killed him. "No. It's not Falcon." Gemma felt a strange bubbling in her chest, threatening to spill out of her, and she realized it was laughter. Bitter laughter. Everyone thought she had loved Falcon, she realized. No one had ever said it, but she realized it now. Even Klaus probably thought so. But that wasn't it at all.

The truth was so much worse.

"I really cared about him." Gemma lifted her head to gaze straight ahead at the long row of glass liquor bottles on the dark wooden shelf behind the bar. "Falcon. But I didn't feel that way about him."

"Gemma." Roy spoke in a gentle tone. "I saw you when we got back to the castle in the Black Forest. You wouldn't leave him. Even though he was gone."

"Because it was my fault." Gemma gripped her mug tightly. "The one time, *the one time* it really mattered, and I didn't take the shot. I failed him, Roy. And it's my fault he's dead. I hold it against me and no one else." Certainly not against Klaus, even if he had loved the woman who'd killed Falcon. It wasn't his fault Viveca did what she did, it wasn't his fault Viveca got into the castle. Klaus hadn't even been there. He was the last person to blame.

"Oh, Gemma." Roy shifted in his seat. He made an aborted gesture with his arm, as though he meant to take her hand or grip her by the shoulder. But Gemma sent him a sharp look, and he dropped his hand to his mug instead. "It is not your fault Falcon is dead."

Gemma had no interest in arguing the point. She wasn't feeling sorry for herself or trying to gain sympathy. "So you see. It's not about Falcon."

"Then what is it about?"

"What do you think?" Gemma reached for that laugh trapped in her chest, but it was gone now. There was only a dark, hollow pit where it had been. "*Who* do you think?"

Roy was silent for a moment. Then he said, "Viveca."

"Viveca." Gemma suddenly raised her mug to her lips and drank from it, even though, as she'd predicted, her stomach did not thank her. The lukewarm ale slid down her throat and into her chest, giving off an uncomfortable burn. It was a distraction, a way to disguise what she didn't want to acknowledge. What she didn't want Roy to see.

Her shame.

"Klaus loved Viveca," she said. "And I killed her."

"To save his life!"

Gemma made a rueful noise. "That's not why I did it."

"No," Roy said grimly. "It's not why I would have done it either."

Gemma finally looked at him head-on. There was a hard look in Roy's eyes. Gemma understood. Falcon had been Roy's best friend, the two of them the pair of archers in Prince Garrett's company. Now Roy was the only one.

"But," Roy went on, "you did save his life. Klaus might have loved Viveca, but she was going to kill him. And he knew it. Prince Garrett told me how it happened, all right? Whether you meant to or not, you saved Klaus's life."

The problem was, Gemma was not sure Klaus had wanted to be saved. He'd spared Viveca and turned his back on her, knowing full well what she was. What kind of a person she was. Klaus had loved Viveca, but Gemma didn't think he was delusional about her. And yet he'd turned his back on her.

She let out a long exhale. "There's too much there, Roy. He can't love me." She heard the pain in her voice and wondered at it. Did it hurt to think Klaus could never love her? Why should that hurt?

She didn't want to examine the obvious answer.

"Look." Roy's voice was soft and serious. "I wasn't there, in the southern wood. When you were injured by that witch. But Sabine was there, and when she stopped by here a couple of months ago, she told me about it."

"You and Sabine were talking about me?"

"Sure we were. Klaus doesn't have a monopoly on worrying about you, you know. This was only a few weeks after you all had returned. Sabine was worried. So was I."

"Now you're going to tell me you and Sabine are in love with me too."

The grin he flashed her was a bit weak. "Ah, Gemma. You're too good for me. Can't speak for Sabine." He sobered. "She told me, Gemma. That when you were first injured, when you returned to the village with Prince Garrett, Klaus only cared about you. Garrett was in a right state too, but Klaus left his side to go find you, to see to *you*. Leaving Garrett completely unguarded, I might add."

Gemma fiddled with her napkin, clenching and unclenching her fingers into its scratchy folds. "Yes, well, Klaus has never been the best guardsman. I think we all know that."

"And when the news came about your sight, Sabine said..." Roy shook his head. "Look, Klaus isn't the most effusive person. But Sabine said he really clammed up. In a way that was just—off. She said he was scared for you, Gemma. Really, really scared."

Gemma scoffed. "Klaus doesn't get scared."

"Exactly."

Gemma clenched her fingers into her napkin one more time, then tossed it onto her empty plate. Her throat felt weird, weirdly full, as though something was swelling up inside her. She felt...stones, she didn't know what she felt. "He can't love me, Roy," she said for the fourth time. This time, the words came out like a plea.

Roy sighed. "Look, maybe it doesn't make sense to you. But who we fall for and why, well. It doesn't always make sense."

And it doesn't always work, she thought.

She and Klaus could never work.

"I should go." Gemma shook herself, rubbing a hand over her forehead. "I work tonight."

"Sure. I'll see you later, Gemma. And...I hope I haven't made trouble, Gemma. For you."

"You haven't. Don't worry about it, Roy."

Gemma thought she was desperate to leave the noise of the tavern, but when she stepped outside onto the nearly empty street, the quiet was too much to bear. The sun was low in the sky, casting long shadows across the cobbled stones, but there was still daylight left and a couple of hours until her next shift guarding the princess. She had thought to kill more time at the tavern, but she couldn't stay there. Not with Klaus hanging about.

But she didn't want to go back to the castle either. So she turned down the street, heading into the center of town. Into the hustle and bustle of Glen City. She walked the streets for hours, passing from dilapidated wooden apartments to great stone townhouses, relatively modern, yet already stained with grime. She walked over broad paved avenues and through narrow alleys and lanes, she ducked out of the way of wheeled carriages, horse-drawn and gear powered alike. She listened to young boys and girls call out as they hawked papers and penny dreadfuls, she inhaled the pleasant scent of warm, roasting chestnuts as vendors scooped them into folded paper bags.

It was a welcome distraction, the city. Gemma hadn't been in town much since her injury. It had been difficult to be out in such a crowded venue, back when she saw nothing but dark shadows through her right eye. And even when her sight began to return, blurred and uncertain. But now she could manage on the city streets. And she was grateful for that. Gemma would never be a city girl, but sometimes she enjoyed the distraction of town.

Dusk was fast approaching as she wandered to the city's outskirts, into the south side. Here, where the magnificent townhomes and businesses faded into the distance, petering out into older homes and small factories, Gemma could see the train depot, its steel tracks and wooden platforms the last bit of civilization before the forest took over. It looked as though a train had arrived just a little while ago, Gemma thought, as she stood at the iron railing separating the street from the station. The platform had mostly emptied of passengers, but the crew and engineers bustled about, cleaning up, working small repairs, making their checks. Or whatever it was they did, Gemma thought, bemused, once a train arrived and everyone disembarked.

"It's a big city," said a voice in her ear, "but it's true what they say. You always run into someone you know."

Astonished, Gemma turned to see a familiar face. The face of someone she'd just been talking about not too long ago. "Sabine? What are you doing here?"

Sabine smiled. She looked much as she had the last time Gemma saw her, three months ago, in the southern Glen wood. Her sharp cheekbones were accentuated by her severe hairstyle, her black hair pulled into a tight, high knot behind her head. Sabine had been a soldier in the guard once, though not for long. She'd been one of the new recruits last spring, brought in to build up Princess Briar's guard. But she'd left her post to serve the royal family in another way: as a supernatural investigator, working with her partner, the former prince Demetri.

From what Gemma gathered, Sabine was very happy in this new job, but she was constantly on the road now, not often in Glen City. Which was a shame, because Gemma rather liked Sabine. She was practical and quiet and altogether pleasant to be around.

Now Sabine gestured towards the arched brick entrance to the train depot, where a small traveling trunk sat. Sabine's, presumably. "I just got in," she said. "Trying to decide if I'd be more comfortable taking a room in town or staying with you lot in the barracks."

Gemma snorted. "I can tell you where you'd be more comfortable."

Sabine's smile widened. "Trying to decide if I prefer companionship and saving a little money, then."

"It's a tough choice."

"Yes, it is."

"I assume Demetri is about somewhere too?" Gemma lifted her gaze. "Surely he'd prefer a room in town."

"He's not here." Sabine adjusted the satchel over her shoulder, then turned to stand abreast of Gemma, looking out over the emptying train station. She lifted a boot, resting her heel over the lowest rung of the railing. "He's taken some personal time. The job we just wrapped was in the Mariner Kingdom, and...he decided to go visit some of the naiads there."

"Does he do that often?"

"In fact, no, he does not. This is his first time speaking with any of them since..." Sabine trailed off meaningfully. "Well, since last summer."

"I see." Since the naiad Perpetua had died, she meant. The naiad Demetri had been in love with. Gemma didn't really know the details, only the garbled stories she'd heard in the barracks from the soldiers who had been there.

Sabine's tone was subdued. "It's a big step for him, I suppose. I wanted to go with him, but. He insisted on going it alone."

"He'll be all right," Gemma said, because it was the sort of thing one said in these situations. She didn't really know Demetri, but he seemed resilient. "He's been through a lot. Come through it all."

"Yes." Sabine sent her a sidelong glance. "He's not the only one. How are *you* doing, Gemma?"

Gemma let out a humorless laugh. With respect to Demetri, she was sure she wasn't doing as poorly as he was. She couldn't be. He'd lost not one but two girls he'd cared about, one to literal death, the other to his best friend. He'd also lost his kingdom and his family, thanks to a djinn who'd locked him up in some kind of magical prison for eighty years. Gemma really did wish him well, but he was the gold standard for "having been through a lot."

She, Gemma, had only suffered an injury at the hands of a witch and nearly lost her sight. It didn't compare. In fact...

"I'm just fine." Gemma slung her arms over the railing, leaning forward. In the fading daylight, the metal had grown cold, and she felt it through her coat sleeves. "If you ask my physicians, I'm better than fine. They say my physical exams show my eyesight is back to normal. All healed up."

Her tone was noncommittal, but Sabine must have read something in her. Some tension Gemma didn't know she was holding. Because the look Sabine cast her was shrewd. "Happy news. But you don't sound happy about it. Why is that?"

"You know why," Gemma said quietly.

It was the reason she'd said it at all. The reason she'd been able to tell Sabine this news when she hadn't told anyone else. Not Kinsley. Not Klaus.

Neither of them had been there when Gemma first learned about her damaged sight. But Sabine had been.

Sabine sighed. She leaned forward, taking the railing in both hands. Pulling herself into it. "You're talking about what Jesine told you."

"Of course I am."

Jesine was a good witch, the good witch who had aided them down in the southern wood when Prince Garrett had gone after that coven. It was thanks to her that Gemma was even alive. The bleed in her brain would have killed her if Jesine hadn't healed her.

But Jesine couldn't heal her completely. She couldn't prevent the damage done to Gemma's sight, even if it was temporary. And even if it *was* temporary, even if her physical sight healed, Jesine had warned her she might suffer other ill effects. Because the injury done to her had been caused by magic, magic twisted by darkness and witchcraft.

"You might experience other symptoms," Jesine had told her. *"Strange symptoms. Hallucinations. Visions of people or things that aren't really there. Like your mind playing tricks on you."*

Visions. Hallucinations. Her mind playing tricks on her.

That was the worst of it. Not the blurriness that had obscured her vision. Not the possibility that she couldn't be a sharpshooter anymore.

She couldn't trust what she saw. She couldn't trust her own mind. That was her life now. Treading a line between what was real and what wasn't.

So when she was sure that the dying girl she'd seen in the woods was Princess Solena, how could she really be sure? How could she be sure she'd seen any girl at all? When she saw skeletons in the mirrors and strangers stepping out of shadows...how could she be sure any of that was real?

Sabine was the only one who knew. Well, besides Jesine. Sabine was the only other one who'd been there when Jesine had given Gemma this news. And Gemma had sworn them both to secrecy. She would tell someone when she needed to, she'd decided.

Only she hadn't. She couldn't. She didn't want to make it real.

But here was Sabine, right beside her, and it *was* real. She knew the truth.

Sabine blew out a long breath. "I wish Jesine had never told you."

"What?" Gemma straightened, turning to stare at Sabine. She didn't bother to hide her incredulity. "What do you mean? She had to tell me. I needed to know that I can't trust my own eyes—"

"But that's the problem." Sabine folded her hands over the railing and rested her chin atop them. "She's made you lose faith in yourself. And you have to trust yourself, Gemma. You don't have to go back to being a sharpshooter—"

Gemma tried not to react to that, but her stomach squirmed uncomfortably.

"—you don't even have to keep being a soldier, not if you don't want to. But you do have to trust yourself. Whatever you do, you've got to be able to do that."

Gemma cast a glance over the train station as a sharp whistle rang out, some of the crew calling to each other from across the tracks. "And what if I can't?" she said softly. "What if I can't anymore?"

Sabine gave a shrug. "Then find someone to do it for you. Find someone to be your eyes. Someone who can tell you what's real and what's not. Someone *you* can trust." She slanted her gaze sideways at Gemma. "I'd volunteer, but I'm not really around much. I'm only here for a day or two, to make my report to the king. Then I'll be off again."

Gemma strove for a light tone. "Well, maybe I'll quit the guard too. Become a supernatural investigator like yourself. Surely you and Demetri could use one more?"

They both shared a smile at that joke, but the uncomfortable feeling in Gemma's stomach persisted. Because she wasn't entirely sure she was joking.

◆○◆

Gemma arrived for her shift guarding Solena that evening to find the princess was in a foul mood. Which was just what Gemma needed after the events of today. Solena claimed she, too, hadn't slept well after the ruckus with the intruder last night, and she blamed Gemma for it—which she made all too clear through a ten-minute dressing-down. Gemma, of course, could do little but stand there and take the reprimand. When Solena finally finished with her, Gemma offered a cool apology, to which Solena gave an inelegant snort. But then she waved an impatient hand, dismissing Gemma.

Gemma sketched a quick bow and stepped past the princess, moving through the open doorway into the next room. But as she crossed the threshold, she nearly tripped as she stepped on something lying on the floor. Frowning, Gemma bent down to look.

The thing she had stepped on was...something strange. A bundle of some kind, a handful of dried flowers bound together with a large white feather and...Gemma sniffed as she lifted the bundle to her face...were those cinnamon sticks? Or something similar—clove or cardamom, something sharp and sweet—

She straightened, gazing at the bundle in her hand. She felt strangely entranced by it, yet at the same time, strangely repelled. Something about it pulled at her. Maybe it was the scent of the spices, bringing some long-buried childhood memory to the surface, or the morbid beauty of the dead flowers, pressed and preserved beyond their time. Whatever it was, Gemma didn't want to look away.

But she forced herself to do just that, giving herself a shake as she raised her head. Her gaze fell upon one of Solena's handmaidens, passing by with a pile of clean linens. It was the tall, gangly, black-haired girl—the friendlier of the two maids. "Pila," Gemma called to her, drawing the handmaiden's attention. "Do you know what this is?"

Pila turned and glanced at the bundle. A look of dismay passed over her face. "Oh, who left that lying around?" She bent to lay her stack of linens in a basket at her feet, then reached out and took the bundle from Gemma. "I'm sorry about this. One of the other servants probably dropped it…or maybe they meant to leave it for the princess."

Gemma felt both oddly relieved and oddly reluctant to part with the bundle. She felt lighter once she'd released it, as though it had been heavier than she'd realized. "But what is it?"

"It's a bit childish, really. Some people carry them around. It's a…" She frowned. "It comes from one of the archaic Desert languages—I don't think there's a word to translate it. I suppose you could call it a talisman."

"A talisman? Like a good luck charm?"

"Not quite. It's meant to ward off ghouls."

"Ghouls?" A chill swept over Gemma, as though an icy draft had entered the room.

"Yes. It's all silly, of course."

"Because ghouls aren't real?" Gemma thought she remembered Prince Garrett saying that once. She could hear his voice plain as day, as though he were in the room with them. *There's no such thing as a ghoul.*

But Pila startled her. "Oh, they're real enough." The handmaiden cocked her head to one side. "You don't have them here in the Glen Kingdom?"

Gemma considered this. It wasn't that she didn't believe in monsters, of course. She'd seen monsters aplenty serving Prince Garrett. Rotting corpse creatures, were-wolves, demons. But… "I've never seen one," she said.

Pila smiled uncertainly. "Well, you wouldn't know, would you? Ghouls are shape-changers. They can take the form of any person."

Shape-changers. Without thinking, Gemma said, "What, like a djinn?"

"You've heard of djinn but not ghouls?" Pila ran a hand over her black head of hair, tucking a stray lock behind her ear. "Ghouls aren't as powerful as djinn. A djinn can weave any illusion, take any form it wants. Real or imagined. But a ghoul is limited to the form of an actual person—someone who was once living. Without a body, they are only shadow. Belonging to the dark, nether reaches of the world."

"Shadow?" Gemma echoed. She felt as though she'd been struck by lightning, a flashing current pulling her body taut and rooting her to the floor. She thought of the intruder, clad in black, stepping straight out of the shadows. She thought of the shadows themselves, slithering down the stairs. "So a ghoul can take the place of anyone? Any living human?"

"Not a living human," Pila corrected. "Someone who was once living but is now dead. To take the form of a human, you see, a ghoul must consume their remains."

It was a moment before Gemma understood. "The ghoul *eats* the human?"

"Yes. At least some part of them must be devoured. To the bone. But ghouls don't usually feed on those still living. Only those already dead. They're known to haunt graveyards or battlefields. Places of death. They feed off remains, but most stories say the...fresher..." Pila wrinkled her nose "...the better. I'm sorry," she added with a look that was half a smile, half a grimace. "This isn't the most pleasant conversation, is it?"

But Gemma hardly heard her. An image flashed through her mind, vivid and perfectly recalled. The dying girl she'd stumbled upon in the woods, sprawled across a bed of bloodied leaves.

A girl who'd been savaged. A girl who'd been missing a hand.

A girl who'd looked exactly like Princess Solena.

The chill that went through Gemma this time moved slowly, creeping vertebra by vertebra, slinking down each notch in her spine. But, she thought, trying to reason with herself, Pila made it sound as though ghouls didn't kill anyone; they just stole the forms of the recently dead. Still, that didn't mean they couldn't kill someone—if they were after a specific form.

Like that of a royal princess.

13

AWAKENING

GEMMA BLINKED HARD AS she left Solena's quarters, pressing two fingers into her right temple. She was getting a mean headache. She should have been off duty a while ago, but she'd ended up pulling a double shift and guarding the princess through the night. Now, as she exited the castle, dawn was approaching. Though it was slow coming. Clouds crowded the sky, muting the first golden flecks of the sun. By the time Gemma reached the barracks, the sun had disappeared completely behind a low bank of gray clouds, and blacker, meaner clouds were on the horizon, descending over the castle like a pool of darkness. Gemma scented rain on the air.

She wandered through the open doors into her barracks building, stepping beneath the arched entry. There, she slowed to a stop, eyeing the looming staircase with reluctance. Stones, she was so tired of climbing stairs. She stood for a moment, lingering in the shadows cast by the light fixtures jutting out from the walls. The wind was picking up, gusting through the open door, but Gemma barely felt it. She should head straight up to her bunk, she told herself. Get sleep while she could. Gemma thought she could probably sleep the entire day, she was so exhausted.

But there were so many thoughts racing around her brain. So many troubling thoughts.

Ghouls are shape-changers. They can take the form of any person. Someone who was once living.

This was it. This was the answer. Everything fit. The mangled body of Princess Solena that Gemma had discovered in the woods—the *real* Princess Solena, probably. The skeletal visage she'd glimpsed in "Solena's" mirror. The stranger in black who'd stepped out of the shadows. It all fit with what Pila had explained about ghouls. Even the things the stranger had said. About tasting like a grave and being released from the shadow and disappearing into bones...

Only, that was where it fell apart a bit. Because the stranger had said all that about Gemma. And Gemma wasn't a ghoul. From what Pila had said, she would know if she was.

No, she wasn't a ghoul. But she might be a little mad.

Gemma closed her eyes, leaning forward to rest her head against the stairwell's cold metal banister. It was probably time she told someone of her suspicions. Because she seemed to have lost her ability to look at any of this objectively. Or maybe she'd never had any objectivity to begin with. Not since that witch damaged her sight.

But right now, she needed sleep. With a sigh building in her chest, Gemma straightened, lifting her head and opening her eyes.

And found herself standing in a dark, dead world.

Gemma stared. Uncomprehending. Unmoving. The metal staircase was gone. The barracks were gone. Where a moment ago she had stood in the stark, sterile foyer of her building, now she stood in a shadowy husk of a world, everything decomposing around her. Only...it *was* the barracks, she realized. It was the barracks, but in a state of utter decay. The brass finishings in the foyer, the tiled floor, the glaringly bright gleam of the gear-bulb fixtures—all had been replaced by a decrepit version of themselves. The metal railing on the staircase was tarnished and rusted through. The tiled floor was cracked and covered in grime. The light fixtures had shattered, their bulbs long dead.

The place looked ancient. As though she was gazing back on the barracks from a thousand years in the future.

For a full ten seconds, Gemma did not move. She simply stood, hardly breathing, still as a statue. She was sure that moving would break the illusion. But it was more than an illusion. It had to be. Everything reeked of decay, the air foul and musty and...almost charred...as though something was burning nearby. Gemma could practically taste ashes in her mouth. But the wind that whistled behind her was frigid and cold. It skimmed over Gemma's boots, sifted through the dust coating the floor, then rose, enveloping Gemma, chittering, whispering.

It was all *real.* So very real. Only it couldn't be, because it was impossible. That she had been standing in the barracks one moment, and now been transported to some colorless afterlife, some dark realm. Had she fallen asleep? Was she dreaming? Hesitantly, terrified, Gemma took a step forward, moving her head from left to right. And still, this forbidding vision did not disappear. Gemma blinked up at what should have been the ceiling, but instead was only a black dome, blanketed in shifting darkness.

This had to be a dream, she thought. It had to be a dream, because there was only one other explanation. She was—

An ominous creaking sound rose in the air, low at first, then growing in volume until it became an earsplitting *crack* that shook the rusty furnishings, sending debris raining down around her. That sound cut through Gemma like a blade burying itself in her ribcage. She watched as a long crack in the crumbling wall began to widen, and something oozed from it—crimson blood, startlingly vibrant in this dark place. The blood came thicker and faster until the wall was weeping with it, weeping blood, rushing down onto the floor and sweeping towards her—

Her pistol was in her hand before she could think about it. The bleeding crack in the wall yawned wider, larger, and Gemma stumbled back, clutching her pistol tighter than ever but with no one to fight, nothing to shoot—

"Gemma—*Gemma*. Gemma, it's me!"

Gemma blinked hard. Someone stood in front of her. The figure was a little hazy, a little blurry, and Gemma blinked again until they came into focus. Until she recognized the person as someone she knew.

Someone she was pointing her gun at.

"It's me, Gemma." Klaus had both hands raised at his sides. His eyes were a little wild, his usually deadpan expression fixed in a look of alarm that was almost funny. If anything about this could be called funny. "It's just me."

Gemma's breath hitched in her throat. Her entire body shook, including the arm that was stretched before her, holding a pistol. Pointed at Klaus. Her gaze darted left and right.

The blood had disappeared. The crack in the wall had disappeared. The dust, the decay, the darkness—all of it was gone. She was back in the barracks, the perfectly clean and intact barracks. She was in her own building, standing in the foyer.

"*Gemma*," Klaus said, and she was still pointing her gun at him, Gemma realized. Inhaling deeply, forcing air down into her lungs, Gemma lowered her gun, dropping it to her side.

"Gemma." Klaus sounded like he was striving for some normalcy, for an even tone. "What is going on?"

Gemma looked at him. She was coming back to herself, breaking free of the hold that shadowy vision had caught her in. But she couldn't be calm. She couldn't relax. Her shaking only increased, her chest tightening as she struggled to draw breath.

"Gemma—" Klaus repeated, and suddenly, Gemma needed to get away from it, from him, from the sound of her name, she just needed *to get away*—

She pushed past Klaus and ran out onto the parade grounds.

Outside, the wind had picked up, winnowing through the courtyard as dark clouds rolled across the sky. But Gemma didn't feel it. The barracks' iron gates loomed ahead, one standing open and the other swinging in the wind. Gemma ran towards it.

"Gemma!" Klaus called from behind. "Wait!"

But Gemma didn't wait. She left the barracks and kept running, tearing across the open hillside. She ran until she reached the wooded land dotting the hill, the dense copse of trees that sloped down into the glen towards the city.

She didn't want to go into the city. She just wanted the trees. She wanted their sap-laden fragrance, she wanted the cover they provided. She wanted them to surround her, to hold her close. Sheltering her. Hiding her.

She reached the trees as the rain began to fall. Just a smattering at first, hard but fleeting, the product of a single passing rain-cloud. But the reprieve that followed was short, and as Gemma delved into the wood, the rain came down again, big, heavy drops pelting her through the forest canopy. The copse was dense but made up of pines and hickory trees, their needles and bare branches scant cover.

She lurched to a halt, pushing damp hairs back from her face. Squinting, Gemma lifted her face to the rain, letting it slide down her cheeks like tears. But they were not tears, or at least, they weren't hers. *Tears of the earth*, her father used to say when it rained.

She hadn't cried since Falcon died.

"Gemma!"

Gemma turned. She should have been annoyed, she thought. Annoyed that he had followed her, annoyed because he was still calling her name. As though he'd forgotten how to say anything else. But all she felt was tired. The shock and agitation dribbling out of her with the rain.

"Gemma." Klaus, jogging, slowed to a halt five paces from her. His dark-blond hair was darker than usual, already soaked, and the ends of his rumpled uniform coat dripped. He ran a hand over his face, wiping rain from his eyes. "What's going on?"

Gemma didn't answer. She wasn't trying to be obstinate. If she'd had the faintest idea how to answer him, she would have.

Klaus took a step towards her, studying her. As though he could find the answer to his question on her face. "What happened back there?"

"What do you think happened?" she asked. Really, really wanting to know. "What did you see?"

"I—" Klaus ran another hand over his face, then back through his hair. "I don't know, Gemma. I saw you, looking like—I saw you. Pointing your gun at nothing. I don't know."

A hollow laugh escaped Gemma. "You don't know? *I* don't know, Klaus. That's become my everything, my every day, every waking moment. That's become my life. *I don't know what I saw.*" The words poured from her. "I can't trust anything—I don't know what's real anymore, Klaus. I don't know what's real."

Klaus shook his head like a dog shaking water from its face. Thunder rumbled in the distance, but at the same time, the rain lightened, the steady storm becoming a more forgiving shower. Moving forward another step, Klaus asked, "What do you mean?"

And Gemma almost told him. She was on the verge of it, the truth ready to spill out. Not her suspicions about Solena. But the real truth, the truth only Sabine and Jesine knew. The truth she had been hiding from everyone. Even from herself.

Hallucinations. Your mind playing tricks on you.

But she couldn't say that. She couldn't. So instead she said, "Something's not right with that princess. With Solena. I don't have any proof, nothing solid, but I know it." Trying to convince herself as much as him.

Perhaps Klaus understood this because something changed in his eyes. A softening. He took another step. "I know."

"I know I'm right about her." Gemma ran a hand over her wet braid, clutching the end of it. "She was the intruder, the one in the king's apartments—"

"Gemma." Another step, and Klaus held up both of his hands, as though to slow her verbal onslaught. "I believe you."

"She's a ghoul."

"I believe you." He frowned. "Wait, a what?"

"It's this—creature." Gemma made a vague gesture. "I think they're from the Desert Kingdom. Or maybe not, I don't know. They can shape-change, steal someone's identity, only they have to eat them first—usually someone already dead, they haunt graveyards and battlefields, but I think this time, I think—" She broke off, meeting Klaus's gaze without meaning to. She hadn't realized how close he'd gotten.

There was a troubled look in Klaus's eye. "Where did you hear about these ghouls?"

Gemma dropped her gaze, staring at the dull brass buttons on Klaus's coat. "They're shape-changers. Changelings. Without a human body, they're just shadow. I think they can *move* in the shadows, I think—" The rain let up even more, becoming a misty drizzle ghosting through the trees. "I saw—"

But she couldn't say it. What she'd seen. None of it.

"What?" Klaus leaned towards her. "You can tell me."

"I can't. I'm—I told you, I don't know what's real." She heard the frenetic tone in her voice, so alien, so unlike her. But she couldn't suppress it. "I'm going mad, you'll think I'm mad—"

"I won't. I told you, Gemma, I believe you."

"Why? You don't even know what I'm going to say!"

"Because I trust you." Klaus's tone was a strange mixture of familiar exasperation and unbearable patience. Unbearable because it was oh, so kind. "So I believe what you tell me."

"And what else?"

"What?"

"You believe me." Now it was Gemma who stepped forward, banishing the distance left between them. She had to tilt her head back to look him in the eye, and she wanted to look him in the eye. An agitated defiance rose inside her, born of desperation and fear and the desire to just *be*. To just be Gemma. Not the Gemma who was seeing things, not the Gemma who was damaged and useless. "And what else?"

"Gemma—"

"*What else?*" Before she knew what she was doing, Gemma reached up, gripping his drenched coat collar. "You believe me. You trust me. You worry about me—"

The gleam in Klaus's dark eyes was unlike any she had seen there before. Reproachful, that was familiar on him. But he also looked...almost afraid. Well, she was clutching at him like a mad woman. She'd told him she was going mad.

She would prove it.

"And I'm not allowed to worry about you," Klaus said, "is that it? You've made that clear."

"But you do worry about me." Rainwater clung to Gemma's lashes. Her voice dropped to a low murmur. "And what else, Klaus?" *What else do you feel about me?*

She didn't have to ask. She knew.

Klaus reached up and wrapped his hands around her wrists. She thought he was going to push her away, pry her hands from his collar, but he didn't. His grip on her was featherlight. "Gemma." He spoke in a hoarse, harsh whisper, and he gazed at her, his eyes searching. Asking.

Gemma answered his question.

Her hands slid from his collar to his face, and she kissed him.

She kissed him fervently, ardently, without hesitation. Pouring everything she was, everything she felt, into that kiss. As though all her fear could bleed straight through him, as though he could exorcise it from her.

Klaus responded in kind, just as she wanted, just as she'd hoped, his mouth moving over hers with hunger. One of his hands slipped behind her neck, while the other took her by the waist, tugging her into him. Gemma surrendered into his embrace, into the comfort of his arms and the heat of his chest.

There was such a wondrous, wild inevitability to it all. As though this was always going to happen, as though it had to happen. Gemma remembered all the reasons that it couldn't, but those reasons were dust now, drifting away on the wind. Klaus's lips were molten heaven against hers, and everything fell away as he kissed her, as she kissed him. She pressed into him, hands roaming over the curve of his shoulder and the jut of his collarbone. She slid a hand inside his uniform coat and felt the erratic beat of his heart. And Gemma thought she had never been so close to anyone, never been so deep into a person. She felt like she'd been made anew. Made whole—

And then, slowly, it ended. No one pulled away, neither of them brought it to a halt. It ended as inevitably as it began, their shared ardor fading from a blazing flame to a smoldering simmer. Gemma caught her breath as Klaus lifted his head, and they gripped each other, gazing into each other's eyes.

Klaus shuddered around her. They were so tightly entwined that Gemma felt it rattle through her. "Why?" he asked. "Why now?"

Gemma squeezed her hand against his chest. "What?"

"Why now? Because I've always—but you—" He gave the slightest shake of his head. "Is this just because you think you've gone mad? Is that what this is to you? Madness?"

Gemma stared at him, silent. The truthful answer was yes. Yes, and no. Because that was why she had done it, that was how it started. But after what had just passed between them, after that kiss...

Hadn't he felt it too? How could he ask her that now?

That kiss had kindled something inside her she hadn't even known she wanted. And she never wanted to let it go. Never wanted to let him go.

But she stayed silent too long. Klaus's hold on her slackened. "That is why. Of course. I've known, I've always known—"

"Known what?"

"That this can never happen. Not really. It's always there between us, it always will be—"

"*What?*" Gemma demanded.

He met her gaze. "Viveca."

Gemma released him as though he'd burned her. She stepped back out of his reach. Nothing had ever felt colder or vaster than the small distance between them now. When Gemma spoke, her voice sounded strange and empty, as though all the feeling had been carved out of her. "You still hold that against me."

"What are you talking about?"

"That's your hang-up, Klaus, not mine." Gemma shivered as a brisk wind slipped through the trees. The rain had stopped completely now. Sometime while they were kissing, tangled up in each other, it had stopped, leaving a cool chill in its wake. "I'm so sorry I killed the woman you loved. I'm so sorry I didn't let her kill you. That's what you wanted, right?"

Klaus looked stricken, his jagged scars pale in the low gray light. "What are you talking about?"

Gemma shook her head. "That's your problem, Klaus. Your burden. Your mess to sort out in your head. Don't put it on me."

"I'm not—" Klaus scrubbed a hand through his wet hair, making it even more bedraggled. "It is your burden. Or at least—that's what I always thought."

"What is that supposed to mean?"

"I couldn't kill her." Klaus let out a laugh that sounded as empty as she felt. "I couldn't kill her, so you had to. Because I was too weak to do it myself. Stones, I was too weak to just walk away from her in the first place. And then there's Falcon."

"What about Falcon?"

"She killed him, Gemma."

"I'm aware."

"So, don't you—"

"Enough about Falcon. Forget about Falcon." She said it like an order, a commandment to be followed. Not for Klaus but for herself.

But it was a useless order. Because Gemma could never forget about Falcon. She could never forget that Viveca had killed him, but she, Gemma, was the reason he was dead.

And here it was, here it all was. The reasons this could never work. They all came rushing back at her. Dust solidifying before her eyes, standing between them. Always between them.

It was too much. Too much baggage for either of them to overcome.

Klaus was staring at her, but Gemma closed her eyes. Letting him go. Letting it all go.

Then she ran back through the trees, fleeing the haven of the woods and the memory of what she'd almost had.

14

TRACES

G RYPHON HAD ASKED ROY and Spencer to keep him informed of any further developments in the investigation of the intruder. It was not so unusual. It was the sort of thing Garrett would have done, taking charge of the investigation. But somehow Gryphon didn't think his father would see it that way, which was why he'd bypassed his father and gone straight to the soldiers. Specifically, the soldiers who liked him. (Though it seemed he'd gained the respect of some of his father's guards after saving his life.)

Thankfully, his father was too busy drawing up plans for taking over the Black Forest to notice what Gryphon was up to. Well, in fact, Gryphon was not thankful for that at all, since those plans involved *him*, but for now, it kept Victor out of his hair. And Gryphon was grateful for that when, a few hours after dusk, Spencer came to report that some kind of threat had been left in Princess Solena's quarters.

"A threat?" Gryphon echoed. He was already pulling on his coat and boots, moving quickly to join Spencer in the corridor. "What kind of threat?"

"I'm not sure. Nothing dangerous." Spencer hurried down the corridor, trotting to keep up with Gryphon. "Oh, the princess was having a right meltdown about it, but I saw Gemma, and she didn't look concerned. I mean, it's Gemma, so she didn't look like anything, but. She had the look she gets when she's trying not to look annoyed. If I had to guess, she thought the princess was overreacting. Still, you wanted to stay informed, so..."

"Yes. It's good you came to get me."

Ten minutes later, they stood in the corridor outside Princess Solena's quarters amidst a number of milling guardsmen, Glen and Desert alike. Gemma, he gathered, was inside with Solena, trying to calm the princess—or enduring a severe tongue-lashing for this breach of security, depending on who you asked. Gryphon wasn't going to enter those quarters unless he had to, so he asked that the "threat" be brought out for him to examine. It arrived a minute later, carried in the hands of a blond handmaiden named Tashi.

"This was it." Tashi's expression was slightly revolted as she held her arms out. "This is what the princess found. It was left on her bed."

Gryphon smelled it before he even saw what it was, cradled within the folds of a large cloth.

The carcass of a dead bird. Both its neck and one of its wings broken.

Wrinkling his nose against the smell—a smell that probably only he could detect, as the bird was freshly dead—Gryphon said, "Are we sure this was left as a threat for the princess? The castle does have cats, after all. Maybe one of them left it there."

The handmaiden shrugged. She didn't look terribly concerned herself. "Maybe, Your Highness. But the royal crest of the Desert Kingdom is a sparrow. And this is a sparrow. And also..."

"Yes?"

Tashi turned to deposit the rag full of dead bird in the arms of the nearest Desert guard. Shuddering, she turned back to Gryphon and said, "Is it true you saw this intruder, Your Highness? The one they say was in the king's apartments two nights ago?" When Gryphon nodded, Tashi narrowed her eyes. "What did it look like? That is, if I may ask. Your Highness."

You already did, Gryphon thought, but he didn't mind answering her. "There wasn't much to see. The intruder was completely dressed in black from head to toe. Including black gloves and a large black hood covering their head and face."

Tashi nodded. She didn't look surprised.

"Why do you ask?" he demanded.

"It's just..." Tashi pursed her lips, a considering look on her face. "I thought I saw someone dressed like that. All in black. It was a bit before the princess found the dead sparrow in her bed."

"Where was this? And what do you mean, you thought you saw?"

"I just don't know." The handmaiden didn't seem particularly bothered by any of this. The way she spoke, one would've thought she was merely doing him a favor, rather than helping to protect her princess from potential danger. "It was down there, down the end of the corridor." She pointed in the opposite direction from the way Gryphon had come. "It was only for a second, and then they just...disappeared. Then Lady Kova called for me, you see, and I was startled, and when I looked again—well, if there was someone down there, they were just gone."

Gryphon thanked the handmaiden—for all that she hadn't been much help—and dismissed her. It wasn't her fault, really, but Gryphon wished he had something more definite to go on. He frowned, turning to stare down the way Tashi had indicated. Breaking away from the guards, he started down the corridor in that direction, moving slowly, deliberately. His gaze swept the floor before him and the walls on either side of him, but he wasn't looking for anything, really. He was...

Gryphon paused and lifted his head.

There. *There.*

A familiar scent, lingering in the corridor. A scent Gryphon had caught two nights ago, leading straight to his father's apartments.

The cloyingly sweet scent of rot and decay.

Trailed by a few of the Glen Kingdom guards, Gryphon tracked the intruder's scent all the way down a winding stairwell to the ground floor of the castle, and then outside onto the grounds. The night was black, the half-moon shrouded in a thick layer of clouds, but it wasn't as cold as it had been, the brief chill brought on by this morning's rainstorms driven out by a warm afternoon sun. Even now that the sun had set, it was positively balmy so far as Gryphon was concerned, and he was grateful for the lack of a breeze because it made it easier to track the intruder's fetid stench.

He followed the scent down a broad path carved into the grounds, one that ran all the way around the property. But near the back end of the castle, the trail grew muddled. Gryphon started down one direction only to jerk away to another, and then another. He cursed, turning about, confused. It was as though the intruder had gone haring off in multiple directions.

I need a tracker, he thought. He looked at his guards and opened his mouth, Gemma's name on the tip of his tongue. But then he recalled Gemma was on duty guarding the princess, and Solena wasn't likely to let her go anytime soon, not after discovering this "threat" in her bedchamber. He could insist, of course, but he wasn't sure if Gemma could help him. He'd overheard some talk among the guards; apparently, Gemma had suffered some kind of injury a while ago, one that affected her sight. He wasn't sure if she was a tracker anymore, and he didn't want to offend by asking.

That left him with one option, so far as he knew.

Turning to his guards, he said, "I need a tracker. Bring me Klaus."

Gryphon continued trying to pinpoint the intruder's scent, but by the time the guards returned, Klaus in tow, he'd had no more success than before. He picked up Klaus's scent on the air, coming towards him, before he spotted the bobbing white lights in the darkness, growing brighter and larger as the guards came down the path.

The two guards slowed as they neared Gryphon, but Klaus stopped outright five paces from him. As though he didn't want to get any closer. The flat hostility in his eyes, lit by the light of the lanterns, was unmistakable. An irrational surge of irritation flared in Gryphon, but he said in a deceptively mild tone, "Klaus." He even dipped his chin in a respectful nod.

They could be civil with each other. Even after that completely unfair tirade Klaus had subjected him to the last time they saw each other.

A muscle twitched in Klaus's jaw, but otherwise, he remained unmoving. A short silence passed, a beat too long after Gryphon's greeting. Then Klaus said with only the slightest trace of belligerence, "Gryphon."

The lack of title immediately rankled, even though there were a million reasons it shouldn't. The first being that Klaus had never afforded him a title, even when they'd worked and lived together in the old Forest Kingdom. Klaus might have done some work for him, but he didn't serve him; that had always been clear. The second reason being that Gryphon didn't want anyone to call him "Prince Gryphon." It was awkward enough putting up with it from the other guards.

But that was why it rankled: Gryphon knew the guards were supposed to call him "Prince," and Klaus could not have made it plainer that he hadn't forgotten that. The challenging glint in his eyes made it clear it was a deliberate choice. In return, Gryphon said nothing, allowing another silence that stretched on too long.

But Klaus didn't flinch. He never did.

Mouth twisting grimly, Gryphon shook his head. They didn't have time for this childishness. "Did they fill you in?" he asked Klaus.

"Only that you needed a tracker." Stuffing his hands into the pockets of his coat, Klaus took a couple of steps forward, his demeanor suddenly casual. No challenges, no more hostility. Making it even more clear it had all been for show.

Gryphon jerked his head, indicating Klaus should follow him as he turned to head down the path. "There might have been another sighting of the intruder. Outside Princess Solena's quarters. The witness isn't entirely reliable, but I caught the same scent from before. Followed it out here, but now…" He spread his hands. "I've lost it. Rather, there's too much of it. It gets all muddied here, like they went off in five different directions."

Klaus had already bent low to the ground to examine the path at their feet. Pulling a face, he raised his head to beckon one of the guards, then motioned for his lantern, which the guard handed over. Klaus held it aloft awkwardly from his crouch as his gaze traveled over the ground. "This would be easier during the daytime."

"I know. But if the intruder is still nearby, they'd be long gone by then. And possibly any trail they've left."

Klaus shifted, turning to study the ground from another angle. "And me."

It was a moment before Gryphon understood what he meant. "You're leaving?"

"In the morning. I was just arranging it before you called me out here." He glanced up. "Just taking some personal time. I have a lot of leave, so."

"Right." Gryphon tried not to blink, his tone carefully neutral.

Klaus spared him an ironic smile, his eyes darkly amused. "It's not because of you."

"I didn't think it was."

The smile became an all-out smirk. "Yes, you did."

Gryphon bit back a scowl. Even when they were friends, Gryphon had never liked how easily Klaus read him, how he could pin down exactly what he was thinking or feeling. Klaus knew him better than anyone.

The truth was, Klaus's assessment of him, two nights ago—his claim that he knew exactly how Gryphon would have reacted to Klaus's betrayal, had Klaus returned instead of running off with Garrett—wasn't unfair at all. It was spot-on. That was how Gryphon would have reacted back then.

But there were two things Klaus didn't understand. For one, Gryphon had changed. And for another...if Gryphon had lashed out at Klaus just as he'd described, it wouldn't have had anything to do with Klaus at all. And everything to do with Gryphon and the self-loathing he'd harbored for himself back then.

There was just no point being angry at Klaus for what he'd done. Betraying Gryphon to Viveca. Gryphon knew it was never Klaus's intention to let Viveca get at him; he knew without even having to ask. In fact, he was sure it was quite the opposite. Klaus had never been anything but a loyal friend to him. He'd fallen for the wrong person, yes, he'd let that person take advantage of him, yes. But Gryphon knew better than to question his loyalty.

Which was why it wasn't Klaus's unwitting betrayal that hurt so much. No, what stung was that he'd never returned. That he'd run off with Gryphon's *brother.* As if Gryphon needed any more proof that people preferred Garrett to himself, in every aspect.

It took a while, and taking up a few trails that went nowhere, but Klaus eventually zeroed in on some disturbed soil that took them off the walking path and into a neglected, overgrown courtyard behind the castle. It was less a courtyard and more a maintenance yard, Gryphon thought, noting the large metal pipework housed back here, mostly concealed by tangled vines and shrubs. Intentionally overgrown, then.

Klaus stopped and stood before a thick mess of climbing ivy that ran up the castle alongside a rusting gutter pipe. He examined both the piping and the ivy, squinting in the light of his lantern. Then he asked, "Got any of the intruder's scent here?"

Gryphon went to stand a little closer. "Yes. Why?"

Klaus gestured, lifting his gaze. "Because I think they went up this."

Puzzled, Gryphon eyed the ivy and the gutter pipe. It certainly made for a good climbing spot, but... "Now why," he murmured, "would an assassin who can scale a flat wall need a gutter pipe or climbing ivy to get up here?"

"Maybe those abilities aren't limitless," Klaus mused. "Like Princess Briar. Using up her speed or strength takes a lot out of her. She loses steam eventually. That's why she has to eat a dead mouse every day."

"Perhaps."

"I think the better question is, did they use this way to break into the castle or to get *back* into the castle?"

"Back in? What do you mean?"

"You said you tracked their scent from inside the castle, right? From where the intruder was spotted, outside Solena's quarters."

"And it's led us here," Gryphon said with grave comprehension.

Klaus shrugged. "Looks like Gemma was right. The intruder is...someone living in the castle. Probably someone from the Desert Kingdom delegation."

"It's a possibility." Gryphon swept a look over Klaus, surreptitiously curious. It had almost sounded as though Klaus was going to say something else just then. "Gemma thinks that?"

Klaus shrugged again, but now he looked distinctly uncomfortable. "Seems so. Ask her about it, why don't you." He ran a hand over his head, then said, "Look, you should probably get some people up into that part of the castle. Whatever's up there." He gestured at the high windows far above them, where the ivy and gutter led. "See if there's anything left to find. Unless you need me for anything else?"

Gryphon shook his head. "No. You can go. I suppose you've got packing to do."

Klaus snorted. "Not much. You know me."

"Yes. Yes I do."

Klaus cast him a sharp glance. As though wondering if that had been a dig. But Gryphon wasn't trying to needle Klaus. His irritation was gone. All he felt now, when he looked at Klaus, was a little sad.

He wasn't too proud to admit that to himself.

Klaus turned to go, heading out of the stone courtyard, the lean set of his shoulders and his carefully controlled gait a familiar silhouette, outlined in the bright glare of his lantern. Gryphon watched him go, his gaze intent, until Klaus surprised him by turning back. Gryphon jerked away, turning slightly to make it look like he'd been studying the broken trail of ivy.

"How did you do it, anyway?" Klaus asked.

Gryphon swiveled, turning back with a look of mild surprise. A feigned look, pretending he had only just noticed Klaus was still there. "What? Do what?"

Klaus made an impatient gesture. As though Gryphon should know what he was talking about. "The beast. Your turning. They say you can control it now, and obviously you can. Otherwise you wouldn't be having afternoon tea with the princess. So. How did you learn to control it?"

Gryphon considered his answer. Debating what to say. Once, he wouldn't have hesitated to share the truth with Klaus. Once, when the trust between them had been less fragile. But he settled on the truth after all, if only because he had no idea what else to say. "Well, Isabelle helped me master the mechanics of it. Since she could always control her turning. But mostly, I just...stopped punishing myself."

Klaus's reply was sardonic. "Is that what you were doing?"

Gryphon narrowed his eyes, unsure if he was being mocked.

Klaus lifted his hands. "It's just, it sounds like you're saying we all could have gotten out of that castle a lot sooner had you just learned not to brood so much."

"You could have gotten out of that castle whenever you wanted," Gryphon said coolly. "In fact, you did. And I still enjoy a good brood now and then, thank you very much."

"I'm sure you do."

Gryphon shoved aside his irritation—how quickly it came back—and said, "Look, I had to stop believing everything my father had instilled in me. About what a failure I was, about how I ruined everything. I had to let go of the belief that I deserved my curse."

Klaus stared at him, but his lantern hung down by his side, leaving his face in shadow. "But *how*—" He broke off, shaking his head. "Never mind. It doesn't matter."

"How what?"

"Just forget it."

Gryphon watched Klaus, wishing he could penetrate the mask of shadows concealing the tracker's face. But he could. Hoping Klaus wouldn't notice, he called to the beast, summoning just enough to use his night vision. To pierce through the darkness.

Klaus wasn't looking at him, his gaze fixed on a spot on the ground. But his expression was awash with misery and frustration. And suddenly, Gryphon understood.

Gryphon looked at Klaus and found him looking at himself one year ago.

Klaus hadn't run off with his brother because he was afraid of Gryphon's retribution. He hadn't done it to spite him or punish him, as Gryphon had once believed. Klaus had run off to punish *himself*. Because he believed he deserved Gryphon's retribution. Because he believed he deserved to lose their friendship. This hostility from Klaus wasn't because Klaus couldn't forgive Gryphon.

It was because he couldn't forgive himself. For loving Viveca.

In that moment, the last of Gryphon's hurt and resentment towards Klaus fell away. He released the beast, letting the veil of darkness fall back into place between them.

"It's not easy," he said. "But it helps if you have someone who trusts you. Who values you. Someone who can see you clearly. Even when you can't."

Klaus muttered something in response, so quietly that even Gryphon almost didn't catch it. Then the tracker turned to go, and this time, he didn't turn back. Leaving Gryphon alone in the darkness with those final words.

He'd said, *"And what if you've already lost that person?"*

15

DELUSION

GEMMA WOKE IN THE barracks in the morning and lay still for a long time. The thin, scratchy sheets were twisted around her legs, but she didn't try to untangle herself. She simply lay there, her thoughts percolating as she recalled yesterday's events.

The vision in the barracks. Finding herself in that horrible dead place. And Klaus. Klaus, in the woods.

Kissing Klaus.

Gemma put a fist to her forehead. *Klaus.* She needed to find him. She needed to apologize. Because whether she'd meant to or not—and whatever she felt for him now—she'd preyed upon the feelings she knew he had for her. She'd used him, and that wasn't fair. She needed to apologize.

And hopefully, he'd forgive her. Because she needed his help to figure out what Solena was up to, to expose Solena for what she was. After all, he was the one who believed her. The one who trusted her implicitly.

He was the one who could be her eyes. He trusted her, but more importantly, she trusted him. Even when she couldn't trust herself.

So she rose from her bed and dressed quickly, throwing on the first clothes she found. Hastily bunched up her hair and tied it behind her head. Then she left her sleeping quarters, heading out onto the parade grounds.

It was another one of those bright but chilly days, where the sun overhead felt faint and colorless. Gemma made her way to the officers' building, stopping short of Kinsley's office and looking for the duty roster. A few other soldiers milled about in there, some checking the roster, others helping themselves to the tea and coffee in the corner. Gemma found herself waiting behind another soldier consulting the roster, and when that soldier turned around, she saw it was Roy.

"Oh, Gemma. Hullo." Roy tilted his head. "Thought you had the day off."

"I do." Gemma indicated the duty roster. "I was wondering where Klaus was today. I'm looking for him."

"Oh." Roy looked even more surprised. "Gemma, Klaus—he left. Early this morning."

Gemma heard the words like a gut punch. "What?"

"Yes. I saw him this morning. Thought he would have told you."

"He *left?* He quit the guard?"

"What? Oh, no. He didn't quit. He took leave for a few days. That's why I thought you knew."

"Oh," said Gemma in a small voice. "No. I didn't know."

"He said he'd be back in a few days," Roy offered.

"Right. Good. Thank you." Gemma turned away, feeling dazed.

She stepped outside once again, out onto the parade grounds. It was a bustle of activity right now—mid-morning, she realized. Shift change. Soldiers in navy-blue uniforms crossed the yard, heading into the barracks to rest and eat, heading out of the barracks for their next shifts. But she, Gemma, had no one to guard today, and neither did Klaus, apparently, because he was gone. Taken leave.

When had he taken leave, she wondered? For all she knew, this had been planned. Perhaps he'd put in for this days ago, weeks ago. But that didn't sound like Klaus. He almost never took leave, and surely he'd have mentioned it, if he knew he had leave coming up. No, deep down, Gemma knew when he'd decided this.

Yesterday. After their encounter in the woods.

He'd left because of her.

Gemma leaned against the wall of the officers' building, rubbing her hands over her eyes. Klaus had *gone*. Because of her, because she'd kissed him and then...

But this wasn't all her fault, she thought angrily. Maybe she shouldn't have done it. Kissed him like that, because she was upset, to distract herself from everything going on. But it had meant more to her than he realized. And what he'd said about Falcon and Viveca—stones, of course he thought she blamed him for Falcon's death. Even Roy had said so, hadn't he? But she didn't, she had never—

And now he was gone? Now, when she needed him, when he knew she needed him?

Gemma exhaled, long and low. "You can go to hell, Klaus," she muttered.

Her head was pounding again. It hadn't really stopped, she realized, since yesterday. She'd just stopped noticing it. That dull throb had become a minor nuisance. But standing here in the too-bright courtyard, the sting of Klaus's leaving fresh in her mind and with nothing to distract her—now she felt it. The pounding intensifying, migrating. It was only going to get worse, Gemma thought. She should probably get some rest. Better yet, perhaps she should visit the infirmary. See if they could do any-thing for her.

That was what she should do. But it wasn't what she wanted to do. The last thing she wanted was to visit the infirmary where they would tell her, yet again, that her eyesight was fine. Stones, they'd probably tell her she was imagining the headache too. Perhaps that wasn't fair, but even so, the physicians couldn't give her what she really needed right now. A way to know if what she was seeing was real, a way to understand what was happening to her. Shadows, skeletons, that vision in the barracks…

Hallucinations. Your mind playing tricks on you.

Klaus was gone. So was Sabine, from what Gemma had heard. She'd only stayed in town for one night, taken the train out yesterday afternoon. And stones knew where Jesine was. Even if she was still living in the southern wood, that was too far away for her to help right now.

But…

There was another witch who might be able to help Gemma. One right here in Glen Castle. Or rather, *beneath* the castle.

He could help Gemma. The only real question was whether he would.

Unlike the rest of the castle, the dungeons had never been modernized. There were no gear-bulb fixtures down here, no modern plumbing or metal framework. The stairs were solid stone, carved into the wall with only a makeshift wooden railing to steady Gemma as she descended into the bowels of the castle. There were a few handheld gear-bulb lanterns here and there, including the one Gemma had brought with her, but otherwise, the only light came from old-fashioned torches, smoky and flaming, set in sconces on the walls outside the cells.

The rows of cells were almost completely empty, which was the only good thing that could be said for these beastly accommodations. Most criminals were housed in the city jail, not here in the castle, or else in other facilities in the countryside. These dungeons were almost never used except for temporary emergencies...or for the most dangerous of prisoners.

Such as a witch. Even if he was a witch with an impaired memory and spelled shackles that kept him from using magic.

The jailer on duty directed Gemma to the cell she was looking for but let her find her own way. Gemma wondered if this was because she was a guard—she'd worn her uniform coat to be sure she'd be granted access—or if the jailer was reluctant to get close to the witch. Regardless, she crept along the dank stone corridors on her own, the bright white of her lantern cutting through the darkness. She made her way from rows of uniform cells with constructed walls and cot-like beds into the deeper, older part of the dungeon, where the cells had been dug straight out of the bedrock. The emptiness of the cells was eerier than a dungeon full of prisoners might have been, and this unsettling feeling only heightened as the flaming torches became more and more spaced out. Gemma began to feel as though she was completely alone down here, no jailer, no witch, and she wondered what would happen if she became lost in these corridors, if anyone would ever find her...

She couldn't help it; she faltered at the thought, her steps slowing, the silence intensifying as the echoing ring of her boots against the stone died out. Gemma was used to the darkness, but this was not the darkness of the woods or the darkness of the night. This was the darkness of the earth. This was the darkness of the grave, of things buried and forgotten. What was it the stranger had said? *Dirt and worms and decaying flesh, clinging to old bones...*

Then a voice sounded out in the black, bodiless and unanchored.

"Who's that, coming to visit a witch?"

Gemma came to a complete stop. The voice was low, a rich, smooth baritone. It was uncanny the way the words floated out of the darkness, but as Gemma raised her lantern, the light fell over the pitted stone wall ahead of her. A dead end. She'd come to the right spot, and she knew who the voice belonged to.

Stepping forward, she turned her lantern and her gaze to the left. Peering into the cell at the end of the corridor.

"I know you," said the disembodied voice. "I remember you. You were there."

For a moment, Gemma still couldn't see the owner of the voice. The last torch in the wall was set back nearly ten paces down the corridor, leaving this cell and its occupant in complete darkness. Gemma took another step forward, holding her lantern aloft. Squinting through its glare.

Then a face materialized from inside the cell as the witch stepped forward into the light. "You were there," he said, "when they took me captive. When they put these on me." A pair of arms materialized below the face as he raised them to display the metal cuffs on his wrists. There was no chain shackling them together; they didn't need one. Their purpose wasn't to hinder his movements, but his magic.

Gemma replied in a steady voice, "No. I wasn't there."

The witch, Harper, smiled at her. His teeth shone white from the shadows. "No. You weren't, were you?"

Gemma didn't flinch. Harper was one of the witches Prince Garrett had faced in the southern wood three months ago. He was not the one who'd injured Gemma and damaged her sight—that witch was dead. But they'd worked together in the same coven, worked towards getting revenge. Both witches had harbored a grudge against Ansel, the witch hunter who'd aided Prince Garrett. Specifically, Harper had wanted revenge for his sister's death; Ansel had killed her some years back, though in defense of his own life. Harper had been consumed by his desire for vengeance.

Until Jesine took it away from him.

Jesine had taken all of Harper's memories of Ansel and of his sister's death. She hadn't wanted him killed, so with the aid of the spelled shackles, Prince Garrett had agreed to hold Harper prisoner indefinitely. A dungeon out in the countryside was being prepared for him, but until it was ready, Harper was here, housed in the castle's dungeon.

Now Gemma stared at the witch, and he stared back. "I wasn't there when you were taken captive," she said in a level voice, "because the rest of your coven had left me for dead. Left me bleeding in the brain."

"Yet here you are." Harper's tone was rather blasé, as though he couldn't care less about any of this. Which was probably true. "And I have seen you before. On the train out of the southern wood. You looked just fine to me." His dark eyes burned in the light of the lantern. "Which means you were healed. And only one witch could have done that."

Gemma inched a little closer to the cell. "Yes. Jesine healed me." Her heartbeat quickened and she wondered if he could sense it. If he could hear it. But he was no were-wolf, she reminded herself, with special hearing. He was only a witch without magic. "But she couldn't heal everything. My sight was damaged in my right eye." It felt weird spilling all of this to a witch, to a stranger. Gemma was not the most verbose of people even among friends. And Harper was no friend. "Jesine told me it might never fully heal."

"Well, I certainly can't help you, even without these." Harper sounded bored again as he raised his arms a second time, indicating the spelled cuffs. "Not without great cost to myself. And I have no interest in shaving any years off my life."

"That's not why I'm here." Gemma gritted her teeth, trying to hold on to her composure. "Jesine told me even if my eye heals, I still might...experience other symptoms. Because it was magic that injured me. She said I might suffer hallucinations. See things that aren't really there."

"Ah." Even as Gemma pushed closer to the bars of his cell, Harper retreated, melting back into the shadows. As though the light of her lantern burned him. Gemma would have thought someone left alone in the dark for so long would crave the light, but perhaps a bad witch was different. Perhaps Harper was as at home in this dark as she was in the woods. "So now we come to it." Harper's words echoed within the confines of his cave-like cell. "What have you been seeing, Gemma? What evils have you spied upon?"

Gemma didn't like that he remembered her name. That suggested he'd taken more interest in her than he'd let on.

"Just tell me." Gemma took another step forward, coming so close that she could have reached out and gripped the bars. But she knew better. Even desperate as she was, she knew better. "How can I know? If what I see is real or not? There has to be a way...there *has* to be a way. Something I can do or some magic that—"

Harper let out another chuckle. The sound was soft and forbidding. "Some magic. Would you like that, Gemma? To be touched with magic again? Maybe you liked it the first time. Maybe you've enjoyed the stain of it on your sight. Perhaps it's been a gift for you, giving you a peek into dark and otherworldly places—"

"No." Gemma couldn't keep her voice from shaking, though she tried to harden herself. "I haven't enjoyed any of it. I haven't enjoyed not knowing what's real and what's not—"

"It's all real." Harper's voice became light, almost singsong, and Gemma wondered if he was a little mad. His memories and magic taken from him, locked up down here in the dark...that was more than enough to drive someone insane. "Embrace it, Gemma. Embrace the magic. Embrace the madness." He laughed again, and there was definitely something of an unhinged quality to it. "You'll be much happier."

Gemma recoiled, stepping back from the dungeon cell. Putting distance between her and the witch. This was a mistake, she realized, the thought hopeless and bitter. She should never have come down here. Of course a bad witch would be no help to her, especially if he'd lost his marbles.

Harper only laughed louder and harder as she backed away, and the echo of his laughter rebounded around her as she fled down the corridor, searching for the way out of these oppressive tunnels.

As eager as she was to leave, she flinched when she stepped out into the bright daylight. The sun had gone behind a bank of misty clouds, but the glare of the midday sky was still strong, too strong for Gemma, after immersing herself in the dark of the underground. The throbbing in her head had shifted behind her eye, and now she felt it keenly, a sharp, stabbing pain with each beat of her heart. Gemma winced and pinched her fingers around her eye as she headed back towards the barracks. She really should get some rest. And maybe visit the physicians for a painkiller.

But she met Spencer and Gallia on the way into the barracks, and Spencer's face lit up when he saw her. "Oh, Gemma, I'm glad we ran into you." He exchanged a glance with Gallia as the three of them passed through the open gates. "We've just come off duty from a shift guarding Princess Solena."

"Lucky you," Gemma groused.

Gallia scowled. "She's still making a fuss about what happened last night. The threat she received. And she wants to know what we plan to do about it. She said maybe she shouldn't attend this ball the king is throwing, if she isn't safe in the castle."

Right. The "death threat," the dead bird Princess Solena had found in her bedchamber last night. Gemma had nearly forgotten. Prince Gryphon and some guards had investigated, checked the castle and the grounds for another intruder. But they'd found nothing.

Resisting the urge to rub her fist into her throbbing eye, Gemma said, "Well, I'm not sure what else we can do. That's not already being done." It was difficult to reorient herself into talk of intruders and threats when her mind was filled with witches and visions and magic and ghouls. "We can ask the king for extra security, I suppose."

"I had an idea actually," Spencer said, bringing the three of them to a halt outside the officers' building. "In fact, it was the princess saying she shouldn't attend the ball that gave me the idea. But, Gemma, I don't think you're going to like it."

"Just tell me, Spencer."

"Well—if someone really is coming after Solena, perhaps we could use the ball to draw them out. Use her as a public target, so to speak. Only, instead of risking her life, we have someone else attend the ball in her place. We use a decoy princess."

Gemma mulled this over. It wasn't a bad plan, especially if the princess truly didn't want to attend the ball. But even so... "We'd need someone who looks like her—roughly the same height and build, same hair color, skin color. A guard or a servant, probably. A guard would be best."

"Yes." Spencer's eyes were bright and nervous. "That's exactly what I was thinking."

He stared at her. Gemma stared at him.

"*Oh*," she said with dawning comprehension—and dawning horror. "Oh, no."

Gallia looked her over critically. "I can't think of anyone else who looks more like her than you, Gemma. And you can defend yourself if someone attacks you."

Gemma didn't bother to hide her dismay, but she had to admit Gallia was right. Gemma and Solena were far from identical, but they were about the same height and body type, and their coloring was similar as well.

"We could ask the king to arrange for low lighting too," Spencer suggested, sounding a little more enthused. "That would help. And maybe we could arrange for the guests to wear those, erm, you know, those decorative masks—"

Gemma tuned him out as she thought this over, tapping the toe of her boot against the pavement. But wasn't this all unnecessary? After all, if Gemma's suspicions were correct, then Solena wasn't in any danger from the intruder because she *was* the intruder. She had probably left the dead bird for herself. In which case, they could be playing right into her hands. It might be she wanted to miss the ball. For some reason.

Then again...perhaps taking Solena's place was just the opportunity Gemma needed. To find out more about the princess, about who and what she was. If the girl she'd found dying in the woods was the real princess, if the one here in the castle was an imposter...

Gemma had no one to help her now that Klaus was gone. There was no one she could trust with her own truth, no one she could bear to trust. But she wasn't going to let that stop her. She had to know if anything she'd seen was real, she had to know if Solena was really a ghoul. Not just because it was her job, but for herself. For her own sanity.

She had to know which it was. Which one she was dealing with.

Monster...or madness?

16

GROUNDWORK

KLAUS PULLED OPEN THE door to the tavern and was met with bright light, raucous laughter, and the strangely welcoming scent of stale ale and roasting meat. He took a moment to acclimate himself to the overpowering atmosphere. Then he stepped inside, the door swinging shut behind him.

No one took any notice of him. There was no reason anyone should. Most of the rowdy patrons were too caught up in their own drinking, eating, and talk to hear the door slamming shut.

Klaus cast his gaze around. A long wraparound bar took up a full half of the room, and the rest of it was littered with tables and chairs. There was a massive fireplace in the far corner, and it was there, tucked in a lone booth beside the hearth, that he spotted the person he was looking for. As he neared the fireplace, he noticed—with some amusement—that the young woman had several sheafs of paper spread across her table, as well as a small stack of books and notebooks. One of those notebooks lay open before her, and she scribbled away as he approached. She didn't look up, even when he stopped and stood at the end of the table.

Klaus cleared his throat. "You're reading? In a tavern?"

The girl in question looked up. "Technically, I'm writing. In a tavern."

"Right." Klaus slid into the booth across the table from her. "Hello, Sabine."

"Hullo, Klaus," Sabine replied pleasantly, closing her journal and setting her pen aside. She wore no uniform, of course—though she worked for the crown, it was as a private agent, not a soldier. Somehow, though, she managed to look more professional than he did, her fitted jacket and trousers neatly pressed and tailored.

"Care for a drink?" she asked.

"Sure."

Despite the crowd, Sabine raised her arm to signal a bartender and was promptly acknowledged with a wink and a nod. "Come here a lot?" Klaus asked innocently.

"Yes, actually. It's close enough to Glen City without being *in* Glen City, so it makes a good, central meeting spot for us." By "us," she undoubtedly meant herself and Demetri, her partner. She indicated the fireplace behind him as she bound her journal in a leather cord. "Besides, it has good lighting." She tapped the front of her journal. "We just wrapped a job last week and I've been finishing my report."

"I thought you'd already finished it. Weren't you just at the castle to make a report?"

Sabine smiled. "That was my official report for the king. These are the more personal records I keep for myself. And how did you know I was just in town?"

"Because when I mentioned to Roy I wanted to get in touch, he told me I'd just missed you." Klaus murmured his thanks as the bartender dropped by with a mug of ale for himself and a refill for Sabine—something that smelled sweet and rich, like hot chocolate. He remembered her drinking a lot of the stuff back in Lise, in the southern woods. "So." He slid his mug towards himself. "No Demetri?"

Sabine froze in the act of collecting her papers, looking startled. "You didn't want to talk to him too, did you? Because your telegram didn't say, and I thought—"

"No, I didn't want to talk to him." Truthfully, Klaus was not entirely at ease around Demetri, the former prince. "I'm just making polite conversation, Sabine. As people do."

"Oh. Right." Sabine gave him a lopsided smile as she set her papers aside. "No, he's not here. He's taking some personal time, believe it or not." By the way she said that, Klaus gathered Demetri was not the sort to take much personal time. Something they had in common.

"So are you two..." Klaus coughed. "You know."

Sabine looked confused. Then her eyes widened. "What, involved? Romantically?" She threw back her head and laughed, leaving Klaus feeling rather stupid. "Erm, no. Not in the slightest. He's not exactly my type."

"Right." Klaus took another sip of his ale, wishing he'd never asked in the first place. "Well. I suppose it would complicate things. Since you work together." The words slipped out before he could rethink them. He hoped Sabine wouldn't think too much of it.

Unfortunately, given the knowing look she gave him, she had. Her thoughts had gone exactly where he didn't want them to go. "Maybe," she said. "But not necessarily."

Klaus took another long sip, ignoring this pointed remark.

"Anyway," said Sabine, thankfully moving on from that topic, "what was it that brought you here, Klaus? Your note was fairly vague. Then again, it's hard to be too detailed via telegram, I suppose..."

Klaus set his mug back down, once his face didn't feel so warm. Tapping his fingers against the tabletop, he said, "Back in the southern woods. Remember the day we arrived in Lise—me, Garrett, and Gemma?" He managed not to stumble over Gemma's name.

"Ye-es." Sabine gazed down into her chocolate, then took a quick sip. Licking her lips, she added, "Demetri and Ansel and I had just come from that cabin. Where we found the woman who'd been killed by the demon."

"Right. And we all sat and had a drink in the tavern. And at one point, you lot were talking about what could have been responsible for all the weird things going on in the southern woods, and you listed off all the supernatural creatures you'd crossed off your list of suspects. And you mentioned ghouls," he went on, keeping his voice calm, "and Garrett said, 'There's no such thing as a ghoul.' And you said—"

"'Shows what you know,'" Sabine finished, quoting herself.

Klaus's pulse quickened. "Yes. Exactly." He eyed her expectantly.

She eyed him back, raising an eyebrow.

"So...you've encountered a ghoul before," Klaus deduced.

"Well. Sort of. Not exactly."

"What do you mean, not exactly?" Inwardly, Klaus deflated. He hoped this whole effort—reaching out to Sabine, taking leave, coming out here—hadn't been a waste of time. Not when he was needed back at Glen Castle.

And he was needed. Gemma needed him.

"Well." Sabine picked up a little stirring spoon and swirled it around in her chocolate. "The thing about ghouls is, it's a bit hard to actually see them. Or know if you've seen one."

"Because they can shape-change?" Klaus tried to recall everything Gemma had rattled off about ghouls.

"Supposedly, they can. Which I find incredibly disturbing."

"Why?"

"Because they could be anyone? Any person you meet could actually be a ghoul. I mean, anyone in here, anyone…" Sabine's eyes traveled the crowded tavern, then landed on him. "You could be a ghoul, for all I know."

"Well, can't those—what do you call 'em—those djinn. Can't they shape-change too?"

"Yes, but so far as we know, only one of them is running around the Five Kingdoms somewhere," Sabine said. "The rest of them are confined to their shadow realm. Whereas ghouls, we have no idea how many of them there are. Or where they are. Or what they want. Perhaps they just work individually, hanging around graveyards and chomping up corpses so they can live some kind of normal life. Or maybe they've all banded together to—I don't know. Infiltrate the Five Kingdoms and take them over."

"You may be more right about that than you know."

"Why? What's going on, Klaus? Why do you need my help, and what does it have to do with ghouls?"

"Well. We might have a ghoul in the castle."

He launched into the story of everything that had happened in Glen Castle since Princess Solena had arrived. He detailed how he and Gemma first discovered her in the woods at night, miles from her retinue. He told her about the intruder who could scale sheer walls. He suspected there was more that Gemma hadn't confided in him. When he finished everything, Sabine looked nonplussed. "So how did Gemma learn about ghouls in the first place?"

"I'm not sure," Klaus said honestly, "but parts of it seem to fit."

Sabine rubbed her thumb back and forth over her mouth. "So. She's right that ghouls seem to have originated from the Desert Kingdom, or at least, all the stories about them do. But the place where Demetri and I encountered one—or where we think we did—was here in the Glen Kingdom. Actually, it wasn't far from here. And it wasn't too long ago—it was the last job we worked before meeting Ansel and Prince Garrett in the southern woods." She met Klaus's gaze. "Why is it you're here on your own?"

"Because I prefer doing things on my own."

"No, I mean—did someone send you to consult with me? Kinsley? Because none of this feels very official. Or did you just take it upon yourself?" When Klaus didn't answer, Sabine asked incredulously, "Does anyone even know you're here?"

"I mean, I took leave. I didn't just run off."

"I see." Sabine sounded half-exasperated, half-amused.

"What?" he asked defensively.

"It's just...why are you really here, Klaus? What is this for? Or perhaps I should ask—who is this for?"

"You know, we really don't need to talk about this." *I really don't want to talk about this.*

"Mmm," Sabine murmured. "It's just, when you were telling me everything about this Desert princess and about ghouls—Gemma seemed to factor in a lot."

"Yes, well, she's heading the escort guard for the princess, so."

"Right. And you're helping her with that?"

"I'm also guarding the princess, if that's what you mean."

"Klaus."

"Sabine."

"Look. I meant what I said before." Sabine traced a finger over the tabletop, not quite looking him in the eye. "I don't necessarily think it's a bad idea. Getting involved with someone you work with."

"Yes, well," Klaus grumbled. "When it comes to me and Gemma, I don't think working together is our problem." Sabine clearly wasn't going to let this go, and what was the point of trying to deny it? It was a little childish, wasn't it, when she obviously knew how he felt about Gemma.

"Then what is the problem?" Sabine asked.

Klaus let out a little sigh. "Me."

That was the truth, plain and simple. He could see it now. Falcon wasn't standing between them, and neither was Viveca. From the sound of it, any feelings Gemma ever had for Falcon were in the past. And from the sound of it, she had never blamed him, Klaus, for Falcon's death. She'd never thought him a weak fool for not being able to kill Viveca, for loving Viveca.

She thought *he* blamed *her*. For Viveca's death.

Well, there was a logic to it, he supposed. She had killed Viveca. If he was going to blame someone, he suppose he might blame her. But though he had loved Viveca—more fool him—he also knew her for what she was. Poison, through and through. He didn't blame Gemma for killing her. If anything, he was grateful.

She had saved his life. In more ways than one.

Maybe he hadn't been able to see it at the time. Maybe it had taken him a long time to see it. But he did now. He didn't count the hours he went without thinking of Viveca anymore. He didn't even notice he wasn't thinking of Viveca anymore.

That was all thanks to Gemma.

And maybe he should tell her so. If only so she knew he didn't blame her. But otherwise, he wasn't sure what good it would do. He wasn't sure there was any future for them, even if there was no blame between them.

There was still a hell of a lot of baggage. Most of it his.

"But look, enough about me." Klaus rested his arms atop the table. "You said the place you and Demetri encountered a ghoul wasn't far from here. Can we go there? I mean, do you think that might help us get more information about ghouls?"

"Ye-es," Sabine said. "I think it might."

<hr>

Two hours later, Klaus eyed the landscape before him with undisguised trepidation. "So I tell you the Glen Kingdom is under attack from ghouls," he said, "and you bring me to a graveyard? Where ghouls like to gather?"

"Relax," Sabine said. "There aren't any ghouls here."

Klaus hardly found that reassuring. Overhead, waning moonlight filtered through sludgy clouds, giving the graveyard a ghostly, greenish cast. They'd climbed up a rugged hill to get here with only a pair of lanterns to light their way. But though they stood atop the hill's summit, the graveyard before them did not stretch beneath an open sky, affording them a view of the valley below. Instead, the graveyard was ringed in twisted cedar trees that seemed to hunch, branches tangling together and drooping towards the ground. Great curtains of moss hung from their limbs, enclosing the space even more. A person could get lost in this graveyard, Klaus thought. And wander right off the edge of the cliff in the darkness.

Sabine moved towards a low iron gate. It creaked as she pulled it open, rust flaking off as it swung on uneven hinges, one end dragging through the leaf-strewn ground.

"We think there was a ghoul here," Sabine admitted. Klaus froze halfway through the gate. "But it's gone now."

Klaus flinched as the gate clanged shut behind him. The sound was too loud in the dead quiet, ringing out over the headstones. "So what are we doing here, then? You think the ghoul left something behind?"

"Not the ghoul. But maybe someone did."

Klaus couldn't help but notice the wary way Sabine moved through the graves, despite her assurances they were alone. Then again, perhaps that was just respect for the dead. There were dead here of course, though they were likely long dead, Klaus thought. This graveyard seemed ancient; it didn't look as though anyone had visited here or tended the grounds in many years. The headstones lining the yard in crooked rows were cracked, stained with black lichen and padded with fuzzy moss, or else half-covered in snarls of shallow roots and overgrown vines. Some of the graves even showed signs that animals had been at them, though likely long ago, the soil upturned and bits of bone scattered here and there.

"I told you this was the last job Demetri and I worked before we joined Ansel in the south." Sabine sidestepped the remains of a broken headstone, half-reclaimed by the earth. "Honestly, we never really finished the job. Though we followed up with the locals later and confirmed they hadn't had any more problems."

"What kind of problems?"

Sabine slowed as they ventured beneath a sprawling maple tree in the center of the graveyard. Its gnarled branches were still bare, the ground littered with the crunchy remains of dead leaves. They'd probably been a nice golden yellow when they first fell, or perhaps a deep red. Now they were brittle and brown.

"It was strange." Sabine came to a halt, gazing up at the barren boughs of the maple tree. "It started with the appearance of a young woman in the village. No one recognized her. Well, not really. One old man swore she was the spitting image of a girl he'd loved in his youth, but she died a long time ago, he said. Over sixty years ago. And even if she hadn't, she would've been as old as he is now."

Klaus crossed his arms over his chest and slouched, leaning his hip into the rounded top of a large headstone. "I think I see where this is going."

"Whoever she was, she'd appeared suddenly," Sabine continued, "without any belongings or traveling things. And she was weird, people said. The way she moved. She couldn't walk properly, as though her joints were misaligned or damaged somehow, even though she was a young woman. And the way she acted was strange too. She didn't talk. The way she behaved was more like an animal than a person. Feral. Wild.

"Anyway, she disappeared a few days before Demetri and I arrived. Without anything else to go on, we came to this graveyard because, supposedly, this was where the girl was buried—the one the old man had known, the one she resembled."

"And let me guess," Klaus cut in. "Her grave was dug up."

"Yes. And her remains disturbed. Possibly some missing, though given the state of them, it was hard to tell. Anyway, we didn't know what we were dealing with—I'd heard of ghouls and thought it a possibility, though it might have been a reanimated corpse as well. I mean, Demetri's seen something like that."

"We've all seen something like that," Klaus drawled. "Her name is Briar."

"Well, Briar never died, technically. Or...I suppose she did. But only after her curse had taken hold—anyway, my point is, it might have been something like that. We didn't know. Anything could have been responsible, a witch or a fairy curse. And we didn't know what had happened to the girl. Had she just wandered off someplace? Or—"

"Or, if she was a ghoul," Klaus interrupted again, "maybe she came back here."

"Exactly. And this is the part where we...sort of saw a ghoul. But not quite."

A dry wind stirred through the graveyard. Klaus glanced around, his gaze piercing the ring of trees, and he gave a shiver as the wind whistled past, dragging cold fingers across his skin.

"We thought we were alone here," Sabine continued.

Just like we do now. Klaus cast another glance around, quicker this time. Like some part of him didn't really want to see if there was anything out there, hiding in the trees. "But the ghoul was here," he guessed.

Sabine nodded. "I'm not sure why it came back. From the stories I've heard, ghouls can completely take on a person's identity.

They have access to that person's memories, their personality. Meaning, they can act like the person should. But this ghoul wasn't doing that. It's like there was something wrong with it."

"Well, they haunt graveyards, don't they? Maybe the ghoul felt at home here."

Sabine slid her hands into the pockets of her coat, tugging it tight across her chest. "Maybe. Or maybe it wanted to take another form, dig up another grave. A fresher one."

"What do you mean?"

"Some of the research I've done suggests that ghouls prefer fresher remains," Sabine explained. "No one seems to know for sure, but there's a theory that consuming older remains isn't good for a ghoul. That it somehow messes with the process. That could be why the young woman—the ghoul—was acting so strangely. I mean, the way people described her—the funny way she walked and moved—it almost sounds as though her body didn't work properly. Like the transformation didn't fully take. So maybe it came back here to find fresher remains."

"I doubt it would've had much luck," Klaus remarked. "Doesn't look like anyone's used this cemetery in the last few decades. So what happened here, then? When the ghoul came back? Did it attack you?"

"No, but we heard something. Back here." Sabine turned. Klaus followed nervously, not liking the idea that she was taking him to the place where they'd encountered the ghoul. But as she led him beyond the monstrous maple tree, she said, "It wasn't the ghoul. It was a young man." Hands in her pockets, she tossed out another nod, indicating a colossal grave marker ahead of them—a square headstone so large, it sat upon a low dais and was supported by two pillars on each side. Grand though it was, overgrown grass encroached over its base, and it was so covered in grime that any name on it could no longer be read. It was as old and neglected as the rest of this place.

"We found him here." Sabine pointed to the base of one of the cracked stone pillars. "Collapsed. He'd been wounded badly. There was a lot of blood."

Klaus moved closer and held out his lantern, peering down at the spot. Sure enough, he spotted dark stains at the base of the pillar, stains that looked different from the black lichen spotting the stone.

Blood. Old blood.

"He wasn't talking a lot of sense," Sabine admitted. "Delirious, you know. He was dying. We did what we could for him, but...I'm not sure if a doctor could have helped him at that point. And he never would have made it down to the village to get him one."

"What did he say?"

"He said 'it' was still here. Which put us on our guard. Demetri hung back and looked around a bit, though he didn't go far. I tended to the man, trying to get him to talk. He said he had to kill it. That it was his duty. Though obviously, it got him first. I asked if it was a ghoul, and I *think* he said 'yes,' but again, he wasn't clear. Then—" Sabine's face went gray and serious in the pallid light of her lantern. "He sort of grabbed me. Pulled me close. And he kind of pointed—at least, I think that's what he was trying to do—back towards that big headstone behind him. And he said something like—like *'get them, need them'*..."

"Meaning what?"

"Well, I didn't have time to puzzle it out," Sabine said, "because Demetri shouted and ran off into the trees. I called after him, but he didn't come back, and then there were shots. So I left the young man here and went after Demetri. It was back there somewhere—in the trees—" Sabine pointed into the line of cedars ringing the end of the graveyard. The land before the trees was more deserted and desolate than the rest of the place, lain with dead patches of grass, empty of headstones and markings. Klaus squinted in the light of his lantern, trying to glimpse into the gray gloom beyond the trees, but there was only darkness.

"That's where I saw—what I saw," said Sabine. "It really wasn't anything. Nothing solid. I had my lantern raised, and it seemed like it was right before me, within the light of the lantern, and yet..."

"It was like a shadow," Klaus finished, recalling something else Gemma had said.

"Yes. Just darkness. And then—it was just a flash, just for a moment—but I saw a pair of glowing eyes."

She fell silent, as though caught in the memory. Klaus waited for more, for her to finish her story, but she didn't. Finally he asked, "So what happened to it?"

"I don't know. Demetri shot at it some more, and it just disappeared. Not hard to do, considering how dark it was back there in the trees. We looked around, but there was no trace of it. And when we came back here, where we'd left the young man, he was dead."

Though Klaus had already known how the tale would end—Sabine had said as much—the gravity of it struck him. A death, here in this haunting graveyard. This place where death was soaked into the ground.

"It wasn't until much later that I remembered the last thing the man had said. That I realized he'd been pointing at the headstone, at this grave." Sabine looked down at the ground before the grand headstone. "And he'd been saying *need them, get them*—and I wondered if there was something in here. Something he was trying to retrieve."

"In here...you mean something buried in this plot?" When Sabine nodded, Klaus asked, "You didn't come back and check?"

Sabine gave a regretful shake of her head. "We'd already received the telegram from Prince Garrett. Asking us to meet Ansel in the south. The message was waiting for us when we got back to the tavern. We were literally on our way out when I remembered what he'd said, when I thought about it." She shrugged. "I thought maybe we could swing back sometime later, after we were done helping Ansel. But we never did. Until now."

Klaus felt as though cold fingers had brushed over the back of his neck. Maybe this was it. Maybe buried here—buried with whoever was interred here—were answers. Answers about Solena.

Answers for Gemma.

"Well." Klaus raised his lantern, and its beaming white light fell upon a tumbledown shed at the edge of the graveyard. A few rusted shovels leaned against it, and two more lay on the ground in the mud. He tipped his head in a nod. "I hope you're not superstitious, Sabine. Let's dig this grave up and see what's inside."

17

LEGENDS

G RYPHON HAD ONLY BEEN in Glen Castle, restored to the princely life, for eight days, but he was already growing tired of all the social engagements. One of the things Gryphon had not realized about himself until he was exiled was that he preferred to spend a lot of time alone, or at least, in the company of only a few close friends. Life as a royal didn't much lend itself to such inclinations, so until he no longer *was* a royal, he'd never understood why he found all the parties, outings, high teas, and state dinners so difficult and tiresome.

Most of his social engagements thus far had been on the smaller side, and almost all of them with Princess Solena. That made them a little easier to bear—the smallness of the events, not the princess's company—but even still, it had been something or other nearly every day, and he was growing exhausted. The dinner he was attending tonight, at least, was small and private. Only Gryphon, his father, and a few of his father's closest friends and advisors were attending, along with Princess Solena, her ladies, and her advisors. It was the kind of affair that was intended for the king and Solena's people to talk shop—trade agreements, treaties, oh, possibly a betrothal between Solena and Gryphon, that sort of thing—while Gryphon entertained Solena and the ladies.

Gryphon had been through all of this before when he was still crown prince. He knew how these things went. He knew what was expected of him.

But when he arrived at the dinner that night, Princess Solena wasn't there yet. Neither was the king, for which Gryphon was extremely grateful. He'd much rather make small talk with the princess and her ladies than with his father. He stepped into the sumptuous parlor where everyone was gathering for predinner drinks. Glittering crystal chandeliers hung from the ceiling, emitting warm glows that filled the room with a soft, cozy light. Gryphon surveyed the room, taking in the small groups that had already formed.

Three of his father's advisors stood in the furthest, darkest corner of the room, whispering together, wearing matching serious expressions. Directly across from Gryphon, next to the gilded doors leading out onto the terrace, was a more lively group comprising Lord...what was his name...some viscount, Gryphon thought, a friend of his father's. By the looks of it, he was telling a very amusing tale to a few other lords and ladies listening in. And on the left side of the room, perched on the edge of an upholstered chaise and giggling together, were—

"Prince Gryphon!" Two of Solena's ladies-in-waiting bounded up off the chaise, practically tripping over themselves to come and greet him. Or perhaps their clumsy gaits were due to the little goblets of wine in their hands; Lady Danya's cheeks were pinker than usual. They both wore corseted satin gowns in differing shades of blue, Danya's peacock blue and Ilana's an icy blue.

"I'm sure you're wondering where Princess Solena is." Lady Danya beamed at him. "Not to worry, she'll be here soon. And in the meantime, she sent us ahead to keep you entertained!"

"We're much better company anyway." Lady Ilana, Danya's companion, murmured that comment into her goblet. Gryphon didn't think he was meant to hear it, but thanks to the beast's enhanced senses, he did. After taking a sip of her wine, Lady Ilana smiled widely at him, displaying her perfectly even white teeth. Ilana had thick, dark-golden curls and long lashes that she was constantly fluttering at Gryphon. She had made it perfectly clear—without actually coming out and saying so, of course—that if Gryphon tired of courting the princess, he was welcome to turn his attention to her.

"I'm so happy you could make it tonight, Prince Gryphon," Ilana said, "but then, of course you would. It's not as though you would be cowed into missing your social engagements!"

"Cowed?"

Lady Danya's eyes widened. "All this business with intruders and death threats! But you faced the intruder, didn't you, Prince Gryphon? The whole castle has been abuzz with the talk of how you saved your father's life!"

"Well, I wouldn't say—"

"Ooh, yes, you must tell us all about it." Lady Ilana took him by the arm, squeezing him tightly. Not to be outdone, Lady Danya took his other arm, linking them together. Rather masterfully, the two ladies steered him over to the mahogany bar to get him a drink, all the while demanding to know every detail about the incident with the intruder in the king's apartments.

"I heard you were *wounded*." In the low glimmer cast by the chandeliers, Lady Danya's pink cheeks had turned bright red. "They said you took a knife to the chest."

"Not quite." Almost involuntarily, Gryphon lightly touched two fingers to the wound, just inside his shoulder. It was still bandaged but healing quickly. If he could take a day to himself to spend as the beast, it would heal even quicker. As it was, the skin still felt sore and raw. "Just a scratch."

Ilana sighed in admiration. She was still clutching onto his arm; even when he turned, rather awkwardly, to take his drink from the serving man, she did not take the hint to release him. "But you must have been so afraid. I would have been terrified!"

Gryphon managed a small, polite smile and gave the expected answer. "Not at all. I was focused on protecting my father."

"But you're so *brave*, Prince Gryphon—"

"Danya, Ilana," snapped a new voice. Ilana released Gryphon's arm so fast, anyone watching might have thought he'd burned her. Danya gave such a start that she spilled her wine, slopping it over the front of her gown.

A third lady-in-waiting appeared, Lady Kova, and she did not smile or simper at Gryphon. Her attention was focused on her fellow ladies. Her grayish-blue gown and severe hairstyle emphasized her angular features, giving her a stern look. As did the frown on her face.

"Why don't you two go see what's keeping the princess?" she said pointedly to Danya and Ilana. Her tone made it clear it wasn't a suggestion. "Perhaps Marisel and Berise could use some help getting her dressed and ready." When Danya pouted, looking ready to protest, Kova added, "And perhaps *you*, Lady

Danya, should retire for the evening. You've already ruined your dress."

Danya looked sulkier than ever, but she closed her mouth and bowed her head, chastised. She and Ilana flounced away while Lady Kova watched them go through narrowed eyes. Not until they'd left the room did she turn to Gryphon and smile. Her smile was not like the other ladies'—there was nothing sycophantic or seductive about it. And yet it did not put Gryphon at his ease either. Quite the opposite.

"I'm sorry about that," Lady Kova apologized. "Silly geese, the pair of them. Well. Perhaps not Ilana." She grimaced. "She is far too...predatory to be a goose."

Gryphon took a sip from his crystal glass, watching her carefully. "And which one are you?"

"Oh, neither." Kova spared him another smile. She was a tall woman, tall enough that Gryphon didn't have to stoop to talk to her, as he did with most people. "Then again...well, I am not predatory in the way Ilana is. But perhaps I am something of a predator."

Gryphon took another sip of his drink, trying to hide his study of the lady. She had a strange accent, he'd noticed—barely perceptible, but it was there. That in itself was not so strange; many people from the Desert Kingdom had a bit of an accent. But Gryphon had spent some time in the Desert Kingdom, and Lady Kova's accent wasn't quite like the other Desert accents he'd heard before. There was something almost antiquated about it. As though she were not just from another place but another time.

And yet by the look of her, she could not have been a day over twenty.

Now Lady Kova shook her head, glancing over her shoulder again, towards the door Ilana and Danya had disappeared through. "What were they blathering on about, anyway?"

"Asking about the intruder in the king's apartments."

Kova looked at him sharply. "Were they?" She swept a glance over Gryphon, as though taking the measure of him. It was very subtle—just a flick of her gaze, up and down—but Gryphon took note of it. "I heard that same intruder might have been spotted two nights ago. When the 'death threat' was discovered," she added dryly.

Gryphon looked at her curiously. "You don't sound as though you think much of that death threat."

"I suppose I should, as Princess Solena's first lady." Kova's tone turned from dry to outright derisive. "But I think it entirely possible a cat left that bird on her bed." She cast him a furtive look. "Of course, if the intruder was spotted that night, so close to the princess's quarters..."

Gryphon shrugged. "We don't know for sure. But shouldn't you know? It was one of Solena's handmaidens that made the sighting. Tashi, I think her name was?"

"I didn't know that." Kova rested an elbow atop the bar, leaning against it. She hadn't ordered herself a drink and made no sign of doing so. "What did she say? About what she saw?"

A burst of laughter drew Gryphon's attention, and he cast an idle look across the room. The group of lords and ladies by the terrace doors had gotten bigger. Rather too big, he thought grumpily, wasn't this supposed to be a small dinner? Frowning, he turned back to Lady Kova. "Ah—sorry—she said she saw a figure dressed in black. Her description seemed to match the person I saw in the king's apartments, so..."

Kova looked suddenly intrigued. "Dressed in black completely? Even their face was covered?"

"Well, the intruder I saw was, yes. They wore a large hood that covered their head and face."

"And you were wounded, weren't you? With a knife?"

"Ye-es." Gryphon shifted, turning away from the distracting chatter across the room. Facing Lady Kova more fully. "The intruder threw a dagger at me. Hit me right here." He indicated the tender spot beneath his shoulder.

Kova looked interested in these details, but also troubled, Gryphon thought. A darkness lurked behind her eyes. "That would take a good bit of skill, wouldn't it?" The troubled look lingered on her face a moment longer. Then she wiped her expression clean, and when she spoke, it was with an air of casual indifference. "Well." She smoothed a hand over her chestnut-brown hair, though not a strand was out of place. "I'm glad you weren't seriously hurt."

But Gryphon was not about to be put off. "You seem as interested in the tale as Danya and Ilana were."

"Please," Kova scoffed. "They weren't interested in the intruder. They were interested in *you*."

"Well, yes, I know. But you're not. Is what I meant." Gryphon cleared his throat. "Is there something you know? About the intruder?"

Kova turned wary, her expression closing off even more. "What are you implying?"

"I didn't mean—" Gryphon leaned in towards Kova to set his glass down on the bar behind her. It was still half-full. "When I mentioned what the intruder looked like, you seemed...concerned." *And you weren't before*, he thought, *until I described what they looked like.* "I just wondered if—like the handmaiden—perhaps you'd seen something."

Kova shook her head. "No. I haven't. But..." She hesitated, then drew Gryphon away with a slight nod of her head, indicating he follow her to the chaise Danya and Ilana had vacated. She lowered herself onto the chaise, and Gryphon did too, sitting at the opposite end. Maintaining an appropriate distance between the two of them.

"I'm going to sound as silly as those two geese," Kova said, "but there's this old story, you see. A legend about an elite band of warriors. Protectors. They are like guardsmen, I suppose, only far superior to the average guard. In every respect."

Gryphon frowned, confused and intrigued at the same time. "How so?"

"Their fighting skills. Their skills at evasion and secrecy. They are said to be almost inhuman in their abilities." Kova gave a shrug, as though to remind herself this was only a story. But the look in her eyes was almost spooked. "There are all sorts of tales about where they come from, how they came to be. Some say they are stolen from their mothers at birth and trained to fight from infancy. Some say they are blessed with supernatural gifts from unnatural creatures. But what most of the stories agree upon is that they are sworn to protect the throne of the Desert Kingdom. Sworn to protect the kingdom's ruler and heirs."

"And let me guess," Gryphon deduced, "they're described as dressing in black from head to toe?"

Kova nodded. "Exactly. And I suppose...well, when you described the intruder. It made me think of the stories, is all."

Gryphon nodded too, but absently, his brow furrowed. *But if these warriors are meant to protect the Desert Kingdom heir—Princess Solena—why would they try to kill the king?*

"But they are just stories," Kova said dismissively. "Nothing more."

"Oh, I don't know about that."

Gryphon looked up, and Kova whipped around.

Princess Solena stood behind the chaise, looming over them. As though she had materialized from the shadows, for Gryphon had not seen her enter the room. Garbed in a midnight-blue, off-the-shoulder gown that put all her ladies to shame, she smiled at them both. But when she turned that smile on Lady Kova, the look became somehow feral. Like one cat hissing at another.

"The stories of these elite protectors have never been verified, of course," Solena said, and she still seemed to be speaking to Kova more than Gryphon, "but many believe they are true. And supposed sightings of these warriors have cropped up more and more in the last...oh, ten years or so, they say. That lends some weight to the legend, don't you think?"

Lady Kova dipped her head respectfully, not meeting the princess's gaze. "As you say, Your Highness." Before anyone could say anything else, she rose from the chaise, dropped a curtsy for Gryphon and Solena, then slipped away, vanishing somewhere amongst the growing crowd on the other side of the room.

Gryphon put on a polite smile for Solena and gestured for her to take Kova's vacant seat. With a mischievous glint in her dark eyes, she did so—only, she seated herself rather closer than Kova had been, Gryphon noticed. Close enough that she could easily reach out and touch him. Her eyes, Gryphon noticed, dark though they were, were actually blue—the blue-black of an ocean beneath a night sky.

She was beautiful, he had to give her that. But far too vapid and vain to interest him. Far too like every other noble he had met.

Still, Gryphon was here to play nice with her, so he did. "Is that true?" he asked her. "That sightings of those...protectors...have cropped up more recently?" In the last ten years, she'd said. Interesting, when one considered the timing. The plague that had killed off all the other Desert princesses had been about ten years ago.

Solena snapped a finger at a passing servant and pointed, indicating she wanted a goblet of wine from the bar. Then she focused her gaze on Gryphon and smiled again, turning from haughty to flirtatious in an instant. "Oh, yes," she said. "At least, that is what I've heard from people old enough to know. People older than me."

She turned to accept her little goblet from the servant, who'd rushed it over so quickly, it was a miracle he hadn't spilled it. Solena took a delicate sip, then said, "Of course, it's possible the people who told me that were only trying to placate me. Or impress me. Since this elite force is meant to serve as guardians to the throne—which is me." Her tone turned vicious. "People will say anything they think will please me. I cannot trust anyone, really." She tipped her goblet at him. "That is why I like you, Prince Gryphon. You seem so very genuine."

This time, the smile she flashed him was canny—and rather unsettling, Gryphon felt. He wondered if Princess Solena was not quite so vapid as she seemed.

But that little glimpse of cunning she showed him was the last he got that night. Shortly after his father arrived, everyone was herded into the dining room to take their places at the table—a long table, much longer and accommodating of more guests than Gryphon had expected. He was seated beside Princess Solena, of course, and she talked his ears off throughout the entire six-course meal, from the thick onion soup to the rhubarb tart served for dessert.

He didn't get a reprieve until dinner was over and everyone was herded into another parlor—an entirely different one—for after-dinner drinks. King Victor did not separate the men and women into distinct rooms—he preferred everyone socialize together—but most of the crowd separated themselves just so, the women gathering in a cozy seating area on the far side of the parlor, arranging themselves around painted rosewood tables, and the men circling up in front of the marble fireplace in the opposite corner.

Gryphon took a moment to separate himself from all of them, sidling up to the guards in navy blue who stood, unobtrusively, near the oaken doors. One of those guards was Gemma; she and another woman—tall with short hair—had accompanied Princess Solena to the dinner tonight.

Gemma arched an eyebrow at him when he placed himself beside her, trying to look as inconspicuous as she did. It was unlikely he succeeded; his hulking stature made it impossible for him to be inconspicuous anywhere. "Your Highness," she greeted him respectfully. "Surely you haven't tired of Princess Solena's company already?"

Gryphon sent her an unamused look, which Gemma returned with a rare, faint smile. "It was Lady Kova's company that I found interesting," he told her in a low voice. "She had a rather mysterious story to share with me."

"Was it about ghouls?"

"What? No." That was the last reply Gryphon had expected. "Where did you hear about ghouls?"

"You know what they are?" Gemma sounded as surprised as he was.

"Yes. I lived in the Desert Kingdom for a little while. Never encountered a ghoul—well, so far as I know—but there are lots of stories about them over there. People hang talismans to ward against them in their homes. And ghoul hunting is a rather prolific career."

"Huh." Gemma pursed her lips. Gryphon couldn't decide if the expression was thoughtful or skeptical. "One of Princess Solena's handmaidens told me about them. And I'd wondered...well. I wondered if your intruder might be one. Given the way she managed to appear and disappear, and the way she scaled that wall."

Gryphon considered this. The idea that they could be dealing with a supernatural entity had already occurred to him; there was little other explanation for what had occurred that night, the way the intruder had escaped. And also— "There was a strange scent." Gryphon rocked back on his heels, leaning into the wall. "A bit like a fresh corpse. Something rotten. That was what alerted me to the intruder in the first place. And I caught the same scent a few nights ago, outside Solena's quarters. When that dead bird was left for her."

"Have you smelled it anywhere else?" Gemma asked sharply. "On...anyone? From Solena's delegation, I mean."

Gryphon gave a slow shake of his head. "No. I can't say I have." It was mostly the princess and her ladies he spent the most time with, and he hadn't caught a whiff of anything like that rotting scent around them. But there were plenty of servants and soldiers in her party that he probably hadn't come across. Even some of her advisors. "I'll keep an eye out. Or nose, rather."

He eyed the princess across the room. She was seated at a table with Lady Kova and Lady Ilana, playing at cards. *Ghouls*, he thought. *And an elite force of legendary warriors.* Just stories, he wondered? Mere superstition? Or were they dealing with one of those "stories" here in the castle? And if they were...why did they want to kill the king?

18

Doppelganger

G EMMA STOOD ON A short wooden stool in Princess Sole-na's quarters, bedecked in the most lavish, ridiculous gown she had ever seen. It was the evening of the ball. The king had made the last-minute adjustments needed to ensure their decoy plan would work—the lighting would be lowered in the venue, and the theme had been changed from "springtime dreams"—whatever the hell that meant—to "midnight masquerade." Now all they had to do was attend the ball and wait.

For someone to attack Gemma.

One thing was for sure, Gemma thought in dismay. She had nothing to worry about. Because she was certain no bullet or blade could pierce all this fabric. The gown she wore was a bell-like, flouncy, champagne-colored monstrosity constructed from shiny satin, full of frills and ribbons. Several underskirts peeked out from beneath a heavy overskirt adorned with little crimson bows, giving Gemma the look of a wrapped holiday gift.

She tried not to fidget. Not that she could really move much if she'd tried; the gown was more confining than a full set of shackles. The corseted bodice compressed her torso, squeezing her waist and putting pressure on her ribcage. Yet even still, it was difficult to remain motionless; she had already been in the princess's quarters for three hours. She'd been bathed and scrubbed, washed and perfumed, but the ladies and handmaidens working on her didn't seem to think she would be ready anytime soon.

Aside from her "attendants," the parlor was quite empty. Some of the princess's servants had been assigned to work elsewhere in the castle tonight; they didn't want to trust too many people with this plan. The real Solena would spend the evening here under heavy guard.

Gemma had seen very little of Solena these past few hours, but now, as Pila, the dark-haired handmaiden, knelt at Gemma's feet, the princess walked into the room to assess their progress.

"Forgive me, Your Highness." Pila's face pinched in worry when she spotted Solena. "I need to fix the hem—when I took her measurements before, I forgot she would be wearing heels. I need to let it out—"

Solena waved a negligent hand. "Not to worry. We've got plenty of time."

"Doesn't the ball start in an hour?" Gemma asked, more waspishly than she intended.

Solena cast her a disdainful look. "As if I would ever arrive to a ball on time, Gemma. Arriving on time is for pitiful little baronets and ladies-of-the-court whose names no one has ever heard of. A *princess* arrives fashionably late."

"Right." Gemma's tone was deadpan. "I should have known that."

"It won't take me long." Pila pulled at a thread in the gown's underskirt. "But she still needs her hair done—"

"What's wrong with my hair?" Gemma asked.

"I can see to her hair." Solena clapped her hands together with an air of authority and ordered everyone out—everyone who wasn't helping Gemma get ready. This left the parlor even more empty. It took two ladies-in-waiting and Pila to remove Gemma's skirts for hemming, so that Gemma stood in only bloomers and half a gown—and without any dignity whatsoever. Still, she allowed Solena to lead her to the vanity, placing her in front of a broad gilt-framed mirror.

The same mirror where Gemma had glimpsed a wraithlike visage in place of Solena's reflection.

Gemma tried to school her expression. As she took the seat at the vanity, Solena came to stand behind her. Both of their reflections gazed back at them from the mirror.

And they were just reflections. Solena's face in the mirror looked as it always did. No skeletal visage in sight.

Gemma suddenly wondered if the princess was also thinking of that night when Gemma had come to present herself. She hoped not. She didn't want to arouse Solena's suspicions, and so cast about for something to say.

"I was surprised to see Pila tonight," Gemma remarked. "One of your other servants mentioned she'd been ill."

Solena replied in a toneless voice, "Yes, she was ill. Now she is better. So?"

"I'm sorry, is all. It must be difficult to be without her."

"Thank you, but she isn't much of a maid. I've had better."

Only years of training kept Gemma's face as blank as Solena's, her expressionless mask staying in place.

Something like a smile flickered over Solena's lips. A smug smile. "You think that's awful of me, don't you? You think I should be sorry for her taking ill. Or more grateful for her service."

"Not at all, Your Highness." Gemma spoke coolly. "I would never presume."

"Wouldn't you?" But the princess didn't sound offended. "Now let's see what I can do with your hair. I'm thinking if we leave it down...the style is a bit girlish, but I'm young enough to pull it off. I think if we pin it up, the difference in our jawlines will be too apparent."

"The difference in our jawlines?"

"Yes, haven't you noticed? Your chin is much more pronounced than mine. I've a much softer face. Yours is more mannish. This way, it won't be so obvious."

Gemma gritted her teeth, biting back a retort. But she didn't need to say anything because Solena talked nonstop as she proceeded to brush and style Gemma's hair.

It was strange, Gemma thought, watching the princess. Gemma had expected Solena to be disappointed about missing the ball, but in fact, she seemed weirdly excited about the deception, as though it was a game. As though she and Gemma were playing dress-up. It was even stranger considering this entire escapade had stemmed from a death threat that had been left for the princess—a threat Solena had been very upset about. Then again, if anyone got stabbed tonight, it would be Gemma.

Still. Gemma could not put aside the niggling idea that Solena had left the threat for herself. But to what end, that was the question. To throw suspicion off herself? That seemed the obvious answer, but it was only obvious if Solena had been under suspicion, and—aside from Gemma herself—no one seemed to suspect the princess of anything. The other possibility was she might have done it to get out of the ball. This whole charade had been their idea, not hers, but she had been the one to first suggest she should miss the ball.

One thing Gemma was certain of: there was more to Princess Solena than met the eye. She was more clever than she tried to appear, for one thing. She was full of useful tips and advice—useful and insightful.

"Just remember," she told Gemma, "no one here knows me, so you don't need to worry you'll say the wrong thing. But if you are worried about that—if someone asks you something you don't know the answer to—just giggle and put on the most brainless expression you can. Trust me," she added in a droll voice, "no one will expect any more of you."

Gemma eyed the princess in the mirror. *Is that what you do?* she wanted to ask.

"There, I think that does it." Solena beamed. "What do you think?"

Gemma blinked, looking—for the first time—at herself in the mirror. Rather than pinning Gemma's hair behind her head, as most noble ladies did, the princess had only pulled a few strands back, leaving the rest of it pouring over one shoulder in brushed-out curls. Gemma never wore her hair down; she always wore it braided or pinned back. The effect was a softer and more vulnerable version of herself, and Gemma could not decide if she liked it or not.

Solena pursed her lips. "Now we just need a touch of cosmetics. I'll be right back..."

But Pila and the ladies returned before the princess and helped Gemma into her hemmed gown. Once she was fully dressed, Gemma's fellow guards—her guards, tonight—entered the parlor: Spencer and Beckett. Spencer positively gaped at her, taking her in from head to toe.

Gemma scowled at him. "Keep gawking at me like I've sprouted horns, Spencer, and you'll find out where I've stashed my knives under all this."

Beckett smiled. "That was perfect. Just snap at everyone like that, and no one will think you aren't Princess Solena."

Half an hour later, she was finally ready. To Gemma's surprise, Solena had managed to apply her cosmetics in such a way as to make Gemma look even more like the princess. Gemma's eyes had taken on a wide, hooded look, and her lips seemed smaller and poutier like Solena's.

"And to finish it off." Solena whipped out a painted masque crusted in red and gold beads that framed the eyes and dangled from the bottom. She set it over Gemma's face and tied it behind her head, weaving the ribbons through her hair.

Gemma rose from the vanity and turned to face everyone.

The room fell into uncanny silence. Gemma glanced back into the mirror and understood. She truly was the spitting image of Solena in her shimmering champagne gown, the beaded masque disguising just enough of her features to pull off the deception.

"Creepy," said Spencer.

Gemma's reply dripped with sarcasm. "Thank you."

Solena clapped her hands in delight. "It's perfect! You know, I wasn't sure this would work—Gemma is the same height as me, but she's a bit thicker than I am—"

Gemma nearly choked at that. "*Thicker?*"

"—but dressed like that, no one will notice! Oh, I wish I could go too, just to see how everyone reacts." The princess waved an imperious hand. "Now hurry, you must be off. The ball started nearly an hour ago."

"What happened to being fashionably late?" Gemma muttered as she lifted her skirts and exited the room, surrounded by guards and attendants.

They traversed the long corridors until they emerged into a vast hall surrounded by long bay windows. Starlight glinted through the paned glass, casting dazzling light over the marbled floor. At the end of the hall was a grand stairwell that curved down into the ballroom.

As Gemma's guards fanned out at the top of the stairs, Gemma and her attendants—Kova, the tall, dark-haired, rather unfriendly lady-in-waiting, Marisel, another lady with black hair and deep-blue eyes, and Pila, the gawky handmaiden—stood at the railing and waited. Gemma peeked down into the ballroom below.

The lights were indeed dimmed, the gear-bulb fixtures emitting warm, pulsating glows. Hundreds of miniature bulbs had been strung from the ceiling as well, as though the starlight outside had been harnessed.

It was all very romantic, Gemma supposed, but if she was guarding the princess tonight, she would have hated it. The low lighting would make it difficult to keep a charge in sight. And the room was already full of people, which only added to the difficulty. Dozens of courtiers flitted across the ballroom floor, bedecked in their own ruffled gowns and trimmed coats. Their glittering masques gleamed beneath the lights overhead.

Behind Gemma, Lady Kova cleared her throat. Gemma looked around.

Prince Gryphon had emerged from the other end of the hall. His black tailcoat, though most formal, was almost plain in its lack of adornment, compared to all the frippery Gemma was wearing. But his waistcoat was the navy blue of the royal family and trimmed in gold embroidery to match its gleaming buttons. He didn't fidget or tug at his clothes as he stopped and stood at the top of the grand staircase, waiting to escort her.

Our first test, Gemma thought, as she crossed the hall to the prince. They hadn't told Gryphon about the decoy plan, just to see if he would fall for the ruse.

"Your Highness," said Gryphon, taking her gloved hand and bowing over it. His bow was deep, and Gemma realized he meant to kiss her hand.

But he didn't. Instead, he straightened abruptly. After a moment's hesitation, he inquired, "Gemma?"

Gemma let out a curse. "How did you know?"

When Gryphon answered, he sounded faintly embarrassed. "I, ah—recognize your scent, Gemma. And I know Solena's as well."

"Oh. Right. I should have thought of that."

Gryphon tilted his head. "Why the decoy?"

Gemma explained about Solena's hesitation to attend the ball after the "threat" that had been left for her and their hope to draw out the intruder. She kept her own suspicions about the princess to herself, given that they were surrounded by some of Solena's own people.

"Well." Gryphon sighed as Gemma finished explaining everything. "Princess Solena probably attends enough of these things, I suppose, to mind missing it too much. I know I have, and this is my first ball in over five years."

Gemma smiled as all the guards, hers and Gryphon's, fell in around them. "So you're looking forward to this as much as I am," she said dryly.

"I would imagine so." Gryphon proffered his arm to her. "Shall we get this over with?"

The evening passed with interminable slowness. Gemma spent the entire first hour meeting and chatting with people, though thankfully, she was never alone. First she was accompanied by Prince Gryphon, then, for a short while, by the king. After that—once everyone was satisfied she wasn't going to mess this up, Gemma supposed—she took a turn about the room with only her two ladies for accompaniment. She met so many people that they all became a blur of noble names and painted masques, and one would think the time would have gone by quickly. But it didn't. Gemma felt as though she was counting the minutes, minutes by which her pinched feet ached more and more.

And she was starving. At the end of that first hour, Gemma managed to break away from everyone—including Lady Kova and Lady Marisel, who were relentless taskmasters—long enough to make her way to the banquet table and discreetly stuff a few mince tartlets into her mouth.

"Your Highness?"

Gemma jumped, chewing and swallowing so fast she nearly choked. But she needn't have worried; it was only Pila the hand-maiden. Pila had spent most of the night on the secluded dais where Gemma could retreat to, in case she needed a respite or a private moment.

Pila smiled at her. Her pale skin looked especially sallow in the warm, shaded light of the ballroom, shadows making her face gaunt. Gemma wanted to offer her a few tartlets; she looked as though she could use some feeding. She hoped the maid wasn't still feeling unwell.

"I saw you here and thought you might need this." Pila held out a glass of something cool to drink, the cup so chilled that frosted condensation coated its exterior.

"Oh. Thank you." Gemma accepted the goblet and drank deeply. Chilled wine. "I suppose I shouldn't be stuffing my face. Not very princess-like."

Pila smiled again. "I won't tell if you don't. Did you want to retreat to the dais for a bit? I think you've socialized enough to earn yourself a short break."

"I just might." Taking another sip of wine, Gemma cast a glance around the ballroom. Couples danced nearby, gliding gracefully over the gleaming marble floor, their sequins and beads flashing beneath the twinkling lights. "I—"

But as Gemma gazed out over the gilded ballroom, a strange thing happened. The musty, stagnant scent of decay suddenly enveloped her, as though she'd just walked past some moldering ruin or a fresh grave. A wave of dread swept over her, but before she realized why, the ballroom *flickered*.

And for a moment—just a moment—the lavish hall turned dark. The dancing couples in their opulent masques were swept up in shadow. The savory scent of the food on the table turned foul. The whole ballroom changed, becoming cold and dank. Lavish furnishings decayed before her eyes, wood chipping and rotting, curtains turning frayed and moth-eaten, lights shattering and winking out. The floor creaked and groaned, cracks splitting the marble as though it were nothing. The guests reappeared, materializing from shadow, and though they still smiled and laughed and danced, their faces were covered in blood, rivulets leaking from their scalps and running down their cheeks.

It was the same vision. The same hallucination Gemma had suffered before. Panic squeezed her more tightly than a corset ever could. She closed her eyes against it all. *Not now*, she thought desperately, willing her surroundings away, *not now, not now, not now—*

"Your Highness? Are you all right? Oh!"

Gemma's eyes flew open as her glass of wine slipped from her boneless fingers and crashed to the floor, where it shattered and spilled over the gleaming marble.

The marble. The floor. No longer cracked, but whole and unblemished.

She was back. Back in the real world.

"Oh, no—your dress!"

Gemma blinked. Pila. Of course. The handmaiden was still beside her at the banquet table, only now she was looking at Gemma in concern and dismay. Gemma glanced down and realized the spilt wine had sloshed over her, leaving a crimson streak down the front of her shimmery skirt. An involuntary shudder coursed through her as she was reminded of the blood streaming down all the faces in the ballroom.

"Are you all right?" Pila asked. "Here, come with me—I'll see what I can—"

"No." Gemma placed a hand over her ribcage. She took a few steps, feeling suddenly clammy, overwhelmed by the opulence and the noise and the throng of people and Pila's panicked babbling. "I'm just...I need a moment—"

"Yes, of course, come with me—"

"No, I—I need—" Gemma turned, and an unexpected draft of cool, fresh air wafted over her face. The ballroom terrace, just ahead of her. It was a cold night, colder than expected, so the doors had been kept shut, but there were still guests out on the terrace gathered in small crowds, chatting and laughing at whatever entertainment was going on. Practically staggering in her heeled shoes, Gemma made for the terrace doors.

She fled the sparkling ballroom and everyone in it.

Outside, the night sky was clear and black, the moon a small sliver, providing little light. But there was plenty of other light. The paved terrace, the balcony and the stone steps to the grounds below, was ringed in oil lamps set in tall lampposts. The balcony was more crowded than Gemma had thought, so she quickly took the stairs to her left, down to the grounds. Here there were no lampposts, only iron braziers topped with elaborately wrought designs and blazing with fire. Gemma lingered near one, enjoying the warm little sanctuary it provided. She closed her eyes and forced herself to breathe.

As her panic slowly receded, rational thought returned. She shouldn't have left the ballroom. She should have gone with Pila.

What if someone saw her out here, *Princess Solena*, unaccompanied and dressed in a wine-stained gown?

But no one was paying her any attention. Everyone out here was too caught up in their revels, too drunk, Gemma realized, as she listened to rowdy calls and shrill laughter. Apparently, nobles weren't all that different from common people when they drank too much.

Gemma turned to gaze into the darkness beyond the braziers, the gardens and the grounds amorphous in the black night, a void of shadows. Stones. Who would have thought socializing for an hour could be more exhausting than trekking through the forest all day? And the headache didn't help. It had returned, that dull pounding in her forehead like a hammer between her temples.

Add to that, her feet were really killing her. She was sure blisters had formed around her toes. It was a miracle she'd made it this long, prancing around on those heels. Though she hadn't had any difficulty balancing in them, which Solena had complimented her on. The princess said she "*must* have worn heels before" because they took practice to walk in, but that was nonsense. Gemma had lived her life in backcountry woods, raised by a father who cared deeply for her, but not enough to buy her fancy shoes. They hadn't had money to spend on frivolity, and besides, Gemma didn't have much interest in that sort of thing—well, she'd had very little exposure to that sort of thing. Her father had hated going into town for anything. He had a wanderer's soul, that's what he'd always said.

Looking back, though, Gemma wondered—though it seemed silly—but looking back, she sometimes wondered if they'd been running from something. She and her father. She wondered if her father hadn't been afraid to stay in one place too long. But if they had been running, Gemma would never know what from. Her father was dead now. More than two years gone.

Gemma would never forget finding him that day. They'd been camping in the wilderness, Gemma couldn't remember exactly where. One afternoon, Gemma had gone hunting on her own. She'd been gone for hours, and when she'd returned near dusk, she'd found their camp in ruins and her father dead. His body ravaged and ruined. A bear had gotten to him.

Gemma could still remember with perfect clarity the moment she'd found him. The blinding shock of it. Almost literally blinding, because she remembered that moment but very little of what came after. If she cleaned up the camp, if she left straightaway—she couldn't remember. She only remembered the next day, trampling through the woods on her own. Understanding, now, that she was on her own. That she always would be.

Until she wasn't. Until she joined the royal guard.

The guard who were probably looking for her now, she realized. She really should get back into the ballroom. She sighed, turning away from the grounds—

And then she stilled.

Something at the edge of the darkness caught her eye. Something along the winding garden path on her left, a narrow path lined with an ivy-covered wall on one side and thick trees on the other, their boughs curving overhead. She could barely see the path in the darkness, for it lay beyond the circle of braziers, where the gardens were et up in murky shadow.

Gemma stared into the darkness, and it was like the darkness stared back. There was something deeply impenetrable about it, as though it was not just the dark of the night but something menacing and eldritch. It was a black hole, the garden path a road to some netherworld, right here on the castle grounds. As Gemma watched, transfixed, one of the shadows shifted. Separating itself from its fellows.

Slinking down the garden path.

Before she realized what she was doing, Gemma took a step forward, away from the terrace, out of the circle of warmth cast by the brazier. But she didn't feel the night's cold. Instead she felt hot in her satin gown, her clamminess returning. A line of perspiration lined her forehead, at odds with the brisk chill surrounding her.

Had she really just seen...?

Yes. She knew she had.

A shadow, moving of its own accord. Slithering away from the castle. Just like the shadow she'd seen in the stairwell, the shadow that had concealed the intruder.

Swallowing hard, Gemma cast a glance back at the castle. Raucous shouts and boisterous laughter floated down from the terrace balcony, and a warm glow emitted from the ballroom windows, beckoning her inside.

Gemma turned her back on it all and hurried away from the castle. Beyond the braziers. Down the garden path.

Vanishing into the darkness.

19

STRANGER

G EMMA WAS FORCED TO slow her pace as she made her way down the garden path. The darkness was truly impenetrable, pressing in on her like the steel bars of a cage. There was something eerily vibrant about the darkness, and eerily heavy, as though the shadows themselves were breathing. Gemma quickly grew disoriented. The foliage on her right grew taller and thicker until it was like moving through a maze. The stone wall on her left, too, was quickly replaced with overgrown shrubbery, and Gemma knew even in the daylight, it would have been impossible to see the castle from this remote path. It was taking her along the edge of the gardens; she thought she must be approaching the end of the grounds.

And she hadn't glimpsed that shadow again. She didn't see how she could; it was so dark. Rigid, alarmed, Gemma came to a halt, eyes scanning the path ahead of her. Looking for something, anything she could make out. She rotated slowly, making one full turn, and then another—

Then a light flickered, bright pulses breaking through the dark. Somewhere ahead of her. It flickered again, and Gemma thought it must be a lantern. The light flickered the way a bulb did when it was struggling to draw enough power.

Warily, Gemma moved up the path, rounding a bend, where she found an opening in the shrubbery. An opening that led into another, narrower path of worn dirt and pebbly rock. There were few trees beyond the opening, and the anemic glow of the crescent moon cast broad swathes of light over the land there. The dirt path wound up a shallow rise in the grounds, and atop the rise, Gemma could see, was—

The castle's cemetery.

Gemma stared. The imposing iron gates and fence surrounding the cemetery were visible from here, topped with gear-bulb fixtures. One of those fixtures sputtered, winking in and out—the light she'd glimpsed. A few pine trees dotted the rise, spindly but towering, throwing long, crooked shadows across the dirt path.

As Gemma watched, one of those shadows broke away and scuttled up the hill. Up towards the cemetery.

Gemma watched it go, but for a moment, she couldn't move. Her mind was full of doubt and fear. Fear that she couldn't trust what she saw, fear emboldened by the stabbing pain behind her eye, by the distraction of her intensifying headache.

But she had seen a shadow move like that before. That night she'd met the intruder, the stranger in black. And she had not imagined that. Gryphon had seen the intruder too.

Grimly, she started up the rise. She didn't make it far before she stopped, cursing, her ankle wobbling in her heeled shoe. After a moment's consideration, she peeled off her gloves and kicked off her heels, flinging them away, and then, she reached beneath her overskirt to yank down all her petticoats. She stepped out of them, leaving them behind, and, lastly, she removed one of the knives she'd strapped to her calf, pulling it free of its sheath.

Unencumbered—as unencumbered as she could be without undressing completely—she dashed up the path to the graveyard, knife in hand. When she reached the cemetery gates, Gemma pushed them open with only a slight squeal. The castle's most important dead—the kings of the past—weren't buried here; they were laid to rest beneath the castle in a crypt. But this cemetery was carefully maintained, the outer fence and gates well oiled, the grounds raked clear of the dead needles that shook from the pine trees rimming the fenceline.

Gemma stepped through the gates just in time to see the scuttling shadow dart through the headstones and memorials ahead of her. Gemma followed, her stockinged feet tramping over scrubby grass and hardened mud. Cold as it was, they'd had little rain in the past few weeks, the morning dew the only watering this ground had received recently.

As the shadow approached a line of mausoleums near the center of the cemetery, Gemma slowed, eyes fixed on her target. She watched the shadow stop before a mausoleum's thick, iron-enforced oak door. Then it slipped inside, sliding right beneath the narrow gap at the bottom of the door.

Following, Gemma approached the mausoleum, slow and careful. Apprehensive. This felt very much like a trap. Like she had been lured here deliberately. But did it matter? She had to find out the truth about this intruder. About Solena. She had to know the truth.

When she reached the door to the mausoleum, she tried the handle and was relieved to find it unlocked. She stepped inside.

And stopped dead. Blinded.

The mausoleum was full of hot, blazing light. Iron braziers, like the ones back at the terrace, filled the interior, two at the far end and two on either side of the entrance. For a disconcertingly long moment, Gemma's eyes tried to adjust to the fiery light. Disconcertingly, because someone had lit those braziers.

She hadn't imagined that scuttling shadow. Someone was in here.

Into that disorienting moment, a sibilant voice said, "Oh my. Now what would people say if they found Princess Solena alone on the grounds, stripped down of half her clothes?"

Gemma tensed. Then her eyes adjusted, and the scene before her came into focus.

The mausoleum's interior was mostly stone. Dark-gray stone walls, low stone ceiling. A stone floor, dirty, littered with pine needles and dead leaves. Narrow windows in the walls were set in wooden frames. At the back of the mausoleum were stained-glass windows, small and round, save for one large expanse set into the wall on Gemma's right. The wavering light from the fiery braziers danced over the stained glass, cavorting among the designs depicted there.

But it was the center of the mausoleum that drew Gemma's attention. There, on a low dais, was a mounted stone bier. Carved onto the bier was a white sculpture, a supine figure with crossed arms. A depiction of some dead lord, Gemma supposed. A memorial.

And perched at the head of the memorial, at the end of the bier, was the intruder. The same stranger, clad in black, that Gemma had faced five nights ago.

The oaken door swung shut behind Gemma, not quite latching, and she flinched, resisting the urge to turn back. Instead she stepped forward, eyeing the stranger. She was sure it was the same intruder she'd encountered before. The figure was the same build—slender, of a height with Gemma—and she wore the same black hood, tented forward to disguise her face. She faced Gemma with a pair of knives, one in each gloved hand, twirling them lazily.

Reaching up to her face, Gemma removed her beaded masque, sliding it over the top of her head. She'd almost forgotten she was wearing it.

"If you were hoping to get Princess Solena," Gemma said, tossing the masque onto the floor, "you'll be disappointed."

The stranger let out a laugh. It was a repellent sound, girlish but grating. As though it had clawed its way out of the stranger's throat.

"I don't care about Princess Solena." The stranger hopped off the bier, coming around the memorial. "I'm here for you. Gemma."

Gemma mouth went dry. "What?"

The stranger circled towards her, swiping her knives through the air. The moves were more theatrical than threatening, not a real prelude to an attack. "I want to know all about Gemma. Who is she? Just an ordinary soldier in service to the Glen Kingdom? That's what everyone says. A skilled sharpshooter, once upon a time. But no longer."

Gemma gripped the hilt of her knife, urging herself to ignore the stranger. *She only wants to distract me.* The problem was, it was working. Gemma could not help but be unnerved by this stranger in black who claimed to want to know her.

That didn't make any sense. She was just a soldier, nothing more.

"Odd that you would be assigned to guard the princess," the stranger continued, "useless as you are."

"I'm not useless," Gemma growled.

"No? Perhaps you have other skills?" The stranger pointed with one of her knives. "Are you skilled with that blade?"

"Why don't you find out?" Gemma asked with a lot more confidence than she felt. Her rout with Klaus was still fresh in her mind. The one where she'd ended up disarmed and flat on her back in the dirt.

But a considering silence followed her words. The stranger stilled, no longer circling. She flipped one of her blades around, ever so slowly.

Then the stranger attacked, launching herself at Gemma.

It was a lazy attack. Designed to test, Gemma was sure of it. The stranger swiped at her with one blade, then with the other, quick, overhand strikes that were broad and obvious, telegraphed. Gemma didn't bother to raise her own blade; she simply leaned back, left, then right, easily dodging the blows.

The next test was not so easy. It should have been, were it not for the confounded gown. Even stripped down as she was, Gemma found it difficult to move, to fight. The corseted bodice was like a vice around her, making it difficult to twist and turn, and the heavy folds of her skirt tangled between her legs, tripping her up. As the stranger struck at her again with a wide swing from the side, Gemma crossed one foot behind the other, attempting to sidestep the blow. But she trod on the hem of her skirt and stumbled, barely ducking in time to avoid the stranger's attack. She retreated, regaining her footing.

"Clumsy," the stranger admonished.

"Yes, well, I don't usually fight in skirts."

"Still clumsy," the stranger scolded. "Aren't you trained to fight in any circumstance? No matter your clothing, no matter the distraction?" She didn't give Gemma a chance to answer, lunging forward again. This time, her attack was more pointed. She struck high at Gemma's head, then low at her middle, then high again, from the side, her knife's point hurtling towards Gemma's neck.

Gemma barely managed to block each blow, her knife forgotten, clutched uselessly in her hand. Her forearms became bruised and battered, her breath turned short and quick. Her body grew warm and heavy from exertion, perspiration dampening her voluminous gown.

An overhand blow drew first blood. As Gemma raised a hand to slap the stranger's arm away, the tip of her blade caught Gemma in the palm, slicing through her skin. The pain was bright and hot, like the flames leaping from the braziers, and Gemma clenched her jaw. But weirdly, the stranger retreated instead of pressing her advantage. It was almost as though she didn't *want* to defeat her, Gemma thought, but then, what was the point of this, what did the stranger want...?

Taking advantage of the retreat, Gemma went on the offensive. She ran at the stranger, who raised a knife to strike at Gemma's left side. But Gemma blocked her, blade to blade, then swung for her with a closed fist. Her punch caught the stranger in the jaw, and for a moment—as the stranger stumbled—her hood slid back from her face.

Gemma's heart skittered. She knew that face.

That moment of distraction cost her. Tugging her hood forward with one hand, the stranger reached for something at her waist and threw a fistful of it at Gemma.

Gemma staggered, coughing. The stranger had tossed some kind of...fine powder...into her face. Blinded, Gemma squeezed her eyes shut, falling back. She shook her head furiously to dispel the dust-like cloud engulfing her; she expected to feel the slice of the stranger's knife any second. Trying to open her watering eyes, Gemma coughed again. The powder tasted weirdly like...spices? Sweet and sharp, like cinnamon maybe, or clove...

And where had she smelled that so recently?

But the answer was slow to come. Shaking her head one last time, Gemma rubbed at her eyes, then opened them.

And found herself back in a world of shadow and decay.

Gemma's breath tangled in her throat. The mausoleum had become a husk of itself, a neglected, crumbling ruin. Black scorch marks stained the walls, and the floor was covered in a layer of white ash. The windows, both paned and stained glass, were gone, become gaping eyes in the stone façade, shards of glass heaped beneath them. The dais and its mounted memorial, grimy and gray with age, had toppled over, and great hunks of stone had broken away, leaving a mass of rubble.

"No," Gemma whispered, but in this withering dead place, there was no one to hear. Her lungs screamed for air, but she was drowning in dread. "What is happening, what is *happening*—"

As if in answer, the stone floor began to tremble. The quaking shook through her, and when Gemma glanced down, great cracks appeared in the floor. Crimson blood welled up from the fissures, gushing over her feet, lapping at her ankles. Gemma squeezed her eyes shut, willing it away, willing it all away—

And then, a voice in the darkness.

"What do you see?" a guttural voice demanded. "What do you remember?"

It was the voice of the stranger.

"There must be something," the stranger rasped. "You must recall something!"

Gemma opened her eyes to the bright, fiery light of the mausoleum's iron braziers.

And to a knife whistling through the air, sinking towards her.

The stranger wielded the knife. Gemma caught her by the wrist, halting the blade at the last second, but the stranger wasn't deterred. Using Gemma's grip like an anchor, the stranger delivered a solid punch to Gemma's gut. Gemma grunted, and in the next second, she was falling, for the stranger hooked her foot around Gemma's ankle and sent her toppling to the floor.

She landed hard, flat on her back. On the seamless stone floor that was covered in leaves and pine needles, not blood and ash.

Gemma blinked. Her back throbbed where she'd slammed into the floor, and she gasped and choked, pain and confusion and panic vying to take control of her. Never before had Gemma felt so helpless, so utterly defeated in both mind and body. She could not fight this stranger.

And she couldn't stop those relentless visions of death and decay from haunting her.

As Gemma lay there, the stranger appeared, looming over her. Her cavernous hood framed a face that was nothing but darkness. "You don't remember, do you?" The stranger's tone was vaguely resentful, almost petulant. "You don't remember what you are."

"What—are you—talking about?" Gemma gasped. It was all she could do to draw air into her lungs. She could not calm her racing pulse. She could not find that state of detachment she'd always relied on as a sniper. The world was a jumble, and she couldn't tell what was real. Not anymore.

"You know." In the depths of that faceless hood, the stranger's eyes gleamed with an unearthly light. "You've seen me moving through the shadows. And you saw my true face in the mirror. Only another ghoul could see those things."

The words tolled like a bell in Gemma's ears, a cacophony more pounding and tumultuous than any headache. Inexorable. Inescapable. She thought her wildly beating heart might have stopped entirely.

Only another ghoul...

"What—are you saying?" The words quivered from Gemma's lips. "Another ghoul—what are you *saying?*"

The stranger cocked her head to one side. Then her hand shot out, grasped Gemma by the wrist, and hauled her to her feet.

"Come now." Still gripping her tightly, the stranger inhaled deeply. As though breathing in the death that imbued this place. "You know what I'm saying. Isn't that why you came here, why you followed me tonight? You want to know what I am. And you want to know what you are."

"No." Gemma struggled to make sense of this, but nothing made sense anymore. It was impossible, it *was not possible.* Gemma knew there was something wrong with her, something deeply wrong. But never in her wildest fears had she imagined...

And yet the stranger's words stuck in her mind, striking a horrifying chord. Because in some way—some terrible, surreal way—it fit. For a moment, Gemma went limp in the stranger's clutches, slumping forward, boneless. Everything seemed to leave her, reason, thought, common sense. It all rushed out of her. Even the blood in her veins seemed to go, leaving her a hollow husk, as ruined and wretched and empty as anything she'd glimpsed in one of her hallucinations.

You wanted to know. Monster or madness.

But she'd never thought—*she* couldn't be the monster...

No. No, it could not be true. In an instant, Gemma came to herself, and her fear ratcheted like growing thunder in her ears. Her heart started beating again, her pulse *thump-thump-thumping* beneath the stranger's grip. "Let go of me." Gemma twisted away, tugging back her arm. "I'm not what you—don't—*let go of me!*"

With another great twist, she broke free from the stranger. Reeling, staggering, Gemma tried to keep her footing, but her flailing arm crashed into the stand of the iron brazier behind her. Sending it toppling to the stone floor.

The floor covered in pine needles and dead leaves.

The leaves and needles caught ablaze at once, enormous flames leaping up and racing across the mausoleum. As Gemma fell against the dais and the stranger wheeled around, fire quickly surrounded them both, covering the floor, eating up the walls. Catching at the wood-framed windows. Climbing over the oak door. In a matter of seconds, it was everywhere. Boxing them in.

The fire burned and raged, devouring the mausoleum. With Gemma and the stranger stuck inside.

20

BLAZING

GRYPHON SLUMPED DOWN INTO his chair as his father droned on. The two of them—and a small contingent of guards, of course—were ensconced in a small, stuffy chamber just off the ballroom. Even from in here, Gryphon could hear the sounds of the ball—music playing, glasses clinking, people laughing and talking. But he was stuck in here with his father. He had done his best to avoid the king that evening, but eventually he'd been spotted and guards sent to fetch him, so they could step away from the ball for a "private" conversation.

Gryphon knew exactly what that private conversation would be about, of course: his father's new favorite subject, expanding into the Black Forest. He talked of little else these days. Apparently, he couldn't even spend one evening at a ball without talking about it.

Now Victor was pacing back and forth across the small chamber, hands clasped behind him, going on about making soft incursions into the west—nothing violent, just setting up a few settlements on the fringes of the forest. Gryphon sat in a carved armchair in the corner, trying not to nod off. The lighting in here was as low as it was in the ballroom, only a few shaded lamps glimmering faintly on the far side of the room. Between that and the tedious subject, Gryphon was getting sleepy.

"At the same time, you can start making appearances in the Black Forest," his father was saying. "Nothing too grand, of course, but we can start putting the story out that you're the last descendant of the royal family—"

Gryphon choked at that, coming wide awake. First of all, he wasn't the last descendant—or at least, he didn't think he was. One of Viveca's sisters had escaped the Black Forest last year. And secondly— "I don't think making appearances in the Black Forest is such a good idea," he sputtered, "since several of the villages banded together to have me burned at the stake. And when that didn't work out, I turned into a beast and slaughtered a number of them. So."

King Victor stopped abruptly. "You what?"

Gryphon shrugged. "Wasn't my fault they wanted to burn me at the stake."

"Why didn't you tell me about this before?"

"Never came up, I suppose. I'm surprised Garrett didn't mention anything about it." He was not surprised. He was not surprised at all. He was sure Garrett had explained as little as he could about what had happened in the Black Forest.

"Well." Victor pinched the bridge of his nose. "We might have to amend those plans. Perhaps—"

"Yes." Gryphon leaned forward in his chair. "You will have to amend them." Really, he'd had enough. "Since all of this" –He gesticulated vaguely between himself and his father— "is temporary. I told you when I turned up here, I don't want this life anymore. And as soon as Garrett returns, *I* intend to return to my own life. Far from here. I'm not going to help you lay claim to the Forest Kingdom!"

In an instant, Victor's face turned beet red. "You will do what I tell you to," he snapped, "or I'll have you thrown in a dungeon."

Well, that escalated quickly. Not that Gryphon expected anything less. Rising to his feet, Gryphon faced the king, holding his ire in as best he could. "Why don't you try that," Gryphon said in his softest, deadliest voice, "and see how it goes?"

That caught the attention of the guards loitering nearby. Not that they moved forward or reached for their weapons or anything so obvious as that. No, they simply sharpened, standing alert as they watched the dispute between father and son. Gryphon clocked their attention, and so did the king. His father raised a hand, indicating they needn't worry. But the guards, Gryphon noticed, did not relax.

"You want me to act the prince," Gryphon barreled on. "Pretend like everything is fine here, like you didn't exile me, like all is forgiven and I have my title back. And now you want to use me as an excuse to grab more territory. But in the meantime, you don't even trust me enough to let me walk around the castle on my own! Or do you insist Garrett be under guard every second of the day, with soldiers posted at his door at night to make sure he stays put?"

"Wouldn't matter if I did do that," his father muttered. "He knows all the secret passages in the castle. And I don't doubt he's confided them to you."

"That is really not the point."

"You know, you might try being grateful. Grateful that I have forgiven your exile. It's not all pretend, you know, I can't take that back as soon as your brother returns. I'd look the fool—"

"And that's what matters most, isn't it?" A deep well of old, familiar bitterness rose inside Gryphon. "That you don't *look the fool—*"

"This is about more than just my pride, Gryphon! I am the king of this country, and it is paramount that my people have faith in me to be king! That is what you have never understood, not before I exiled you and apparently not now—"

Gryphon threw his hands into the air. "Then you should be happy I'll never be king, Victor. I know I am." He turned away, crossing the small chamber in a few quick strides.

"Where are you going?" the king demanded.

"Someplace not here." He should go back to the ball, he knew, but he didn't think he could stand to talk to any more preening courtiers right now. Pausing at the doorway, Gryphon indicated the guards. "Well?" he challenged, a pugnacious note in his voice.

His father matched him glare for glare.

Gryphon yanked the door open, marching out into the corridor.

"Just—leave him," he heard his father say. Addressing the guards. "Let him go. It's fine."

That was a surprise. Gryphon hadn't expected his father to capitulate, no matter his complaints. But he was too angry for this small gesture to make much difference. Victor wasn't doing it to show trust in Gryphon anyway. This was just a way to get the last word, to show Gryphon he could be reasonable. But "reasonable" was the last thing his father ever was.

Gryphon turned right, moving away from the ballroom. His boots thudded down the marble corridors as he swept through the castle, fuming silently. He didn't care that Garrett had saved his life; his brother would owe him for all of this once he returned. Courting Princess Solena was the least of it. No, it was putting up with his father's shenanigans that he couldn't stomach. Garrett definitely owed him.

He didn't realize where he was headed until he stood before the door. It was not that far from the ballroom, though far enough that the sounds of revelry had faded even to his ears. The silence echoed around him. Here, on the ground floor of the castle, he stood before a stout door with a simple iron handle. The door was locked, but Gryphon had the key. He'd asked Magan for it only a few days after he'd arrived. Magan had found it and handed it over, and Gryphon had carried it in his pocket ever since. Every day.

But today was the first day he found himself standing here.

Gryphon gazed at the door, incapable of parsing all the emotions stealing through him. Then—before he could second-guess himself—he pulled the key out of his pocket and unlocked the door. It swung open easily, and Gryphon peeked inside.

The room was completely dark. During the daytime, there would have been natural light to see by, for a glass wall ran the length of the right side of the room and curved around the far end. But right now, all Gryphon could see was the faint glimmer of the glass, the night beyond it as black as the depths of the ocean.

Gryphon had been here before, though not since he was a small child. He remembered where the sconces on the walls were, to wind up the gear-bulb lighting. The lights flickered on, and Gryphon cast his gaze around the room. There was the glass wall on the right. The rest was pale stone, including the floors. It was a modern construction, one of the newest parts of the castle, added on within the last fifty years.

It was his mother's old workshop. Where she had worked her magic. Her art.

It had seemed like magic to Gryphon. He had very old, very dusty memories of crawling around the floor here, sitting at his mother's knee while she created beauty out of blank canvases and life out of hunks of marble. Now the workshop was as dusty as his memories. Heavy cloth covered all the furniture. Greenery that had once spilled out of planters and trailed from hanging pots was long dead. But everything had been left as it was, Gryphon realized. As his eyes traveled the room, his memory formed objects from the amorphous white cloth—her easels, her desk, her supply cabinets. With trembling fingers, Gryphon reached for the edge of the first cloth and tugged it back, letting it slip onto the floor.

Beneath it was his mother's tall wooden stool. He could see her perched upon it, tapping her cheek with the end of a paintbrush. Thinking. Dreaming.

One by one, Gryphon went round the conservatory and pulled all the cloth away. Even his mother's supplies were still here, though the paintbrushes looked stiff and the paints long sullied. His heart squeezed tight when he pulled the last cloth back to reveal a canvas on an easel, a painting halfway done. Forever unfinished.

Gryphon sank down onto the stool. Illness had claimed his mother's life before he turned four years old. He'd been left alone in this castle. His father's only interest in him had been as his heir, an interest that had waned when Gryphon showed more inclination to be in this art workshop than out on the training grounds or studying strategy. When Gryphon had discovered, several years later, that he had a half-brother, a brother his father had visited and tended to all his life, well, it only made sense. Victor could afford to lose interest in Gryphon. He had a backup in Garrett.

What might his life had been like, Gryphon wondered, if his mother hadn't died? Would he have been a better prince, a better heir? No, he doubted that. He might have had someone to advocate for him, but even his mother couldn't have made Victor like him. But he wouldn't have been alone. He would have had an ally, someone to relate to, someone who could relate to him.

Oh, there was no point wondering at things like this, was there? And Gryphon had no desire to succumb to maudlin thoughts. He'd spent so much of his life like that, and he knew a better way now. He was happy with his life, and it didn't matter what his father thought. It didn't matter what plans the king made. As soon as Garrett returned, Gryphon would be gone from this place.

He pushed off the stool, then paused as he caught a concerning scent on the air. Not inside the conservatory. In here, musty dead plants and acrid oil paints dominated his senses, but outside the glass wall—

Smoke. He smelled smoke. Anyone else might think it woodsmoke from a hearth or stove, but Gryphon could tell it was more than that. This was smoke from a conflagration. A wild blaze, something huge, a fire raging out of control.

Unlocking the conservatory door, Gryphon stepped outside. He moved quickly through the lush garden that ringed in the workshop, exiting onto a path that led through the grounds near the back of the castle. He called to the beast to enhance his senses, scenting the air and using his night vision to pierce the darkness as he wound his way past cultivated green squares, rows of shrubs, and small groves of trees. When he reached the place where the path turned, climbing a rise in the land to the castle cemetery, he didn't need his sense of smell anymore. There was smoke on the rise beyond the cemetery gates. An inky black stain against a midnight-blue backdrop.

He started up the dirt path, taking it at a run, but he didn't get far before he caught another scent, more familiar this time. Just ahead of him.

Spencer.

"Prince Gryphon!" Spencer appeared around a curve, staggering to a halt. His dark cheeks were flushed red, and his eyes bright and panicked. "Oh, thank the stars, I was hoping—there's a fire!"

"I know. What is it? Where?"

"The graveyard. A mausoleum," Spencer panted. "I think Gemma might be inside—she disappeared from the ball, but someone said they saw her, well, the princess, rather, headed in this direction—"

A jolt of fear fissioned through Gryphon. "Keep going for help," he barked Spencer. "Get back to the castle and alert someone!"

Without waiting to see if his order was followed, Gryphon left the winding dirt path and charged straight up the rise, over tufts of scrubby gray-green grass and rocky ledges cut into the ground. He called to the beast as he ran, allowing more of the creature through. Fur sprouted from the backs of his hands and along the sides of his face. His teeth elongated into fangs, and claws sprouted from his nailbeds. All so he could use the beast's speed and strength, propelling himself up the hill and across the cemetery as fast as he could.

There were several mausoleums in the cemetery, but Gryphon hardly needed to ask which one was in trouble. The stone structure was alight with flame, dark smoke pouring from shattered windows and the gaping entrance, where the wooden door had burned away. The building itself might be stone, but that didn't mean there wasn't plenty else inside to burn. And he wasn't sure how long the mausoleum could withstand such intense heat without collapsing.

As he reached the burning building, someone staggered out of the smoke. But it wasn't Gemma. It was another guard, her freckled face and short hair streaked with soot. Her eyes were weirdly glazed over.

"I couldn't—" She swayed. Gryphon caught her with clawed hands. "I tried to—but there's so much smoke—couldn't see anything—"

"Wait here," Gryphon commanded, gently setting her aside.

Then he ran into the mausoleum, bursting through a cloud of smoke.

The guard was right. Inside, it was difficult to see. Gryphon was still half-transformed, and the wavering glare of the fire obscured the beast's sight, making everything hazy. He coughed and recoiled as smoke filled his throat and nose, as his eyes watered and the heat scorched his fur. The blaze was so violently overpowering, so staggeringly disorienting, that it was a moment before he could make out anything.

Scent, he thought to himself. *Scent the air.*

He tried. The choking smell of smoke overlayed everything, and beneath it, other things burning. Charred wood, leaves turned to ash. Mortar melting, caustic and sharp.

Mortar, melting.

He needed to get out of here. He needed to find Gemma.

He tried scenting again, and there, beneath the odorous smoke, he smelled them. Not one scent but two. One he recognized as Gemma, but the other was only vaguely familiar. He ventured forward, summoning more of the beast. Enough that his clothes began to split, and more fur sprouted along his arms. The fur was hardly fireproof, but the beast's thick hide would provide some protection from the heat. Still, he clamped his lips shut as he lurched through the burning building, a roar building in his chest. There was not much of the floor that wasn't scorched, and he stumbled several times to avoid fiery scraps of wood tumbling to the ground or explosions of embers bursting from the conflagration.

Finally—when he was drenched and dripping with sweat, when he was sure he could not withstand much more heat, when he felt the soles of his feet must be blackened and burnt, when he thought he was about to pass out from the smoke—he spotted someone. Not Gemma, but another young woman, someone with dark hair. Whoever she was, she'd collapsed in a heap on the dais at the base of a mounted sculpture. Shielding his eyes, Gryphon hurried forward. If the woman was burnt or injured, he couldn't tell, and he wasn't going to stop to check. She was unconscious. He scooped her into his arms and turned quickly, looking for Gemma.

"Gemma!" he called. Or tried to call. Her name was distorted by his fangs, and his voice weak and hoarse from the smoke. "Gemma!"

But the fire was only growing hotter, stronger, the smoke thicker and blacker. Gryphon could barely make out his surroundings, and when he tried to scent the air again, smoke clogged his nostrils, irritating his airway. Hacking a violent cough, he turned, looking for a way out. If he could get this woman out, then he could come back for Gemma—

There. A gaping hole in the wall, probably where a window had been. It had been shattered by the heat, burnt out by the fire. Gryphon moved towards it, encumbered by the unconscious woman. He shifted most of her weight into his right arm so he could see his way better—

And then he spotted her. Another figure in the blaze, crouched atop the dais. Hunched over behind the mounted sculpture.

Gemma.

"Gemma!" Gryphon roared. "*Gemma!*"

But she didn't move. She probably couldn't hear him, and her face was turned away. Gryphon would have to go to her. Thankfully, most of the fire back here had burnt out, the floor covered in crisp black ash. When Gryphon reached Gemma, he shifted the other woman again, hefting her over his right shoulder. "Gemma," he croaked, bending down. "Come on. We need to get out of here."

But when he touched her arm, Gemma's head rolled back, her neck limp, her eyes closed. She, too, had passed out, huddled here beneath the sculpture. Gryphon swore. Adjusting his grip on the other woman, he reached for Gemma, trying to get his free arm under her.

Then an ominous *cre-e-e-e-a-k* sounded out overhead. Gryphon's heart leapt into his throat. He looked up.

The roof gave another terrifying creak, the stones shifting before his eyes.

Gryphon scooped up Gemma and slung her over his left shoulder, just as he had done with the other woman on his right. Then he turned towards the gaping window. It was a good five paces from where he stood.

Summoning all that was left of the beast, and all that was left of his strength, he leapt from the dais. An animalistic roar tore from him as he soared over the flames.

They flew through the window. Tumbling free of the flaming mausoleum.

And the stone roof crashed in behind them.

21

DAMAGED

G EMMA LEFT THE INFIRMARY under the cover of a dark night sky. It wasn't so late, but it might as well have been, for the parade grounds were silent and empty. The last shift change was over an hour ago, and those not on duty were sleeping or eating, or maybe in town, having a drink in a pub. At times like these, the barracks looked like a ghost town, the whistling wind the only sound to be heard.

She'd spent twenty-four hours in the infirmary. She hadn't suffered anything from the fire but a bit of smoke inhalation, and her stay in the infirmary had only been a precaution. She'd had a couple of visitors. The first was Kinsley, first thing this morning. After he'd been assured she would be all right, they'd discussed what had happened at the ball last night, why Gemma had left, how she'd followed the stranger to the mausoleum. Gemma had left out a lot of details—in fact, as many as she could—but she'd insisted that the stranger she'd encountered was Princess Solena.

At that, Kinsley had admitted, "Prince Gryphon did pull someone else out of the mausoleum. A dark-haired girl—"

"Solena?"

"No, Gemma." Kinsley met her gaze. "It was Pila. Your handmaiden."

Gemma had been stunned. Dazed, she'd mumbled, "Solena's handmaiden."

"Well, last night she was yours."

"But is she all right? What was she doing there?"

Pila, Kinsley told her, had suffered only minor burns and smoke inhalation. What she was doing there was anyone's guess. Guards were keeping a close eye on her, and once she was fully healed, the king intended to hold her for questioning.

But Gemma shook her head. "No. He shouldn't bother. It couldn't have been her, Kinsley. She couldn't have been the person I fought. I'd just left her in the ballroom. She couldn't have changed her clothes so quickly and gotten out there in time. She couldn't have." Her voice hardened. "It must have been Solena."

"Gemma, I've debriefed the guard contingent that was on duty with Princess Solena last night." A faint line creased Kinsley's forehead. "Thoroughly. They said she never left her quarters. In fact, she went to bed early and never left her room the entire night."

"The window in her bedchamber—" Gemma began.

"—was bolted shut," Kinsley cut in. "Three nights ago."

"It was?"

"Given the death threat she received and the intruder's rumored ability to scale walls, it seemed prudent. For Solena's protection, if nothing else."

Gemma rubbed a hand over her eyes. "And the window couldn't have been pried open somehow?"

"I think we'd know if it was."

"And no one entered her quarters?"

"Everyone on watch said no. They were quite sure."

But I saw her. I saw her face. It had been a quick glimpse during the fight, when the stranger's hood fell back. But Gemma knew it was Solena. She'd recognized her. And besides, everything she'd said to Gemma—

You saw my true face in the mirror. Isn't that why you followed me tonight? You want to know what I am.

Gemma swallowed. Of course, she'd said other things too. Things Gemma was trying not to think about.

Kinsley leaned back in his narrow cane chair, looking uncomfortable. Of course, that might have just been the chair. The infirmary was not known for its comfortable seating. "Look, Gemma." There was no trace of skepticism on Kinsley's face, but Gemma read it in him anyway. "I believe what you're telling me—what you've seen, what you've observed about Princess Solena. More than that, I know sometimes we have an instinct about something we can't quite explain." He sighed. "But we need something more solid to present to the king. Because he will need something more solid to move against Solena. To expel her from the castle, if need be. So. We will continue to monitor the princess for anything suspicious. And you will get some rest. Until the physicians are sure there won't be any lasting damage."

Any lasting damage.

Gemma thought it might be too late for that.

The only person she had seen today—besides the physician—was Roy, who had come in twice to visit her. The first time, Gemma had heard him coming and feigned sleep so she wouldn't have to talk to him. The second time, he'd taken her by surprise. He had little to say about Solena or Pila, but he did have news of Gryphon. Apparently, no one had seen Gryphon since the fire. According to Beckett, who'd been in the graveyard, Gryphon had escaped the burning mausoleum and left Gemma and Pila with her. Then he'd taken off. Help in the form of soldiers and servants was arriving by that time, and Gryphon, Beckett reported, had been almost entirely in his beast form. Gemma gathered he'd wanted to remain in that form for the time being because he would heal faster. He'd almost certainly sustained burns inside the mausoleum.

While he'd been saving Gemma and Pila.

A distant part of Gemma thought she should feel some guilt or shame over that. Over Gryphon being injured, over needing to be saved. But all she felt was numb. A film of shock hung over her, giving everything an unreal quality.

Now as she left the infirmary, she made her way to the officers' building where Kinsley awaited her. When he'd left her in the infirmary this morning, he said he'd want a talk with her as soon as she was released.

She found him in his office, sitting behind his desk. It was a simple desk, rustic, utilitarian. Just like Kinsley himself. A single handheld gear-bulb lamp sat on the desk, adding a little extra light to the rest of the room. Kinsley barely looked up, though he gestured for Gemma to come in. His focus was on a document before him, something he was writing, and a deep crease in his forehead marked his concentration. "Just a moment," he told her absently as she trudged into the room.

Kinsley's desk was not the tidiest. It was littered with papers, rosters and memos and reports, but patches of the honey-colored maple-wood were visible through the clutter. One of those patches bore a burn mark, the wood blackened and scorched.

Likely where someone had toppled a candle over long enough to gouge the desk.

Gemma stared at the burn, her fingers curling in towards her bandaged palm, where the stranger's knife had sliced through her. She stood there as Kinsley scribbled furiously. The quiet in the office was somehow oppressive, unbearable. Just as it had been in the infirmary all day.

Gemma had spent her time in the infirmary trying not to think about everything she hadn't told Kinsley. Her other, more outlandish suspicions about Princess Solena. And what Solena—the stranger, whoever, it had to be Solena—had said to her. She'd told herself it wasn't necessary to tell Kinsley any of that because, well, it was just madness, wasn't it? Solena's madness. Gemma's madness, maybe. It didn't matter. Because it couldn't be true.

You've seen me moving in the shadows. You saw my true face in the mirror.

Only another ghoul could see that.

No. It could not be true.

She, Gemma, was not a ghoul.

It was impossible, wasn't it? From what she'd learned about ghouls—which was admittedly not very much—she would know if she was one. Wouldn't she?

A ghoul is nothing without a human form. Without a body, they are only shadow. Belonging to the dark, nether reaches of the world. Destined to wander, lurking in the lowest places.

But what did that really mean? Did that mean a ghoul without a body had no identity of their own, no memory of what they were? Was it possible that a ghoul could take a human form and not know, not remember, that they were a ghoul? It seemed unlikely to Gemma, but the longer she'd lain in that infirmary bed, the longer she dwelt on it, the uneasier she became.

A shiver stole through Gemma. No. No, it couldn't be true. It just couldn't. Yes, everything Solena had said was unsettling, but in the end, they were just words, ghost stories and words. The words of a masked intruder whom Gemma had no reason to trust. Solena might be the mad one, for all Gemma knew, or she was messing with Gemma, trying to get into her head, trying to make her doubt her own mind. All to throw suspicion off herself. After all, if she, Gemma, was mad, then who would believe anything she said about Princess Solena?

"Gemma? Are you all right?"

Gemma looked up. She was briefly startled to find herself in Kinsley's office; she'd nearly forgotten what she was doing there. She felt wrapped in a fog that separated her from everyone else. Part of it was just exhaustion, she thought. When was the last time she'd had a solid night's sleep, unbroken by headaches or fear or fragmented nightmares? She couldn't recall.

Kinsley set his pen and document aside, and now he watched her closely, concern in his tired eyes. He looked as tired as she was. Dark circles rimmed his eyes, as stark as bruises against his pale skin. "I'm fine," she said. Her voice sounded like her usual self, but she didn't feel like herself. It seemed her voice should have reflected that.

"Good. Well, even if the physicians have cleared you, I'm sure you still need rest. So I'll get right to the point." Despite this direct speech, Kinsley's gaze had strayed back to his papers. "I told you this morning we would continue to monitor Princess Solena closely, and we will. However, I want you to take some time away from her. Five days' leave."

This was enough to pull Gemma from her numb fog. "What? But I'm supposed to work tomorrow—"

Kinsley shook his head. "You've been attacked twice now, Gemma. You've earned a respite."

"I wasn't really attacked—"

"Gemma." Kinsley finally looked up from his papers with a stern expression. "This is an order. Five days' leave."

Gemma set her jaw. "Give me a real reason why, Kinsley."

"Fine." Kinsley's tone became clipped. "Just as soon as you tell me the reason you left the ballroom last night on your own, without telling anyone where you were going."

Gemma's mouth hung open. It was a moment before she found words. "I thought I saw—an intruder." Though that was not why she'd left the ballroom. She left the ballroom because she'd hallucinated. "And I did see an intruder, didn't I—"

"So why didn't you alert your guards?"

The words were vaguely reminiscent of something, and it was a moment before Gemma remembered this morning, when he'd referred to Pila as "her" handmaiden. "I am a guard, Kinsley," she reminded him. "I'm not actually a princess—"

"Except last night you were. And we had plans in place, Gemma. We had a procedure you were meant to follow if you saw anything suspicious. Yet you left without telling anyone."

"Pila knew I was leaving."

"Pila knew you had spotted an intruder?"

"No, she..." Gemma trailed off, remembering how she'd left the ballroom last night. She'd dropped her glass, she recalled, and spilt wine down the front of her gown. She'd half-fled, half-stumbled from the ballroom onto the terrace, desperate for fresh air. She'd left Pila behind—or she thought she had. But

Pila had been babbling about taking her somewhere to see to her dress, to get her cleaned up, so maybe...

Gemma closed her eyes. *Maybe Pila followed me.* Of course. Of course the handmaiden would have followed her, that was her job. She'd probably followed Gemma to the cemetery, and when the fire started, she'd gone into the mausoleum to try and help—

Gemma's shoulders sagged. "I didn't tell her I saw an intruder." She pressed two fingers between her eyes. A dull throb answered her. "But she must have followed me. She wanted to help me. And then she got stuck in that fire because of me." *She could have died because of me.*

Kinsley seemed to know what she was thinking. "This leave isn't meant as punishment, Gemma. It's not a reprimand, certainly not an official one. But..." He sat back in his chair, tilting his head to look up at her. "I think you've gotten too close to this. We had procedures in place last night, and you didn't follow them. You know better, Gemma. I know you do. So I think a few days off will do you some good. Help you reset."

Help me get my head on straight. If only. The problem was, she didn't think time off would help at all. It would only give her time to dwell on...so many other things. Things she wanted to forget. "You don't understand." Gemma's chin trembled. She rested the tips of her fingers on the edge of Kinsley's desk to steady herself. "I can't just sit in the barracks and do nothing." Not while Solena was here in the castle, not while they were investigating without her. Damn it, this was as much about her as it was about Solena. "I can't not be a part of this investigation. Please, Kinsley, I know I messed up, but if you would just trust me—"

For the first time, Kinsley's stoic mask slipped. "The problem is," he said, running a hand behind his neck, "that's a lot to ask right now, Gemma."

Gemma felt as though he'd punched her. Kinsley's tone was not unkind, but to hear him, of all people, say he didn't trust her—Kinsley, who was one of her oldest friends in the guard, Kinsley, who had been a mentor to her. He'd never questioned her judgment. Not once.

But Kinsley did not back down. "What happened last night could have been a lot worse. You, Pila, Prince Gryphon, any of you could have died in that fire. And we weren't there to help—rather, we were there too late—because you left without telling anyone. You left us all in the dark. And according to some of the other guards, you've been acting strangely ever since Princess Solena arrived." He let out a long sigh. "Maybe that's my fault. I told you the king wanted a close eye kept on her, that we shouldn't trust her. Maybe—"

"It wasn't you." Gemma felt very small, shriveling beneath the weight of Kinsley's disappointment. "It's me, I'm—I—" But there was nothing she could say. Nothing she could bear to put voice to. "I can't always tell you everything, Kinsley," she said, her voice little more than a whisper. "Some things are just—they're personal."

"Of course they are," Kinsley said. "We all work closely together, Gemma, but that doesn't mean we aren't entitled to our secrets. But when those secrets put the rest of us in danger? That's when it's not personal anymore. Trust works both ways, Gemma. And you aren't trusting me, which isn't like you."

Gemma felt a lump in her throat. *It isn't like you.*

Maybe that was more true than he knew.

"Ghouls are shape-changers."

"Don't you even know what you are?"

"You taste like the grave."

"Only another ghoul could see those things."

Gemma felt as though the wooden floorboards were rotting beneath her. The earth opening wide to swallow her whole. She couldn't keep ignoring it all, she couldn't forget. Not this.

She stared at Kinsley. Her fellow soldier. Her friend. He didn't trust her. And, Gemma realized, she couldn't blame him. He shouldn't trust her. He didn't know what was happening to her, he didn't know the things she had seen. He didn't even know who or what she was—

Even she didn't know that. She didn't know if she really was Gemma. And even if she was, she didn't know how to trust her own eyes, her own mind. She couldn't trust herself.

Of course Kinsley shouldn't trust her. She shouldn't even be here.

"You're right," she said hoarsely. "I can't be a part of this. Not anymore. I'll go."

Kinsley looked relieved. "Just five days, Gemma. Then we'll reassess and go from there. All right?"

She heard herself murmur an assent. But what she was thinking was, *No. Not five days.*

She had to leave the guard. For good.

She left Kinsley's office in a daze. The night outside had gotten even darker since she'd left the infirmary, and she wondered how long she'd been in Kinsley's office.

It felt like a few minutes.

It felt like an age.

The weight of her exhaustion returned, sitting on her shoulders like two piles of bricks. She didn't know where she was going to go, but if she was leaving, she'd need to take some things with her. Clothes, supplies. She needed to return to her sleeping quarters to pack.

But just the thought of that felt so hard. It was too much. If she was going, she just wanted to be gone.

So she turned, not in the direction of her building, but towards the outer gates. At this time of night, they were shut tight but not locked. As she turned, a shadow shifted on her left, moving across the exterior brick wall of the officers' building. Gemma stiffened, but when she turned to look, it was not a slithering shadow but an actual person, skulking in the dark. A tall, broad-shouldered figure, pushing off the wall.

It was Prince Gryphon.

Gemma looked at him without really seeing him. "You're back."

"Yes," he said simply.

"Are you—injured? From..." She couldn't even form complete sentences. Even that was too hard.

"I'm fine now." As he stepped forward, Gryphon's eyes reflected the light of the nearest lamppost. They were not the yellow eyes of the beast but just his plain brown eyes. "A few minor burns was all. But I needed to stay in beast form for a few hours to heal. I wanted to stay out of sight."

"Of course." Gemma turned to look at the door to Kinsley's office. Gryphon had been standing just outside. "How much of that did you hear?" The door had been shut, of course, and the windows too. But that wouldn't have stopped Gryphon.

"All of it," he said. "You're not staying here in the barracks?"

Gemma said, "No." She would have told Gryphon she was leaving for good. Quitting the guard. She wasn't trying to hide it. She just couldn't find the words. Couldn't make herself say it out loud.

Gryphon studied her for a moment. "Are you all right?"

Gemma shrugged. There was no possible way to answer that. Her entire life was upended. It should feel like the end of the world. And it did in a way. But it also felt like she should have seen it coming.

"Where are you going to go?" Gryphon asked.

"I don't know." Gemma felt empty, hollowed out by fatigue and shock. She could take a room in the city. There were places there she could afford. Or— "I can just. Camp in the woods. It's what I used to do. It's where I used to live."

"If you really want to. But I might have an alternative."

"Why?" Gemma asked in a tired tone. "Why are you helping me?"

The look he gave her was almost exasperated. As if that was a stupid question. Perhaps it was. "Why are you leaving?" he countered.

She managed to answer honestly. She managed to find the words. "Because I think Princess Solena is a ghoul. And I think I might be one too."

22

ABSOLUTION

K LAUS GAZED UPON THE cluster of white lights in the valley below, glittering like a field of stars that had been harnessed from the night sky. Glen City. A layer of gray fog hovered over the glen, giving the lights a blurry look. A part of him was not eager to get back to the city. To be immersed in so-called civilization, to be closed within the castle walls. But there was one thing he was eager to get back to. One person.

So he started down into the valley, descending towards the city.

When he reached the barracks and slipped inside the gates, waving to the guards in the watchtower, he crossed the parade grounds, heading straight to Gemma's sleeping quarters. He had no idea if she would be working or not, but it was getting late. If she wasn't working, she was probably in bed.

But she wasn't there. No one was. The room was empty.

He headed for the officers' quarters next. Not because he had any reason to think she was there, but someone would be, some-one who could tell him where she was. His body thrummed with nervous energy as he hurried back across the parade grounds, the lampposts ringing the courtyard lighting his way.

Just outside the officers' building, he ran into two familiar figures: Roy and Spencer. For some reason, they both froze when they saw him, Spencer's eyes darkening and Roy looking vaguely uncomfortable.

"Klaus," said Roy in a voice that was strangely strained and strangely friendly.

"Roy," Klaus returned, frowning.

"Thought you were on leave," Spencer said shortly.

"I was. Still am." Klaus turned his frown on Spencer. "I'm looking for Gemma. Either of you seen her?"

Roy and Spencer exchanged a glance. "Ah. You should check with Kinsley," Roy said. "About that."

"About what?"

"About where Gemma is."

"All right." A sense of disquiet swept over Klaus. Something was wrong. Something with Gemma? He shot the two soldiers another look, then strode past them into the officers' quarters. Where he'd been headed in the first place.

He found Kinsley in his office, standing behind his desk, frowning over a sheaf of paper. Klaus had already stepped inside before he realized Kinsley wasn't alone. Gallia was there too, leaning against the far wall with her arms crossed. By the sound of it, Klaus had interrupted some discussion they were having. But they both fell silent when he walked in.

"Klaus." Kinsley dropped his papers onto his desk. "I thought you were on leave."

"I am. Technically." Klaus threw a quizzical glance at Gallia. "Sorry. I didn't realize you were in a meeting."

"It's fine." Kinsley tossed Klaus a quick, underhanded glance. His face was paler than usual in the harsh gleam of the light fixtures, giving him a sallow look. "Actually, I'm glad you're back. If you don't mind coming off your leave early, we could really use you around here."

"I don't mind, but...what's going on?"

Kinsley tapped an idle finger against the top paper on his desk. "I've just received a telegram from Princess Briar. She's asked for a few of us to go join her and Prince Garrett." He indicated the young woman on his right. "Gallia's going too, and one or two others. So we'll be short-staffed here."

"Are Garrett and Briar in trouble?"

"She didn't say. Only that she wants us to come. It's terrible timing, but we've got to go. We leave first thing in the morning."

Terrible timing. That was an understatement. "Right. Ah, have you seen Gemma?"

A pointed silence met his words. Not just from Kinsley, who for some reason seemed hesitant to answer a simple question. But from Gallia too. The silence stretched on for a beat, and then Gallia said, "I'm going to go. We can finish up later, Kinsley."

"Right," Kinsley said, his voice a little too brisk. Klaus turned to watch Gallia go, then turned back to face Kinsley.

"What's going on?" he demanded.

"Klaus." Slowly, Kinsley came around his desk to face him. Only, he didn't really face him because he wouldn't look him in the eye. His gaze hovered somewhere around Klaus's shoulder. "I know you weren't gone long, but you missed quite a bit. There was an...incident yesterday. With Gemma."

Klaus felt an uncomfortable tightening in his stomach. "What do you mean? What kind of incident? Is Gemma all right?"

"Physically, she's fine," Kinsley assured him. "No one was hurt. But...well, I discussed it with Gemma earlier this evening. And she agreed it would be best to take some time away. She's on leave for the time being, and apparently, she decided to take that leave away from the barracks. Away from the castle. To get some space, I expect."

Klaus stared at him for a moment. A long moment. He could see that Kinsley was growing uncomfortable with his silence, but Klaus let it stretch on. Finally, he said, "All right. I understand."

Kinsley looked surprised. "You do?"

"Or, well, I would," Klaus said, "if that had been anything like a clear explanation."

Kinsley sighed. "Klaus."

"You said 'apparently' she decided to leave the barracks. So she didn't tell you she was going? Or *where* she was going?"

"No, she didn't, but—"

"Because, see, the Gemma I know would never just up and leave the castle. The guard is her life. And you have no idea what she's going through right now. How could you just let her leave?"

"It was her choice to go," Kinsley said curtly.

"I don't believe that. And I can't believe you'd just abandon her like this."

Kinsley bristled, taking a step forward. "I haven't abandoned her. But you're one to talk. What about you, Klaus? Where have you been? If Gemma's really going through something right now, why did you leave her?"

"I was trying to help her," Klaus snarled. "I went to find help, to find information. I was trying to—" He broke off. "Never mind. I don't need to justify myself to you."

"No, you don't." Kinsley sounded tired. "But if you have information that can help us, Klaus, I would like to hear it."

"Would you? Well, I don't feel like sharing." Stuffing his hands into his pockets, Klaus said, "If Gemma hasn't trusted you with her suspicions, then I won't either. Because I still trust Gemma more than I trust anyone else here."

Klaus turned to go without looking at Kinsley. He didn't want to see his reaction. He was angry, *stones*, he was angry. He didn't understand how Kinsley could have let this happen. But Kinsley was also one of the few people he actually liked, and he didn't want to see his face. Not right now.

Gallia was waiting right outside the open door, arms crossed, scowling as usual, and it was obvious she'd been listening. "So is that it?" she asked. "You're leaving too? You're, what? Quitting the guard?"

"Don't be stupid," Klaus snapped. "I'm still on leave for another two days."

He swept down the parade grounds, turning towards the outer gates. But when he reached those gates, he stopped. He had no idea where Gemma had gone, no idea where to find her. He tried to recall if she'd ever mentioned somewhere, a place in the city or a hideout in the woods. He doubted she'd go far. He would just have to track her, he thought. Which would be difficult in the dark but not impossible.

But before he could push open the iron gates, one of them swung open, and he was met by three of his fellow guards. Klaus did not recognize any of them, so he was surprised when one said, "Klaus?"

Warily, Klaus answered, "That's me."

"If you'll come with us, please," said another of the guards. "Prince Gryphon requests your presence."

Again? Considering how things stood between them, Gryphon was calling on him quite a lot. And hadn't he told him, Klaus thought grumpily, as he motioned for the guards to lead the way, that he was taking leave? How had the bloody beast even known he was back? Or had he "requested his presence" while he was gone too, only to be told that Klaus wasn't here?

Much like before, the guards led him, not inside the castle to Gryphon's quarters, but to someplace out on the grounds, a small courtyard square in the eastern gardens, ringed in stone benches and lit by lampposts in each corner. Gryphon was already there, pacing back and forth across the courtyard, looking preoccupied. As soon as the guards had deposited him there, they spared deep bows for Gryphon and departed, leaving him and Klaus alone in the dark of the night.

Klaus raised an eyebrow at the retreating guards. "Well, you've certainly won everyone over, haven't you?" Those had been *very* deep bows.

Gryphon behaved as though he had not heard this remark. He faced Klaus, hands clasped behind his back, and said, "I'm glad you're back. I told the guards in the watchtower to let me know as soon as you returned."

So that's how he knew. "Look, I'm still on leave, so if you need someone to track some trail for you, you'll have to find someone else. I haven't got time to go sniffing around the castle, I've got to find—"

"Gemma?" Gryphon interjected.

Klaus blinked. "How did you know?"

"I suppose Kinsley told you she left? That he put her on leave?"

Klaus nodded. "If you're telling me you had something to do with it—"

"I had nothing to do with it." Gryphon's voice turned as hard as Klaus's, an undertone of exasperation lining his words. "But I spoke to her before she left, and there are a couple of things you should know. And yes—" He raised a hand to forestall Klaus, who had opened his mouth to speak. "One of those things is where you can find her."

That was the last thing Klaus had expected to hear. "You know where she went?"

"I told her where to go. There's a little house outside the city, out in the woods west of here. A cottage. It's mine." Gryphon cleared his throat. "Well, no, it's Garrett's, but he acquired it so Isabelle and I could stay there when we're in the area. Only, Isabelle's not there now, and neither am I, so. I told Gemma she could stay there."

"And you're sure she went there?"

"She said she would."

Klaus nodded, grudgingly grateful. "How long will it take me to get to this place?"

Gryphon shrugged, his manner deliberately blasé. "Takes me a couple of hours. In beast form."

Klaus sent him a flat look. "So about double that for me."

"I can get you a horse, if you want...?"

Klaus shook his head. "That will just slow me down in the dark." Especially since he wasn't a very good rider. As Gryphon well knew. He frowned, staring into the darkness of the grounds beyond the courtyard. Not bothering to hide the mistrust in his words, he asked, "Why are you being so helpful, anyway?"

The look Gryphon shot him was full of irritation. "The pair of you," he grumbled.

"What? What pair?"

"You and Gemma. You don't trust anyone, either of you."

"I trust Gemma."

"You trusted me once too." Though he still stood with his hands clasped behind his back, the pose reserved and professional, Gryphon sounded a little more like the person Klaus had once known. A little bitter, a little moody. "Before you ran off with my brother."

Klaus folded his arms across his chest. "So that's what you're upset about? You don't care that I betrayed you to Viveca, but you're upset I left and joined Garrett's—"

"Of course I'm upset about that!" Gryphon exploded. He threw his hands up in the air, his exasperation on full display. Stunned, Klaus retreated a step—not out of any fear but just in plain surprise.

"We were supposed to be friends, you idiot," Gryphon ranted at him. "We *are* friends, which is why I'm helping you, by the way. And you know what, yes, maybe I would've been angry with you if you'd returned, back in the Forest Kingdom. Maybe I would have been just a little bit angry that you ran off. But you can't honestly think I would have blamed you for what happened between you and Viveca."

Klaus could not believe what he was hearing. "Of course I expected you to blame me. Why wouldn't you?" Despite the chill in the air, Klaus felt suddenly warm beneath his traveling coat, heat suffusing him from the inside out. "I let Viveca into the castle. It was my fault you got out, and it could have been so much worse, all because I was too stupid to—because I had feelings for her—"

"Klaus." Gryphon closed his eyes. "I made the same mistake. Here, in this castle, when I was fourteen years old. It's the reason my father exiled me, remember?"

Klaus's half-formed retort died in his throat as Gryphon's words sank in. Gryphon had fallen in love with a witch who had convinced him to let her into Glen Castle for some spell she wanted to perform. Garrett had been injured in the process, and King Victor had come away with the impression that Gryphon wanted to harm—perhaps even kill—his little brother. There had been some politics involved too, from what Klaus understood, but essentially, that was why Gryphon had been exiled.

"Well," said Klaus lamely. "Yes. I—do. Remember that. So."

"So." Gryphon exhaled, his shoulders heaving. "So I don't blame you for Viveca. I don't blame you for what *she* did to you." He fixed Klaus with a direct stare. "And you should stop blaming yourself."

Klaus's stomach gave a flip. He dropped his gaze and said, "Well, I don't think that's quite fair." He scuffed the toe of his boot over the paved yard. "You spent a number of years punishing yourself. It's barely been a year for me."

Gryphon rolled his eyes, but Klaus could tell it was in good humor. "Yes, well, you need to get your act together now." The humor vanished from Gryphon's face, his expression turning sober. "Gemma needs you. There's something else you need to know about her, Klaus. Something she told me."

23

KNOWN

KLAUS FOUND THE COTTAGE easily enough, following Gryphon's instructions, though it took a blasted long time to get there. It was beyond the outskirts of Glen City, a little ways into a wooded area southwest of the glen. The cottage boasted a ramshackle wooden porch at the front door, hung with ivy that was no doubt infested with spiders. Grimacing, Klaus balanced his lantern on the uneven railing as he bent to work at the lock with his pins. He supposed a normal person would've just knocked, but, well, it was past midnight. If Gemma was sleeping, he didn't want to wake her.

It took him longer to pick the lock than it should have, thanks to the low light, but once he got it, the door opened easily without a single squeak. Stowing his pins in his pocket, he lifted his lantern and stepped inside.

The interior was dark. Klaus eased forward, raising his lantern higher to get a better look at everything. It was a tiny place, just a front room here, and beyond it, a wide opening that led into—

Click.

Klaus froze. Something hard and cold dug into his back, right between his shoulder blades. Something that felt very much like the barrel of a gun.

"Thought you said I'd never get the drop on you again," said a familiar voice.

Klaus relaxed. "Gemma."

"Expecting someone else?"

"Expecting a warmer welcome, more like."

"Not sure why you'd expect that."

Klaus turned around as Gemma lowered her pistol. Her familiar flat expression was barely visible in the dim glare of the lantern, and his stomach dropped, remembering the last time he'd seen her. Remembering how they'd left things.

"Right." Klaus blew out a breath. "You're probably wondering where I've been. I'm sorry about that, but—"

"Klaus. I don't care where you've been." Gemma gestured at the front door with her pistol. "I was talking about the fact that you broke in. Didn't exactly give me reason to think it was a friendly coming in."

"Oh. Well. I didn't want to wake you."

"I wasn't asleep."

"Well, I know that now."

Gemma's shoulders lifted in a silent sigh. "What are you doing here, Klaus?"

"Looking for you." Klaus turned and placed his lantern on a small square table, then, spotting a floor lamp, stepped back to wind it on. The glow it shed was faint, but it cast a wide circle, allowing him to see everything more clearly. Not that there was much to see. The table, the lamp. A wide, cushy, slightly worn armchair. The tiny kitchen nearby. "Went to the castle first, to the barracks. Heard Kinsley ordered you on leave. The idiot."

Gemma didn't flinch. She didn't do much of anything. She looked...strange. Not quite like herself. Though perhaps that was just her attire. She wore a boxy, oversized wool sweater, a garment that certainly did not belong to her. It looked sized for a man, for one thing. A large man.

Gemma said, "He didn't force me to go."

Klaus snorted. "Oh, right. You agreed to it, is that it? It was all your idea?"

"Not really, no. But what does it matter. I'm here now."

Klaus frowned. The muted lamplight showed a wan and tired Gemma, and he suddenly realized that flat expression she'd turned on him hadn't been quite right. It had not been flat with irritation or annoyance. She was just...flat. As though all the emotion had seeped out of her. As though she was just a body. Gemma was not a particularly emotive person, but even so, something was wrong. Something was wrong with her.

"Look," he said, "they didn't fill me in on the details of what happened. But it doesn't matter. I left to meet with Sabine. She has some experience with ghouls—not a lot, but more than us. And we found something, something important. If Solena is a ghoul, then we might have something we can use to fight her."

He stopped to gauge Gemma's reaction to all of this. But her face remained inscrutable. Folding her arms around herself, she circled Klaus, moving towards the wide, lumpy armchair. "So again I ask, why are you here? I'm not in the guard anymore. Why aren't you telling Kinsley this?"

"First of all, you're not in the guard *right now*. Kinsley said you were on leave, not that you'd been sacked."

"He didn't sack me." Gemma stood with her back to him, and for a moment, he saw her stiffen, her shoulders lifting slightly. "But I quit. I'm quitting the guard."

Klaus blinked. It was a moment before he understood what she was saying, before he could process it. Because he had never, ever thought he would hear those words from her. Utterly gobsmacked, he said, "*What?* You can't—you would never."

"Well, I am, so. Shows what you know."

"But..." Klaus shook his head. She couldn't mean that. It was the stress talking. There was no way she would ever quit the guard. "Look. Never mind that. Whether you're in the guard or not, I still trust you a hell of a lot more than I trust Kinsley. Or any of them."

He thought for sure this would get some kind of a reaction from her—that it might lift her spirits to hear he still trusted her. But Gemma did not look lifted. She did not look cheered. She sank onto the armchair, turning to lean her head into its cushy back.

She wasn't just tired, Klaus realized. She was exhausted. All the fight had gone out of her. Whatever had happened while he'd been gone, it had defeated her. His heart ached to see it. Gemma was not one to give up. She had not given up when Viveca killed Falcon in the Black Forest. She had not given up when that witch in the southern wood ruptured her brain. And she had not given up when that rupture damaged her sight. She just kept going. That was Gemma. That was what she did.

But here, now—curled up in that armchair, rubbing one hand over her baggy eyes—that Gemma was not here.

"You trust me." She dropped her hand from her face and looked at him. "Klaus. You don't even know who I am." She let out a hollow laugh. "Or what I am."

And that's what this was about, of course. This was what had driven her past the point of coping. What she'd said to Gryphon, and what Gryphon had related to him. It sounded about as impossible as her quitting the guard, yet strangely, he also felt more comfortable dealing with it. It felt more in his wheelhouse, somehow.

"Yes, all right. Let's talk about that." Klaus grabbed a chair from the table and dragged it out, all the way over to where Gemma sat. The thudding *scr-a-a-a-pe* it made over the floor seemed overly loud in the tiny, sparsely furnished cottage. Klaus set his chair facing Gemma, leaving a few paces between them to give her space. Then he seated himself, his long legs sprawling before him.

"So," he said, his tone indifferent, "you might be a ghoul."

This, finally, elicited a reaction. Gemma threw him a startled look. "How—you know?"

"I talked to Gryphon. How do you think I knew to find you here? And he told me. Everything you told him. About Princess Solena, about the things she said to you. I have to say, I'm not entirely convinced, but—say it's true. Say you're a ghoul." Klaus spread his hands wide. "Where's the problem?"

Gemma stared at him. "Where's the—*what?*"

"Look, I've done this before. Remember? With Isabelle." He leaned back in his chair, lacing his hands behind his head. "In the Black Forest, when she realized what being bitten by Gryphon meant. She was very—*What's going to happen to me? What's going to become of me? Oh, no!'"* He pitched his voice higher in his best imitation of Isabelle.

The flat look Gemma gave him was much more like the one he remembered. Tinged with annoyance.

"And then, look. She was just fine. She turned into a beast, got it under control in time to keep from mauling Stefan, and then she was fine. A few days later she was out in the woods, fighting off were-wolves like she'd been doing it all her life. Best thing that ever happened to her, I'm sure."

"I'm sure," Gemma said, her voice stony. Oh, yes, she was definitely annoyed with him.

"And what about Princess Briar? Granted, I wasn't there for her transformation, but. She wasn't always a rotting corpse person, was she? But now she does all right for herself. Living happily ever after with Garrett and inventing all sorts of mad things." Klaus lifted a shoulder in a shrug. "I'm just saying. I think you're being a bit melodramatic about this 'being a ghoul' business. I mean, so what? So you can practically become invisible, hide in shadows? Is that so terrible?" He paused. "Can you do that? I mean, have you tried it?"

"No. But I suppose I could. Maybe." Gemma's gaze was disturbed.

"So seriously, why are we upset about this?"

Gemma's dark eyes flashed at him, and Klaus was glad for it. Glad to see some life in her. "Why am I upset? Why do you think? All right, so we know what I am. But who am I, Klaus?"

She rose suddenly from the armchair, pacing in the distance he'd left between them. Turning one way, then the other, her footsteps silent against the hardwood floor. "The person who signed up for Prince Garrett's company, who's served him loyally these past two years. The sharpshooter, the tracker, raised by her father—stones, that man probably wasn't my father." She touched a hand to her mouth. "Maybe he thought he was. Or maybe he was a ghoul too. Or maybe he was Gemma's father, only I'm not Gemma, am I? Gemma is probably someone I killed. Someone I—" She stopped abruptly, a visible shiver running through her. "And *that*. I haven't even touched on the things I've done. To become Gemma, to become—who knows who else."

"Gemma," Klaus reasoned, "we don't know what you've done."

"We know some, if it's true I'm a ghoul."

"If it's true. Which we don't know for sure."

"Klaus, I—" Gemma flexed her hands. When she spoke, she still sounded deeply shaken. "I don't remember. My life. My life as Gemma. I mean, I have some memories of wandering with my father, before I joined the guard. But before that...memories of my mother. Memories of my childhood. Everything is fuzzy. It always has been."

"Plenty of people don't remember being a child. Early memories are usually fuzzy. Oh, sure, you hear people talk about remembering being in their cradles, but I think that's hogwash. I don't have any solid memories before the age of...about six, I'd say."

Gemma met his gaze. "I don't have any solid memories before the age of ten."

"That's still not proof of anything. I mean, you're not really the type of person to dwell on the past, are you?"

"And the memories I do have of my life with my father." Gemma ran her hands over her face. "On the road. I think we might have been running from something, Klaus. Perhaps we were both ghouls, and we'd done something, or—I don't know, perhaps we were running from other ghouls—"

"Now you're just coming up with random theories, Gemma," Klaus said, trying to sound reasonable.

"No, I'm not. Solena told me—"

"Solena." Klaus snorted. "We're believing her now?"

"I don't have anyone else to ask, Klaus!" She spun on her heel, retreating back to her chair. Perching on its broad arm, she curled one knee up to her chest, looking for all the world like a vulnerable child. "Solena seems to know what I am. Who else am I supposed to ask?"

"Me," Klaus said bluntly. "I know you, Gemma."

"No, you don't."

"Excuse me." Klaus rose to his feet. "Yes, I do. I know you. You..." He took a quick moment to think. "You *are* a sharp-shooter. Even if you can't shoot anymore, that's still part of you. Because you're quiet and observant, and you know how to tune everything out and just focus." He crossed his arms over his chest. "And you're a tracker. You see with more than just your eyes. You can smell rain coming and hear the difference between a bear or a wolf trawling through the brush. You can tell how long ago a fire was lit by what kind of ash was left behind and how it feels to the touch."

Gemma's chin quivered. "None of those things matter."

"You prefer green apples over red ones." Now he was saying the first things that came to mind. "Probably because they're sharp and sour. Like you."

She rolled her eyes.

"But you'll eat whatever kind of apple you're given," he went on, "because you don't like to complain. You don't like to make yourself a burden. You'll also take any shift you're given, but you prefer late at night or very early in the morning. Because you like the quiet and the dark."

"Sure you aren't describing yourself?"

"I'm not. But we are similar in some ways. Not every way. You don't like to hear yourself talk as much as I do."

"Well, that we can agree on."

"In fact, you don't say much at all." He stepped towards her, closing the distance between them. "Not because you're shy. You just don't need to say anything unless it's really important. Which is a good quality to have because, when Gemma's about to say something, everyone knows to shut up and listen."

Gemma looked at him now, all the annoyance gone from her face. Her eyes locked on his. Gone was her impassive expression. Her gaze was more open and uninhibited than he had ever seen from her.

"And when you're not in uniform, you wear a lot of green," he added quietly. "Probably because it helps you blend into the woods. Where you feel most at home. Where you feel safe." He hesitated, then reached out to tuck a strand of hair behind her ear. "Which doesn't sound very ghoulish to me. Aren't they all about graveyards?"

"But that's just it." Gemma's voice was little more than a croak. "That's not me, Klaus. Maybe none of it is. That's *her*."

"Her who? You talk like there's some other Gemma running around out there, and she's the real one. But you are her. And I don't care how you came to be her."

Gemma hugged her arms around herself, looking away. "Even if I killed and ate her?"

"Even if," he said simply. "But I know you. It doesn't matter what you are. I know, at the heart of it all, you're a good person. You might be a fighter. You might even kill when you need to. When you're called upon. But you're not a murderer. There's a difference." He reached out again, gently placing his hands on her shoulders. "And you don't have to fight alone. I'll fight with you. That's why I left, why I went to find Sabine. To see what she knows about ghouls."

He had mentioned this when he came in, but Gemma seemed to hear it for the first time. "That's why you left? I thought—I mean." She ducked her head, pulling her long, dark hair over one shoulder. "I thought you left because of me."

"Well. I did. You were upset about Solena, about this idea that she might be a ghoul. So I left to find out what I could."

"No, I mean—I thought you left because of what happened between us. In the woods. Because of...what I did. What I said."

Klaus shook his head. He dropped his hands and stepped back.

"Klaus?" Gemma prompted.

Klaus turned away from her. He felt jittery and unstable, like old dynamite buried in the earth too long. "That's not why I left, but. I did need some time. To think about it."

"I'm sorry," she said in a low voice. "That I kissed you. I mean—no, I'm *not* sorry, not about that, but. If you felt like I was using you. I'm sorry."

"Gemma, it wasn't you." With some effort, Klaus turned back to face her. "I needed time because—look, I always thought I could never be with you. That you would never want to be with me because I'm weak. For loving someone like Viveca."

"Klaus. I've never thought you weak."

"Broken, then." His voice turned rough. "Because for years, I loved a woman who didn't love me back." He ran a hand over his face. "It's only just now that I can even say that. That I can admit it. She didn't love me." Klaus reached back to grasp his chair, leaning into it. "I always knew what Viveca was. I wasn't blind to that. But I always told myself she did love me, just. In her own way. In whatever way she could." He clenched his hand around the chairback. "But the truth is, Viveca wasn't capable of loving anyone."

He chanced a glance at Gemma and found her watching him steadily. There was no pity in her eyes, and he thanked the stars for that. He didn't think he could bear her pity. But there was pain there. Pain for him.

He didn't want her to hurt, but even so. It was strangely comforting.

"Anyway." He tried to clear his throat. "Doing that for as long as I did—for years—loving someone who doesn't love you, and lying to yourself about it—it does damage. It damaged me. So it's hard for me. To believe that I could deserve someone like you, Gemma. Someone good."

He stopped talking then. It was a lot more talking than he had done in a while. A lot more talking—a lot more *honest* talking—than he had ever done, in fact. But Gryphon had been right, Klaus realized. He'd had time to think it over, on the four-hour trek out to this blasted cottage. It wasn't Gryphon or Gemma or anyone else blaming him for his relationship with Viveca. It was he himself doing that.

He wasn't sure how to stop. It was the sort of thing that would probably take some time. But he had a feeling it might be easier with someone like Gemma by his side.

They were both silent for a moment. Klaus thought maybe Gemma was waiting to see if he would say anything else. He hoped he hadn't horrified her into silence. But then she said, "See, I thought you blamed me. For killing Viveca."

Klaus stared at her. "How could you think that? You saved my life that day."

"I know, but I thought—stones, I don't know. I just thought it was too much. Too much to be between us, too much to overcome."

Klaus pushed himself away from the chair. "I thought so too, for completely different reasons. Took some chatting with Sabine to help me see maybe I was wrong." *And Gryphon,* he thought, though he wasn't going to admit that.

Gemma made a disparaging sound. "Sabine. Whereas it was Roy who told me I was being stupid about it all. About you."

Klaus took a couple of steps towards her, coming within reach of her. "Why is everyone so interested in us?"

Gemma gave a casual shrug. "We're two competent, beautiful people. They're jealous."

Klaus snorted. "You're beautiful." The words slipped from him before he could second-guess himself. "I'm not. Not with these." He gestured, indicating his scarred face.

"Oh, please." Gemma, still perched on the arm of her chair, braced her hands on either side of herself. "You like to think that, I know. You like to throw yourself a right little pity party. But—" She reached out to him and ran a hand down his arm. "Everyone knows scars are sexy."

Goosebumps prickled at Klaus's skin, though he felt oddly warm inside. "Really?"

"Of course. Ask anyone."

Klaus met her gaze. Her hand came to rest in the crook of his elbow, and he felt alight beneath her touch, jittery in a different way than he had been before. There was very little space left between them, and—holding his breath—Klaus shifted forward, moving to occupy that space. Moving until his knees touched hers.

Gemma displayed her complete assent to this closeness by reaching out to lay another hand against his cheek. Klaus felt seen in a way that he never had before. It was terrifying and exhilarating all at once. Making him bold and vulnerable, all at once.

Klaus leaned into Gemma. He gripped her lightly around the middle and watched, his lips hovering over hers, as her eyes fell shut in anticipation.

He didn't make her wait. He kissed her.

There was a slowness to this kiss. A savoring. There was none of the frenzied desperation like the kiss they'd shared before. No, there was a slowness. A carefulness. But also a renewed sense of understanding. A sense of belonging. Klaus reveled in each brush of her lips over his. He reveled in the taste of her as he slipped his tongue inside her mouth. He wrapped his arms behind her, pressing into the small of her back, the warmth of her such a wonderful thing.

Gemma's hand skated down his chest, slipping inside his unbuttoned coat. She had his shirt untucked in a matter of seconds, and then her hand was on his bare chest. Her touch was like lightning, electrifying and thrilling, and nearly every thought left

Klaus's head as Gemma urged him closer, as she tumbled back into the armchair, her legs tangling around him as she pulled him down—

Nearly. Nearly every thought left his head. There was still that one, intrusive thought that would not leave, that broke through the pleasurable haze of Gemma's lips trailing kisses along his jaw. And as unwanted as that thought felt, perhaps it was not such a bad thought to have—a small part of his brain, looking out for him.

"Uh." Bracing one arm beside Gemma, Klaus leaned back. "Gemma."

Gemma gazed at him. She was such a lovely vision, her cloud of dark hair pooling around her, her eyes hooded with desire. "Yes?"

"It's not that I don't want to—because I do, I really, really do—*really*—" This was extremely difficult to put to words, especially like this, hovering over her, her knees pressing into him. "But..."

Some of the desire in her gaze was replaced by confusion. "But?"

"But..." He really could not do this. Not like this. He pushed himself back. "Look. I very much want you. But my relationship with—" He did not want to say her name. Not in this moment between them. "Well, you know with who. My relationship with her was...extremely physical. Almost entirely so. I mean, that's all it was."

Gemma pushed herself up too, carefully sliding out from beneath him. She tucked one leg beneath her, watching him. Letting him talk.

"So…" Klaus raked a hand through his short head of hair. "You're so much more to me. Than just that. And I don't want to—honestly, I'm just not—"

"Not ready," Gemma finished. "To take things that far. Right now." It sounded humiliating when she said it out loud, but when Klaus dared to look at her, there was only a calm acceptance on her face. Nothing to make him feel ashamed.

"Right. Yes," he said. "Just, after everything with her—"

"I know. Klaus, I understand." She rubbed a hand over her collarbone. "I won't pretend I'm not a little disappointed right now—"

"Oh, believe me," Klaus said wryly. "You're not the only one."

"—but that will pass." Her eyes darkened, a shadow passing through them. "But you will stay here, won't you? Tonight. It doesn't have to be—"

"I'm not going anywhere," he assured her. "Not tonight. Not tomorrow." He took her hand, lacing his fingers through hers. "For as long as you'll have me, Gemma. I'll be here."

24

USURPER

G EMMA WOKE SLOWLY, UNSURE of where she was. Filmy sunlight filtered into the room through bottle-blue curtains. The air was cold, but Gemma felt warm, her face pressed into something solid and comforting.

She raised her head.

Of course. She was in the cottage Gryphon had loaned her, sleeping in the single bed in the back room. And beside her was Klaus. Gemma remembered falling asleep ensconced in his arms, her head pillowed on his chest. Sometime during the night, they had become disentangled, leaving only their arms entwined. Gemma surreptitiously wiped his sleeve, noting she had drooled a bit.

She sat up quietly, not wanting to wake him. Watching the gentle rise and fall of his chest. Then she ran a hand over her eyes, wondering what time it was. It was difficult to gauge through the curtains, but it seemed like quite a bit of sunlight was coming through. It must be late, perhaps already past noon. For the first time in weeks, Gemma felt well rested. Still, she looked around the room, taking in every shape, every detail. As was her custom when she woke in a strange place. There wasn't much there; the room was sparsely furnished. A small, rustic chest of drawers. Gemma had left her breeches there, neatly folded. A wobbly little table at the bedside holding a candle in a cast-iron sconce, which they'd blown out before they'd gone to sleep.

That was it. And everything seemed all right. Silent as a mouse, Gemma slipped from beneath the quilted blankets, careful not to disturb Klaus. The room was cold, and gooseflesh rose along her bare legs until she pulled on her breeches. She stepped briefly into the tiny washroom, where a small stand with a basin and a pitcher of water stood against the wall beneath a dirty little mirror. Gemma poured some water into the basin and splashed it onto her face. Chin dripping, she raised her head and gazed into the mirror.

Her own face stared back at her. A little sallow, a little bleary from a long night's sleep. But it was her face. No ghoulish visage. Just her.

She gripped the stand holding the basin. She wasn't sure what to think anymore, about what she was. What she might be. If she was a ghoul, or if Solena was lying. If she was just insane, her ruined eye and those death-like visions driving her mad. But this morning, she didn't feel mad. Her grip on reality felt firmer than ever. Perhaps that was due to finally, finally getting a full night's sleep. Or perhaps that was due to Klaus. His familiar, comforting presence had returned a sense of normalcy to her, even when nothing was normal. It felt at last like no matter what happened, she would be all right.

So long as Klaus was by her side. So long as he was there to remind her who she was.

She left the washroom. The rest of the cottage was as empty as it had been last night. The few things Klaus had brought sat on the table, his gear-bulb lantern, his traveling satchel. His pistol and his rifle. That was sloppy; he should have kept one of those in the bedroom with him. His coat was slung over the back of a chair—a traveling coat, not his uniform coat.

With a smile, Gemma drifted towards the table. *So he does own another coat*, she thought, picking up the garment up to shake it out. But there was something heavy at the bottom, weighing it down, and, frowning, Gemma reached down into the coat's deep pocket. Her fingers came into contact with something hard and angular. Grabbing a hold of it, Gemma pulled the pocket open wide and withdrew the object.

She held it before her, studying it. It was a small, rather unobtrusive black box. The only thing remarkable about it, she noted, peering closer, were the strange markings carved into every side.

"So I've thought about it."

Gemma jumped, nearly dropping the box. She glanced over her shoulder.

Klaus had woken up. He stood in the doorway of the bedroom, his dark-blond hair tousled. He yawned, then went on, "I think that sweater you're wearing must be Gryphon's."

Gemma suppressed a roll of her eyes. "Well, I hardly thought it was Isabelle's."

"It's just wrong," Klaus commented. "I slept next to that sweater all night."

"With *me* in it." Gemma turned to face him. Still holding the box in her hand.

Klaus had opened his mouth to retort, but his face froze when he spotted the box. His eyes flared wide. "Ah—you probably shouldn't touch that."

"Too late for that. What is it?"

Klaus pushed off the doorframe and came to join her. "Well, supposedly it contains a weapon—one that can be used against ghouls. Supposedly, those markings on the box are wards against ghouls. To keep them from touching the box."

Gemma couldn't repress the shudder that spasmed through her. An overwhelming urge to drop the box came over her, but she was already holding it, wasn't she? And it hadn't hurt her, so far as she could tell. "So these wards don't work?"

"Maybe." Klaus narrowed his eyes at her. "Or maybe you aren't a ghoul."

With another shudder, Gemma handed the box over to him. She wasn't sure she wanted to place her hopes in that just yet. She wasn't sure she wanted to allow herself to believe that she wasn't a ghoul. It was easier, for the moment, to accept that she was. "What's in it, then? And where did you find it?"

Klaus launched into an explanation, relating where he'd gone with Sabine and why. As he spoke, they ambled back into the bedroom, both seeming to agree it was too cold to stand out here and talk, since neither of them felt like building a fire. Klaus retold Sabine's story about what had happened in the graveyard, the shadowy creature she'd glimpsed, the young man who'd died. And he told her what had drawn Sabine there in the first place. The strange, wild girl who had appeared in the local village. Looking an awful lot like someone who was known to be dead.

"Wait..." Gemma frowned, thinking over what he'd told her. They'd both climbed back into bed and pulled the blankets over their laps. Gemma clutched the blankets so tightly that her knuckles began to turn white, and she forced herself to relax, smoothing out the sheets. "So Sabine thinks if a ghoul consumes old remains, it can mess with them? With their ability to act human, to *be* human?"

Klaus nodded. He wrapped up his story as he explained how Sabine had thought there could be something buried in the graveyard there, something the dying man thought might help him against the ghoul.

"Sabine looked into it the next day," Klaus went on. "I wanted to get back here, but I stayed long enough for her to poke around the town and find out what she could. Apparently, the locals have an old tale about some man who traveled here from the Desert Kingdom. Some hundred years ago. The tales differed on whether he was a king or a warrior or a holy man of some kind. Stones, he was probably just some common bloke. But the story goes that he died in their little backwoods village, and all his things were buried with him. Evidently, the locals believed he was someone great, because they took out that grand headstone for his burial plot."

"Which you dug up. And that's where you found that," Gemma guessed, nodding at the box in Klaus's lap.

"Yes."

"But what's in it?"

Klaus eyed her shrewdly. As though hesitant to show her this weapon he'd discovered. "You first. What really happened to you while I was gone, Gemma? What happened with Kinsley and the guard? Why were you put on leave?"

"Didn't Gryphon tell you?"

"Only the bit about thinking you're a ghoul. That's all."

"Well." Gemma darted a glance at him. "I sort of started a fire."

"A *fire?*"

"I burned down one of the mausoleums in the royal cemetery."

Klaus stared at her for a long, long moment. Then his lips twitched.

"Klaus," she said warningly.

"Look, I'm sure it wasn't funny at the time—"

"It wasn't. I could have died." And Gryphon and Pila.

"But really." A soft chortle escaped him. "What were you even doing in one of the mausoleums?"

"That's why I really got into trouble. Because I shouldn't have been there. I was at the ball—the ball for Gryphon. I'm sure you heard about it before you left. And I snuck away on my own. Without telling anyone where I was going. I broke protocol."

"Why?" Klaus bent his head to look at her, all traces of laughter gone from his face. "That is—can you tell me?"

She could. She could tell him, she realized. She looked into his scarred face, taking in his rumpled hair and intent dark eyes. He was the one person she could tell anything.

So she did. She started from the beginning, relaying it all, everything she'd seen and experienced around Princess Solena from that first night in the woods. She told him everything, even though he knew some of it already, because she couldn't stop to think right now about what he knew and what he didn't. And Klaus let her tell it. She explained about the ball and their plan to use Gemma as a decoy in place of Princess Solena. She ended with everything that had happened in the mausoleum. And the fire afterwards, which they'd only escaped thanks to Gryphon's intervention.

She didn't tell him about the hallucinations she'd had or what the physicians had been saying about her vision. She didn't confide what Jesine told her all those months ago. It wasn't that she wanted to hide any of that, not anymore. It just didn't seem important right now. Solena was what was important, and all of Gemma's suspicions about her.

When she was done—when she'd told it all—Klaus leaned back against the bed's headboard. He was quiet for a moment, his expression unreadable. Gemma watched him and swallowed, wishing she had a glass of water. Her throat was dry after all that talking.

When Klaus finally spoke, it was the plot he focused on. Which Gemma appreciated. It was the most important thing right now. "So if Solena is a ghoul," he mused, "and she killed the real princess in order to replace her...then this must be some kind of power grab, yes? She thought she could come here, marry the crown prince, and assume a position of power in the court. I mean, there are a lot of people out there who would want that; why not a ghoul?"

"Ye-es. I suppose that would be her plan."

"But the thing is," Klaus continued, "the crown prince isn't here. He never was, since Garrett took off before Solena arrived. So what is her plan now?"

"Well..." Gemma hadn't thought much about that. Court intrigue and political scheming weren't really her strong suit. "Perhaps she thinks she can marry Gryphon instead?"

"Maybe. Or maybe she'll take a more direct route to the throne. Maybe she'll become the king."

Gemma straightened. "What do you mean?"

"I mean, why was she in the king's apartments that night? With a knife?" Klaus looked grim. "Ghouls can become anyone, right, if they consume their remains? So maybe her new plan is to kill the king. And take his place."

Horror sluiced through Gemma. Of course. Why hadn't she thought of that? But— "Why hasn't she done it yet? I mean, that attack on the king was a week ago—"

"And he's been closely guarded ever since," Klaus pointed out. "Very closely guarded. Perhaps she hoped to get to him that night in his apartments, without anyone knowing. Only, Gryphon happened to be out wandering and discovered her. Now she's got to be more careful. Find a way to take the king, kill him, and replace him without anyone knowing. She's probably used this time to observe and plan. To find just the right time to do it."

"If you're right—if this is true—then we have to do something. She could enact this plan at any moment. I don't care if Kinsley's put me on leave, we have to warn the king and stop Solena." Gemma looked at Klaus. "We have to go back to the castle. Now." She pointed at the little box. "And we're taking that with us. You can explain what's in it on the way."

⸻◆⸻

By the time they reached the castle, the sun was sinking beyond the horizon, the sky a dark cobalt in the east. Impatient as she was, Gemma agreed to wait in the copse of trees—the copse where she and Klaus had first kissed—while he slipped into the barracks to find out about the goings-on in the castle tonight. Gemma, weary from the trek back into the city proper, sat on the forest floor while she waited for Klaus to return, picking apart pine needles in an effort to distract herself.

Happily, Klaus was only gone for about fifteen minutes. When he returned, the first thing Gemma asked was, "Did you get it?"

Klaus nodded, removing a long barrel pistol from beneath his coat and handing it over to Gemma. It was one of hers, an older model she didn't use much anymore. "Already loaded," he told her.

"Good." She hung it in her holster opposite her other pistol. "What did you find out?"

Klaus reported that a state dinner was taking place tonight, and King Victor, Prince Gryphon, and Princess Solena were all expected to attend. "Gryphon and the king might already be there," Klaus said. "Princess Solena, I don't know."

"I doubt it. A princess must always arrive *fashionably late*. She's probably still in her quarters, getting ready."

After some debate, they decided Klaus should go ahead to the dinner to warn Gryphon and the king. Gemma, meanwhile, would sneak into the castle and track down Solena. They wondered briefly if they should try and recruit other guards to their plan, but Gemma didn't see the point. "We don't have time to try and convince anyone."

"I don't disagree," Klaus said heavily. "But you'll have to be careful moving about the castle."

"Klaus. It's me."

"Right, I forgot." Still, he looked edgy, uncertain.

"Klaus." Gemma held his gaze with hers. "I'll be fine."

"I know. I know you will."

But he was still worried. Gemma could tell. Standing on tip-toe, she leaned in towards him, placed a hand upon his scarred cheek, and kissed him. It was a long, lingering kiss. Long enough to steal her breath away. Long enough to calm her own nerves.

When they broke away from each other, Klaus's face was warmer beneath her hand than it had been before. "Right," he said, his voice low in his throat. "I suppose we'd better go."

"Yes. We'd better." She dipped her chin, indicating the rifle slung over his shoulder, and asked in a deadpan tone, "Are you sure about using that?"

The look Klaus gave her said he knew she was teasing him. "I may not be a sharpshooter, but I can use a rifle. I had to bring a certain beast down once or twice, using this." He gestured to the pistol strapped to her waist, the one he'd brought her. "Are you sure about that?"

Gemma spared him a wry smile. "I told you before. Even I can't miss if I'm close enough. I just have to get close enough."

Klaus headed straight into the castle to get to the king's state dinner, while Gemma found her own way in. She wore a coat of Isabelle's that she'd found in the cottage, one with a deep hood that she could pull over her head to conceal her face. The coat was a little tight, but Gemma didn't need to fasten it. She just needed the hood.

Disguised as she was, getting into the castle was easy enough. Prince Garrett wasn't the only one who knew secret ways in and out of the castle. The tough part, she'd figured, would be getting into Princess Solena's quarters; now that the window was bolted, there was only one way in or out—through the front door. Gemma had a couple of different ideas to try, but as it turned out, she didn't need either of them. Because Solena wasn't in her quarters.

"Careful, there," one servant admonished another as they nearly ran into each other. They were down on the ground floor of the castle in the back service corridors. Gemma, crouched at the top of a staircase leading out from the depths of the castle, listened and watched from around the corner.

"Sorry." The servant, a square-jawed woman carrying a stack of towels that was taller than her, looked flustered. "Princess Solena's decided to bathe down in the old stone baths. Last minute, of course, we had nothing prepared for her."

The other servant, a reedy man, chuckled. "And she needs a hundred towels, is that it?"

"She's a princess. She needs a thousand towels."

Gemma waited as both servants hurried off in different directions. Then she headed down the corridor in the same direction as the square-jawed woman, taking care to keep a distance between the two of them, remaining unobtrusive.

The old baths were here on the ground floor in a massive chamber built from stone with large sunken tubs. The castle had been fitted with modern piping nearly twenty years ago, so most guest quarters had their own bathroom and tub, including Princess Solena's. But the old baths were still in use, and occasionally, guests enjoyed them as a kind of novelty. Traditionally, the baths were public, but Gemma assumed Princess Solena would use one of the private tubs in the chamber. Or she might have reserved the entire baths to herself. They were not much in demand anyway.

Gemma felt the air change even before she reached the baths, the stone walls on either side of her growing moist, the scent of herbal oils in the air—fragrant lavender, stinging verbena, and bright lemon. She slowed as she reached the wide opening in the corridor up ahead and eased around the corner, entering the baths.

The stone chamber was entirely lit by flickering candles lining dozens of recessed shelves carved straight into the walls. Thick whorls of steam spiraled up from the hot water filling the sunken tubs; the baths were fed by a natural spring and heated beneath the floor itself. The steam was thick enough to provide some cover, but it also meant Gemma couldn't see anyone coming until they were nearly upon her. This was demonstrated almost immediately when she stepped into the chamber, then quickly backpedaled, spotting the square-jawed woman with all the towels nearby. Thankfully, the servant had her back to Gemma and was soon out of sight.

Releasing a silent breath, Gemma slipped into the chamber again and crept between the sunken tubs, dispersing clouds of steam as she moved through them. Her gaze darted in every direction, each step she took wary and deliberate. The tubs were lined with decorative modern tiling, which Gemma thought quite foolish, given how slippery tile became when damp. So she moved carefully, slowly planting the soft soles of her boots over the floor while her gaze scanned from left to right. Keeping an eye out for Solena or anyone else.

But the deeper Gemma ventured into the baths, the emptier they seemed to become. Gemma's skin grew sticky with sweat beneath her clothes, and her thick hair frizzed, escaping the loose knot she'd bound it in. Her spine grew more rigid with every step she took, muscles tensing, shoulders hunching. Where was the princess? Even if she'd reserved the baths to herself, shouldn't there have been plenty of servants here to attend her? Perhaps her ladies as well?

Edging around one of the enormous sunken tubs, Gemma squinted, leaning to peer down into the tub. But it was empty and undisturbed, only lightly rippling as fresh water pumped in and out. Gemma approached another tub, billows of steam surging from it, but this one, too, was empty. How many more tubs were there? Gemma had become lost in the steam; she wasn't sure where in the chamber she was, or how much of it she had searched. With every passing second, her sense of unease grew, her heartbeat quickening until it felt like it was tripping over itself.

This wasn't right. Solena wasn't here.

"Excuse me, are you supposed to be here?"

Gemma whirled, barely catching herself as her heel slid over slick tile. Her mouth was already open to spin some lie for a servant.

But it was no servant who stood before her.

It was a hooded figure, clad in black from head to toe.

Gemma froze. Every little hair rose on the back of her neck, despite her clammy skin. For a moment, she and the masked figure stood eyeing each other. The figure, brandishing a dagger. Gemma, gauging the distance between them. Trying to figure out her next move.

She didn't figure it out fast enough. The dark figure shot forward, moving more quickly than Gemma expected. She snapped an arm out, slamming the hilt of her dagger into Gemma's left temple.

A shock of pain erupted inside Gemma's head. Stars exploded before her vision, and the floor beneath her seemed to tilt.

Her knees buckled and she collapsed to the floor, unconsciousness tugging at her. But before she gave in to it, her vision cleared—just for a moment—and she looked up.

The hazy black-clad figure wavering above her removed her hood.

It was the last person Gemma expected to see.

Then darkness stole over her, and she saw no more.

25

CAGED

G RYPHON STOOD IN THE murky darkness of the castle crypt and gazed up at the stone sculpture carved into a likeness of his mother. The sculptor had done a good job at capturing her thick, curly hair, her graceful figure, her rounded face. Plum cheeks and wide eyes conveyed her softness and curiosity. At least, that was how Gryphon remembered her, soft and curious. But he had precious few memories to inform him of her character, and the only person who could give him more had always refused to do so.

His mother was entombed down here with all the other Glen kings and queens of the past. This shrine to her memory had been constructed within a cavernous grotto, closed off from the crypt's long corridor by an embellished iron gate. The grotto housed her remains, marked by the stone sculpture carved in her likeness. Because she'd hailed from the old Forest Kingdom, whose people had valued battle and valor above all else, the stone walls of the grotto were hung with swords and axes, family heirlooms she had inherited from her father. They were fine weapons, Gryphon supposed, but he couldn't help but feel that her paintbrushes would have been more fitting adornments.

He stiffened as footsteps rang out behind him, echoing beneath the low stone ceiling. The crypt was full of ornate caskets, stone memorials, and decorative reliquaries, but the only company to keep down here was the dead, and Gryphon would have preferred to remain alone with them. With her.

Unfortunately, that was not to be. Someone stepped up beside him, a tall, solid figure, though not quite so tall as Gryphon. They stood in cold, empty silence for a minute or more, but Gryphon was not silent on the inside. On the inside, he was seething, anger mounting with each passing second. Finally, into that dangerous silence, King Victor said, "She was beautiful, your mother."

"Don't you dare." It really didn't matter what his father said; Gryphon was ready to snap. His anger had been building all this time, he realized. Ever since his father had discovered Gryphon's heritage and come up with his insane—no, his *offensive* plot to use him to lay claim to the Forest Kingdom. But for him to speak of Gryphon's mother, for him to *praise* her— "Don't you dare act as though you had any regard for her."

"I did." The king turned to him, and though Gryphon saw some of his own outrage mirrored in his father's face, what he mostly saw was confusion. "I loved Alivia—"

"I don't know how you can even say that." Gryphon's voice was a low growl. It felt like the beast was very close to the surface, prowling restlessly beneath Gryphon's skin. The beast always came awake with Gryphon's rage, especially when that rage was colored with the hurt and betrayal and rejection his father had visited upon him for his entire life. "You never talk about her.

Even when I asked, even when I wanted you to. And you betrayed her as soundly as you betrayed me, you—" He broke off, trembling with the effort of keeping himself contained.

"I didn't betray her," Victor said softly.

Gryphon scoffed at that. "We never talk about it. You've never addressed it. But I'm not a child anymore, Victor. I have realized, you know, that Garrett is only a year younger than me, yet I was three years old when my mother died—"

When the king spoke, his voice was calm and steady, and that only angered Gryphon more. That his father dared stay calm when Gryphon was itching to burst out of his own skin. "I didn't love Garrett's mother the way I loved Alivia," Victor said. "She was a lovely person, but I was never in love with her."

"And that makes it all right?" Gryphon exploded. Stones, it made it worse. Especially for poor Garrett and his mother.

"Your mother was the love of my life," his father said, and still, he was calm. More than calm. His tone, his entire demeanor, was subdued. "But she didn't feel the same way about me."

"What does that mean?"

"We were very good friends," Victor said simply. "We had been since we'd first met. For me, that friendship quickly grew into something more. For Alivia...it didn't." Something almost like a smile touched his face. "And she was very clear about that. Not at first, but eventually. She was even more direct a person than I am. She wasn't trying to hurt me. She just believed in being plain about her feelings."

Gryphon stared at his father. There was a pained expression on his face, though whether that stemmed from recalling such sore memories or from having to speak of this at all—his father never, *ever* spoke about anything so common as love or feelings—Gryphon could not say.

"Our marriage was political," the king continued. "I always knew that. But I suppose I hoped that someday..." He trailed off. "Eventually, I accepted it. She was aware of my relationship with Garrett's mother. She had no problem with it, believe me."

Gryphon let out a terrible, empty laugh. "I suppose you'll have me believe she had a similar arrangement."

"She may have." His father's voice became very quiet. "I don't know. I didn't want to know."

Gryphon tried for another disbelieving laugh but couldn't quite manage it. He turned and stalked away from his father, clasping his hands together behind his head. Was he supposed to feel sorry for Victor? Was that why he was telling him this, so all would be forgiven, and Gryphon would agree to go along with his father's mad plans to invade the Black Forest? But there were plenty of other sins his father hadn't answered for yet.

"And what about me?" Gryphon spun around to face his father. "What about how you betrayed me, Victor? How do you think she" —He stuck a finger in the air, pointing at the sculpture of his mother— "would feel, knowing what you did to me? Knowing you exiled her only son!"

He waited for his father to shout back at him. He wanted that, stones, he wanted his father to shout like he always did. But still, Victor only said in a tired voice, "I did what I thought was right. At the time."

"What was *right*—" Gryphon curled his fingers in towards his palms, his hands becoming clenched fists. "You avoided me my entire life. You made it perfectly clear with every passing year that you held less and less interest in me. That you were disappointed in the heir you had. So let's stop pretending, Father." The word slipped from him without Gryphon even realizing it. "You were just looking for an excuse to get rid of me, weren't you? You couldn't wait to replace me with Garrett. The truth is, my mishap with that witch provided you with the opportunity you'd been waiting for!"

Victor met his gaze, and the look on his face was grim. Grim—and remorseful.

It should have been vindicating. Instead, Gryphon felt it like a blow. A blow from his own father. "You're not going to deny it, are you?" he asked numbly. He had expected a denial. Some small, pitiful part of him had wanted a denial.

His father closed his eyes. "You don't see it."

"See what?" Gryphon raked a shaking hand back through his hair, then pressed the same hand to his chest. Stones, he felt furiously unstable, desperate to escape, desperate to let the beast surge out of him. He could feel it snarling in his chest, eager to be unleashed. Not so he could strike at his father, not so he could rend and kill. No, he just wanted to flee. He wanted to run from this place, tear into the countryside and never come back.

"It was never you, Gryphon," his father said.

"Oh, please," Gryphon snapped. "I told you, I don't want to pretend anymore, so if you're going to spout some nonsense about the politics of it all, and give me that same old line about placating the Mariner king, I don't want to hear it—"

"That's not what I was going to say." The king's voice turned exasperated, and Gryphon saw a glint of anger had finally entered his father's eyes. "But perhaps you're right. Perhaps we should stop pretending, Gryphon. You're always going on about how you can't wait to get out of here and return to your new life you're so happy with. So why don't you stop pretending this didn't all work out for the best for everyone. Yourself included. Stones, if we're really going to stop pretending, then you should be thanking me!"

"*Thanking you?*" Gryphon could not believe those words had just come out of his father's mouth. "Thanking—stones, do you have any idea what I've been through these past six years, any idea what I've had to—" He whirled around, turning his back on the king. Afraid of what he might do if he had to look at him a minute longer.

"I was fourteen years old when you sent me from this castle," Gryphon fumed, pacing back and forth, "with only a boy younger than ten for company. I had no place to go, no one to turn to. I slept in abandoned homes, I slept in the woods, I traveled to the Desert Kingdom and back—"

"That's—you didn't have to live like a vagabond," his father sputtered. "I secured an old manor house for you in the Mariner Kingdom—"

"Like I was about to go live there! When the Mariner court and their superstitious fears were the reason you exiled me! Of course, I finally found myself in the Black Forest, I finally found my way into that accursed castle, and then I spent two years, *two years*, locked up in my own dungeon every day, terrified that I would escape and kill someone. I can control it now, but for six hundred and ninety-four miserable days, I became the beast against my will. For six hundred and ninety-four days, I was trapped in that castle, for six hundred and ninety-four days, I didn't see the sun."

Gryphon slammed a fist into the wall, so hard that the stone cracked and the crypt shook around them. One of the swords affixed to the wall fell to the floor with a great clatter. "And you want me to thank you!"

He wheeled around to face his father. The king was white in the face. Gryphon was suddenly struck by how small his father seemed, how small and old. King Victor was nearly fifty years of age, but no one would ever have called him old or frail. Yet in this moment, he seemed so.

His father opened his mouth to respond, but before he could, a long, grinding *squeal* sounded out above them, like stone scraping over stone. This was followed by a resounding *thud* that echoed ominously around them, booming down the crypt's long corridor and resounding off its cavernous walls.

Gryphon recognized the sound. It was the crypt's heavy stone door slamming shut. Only, that door was never shut before midnight.

Filled with foreboding, Gryphon exchanged a look with his father. "Where are your guards?" he asked, realizing for the first time how alone they were here. His father always had guards with him, especially since they'd discovered that intruder in his apartments last week.

"I left them upstairs, of course." Victor did not sound worried. Only vaguely irritated. "Like you told me to."

"Like I told you to?" Gryphon was baffled.

"In that note you sent me, asking me to meet you here before the state dinner."

"What are you talking about?" Now Gryphon was becoming irritated. "I didn't ask you to meet me. You sent a messenger to me, telling me to come down here—"

He broke off. Gryphon stared at his father, and his father stared at him. Comprehension seemed to dawn upon them at the same time.

"Damn," said his father in a remarkably calm voice.

"Yes." Gryphon cast his gaze around. The iron gate separating this grotto from the crypt's main corridor stood open, just as Gryphon and his father had left it. But before Gryphon could take even a single step towards it, the gate swung shut with a great *clang*. He watched in dismay as five familiar figures appeared on the other side of the gate, all dressed in black from head to toe. Just like the intruder in the king's apartments.

All of them held a knife in each hand. Ten knives altogether.

Completely at ease, King Victor stepped around Gryphon to pick up the sword that had fallen to the ground.

"What the hell are you doing?" Gryphon demanded in a whisper.

"We can take them," his father said confidently.

Oh, by the Gift. Gryphon didn't know whether to roll his eyes or laugh hysterically or maybe even cry. "There are five of them."

"Yes. Exactly."

"I'm not even sure they can be killed."

The king frowned at him as he held his sword aloft, adjusting his grip on its hilt. "What do you mean?"

"Well, depending on which story you believe," Gryphon said in a droll tone, "they're either ghouls or a legendary secret force of elite assassins. Or both."

"Ah." Still, his father did not sound dismayed. Only briefly stymied. "Well. We can at least hold them off. Surely you can manage several of them on your own? If you turn into that beast thing?" He eyed Gryphon with a measure of trepidation, the first sign of concern he'd showed at all. "You did say you can control it? I mean—" His father coughed. "You won't be at risk of, er—killing anyone you don't intend to?"

His meaning could not have been plainer. His father wanted to know if Gryphon would be in danger of killing him. "I've managed to stay in control before," Gryphon said in a level voice, "around people I care about."

The silence that followed was extremely pointed. Victor and Gryphon eyed each other, obviously both wondering the same thing.

"Well," his father said, "I don't see that we have any other choice."

Gryphon sighed. "No. I suppose not." He began to remove his clothes, quickly unbuttoning his coat and shrugging out of it. If they lived through this, he'd rather not be stuck down here with his father, completely nude, for who knew how long.

Once he'd divested himself of most of his clothes and tossed them, rather neatly, into a pile in the back corner of the grotto, he stepped abreast of his father, who stood at the ready, still wielding his sword as he faced down the hooded assassins on the other side of the gate. "What are they waiting for?" his father murmured.

"No idea," said Gryphon, "but I'd wager we don't want to find out." He exchanged a quick glance with Victor, who gave a sharp nod in return. "Here we go," Gryphon muttered.

He called to the beast.

And the beast, eager and ready, burst free.

26

CHANGELING

KLAUS STOOD NEAR THE front door of the grand stateroom, trying to be inconspicuous as he searched the growing crowd for Gryphon. Guests were already gathering for the state dinner, but Klaus did not see the king yet, and that was worrying. Unlike Princess Solena, the king of the Glen Kingdom did not usually arrive *fashionably late* to his events.

Klaus began to circle the luxurious hall, relaxed on the outside and tense within. It was a long room, built to hold the long dining tables set in rows down the center of the chamber. Crystal chandeliers hung from the high ceilings, bright but tasteful, not so gaudy as the colossal fixtures that hung in the throne hall. Beneath those glaring, glistening lights, Klaus spotted a uniformed Roy standing guard near a side entrance. Roy met his gaze before Klaus could decide whether to talk to him or not. Roy's dark eyes widened, so Klaus headed towards him.

"Klaus," Roy said in a low voice, "you're back. Did you find Gemma? Is she—"

"Where's Gryphon?" Klaus asked brusquely. "I need to talk to him."

"I don't think he's arrived yet." Roy glanced past Klaus, scanning the room. His eyes alighted on someone, and Klaus spun, expecting Gryphon's burly form. But that wasn't who Roy was looking at. "Here's Princess Solena. I wasn't sure if she would come tonight."

Klaus followed Roy's line of sight. This long hall didn't boast any grand stairwells like the one in the ballroom; it was set in a single story. But there was a wide dais at the back of the room, leading out from a discreet door to a private chamber where royal guests could make themselves comfortable before entering the hall. This was where Princess Solena entered, flanked by two of her own Desert guards in their red and gold uniforms. The princess had dressed to match them, bedecked in a bloodred gown with golden pleats peeking out from beneath her full overskirt. She even wore a golden sash like her guards, fastened diagonally across her chest from left shoulder to right hip. The gown was resplendent, rich enough for a princess, but also severe in its lack of bows and frills, giving her a marshal quality. As though she had dressed for battle, not dinner.

As Solena stepped forward—as she paused while she was announced, then descended into the room—Klaus watched her. If Solena was already here, then Gemma must have missed her. Or, he thought with a chill, he hoped she had. Because if Gemma had encountered her, and the princess was still here...

Then something had happened to Gemma.

Still, if Solena was here, then she wasn't going after the king right now. And Klaus wasn't about to let her. He started forward, ignoring Roy, who said, "Klaus? Klaus, what are you doing?"

Klaus wove through the growing crowd and strode right up to Princess Solena, aware that his own uniform was not as smart or pressed or clean as it should be, aware that he wore a day's worth of stubble on his chin. Still, he stopped before the princess—close enough that her guards went on alert, shifting towards her—and made a crisp bow. "Your Highness."

"Klaus," the princess greeted him, half-turning from the small group of nobles she'd been about to greet. Her dark hair was swept up behind her head and secured with a sparkling tiara, making her look even more regal than usual. And yet, Klaus swore he detected a hint of something in her voice—alarm, maybe—something that edged her tone.

But when he rose from his bow, she looked like she always did—a little haughty, a little bored, her dark eyes unfathomable. "I haven't seen you in some time," she said to him.

"I took some personal leave, Your Highness."

"Hmm." Solena's tone turned petulant. She ran a gloved finger across her bottom lip as she eyed Klaus, then asked, "Have you seen Prince Gryphon? He was supposed to escort me, but he didn't turn up. I fear I shall find this whole affair dreadfully boring without him."

Klaus looked at her for a moment before he answered. Not only was there an edge to her voice, he thought, but now there was something in her eyes too. As though she was trying to communicate something to him. Seized by a sudden thought, Klaus said, "Yes, Your Highness, I've just seen him. He only just arrived." He proffered her his arm. "Shall I take you to him?"

Solena's guards shifted again, but the princess stepped forward with alacrity before they could close in on her. "Yes indeed." Solena took his arm. "Take me to him."

Holding her a bit more tightly than necessary, Klaus led Solena through the room. More and more people were arriving, the sparse crowd becoming a packed throng, the stateroom bursting with lords and ladies dressed in their finest. Klaus was glad for this; it made it easier to isolate the princess from her guards, whom they quickly left behind as they wove through the room.

"I suppose this isn't quite appropriate," Klaus murmured, "a lowly guard escorting a princess. Aren't you afraid of what people will say?"

Solena's smile looked more like a gritting of teeth, and when she spoke, she sounded that way as well, grinding the words out. "I'm far more concerned with putting distance between me and my guards. Since I am quite sure they are trying to kill me. Pick up the pace, will you?"

Klaus nearly stopped dead at those words. Solena tightened her grip on his arm, practically dragging him forward, and he caught himself before he could stumble. Lowering his voice further, Klaus leaned towards the princess. "Why would you think that?"

Solena squeezed his arm again. "Get me out of this room, and I'll tell you."

Klaus was only too happy to do so. That had been his plan to begin with. He smoothly guided the princess to one of the covert side entrances, a broad door concealed to look like another gilded panel in the wall. Together, they slipped from the stateroom into a little-used side corridor—where Klaus had stashed his rifle.

He didn't immediately retrieve the rifle. But as soon as the side door was firmly shut behind them, Klaus gripped the "princess" by the arms and pushed her against the wall, pinning her there. Leaving very little space between them. A brief look of surprise passed over Solena's face, but it was gone in an instant. She made no pretense at outrage this time. She said in a rather toneless voice, "Such rough treatment from my favorite guard."

"Yes, well." Klaus was glad she had decided to drop the princess act. "I know what you are."

"If that's true, then you should realize how easily I could get away from you," she said. "If I wanted. You should realize how easily I could slip away. Into the *shadows*."

Klaus searched her face, looking for some clue as to her motives. But the edgy look he'd glimpsed in her eyes was gone. Her expression was impenetrable. Grudgingly, Klaus released her, dropping his arms. But he didn't step back to give her any room to maneuver.

Solena reached up to pat a hand over her intricate hairstyle, then adjusted her tiara, which had fallen slightly askew. The gesture could have been self-conscious, but Solena made it look imperious. "So she told you everything."

"Who?"

"Gemma." Solena's eyes flashed. "Where is she?"

"She was going to look for you up in your quarters," Klaus said in a tight voice. "If you've done something to her—"

But Solena cursed softly. "Then they might already have her."

"Who might?" Klaus demanded. "You've admitted you're a ghoul. Your guards have obviously discovered you if they want you dead. So who could have Gemma? Or are you saying they know she's a ghoul too?"

"You've got it all wrong," Solena shot back. Her hands clenched into fists down by her sides. "My guards want me dead because they aren't taking orders from me. Not anymore."

This was getting more confusing with every word. "You're not talking sense."

Solena tipped back her head, looking exasperated. "That's because you think you know everything. But you don't. You think I'm the only ghoul here. You think I've been working on my own this whole time, don't you? But you're wrong. This has never been my plot. I was only a part of it."

Without quite meaning to, Klaus stepped back from her, scrubbing a hand through his hair. Absorbing this new information, thinking through the implications. If what Solena said was true...and that was a rather tenuous "if"...then she was right, they had this all wrong. If it was true there was more than one ghoul among the Desert Kingdom delegation, then the king—and Gemma—were still in danger, even though he had Solena cornered. Mind racing, Klaus asked, "Who else? Who else from your delegation—"

"Originally, it was just me and my ladies-in-waiting." Though he'd given her space, Solena didn't move away from the wall. She smoothed her hands down her bloodred skirt as though chasing away wrinkles, then braced her arms on either side of her, pressing them into the wall. "It's true that most ghouls do operate alone. But we've been together for a long time. A cabal of us. My ladies and I."

Klaus narrowed his eyes at her. "But you weren't always Princess Solena. Were you? You killed her and took her place that first night we met. Out in the woods, on your way here."

"Yes." Solena's tone became scornful. "That little weakling. She'd gotten cold feet, you see. Decided to come and warn King Victor. So she had to be replaced."

"Cold feet...wait, what?"

"She wasn't human, Klaus." Solena spoke slowly and clearly, as though she thought him hard of hearing. Or perhaps just an idiot. "She wasn't the original princess. She was a ghoul herself. A changeling. She replaced the real Princess Solena years ago when she was just a child. When the human Solena died."

And then Klaus understood. "In that plague."

"Yes." Solena pushed herself off the wall, taking a wary step forward. "All the Desert princesses died in that strange plague. That was when we came up with the idea to replace one of them. But it was tricky. The princesses were all sequestered while they were ill. And no one was allowed near their remains. The contagion, you know. But finally, we got to the last one. Princess Solena. She wasn't even a direct heir, only the daughter of the king's sister. But if she had lived, she would have been heir after all the king's daughters died. She was only eight years old. We got to her remains, and one of us took her place."

"One of you," Klaus repeated. "So this other ghoul was 'Princess Solena.' All these years. Until you killed her. Less than a league from the castle."

"Dear little Lena." Solena gave a mocking sigh. "Stones, she really was a weakling. Oh, don't look so stricken, Klaus. She was a ghoul. She can be remade one day, claim another set of bones." Solena took her voluminous skirt in her hands and spread it wide as though to indicate her human body. "We die as easily as other humans when we inhabit bones like these. But that isn't truly an end for us. We continue to exist, but as nothing. Lost to the shadow, trapped in death and darkness. And it's not easy to claw our way free. It can take decades. But eventually, we emerge to consume another set of bones. Lay claim to another identity."

"So you killed her," Klaus said. "The 'other' Princess Solena. It was her Gemma found in the woods that night, dying. But what happened to—" Before he could complete the question, he remembered what she said and put it together. That she was working with a cabal of ghouls, her ladies-in-waiting. "Let me guess. Some of your ladies were there too that night. They took the previous Solena's body. Made it disappear. While *you* approached us as the new Princess Solena."

Solena dropped her skirt, smoothing it over again. "Yes. The transformation usually takes time, but we can force it more quickly. But it's not easy, and there's a price to pay." She pulled a face. "I wasn't lying, my first few days here, when I complained of headaches. I'd also taken the identity of a boy to sneak up on Lena before I assumed her identity. Those rapid transformations took their toll."

"Then the plan was to infiltrate Glen Castle's court?" As he and Gemma had deduced. "Marry the crown prince? Take up a position of power here?"

"Yes. Only when I arrived, I discovered the crown prince wasn't here. So everything went wrong from the start. And I suppose that's why my superior decided to step in."

"Your superior?" Klaus echoed. "You aren't in charge?"

"Why would I be?" Solena almost sounded amused, but there was something bitter in her words as well. "Because I'm the princess? But I've told you. Only a few weeks ago, I was among the princess's ladies-in-waiting. Any one of us could have been chosen to become the new Solena. Princess Solena is nothing more than a pawn in this plot."

"Somehow, I have trouble imagining you as a mere pawn," Klaus said dryly. "So this superior of yours. Who are they? Are they among your delegation?"

"Yes, but I don't know who they are. I didn't think she *was* among us. She was meant to stay in the Desert Kingdom. But I think she must have been here this whole time. She could be anyone."

"Then how can you be certain she's here?"

"Oh, she's here," Solena said grimly. "One of the ladies told me. Not out of loyalty or friendship, you understand. My ladies are loyal to her, not me. Lady Marisel was quite smug when she told me I would be punished for straying from our plans. Little idiot," she added scathingly.

"What do you mean, straying from your plans? What did you do?"

Solena gave him a pitying look. As though he should have understood this by now. "I've been following my own agenda ever since I began to suspect Gemma was a ghoul. I thought the crown knowingly had a ghoul working for them, I thought everything had gone wrong from the start. First the crown prince was spirited away before I arrived and replaced by his disowned brother. And then to find the king had a ghoul serving him, well, I thought we'd been found out. I confided my suspicions to my ladies, and the next thing I knew, we received new orders. New orders that made me even more suspicious—but not of your people."

"I don't understand."

"I didn't go to your king's apartments that night to kill him, Klaus," Solena said impatiently. "I went there to make sure he hadn't already been killed. To make sure my superior hadn't taken his place." Her tone turned resentful. "And then I ran into Gemma. And I realized, for the first time, that she didn't know what she was. And that's a problem, you see. Because my superior knows all about her. She knows more about her than Gemma herself knows, more than I ever guessed. Gemma has no idea how much danger she's in."

27

GHOULISH

G EMMA'S HEAD WAS ACHING again. That was the first thing she noticed, even before she opened her eyes. But it was a different pain than the one she'd dealt with over the last few days. This was not a stabbing pain behind her eye, but a dull throb that ran from the crown of her head to the nape of her neck.

Wincing, she opened her eyes.

And found herself in a gloomy, blackened, burnt-out husk of a ruin.

Gemma lurched upright and immediately regretted it, the throbbing in her head intensifying. Panic threatened, building in her chest, but as she looked around, her tangled hair falling around her face, Gemma realized she was not stuck in another hallucination. Frighteningly familiar as this state of decay might be, there was a *realness* to it, a gritty, solid feel that was nothing like her prior visions. The floor beneath her was solid stone, though a fine layer of ash lay over it, and streaks of soot marred its surface. Iron braziers set atop tall metal stands stood in the back corners of the ruin, great flames and dark smoke rushing out into the night.

Gemma looked up. The roof of this building was almost entirely gone, leaving it open to the sky. And that's when she realized where she was.

It was the mausoleum. The one where she'd fought the stranger. The one she'd set on fire. It was chillingly similar to the vision she'd had, here in this same place.

But this wasn't a vision. It was real.

"Good, you're awake. I was afraid I hit you too hard."

Gemma snapped her head around. A thrill of shock flashed through her when she saw a young woman, clad in black, step into view, but then she remembered: she'd already seen her. In the baths, right before she blacked out.

The girl who'd knocked her out, the girl who stood before her now...was *Pila.* Princess Solena's handmaiden.

Gemma shook her head in rueful disbelief. "You're a ghoul."

Pila laughed quietly. "I'm *the* ghoul," she said, coming within the blazing light of the braziers. The flames cast dancing shadows over her pale face.

Unobtrusively, Gemma's hand strayed to her waist, looking for her long barrel pistol. But it wasn't there. None of her weapons were. She'd been disarmed. Vexed but trying to hide it, Gemma said, "Were you Princess Solena? And now you've killed Pila and taken her form instead?"

Pila sneered down at her. She was so different, Gemma thought. So unlike the deferential handmaiden she had come to know. Her jet-black hair was pulled back into the same smart knot Pila always wore, but rather than a simple maid's dress, she wore a sleeveless black robe that was so long, it trailed the dusty stone floor. Beneath it, she wore black trousers and a tailored black shirt, cuffed snugly around her wrists and neck.

"I was never *Princess Solena*." With a dramatic sweep of her robe, Pila turned to climb the dais that had housed the mounted memorial of some great lord. The memorial itself, the sculptured likeness, had been removed, no doubt to be restored. In its place was a plain, black ceramic bowl and a stone mortar and pestle. As the ghoul turned her attention to these bowls, she added, "But, yes. I killed Pila and took her form last week. I needed a new form, and Pila was spilling secrets. Well. She didn't know she was. But she was a convenient replacement, and I enjoyed the irony."

Spilling secrets. Of course. Pila—the real Pila—was the one who had told Gemma about ghouls, told her they were shape-changers that haunted graveyards and battlefields, looking for fresh remains.

"That was why 'Pila' was so ill afterwards," Pila continued. She poured the contents of the stone mortar into the ceramic bowl, then began mixing them together. "The transformation took its toll, as it always does. It was only in the last few days that I recovered, or I would have acted earlier to curb *Solena's* insolence. And I would have taken you before now."

So Solena wasn't the only ghoul here. Gemma wondered how many of them there were, but that wasn't her most pressing concern right now. Her most pressing concern was finding her pistol. "Then Solena wasn't in charge of all this?"

Pila made a disparaging sound. "Of course not. Though Solena certainly fancied herself in charge. She didn't know I was here. She didn't know who I was."

"So that was you." *The night of the ball. That wasn't Pila who accompanied me.* It was this ghoul before her now. And... "Were you the one I fought in the mausoleum?" But that didn't quite fit. Gemma tried to remember all the things the stranger had said to her that night before the fire broke out...

"Yes, I accompanied you to the ball," Pila said, "but no, I didn't stoop to fighting you." The ghoul turned away from the stone mount to face Gemma. "Don't you understand? That was Solena. She thought she was so clever, finding a way out of attending the ball. Luring you to the cemetery, someplace private and secluded, where she wouldn't be interrupted. She wanted to find out if her suspicions about you were correct."

"Her suspicions?"

"But I followed you." Pila ran a finger across the top of the stone mount, then lifted it to inspect the ash she'd picked up. "It was careless of me, getting caught in that fire. Solena escaped, but I passed out from the smoke. I was still weaker than I thought." Pila rubbed her thumb and forefinger together, flicking away the ash. "But weak though I might have been, Solena never had any real authority over anyone. As much as she wishes otherwise. I fear she thinks to supplant me." Pila clicked her tongue. "No matter. I will deal with her once this is over."

Gemma shook her head, then pushed her disheveled hair back from her face. "You said Solena lured me here to see if her suspicions were correct. What suspicions?"

Pila cast her a blistering look. "She thought you were a ghoul, of course. The fool. Even after her little blood test didn't work, she still clung to that belief."

The words rocked Gemma like a surging tidal wave. That wave crashed through her, flooding her with a whirlpool of emotions she wasn't prepared for. At the forefront, shock. Disbelief. Brimming hope.

"You mean…I'm not a ghoul?" Gemma hardly dared speak the question.

Completely unaware of the upheaval taking place inside Gemma—or perhaps simply uncaring—Pila said witheringly, "Of course not."

"But—" Gemma struggled to think, struggled to order her thoughts. But her relief and confusion were so enormous, it was hard to see past them. She couldn't figure out what to address first. "Solena said only a ghoul could see what I've seen. I saw her in the mirror, she looked like—she was a skeleton—and I can see her when she's moving in the shadows—"

"She isn't wrong," Pila admitted with a sniff. "And I confess I, too, was confused about you at first. But then I discovered an ally here in the castle, one who could help me learn about you. One with the knowledge to understand why you might be able to see what you've seen. He agreed to help confirm our theory about you."

"Ally?" Gemma echoed sharply. "Who?"

Pila didn't answer, a smirk twisting her lips.

A flash of movement caught Gemma's eye, and she jerked around, scanning the mausoleum. In the back corner, beneath the only bit of roof that hadn't fallen in, the flames of a brazier cast shadows over the blackened stone wall. As Gemma watched, those shadows shifted—and a figure stepped out from behind the brazier. His dark head appeared first, followed by a long, lean body, clothed very differently than the last time Gemma had seen him. Now he wore a serviceable three-piece suit instead of dirty rags.

It was Harper. The witch. The one she'd visited in the dungeons.

The one who should have still been in the dungeons.

Gemma swallowed. "You can't be here."

"Oh, I can." The smile that broke over Harper's face was disturbingly charming. He was a handsome man; there was no denying that. Not that his good looks meant anything under these circumstances. "All thanks to my new friend." Harper gestured towards Pila. "I admit, I've never worked with a ghoul before. But my kind and hers have a long history of cooperation."

Gemma's gaze darted to the witch's wrists, looking for the spelled cuffs he should have been wearing. Harper noted her gaze and smiled again, raising his arms for her to see. As he bent his elbows, his sleeves rose enough to display his bare brown wrists. "Oh, yes. She also removed those tacky cuffs. They didn't go at all with my new suit." He dropped one hand and used the other to brush imaginary dust from his shoulder. "Nice, isn't it? Not too flashy, but then, that's never been my style."

Gemma fought to maintain a stony expression, but she couldn't help the awful knot that grew in the pit of her stomach. Her mouth felt dry with fear. The last time she'd faced a witch—a witch free and full of magic—she had not fared well. Stones, she'd nearly died. Come as close to it as she ever had.

"Oh, don't worry." Harper seemed to sense her discomfort. "I'm not going to hurt you. Gemma. In fact, I'm going to help you."

"Help me how?"

But Harper didn't answer, exchanging a silent glance with Pila. The ghoul turned back to the dais. As Gemma watched, she retrieved the black ceramic bowl she'd left upon the stone mount. Gemma couldn't see inside the bowl, but its contents were steaming. As Pila descended the dais, Gemma caught a whiff of whatever was inside and nearly gagged. The steam gave off a foul, bitter stench.

Dread rose inside Gemma as Pila and Harper approached her from opposite sides. Harper, on her left, raised his hands with his palms facing her and began to chant in a low voice, while Pila, carrying the steaming bowl, closed in from the right.

It wasn't until Pila was nearly upon her that Gemma realized what she meant to do.

"Drink," Pila commanded. Gemma tried to wrench away, but Pila had her by the chin before she could. The tips of her fingers dug into Gemma with bruising force as she forced Gemma's jaw open. "*Drink.*"

And she tipped the contents of the steaming bowl down Gemma's throat.

A scream erupted deep within Gemma, a scream begging to tear itself free. But it couldn't. Some of the liquid sloshed out of her mouth, trickling down Gemma's chin, but it was the liquid being forced down her gullet that she was concerned about. Her throat seemed to sizzle and burn, as though Pila had forced her to swallow hot coals. Gemma's scream caught in her chest, trapped there, and as the steaming hot liquid sluiced through her, spreading across her ribcage, it killed the scream for good. And then—

And then the burning was gone.

Pila was gone. The mausoleum was gone.

A darkness built from shadows and smoke descended upon her, obscuring her surroundings entirely. The darkness brought a stench with it that had become familiar to Gemma: musty decay, charred ash on the air. The shadows enveloping her began to solidify into clear shapes, rot and ruin, a decomposing world—

But instead of falling into another vision, the darkness dissipated. The shadows lifted, the smoke cleared, as though swept away by a strong wind—

—and with a hoarse gasp, Gemma found herself back in the mausoleum, hunched over on the cracked, sooty stone floor.

The change was maddening, disorienting. Gemma reeled, feeling sick to her stomach. No, worse than sick. Her insides hurt, her chest burned, her throat raw and stinging.

"Well?" Pila's voice was both eager and furious. All Gemma could see of her was her boots, her heels ringing against the cracked stone floor as she paced back and forth.

"You were right," was Harper's reply.

Shoulders heaving, Gemma managed to raise her head. She swallowed roughly, but the pain in her throat was slowly receding. "Right about what?" she demanded.

"You tell me." Pila halted in front of Gemma. Placing her hands on her hips, she leaned down to gaze hungrily into Gemma's face. "What have you seen? What dark, dreadful things have you seen these past few days?"

The visions. That place of death she'd been hallucinating. Somehow, Pila knew about it. And while one part of Gemma—a large part of her—was desperate for answers, desperate to understand what was happening to her, another part of her cautioned against giving Pila anything she wanted. "Nothing." The word croaked from Gemma's sore throat. "I haven't seen anything."

"Now that isn't the truth, is it?" Harper stepped into her line of sight, a knowing gleam in his dark eyes. "You don't have to be afraid, Gemma. Not of me and not of what you've seen. I told you before, didn't I? When you asked how you could tell if what you were seeing was real or not. I gave you your answer then."

Gemma didn't have to struggle to remember, she didn't have to cast her mind back. She recalled the scene down in the dungeons perfectly, Harper's singsong words floating to the forefront of her mind. *"Perhaps it's been a gift for you, giving you a peek into dark and otherworldly places. It's all real. Embrace it."*

"That's not…" Gemma closed her eyes and shook her head. A kind of understanding began to dawn on her, but it was a vague, broad understanding. She still couldn't grasp the details, couldn't make sense of it. "You're saying everything I've seen—those visions I had, that horrible place I—you're saying it was all *real?*" Too late, she realized she shouldn't have mentioned the visions. But she couldn't take the words back now.

"As real as the skeletal face you saw in Solena's mirror." Pila sounded smug. "As real as the shadows you've seen her moving in."

"You were touched by magic, Gemma," Harper said. "And that magic changed you."

Jesine had said as much, Gemma recalled. Only, not quite. "Jesine said I might see things that weren't really there. She said I might suffer hallucinations, that my mind would play tricks on me—"

"I assure you," Harper said, and his voice *was* strangely reassuring, his deep baritone low and smooth, "you haven't been hallucinating. You've been gleaning. Catching glimpses into other spaces beyond our own. Spying into the nether reaches of the world."

"Such as into the place we ghouls dwell when we have no form," Pila inserted. "The place we dwell when we have no identity. A realm of death and shadow."

Death and shadow. Gemma wanted to refuse to believe any of this. She still didn't really understand, and it was easy to think they were lying to her, trying to confuse her. But parts of it felt right. Parts of it began to fall into place, her thoughts finally ordering themselves. She herself had thought of that place in her visions as a world of death and decay, of shadow and smoke. That was exactly what they were describing now.

"Your sight wasn't damaged, Gemma." Harper folded his arms across his chest. "Well, it was. Physically. But something else happened too. Your sight was first touched by dark magic, magic that had been corrupted by violence and death." The faint smile that came to his lips was somewhat sardonic. "All magic used by bad witches is like that. And then you were touched again—healed this time—by Jesine's magic, which is unlike any other magic in this world. Jesine's magic, from what I understand, is raw and unrefined. Straight from the bedrock, deep in the earth."

Harper spread his hands wide. "Your sight has been changed by the unique combination of both of those magics. By the death you came so close to, in more ways than one. It's fascinating, really. And it's left you with an uncanny ability."

"An ability that should prove most useful," Pila murmured.

"I suppose." Harper sounded indifferent. "Me, I'm happy enough with my own magic. So. I've fulfilled my part of our bargain. I assume I'm free to go?"

Pila didn't even look at him. Her gaze was fixed on Gemma, and the look in her eyes filled Gemma with trepidation. "Yes, I'm quite satisfied. You may go."

Harper tipped his head in a little bow for the ghoul. Then he turned towards Gemma, casually saluting her with two fingers at his temple. He raised his arms again, and the air around him rippled, blurring his form and his surroundings together until they could not be distinguished.

Then the air settled, and he was gone.

Gemma ran her tongue over her bottom lip. She was torn by the desire to understand everything and the desire to take control of the situation. But she still needed time to find her pistol. So perhaps she could satisfy both desires at once. "What did you mean," she asked, "when you said ghouls dwell in a realm of death and shadow?"

"Exactly that. Think of it as a realm that exists between this world and the next. A liminal space." Pila pursed her lips. "It's why you can see us when we move in the shadows. A shadow isn't a cloak, after all. It's nothing solid. We can't literally step into it. When you see us do that, we're stepping into that liminal space. Briefly departing our human forms and taking up the shadow."

"And when I saw Solena in the mirror?" Gemma darted a quick glance around the mausoleum, searching for her weapons.

"You saw the truth of her, as she might be seen in our nether-world. Probably because she had just assumed a new form and was still recovering."

"But the visions I've had." Gemma didn't mean to, but her attention strayed from her search, turning to this—this last part she was most desperate to understand. "What was I seeing then? Just random glimpses into that that liminal space? Is that just going to keep happening to me, is it—"

"You haven't figured that out?" Pila's lip curled. "Those visions were triggered by that 'talisman,' you little idiot. The one you found, the one poor Pila told you about. It wasn't really a talisman, of course," she added carelessly. "Solena only constructed it to look that way so no one would think anything of it. But she left it there deliberately for you to find. She bound it with some rather specific herbs, you see." She pointed to the black ceramic bowl that had contained the liquid she'd forced down Gemma's throat. "Herbs designed to trigger the subconscious mind."

"But why—"

"It was part of her crusade to prove you were a ghoul. If you *were* a ghoul and lacking your memories—it happens sometimes, though rarely—then those herbs would have brought those memories back. Reminded you what you were. But since you aren't a ghoul, the herbs worked differently. Triggered your latent sight."

Of course. That first vision had come the morning after her shift with the princess, after she'd discovered the so-called talisman. And that powder Solena had blown into her face when they'd fought here in the mausoleum—they had been the same herbs. Gemma had recognized their scent but couldn't quite place it.

"She should have realized when she first tasted your blood," Pila said derisively. "She should have known then you weren't a ghoul. We know the taste of our own kind. But the fool wouldn't be dissuaded. She tasted something in your blood, something wrong. The magic you've been touched by, no doubt. So she persisted." Pila shook her head. "But you are not a ghoul, Gemma. You are perfectly human...though with a rather unique gift." She smiled evenly. "A gift I mean to use."

Gemma could not hold back the relief that sluiced through her, and for a moment, she slumped in on herself. She was *Gemma*. She was herself. She was not a ghoul. The idea of being changed by magic, being able to see things she did not want to see, was disturbing in and of itself, but she could live with it. She could figure that out. It might even, as Pila said, be useful.

But first, she had to deal with Pila. She had to put an end to the ghoul's plot to take over the Glen Kingdom. She needed to find her pistol, she needed to—

Before she could form any kind of plan, the sound of people coming caught Gemma's ear. Still crouched on the floor, she turned and saw three imposing figures in black approaching. They were all dressed in the same garb the stranger had worn before—that Solena had worn before. Black trousers, boots, and gloves, along with long, voluminous black frock coats. Deep hoods hung from beneath the upturned collars of those coats, pulled back now, revealing their faces. Faces that Gemma recognized.

They were Solena's ladies-in-waiting. Three of them.

And, Gemma guessed, all three ghouls.

The ladies stepped into the hollowed-out remains of the mausoleum. "Exalted One," one of the ladies said, addressing Pila, and Gemma rolled her eyes. *Exalted One?* "We've got the king. We have him cornered down in the castle's crypt."

"Excellent," Pila said with relish.

"But you will need to move quickly. The others have him cornered, but he's not alone. His son is with him."

"The beast," Pila scoffed.

"Yes. And others in the castle have been alerted to some danger. The king's guards are searching for him everywhere, and for intruders on the grounds. If you're going to become the king, you'll need to do it now."

Become the king. Gemma's heart lurched.

Pila said, "Very well. Then I need you three to keep this one here." She pointed at Gemma. "She's going to be a very useful tool, but I need to find out who she's been talking to first. Who she's confided in about ghouls. So keep her here, and when I return—when King *Victor* returns—I will deal with her myself."

She turned to go, stepping down from the dais. Gemma scrambled to her feet, but the ladies closed in on her, blocking her from following Pila.

And Gemma watched helplessly as the ghoul strode from the mausoleum, her dark form vanishing across the cemetery.

28

SIGHTED

GEMMA TURNED HER BACK on the graveyard and eyed the ladies in black surrounding her. Her tangled hair had completely fallen free around her shoulders, wispy pieces sticking in her face, so, slowly, she reached back to braid and coil it behind her head, tucking the ends in to secure it. The entire time, she never took her gaze off the ladies, eyeing them each in turn.

"Don't even think of attempting something foolish," one of them warned. Lady Ilana. Broad-shouldered with dark-gold hair.

Gemma smiled evenly at her. "You must know I have to attempt something." It probably would be foolish, but if she could just distract the ladies for long enough, if she could slip past them...

"There is nothing you can do," another of them said, her voice disdainful. This one was Marisel, black-haired and blue-eyed.

"You will never defeat us," said the third. This was Lady Kova, tall and lithe with chestnut-brown hair. "We have trained for decades. We are the best."

"Maybe I've trained too." Gemma adopted the casual drawl Klaus used so much. "Maybe I'm better than you think."

Lady Kova whipped out two little knives from inside her coat, flourishing them before her. "I saw you the day after we arrived here." Her tone was dismissive. "Training in the fighting yards. I saw another soldier take you down. Easily."

"Maybe I was holding back. Faking him out."

"No one can pretend to be that bad."

Gemma opened her mouth to respond, then stopped. A whisper of movement at the corner of her eye drew her attention, and she eased around surreptitiously, as though turning her attention from Kova to Ilana. But it was behind Ilana she was looking at. It was at the shadows cast by the flaming iron braziers.

One of those shadows broke away from the rest, slithering over the ashy stone floor. Like a black serpent, readying itself to strike.

Gemma smiled again.

All three of the ladies began to circle her, knives in their hands. Gemma watched them, taking them in. "So you're the best, are you," she said. "But what about Solena? How good is she? Better than all of you?"

"Better," Kova admitted grudgingly.

"But she is not here," Marisel said.

"No one is coming to help you," Ilana jeered.

"Maybe not." Gemma didn't know if Solena would help her. Pila claimed the princess had begun to work against her. Even if that was true, that didn't necessarily make her an ally. But Pila also said she would *deal with* Solena. Gemma didn't know exactly what that would entail, but it didn't sound good. "But she might help herself."

Before any of the ladies could respond—before they had a chance to comprehend what this meant—a figure materialized from the shadow on the floor, stepping free of the darkness. A figure in a bloodred gown.

Solena.

She struck before any of the ladies knew what was happening. She struck at Marisel, darting in at her. Marisel's eyes widened. She raised one blade before her, and the other she held low, coming in for a thrust. But Solena swatted her away easily, delivering such a quick, snapping blow to the lady's forearm that Marisel dropped her blade. As it clattered to the floor, Solena caught Marisel's other wrist in her hand and twisted her arm back, whirling around behind her. Marisel let out a squeak of pain as her second blade fell from her twisted wrist.

Solena caught Marisel's knife as it fell.

Then she slashed it across the lady's throat, slicing it deep from ear to ear.

A shocked silence followed this attack, punctuated only by Marisel as she collapsed in a heap, choking on her own blood. The entire thing—from the moment Solena had appeared—took less than five seconds.

Still holding one blade, Solena bent to pick up the other one Marisel had dropped.

"Thank you," she said, neatly stepping over Marisel's white-faced corpse. Blood had sprayed over the front of her gown, but it was hardly noticeable due to the color. "I was closely watched when I dressed tonight. I didn't have a chance to arm myself. But these will do nicely." She eyed the remaining ladies the way a lioness might eye her prey. "For the two of you."

Ilana sucked in a breath. Kova let out a curse.

Then they both ran at Solena, coming in to attack.

They came at her from both sides, knives flashing. They were fast, but Solena was faster. She kept their barrage of attacks at bay, blocking and parrying, left, then right, left, then right again. She ducked swinging overhand blows and hooking side strikes, she met low thrusts and dodged snapping kicks. She answered with her own blades, stabbing at Ilana, slicing at Kova. Kova hissed as the sharp edge of Solena's knife drew a thin line of blood from her cheek.

One thing was for sure, Gemma thought, momentarily mesmerized by the level of skill on display before her. Well, two things. First, Solena had been fair to criticize Gemma's struggles with fighting in a ballgown because she had no trouble with it at all. And second—Solena had *really* been holding back when she'd fought Gemma here in the mausoleum. She'd really, really been holding back.

Gemma watched a moment longer as Ilana spun, coming at Solena from behind. But the princess sidestepped away, purposely dropping one of her knives to catch Ilana by the arm. She delivered a low, hard kick to the lady's gut, then flipped her onto her back.

Gemma shook herself, looking away. Now wasn't the time to spectate. She needed to find her pistol and get after Pila, she needed to stop her before she reached the king. The crypt wasn't far from here, especially if Pila was familiar with the servants' corridors, which Gemma bet she was.

But what had the ghoul done with her weapons? They might not even be in here, but Gemma needed to be sure. She turned in a slow circle, her gaze sweeping every inch of the dusty floor. A pile of debris lay in the opposite corner, crumbled stone rubble mixed with slivers of blackened wood. Gemma bent to pick through it, dirtying her hands, but there was nothing there. She didn't really think Pila would have hidden her weapons like that anyway.

Rising to her full height, she scanned the back of the mausoleum. The ghouls were fighting there, in full view beneath the light of the braziers' flames. Their shadows were cast upon the scorched stone walls like giants mirroring their every move.

As Kova aimed a high kick at Solena's head, Solena retreated, backing up onto the dais, then leaping onto the memorial's empty stone mount, her skirt lifted high to expose her knees. Ilana ran at her, and Solena delivered a spinning kick to her face, sending Ilana reeling.

Warily, Gemma crept closer to the fighting ghouls, trying to remain inconspicuous. Trying to remain out of sight. She circled slightly to the left, then to the right, searching the sooty base of the mount for any trace of her pistol. There was another small debris pile in the far back corner where Harper had first appeared, beneath all that was left of the roof.

Keeping one eye on the ghouls, Gemma pressed herself into the gritty wall, inching back to that corner. Ilana and Kova were both on the dais now, fighting Solena, but Ilana was on the far side, and Kova's back was to Gemma as she stabbed at Solena's legs. The princess jumped to avoid the blow, then came down to one knee. Kova swung at her face, but Solena parried the blow and slashed with her other hand. Her blade caught Kova on the chin, making another gash.

Kova shook her head, practically growling as she backed up to the edge of the dais.

That was when she glanced back. Her gaze locked on Gemma and pinned her with a vicious glare. She didn't speak, but her expression said it all. *Where do you think you're going?*

As Kova leapt off the dais towards her, Gemma pushed herself off the wall and darted into the back corner, concealing herself among the shadows. It was darker here beyond the light of the braziers, partly because of the cover provided by what was left of the roof—cracked stone and charred beams of wood, hanging on overhead.

Using the toe of her boot, Gemma quickly sifted through the small debris pile at her feet, but there was nothing there. Not her pistol or any other weapon.

"Hiding won't help you!" Kova called out. Her voice was very near.

The truth was, this was no hiding spot at all; Kova knew exactly where she was. And while she might have orders to keep Gemma alive, that didn't mean the ghoul wouldn't do whatever it took to disable her. Break an arm. A leg. Stab her in a non-lethal spot.

As Kova's shadow fell across the floor, Gemma's gaze latched upon the fiery brazier in front of her. Its wrought-iron basket, holding a bundle of coals, was mounted upon a long metal pole.

Gemma reached out, wrapping both hands around the pole. The basket itself would have been too hot to touch, but the stand holding it wasn't.

Kova appeared before her, a triumphant look upon her face.

Gemma smiled in return. Then she swung the iron brazier around like a quarterstaff, aiming the fiery end at Kova's head. She caught a quick glimpse of Kova's horrified expression before white-hot coals flew from the brazier, red embers showering the ghoul.

The brazier struck Kova, making contact with her face, and she let out a thin scream as the blazing iron casket branded her. She flailed and writhed, but not for long.

A carefully aimed blade zipped through the air and embedded itself dead center in Kova's back. Kova's screams died as she slumped over, first to her knees, then onto the mausoleum floor. She fell face first into the debris pile.

Gemma looked up. Solena had thrown the blade. She stood atop the memorial's stone mount, her arm still outstretched. Behind her, Ilana backed off the dais, retreating several steps. Her wide eyes flew from Gemma, to Solena, then to Kova's motionless corpse.

Then she turned and ran, fleeing the mausoleum.

Gemma cursed softly. Without a glance for Solena, she hurried around the dais, dashing after Ilana. Her boots tracked through ash and debris over the stone floor, then over dewy grass as she passed out of the ruin and into the graveyard.

She spotted Ilana fleeing through the headstones, but, Gemma thought, skidding to a halt, it didn't really matter if Ilana got away. She just needed to find her pistol and get after Pila—then again, maybe Ilana could tell her where the pistol was—

That last thought had no sooner crossed her mind when a second figure materialized on the hill, stepping out of the long shadow cast by a massive headstone. Solena, her bloodred skirt billowing in the wind, appeared again out of the shadows—right in the path of Ilana. As the clouds shifted overhead, a sliver of moonlight peeked through the haze, and by its pale glimmer, Gemma spotted the glint of Solena's knife.

With a swift slash, the ghoul princess cut Ilana's throat. Gemma couldn't see the blood that must have gushed from the lady, but she watched Ilana thud to her knees, then keel over sideways. Dead.

Solena looked up and met Gemma's gaze across the graveyard. As she started forward, closing the distance between them, Gemma clenched her hands tight, itching for a weapon. But Solena stopped short of her, and she and the princess stared at each other, gazes equally hard.

Then Gemma said, "I wish I could learn that shadow thing." It was possibly her one regret about not being a ghoul.

Solena bared her teeth in a catlike grin. "If you were a ghoul, I could teach you."

"I'm not a ghoul. But you could teach me some of your knife tricks—if I decide not to kill you."

Solena arched an eyebrow. "I just saved your life."

"They weren't going to kill me. Pila ordered them not to."

"Pila?" Solena sounded surprised, but then she cursed. "I wondered if it was her. After she was ill. But I didn't get much chance to speak to her myself." She extended an arm towards Gemma, then seemed to realize this might come off as threatening since she was still holding a knife. Dropping her arm, she said, "Look. I wasn't trying to kill your king that night Prince Gryphon found me in his apartments. I don't want that."

Gemma cast a distracted glance behind Solena, her gaze searching the hillside. Where was Pila now? How far had she gotten? The time the ghouls had spent fighting in the mausoleum had felt like forever, but Gemma knew it had only been minutes. "And what do you want?"

"Only to rule the Desert Kingdom." When Gemma shot the princess an incredulous glare, Solena shrugged. "I am the only one left who can. Without plunging the whole realm into civil war. You might not believe me, but that is one of the reasons I agreed to our cabal's plan to replace a Desert princess in the first place. For the good of the kingdom."

Gemma gave a suspicious snort. "Why do I get the feeling there's more to it than that?"

"Oh, there is." For a moment, Solena was every inch the princess again, her tone both haughty and girlish, her expression lofty and her dark eyes coy. "Don't get me wrong. I love the gowns, the balls, the riches. The attention. The power." Then her face darkened. "But *Pila's* lust for power far outweighs mine. She won't stop at the Desert Kingdom, nor at the Glen Kingdom. And she will do anything to get what she wants."

Yes, she will. Unless they could stop her first.

"Gemma!"

Relief filled Gemma as a figure appeared behind the princess, charging over the hill towards them: Klaus, his uniform more rumpled than ever and his rifle slung over his shoulder.

"Sorry I'm late," he panted as he reached her. He half-gestured towards Solena and bent over, hands on his knees, to catch his breath. "I can't travel through shadows like this one."

"You might be just in time." Gemma pointed at his rifle. "Please tell me you haven't used yours because I don't know what Pila did with mine. She must have taken it when she subdued me. And now she's gone to kill the king." If they were lucky, Pila might not have reached the bottom of the hill yet. Which meant Gemma could still get to her.

Klaus hefted his rifle, adjusting the strap over his shoulder. "Haven't had anyone to use it on. Yet." He shot Solena a sidelong glance, who eyed him back just as consideringly. "We'll go after her. If we run, we can probably catch her and—"

"No," Gemma interrupted. "I mean, yes, you and Solena should go after her, but—" She held out her hand. "Give me the rifle, Klaus."

"Why all this bother about a rifle?" Solena demanded. "A blade will put a stop to her just as well as a bullet. For the time being anyway. Until she claws her way out of the shadow."

But Klaus ignored her. He seemed to understand Gemma's meaning, his expression sharpening, his nostrils flaring. Locking eyes with her, he asked, "Are you sure?"

Gemma held his gaze. She extended her hand further to him, and it was as steady as a leaf on a windless day.

"I'm sure," she said.

Two minutes later, Gemma lay flat in a prone position atop the roof of one of the cemetery's mausoleums—one that hadn't burned down, of course. The damp cold of the stone leached through her clothing, chilling her to the bone, but she didn't feel it. She was heedless of the cold night air numbing her nose and cheeks. Flexing her fingers to keep them from growing stiff, she took note of the wind long enough to judge its strength and direction, eyeing the way the needles bristled and blew on a nearby pine tree.

She breathed in, deep and even. Settled into herself.

She bent her head to peer through the scope of the rifle, perched at the edge of the roof before her.

Pila, her long black robe trailing behind her, was nearing the bottom of the hill. Gemma spotted her by the bobbing light of the single lantern the ghoul carried. She'd taken the cemetery's winding path, Gemma realized, rather than cutting through the headstones straight down the hill, which would have been faster. Pila was that confident. That sure of herself and her plan. Now she approached the opening in the hedge at the bottom of the rise. Once she disappeared through there, she would be beyond Gemma's sight. Beyond her reach.

Gemma's finger rested on the rifle's trigger. With both eyes open—her vision clear and crisp—she breathed in again and sighted her target.

She released her breath.

She squeezed the trigger.

She took the shot.

29

ANCIENT

K LAUS AND SOLENA WERE near the bottom of the rise
when the powerful shot rang out, a loud *crack* splitting
the night. They exchanged a quick glance and then quickened
their strides, though they were already running. A minute later,
they rounded a rugged curve at the bottom of the hill, and Pila
came into view. The ghoul masquerading as a handmaiden was
down on one knee, trying to push herself to her feet. She jerked
around as Klaus and Solena approached. Klaus placed a hand on
the pistol holstered at his waist, and the princess had her knives
out, one in each hand. They circled behind Pila, the two of them
boxing her in.

Pila noted their wariness and let out a hoarse laugh. As Klaus
came around to face her, he spotted the dark stain at her back,
turning her black robe even blacker.

"You" —Pila struggled to speak, though her tone was defi-
ant— "*missed.*"

"No, she didn't," said Klaus. His hand still rested on his pistol, but he relaxed as he faced her, seeing no weapons in her hands. "And I wouldn't try to get up if I were you."

"Why not?" Pila snarled. "I'm not planning to stay in these bones for much longer, boy. Once I take another form, I'll be as fit as ever I was. As fit as a *king*."

"Gemma didn't miss." Klaus gestured to indicate the wound in her back. "She wasn't trying to kill you. At least, not in the traditional sense. Because you don't die in the traditional sense, do you? We put a bullet in your head or a knife in your heart, and you're just going to come back eventually."

"It might take her a while." Solena's voice was hard. "But yes, she'll be back. In ten years. In fifty. In two hundred."

Klaus shook his head in mock-dismay. "And you'll turn back to the same scheme. Kill and consume a king or queen. Take up a position of power in a royal court. We could keep an eye out for imposters, send word to the other kingdoms. Pass it all on to their descendants, but frankly, that sounds exhausting. And I wouldn't even be the one to do it."

Circling around Pila, Solena leaned in toward her. "There's something you should know about that bullet, Pila dear."

"What do you mean?" Pila's hand went to her hip, and she winced, her fingers digging into the folds of her robe. "It's just a bullet."

"Yes," Klaus said. "A bullet. Crafted out of the remains of some long-dead fellow. Bones ground down into fine dust. Mixed in with the lead."

Pila's eyes flared wide.

"Found them in the possession of someone who seemed to be a ghoul hunter," Klaus said. "Though I don't know that for sure, since the poor man was dead himself. But he left the bullets in a little case with a note explaining what they were and how they were made."

"How old were the bones?" Solena asked viciously.

"Oh, about eight hundred years old. The bones had been found and preserved out in the desert, you see. Apparently, bones can last for a long time in that kind of climate. And no telling how old the bullets themselves are, so the remains are probably even older now..."

"Eight hundred years." Solena flourished her knives with relish. "Maybe a *thousand* years."

"Funny thing." Klaus finally dropped his hand from his pistol. "A friend of mine told me a story about a ghoul who consumed bones about sixty years old. She was all kinds of messed up. Couldn't really speak, couldn't even walk properly. As though her bones hadn't quite formed right. Seems the remains were too old for the transformation to work."

"And those bones were only sixty years old," Solena said. "Imagine consuming bones that are over *eight hundred* years old."

Pila listened to all of this with a look of growing horror on her face. "But I didn't consume them!" she burst out, the words tumbling over each other. "I didn't, I haven't—"

"I don't think it matters. They're in you." Solena squinted at Pila. "Lodged in your digestive track, I'd say."

"Like I said," Klaus repeated, "Gemma didn't miss."

"No—but—I—" More words sputtered from Pila's lips until she couldn't speak anymore. A ragged cry escaped her, and she doubled over, falling to hands and knees. Klaus expected something like what he'd seen when Gryphon turned into the beast—bones snapping and lengthening and reforming, as the ghoul transformed from one person into another. But instead, shadows rippled over Pila's hunched form, darkness flitting over her like a murder of crows beneath her skin, fighting to get free of the body's confining form. A strangled scream keened out of the ghoul, and then she threw back her head, lifting her face to the sky.

Klaus gave a start. The skin covering Pila's face puckered and shriveled, as though he was watching a corpse desiccate in rapid time. As the skin tightened and drew back from the skull, Pila's eyes bulged and then burst, liquifying in their sockets. Her teeth detached from her gums and fell from her mouth, and her hair disintegrated before their eyes. Then the last of the ghoul's withered, discolored skin rotted away, until all that remained was a naked skull protruding from the collar of Pila's black robe.

Klaus recoiled, taking an instinctive step back from the skeletal ghoul, and even Solena looked repulsed. Now the skull itself began to fracture and crumble, turning to dust. That dust flew away on the wind, and so did an undulating darkness, what looked like flecks of ash collapsing and fragmenting until the wind scattered it all to the corners of the earth.

When all was said and done, there was nothing left of the ghoul. Nothing but a pile of black clothing at the bottom of the hill.

30

AMENDS

GRYPHON WINCED AND PUT a hand to his shoulder as he arched his spine, a bone in his back cracking. The beast's curse had made him stronger and sharper in many ways, but sometimes he wondered if all the strain on his body was aging him prematurely. One thing was certain: he longed for a hot bath to soothe his aching muscles. Though most of that aching was probably from the fight, not from the change.

Not that it had been much of a fight.

The grotto that held his mother's remains was filled with carnage. The iron gate separating the grotto from the corridor lay askew, half-propped against the stone wall. Gryphon—or rather, the beast—had ripped it from its hinges and tossed it aside to attack the assassins. Those assassins lay dead now, mauled, bloodied, and tattered. Gryphon didn't know if they'd been ghouls or elite warriors, but either way, they'd died easily enough once the beast got at them.

"That looked like it hurt."

Gryphon blinked, glancing over his shoulder. Uncertain as to whether or not his father was talking to him, though he supposed there was no one else he could be talking to. They were still alone down here. But his father's gaze was on his sword, all his attention bent on it. He'd removed his coat, his shirt sleeves rolled up to his elbow, and now he used his coat to wipe the blood from his blade.

When Gryphon made no response, his father glanced up in question. Gryphon needed another moment to recall and process what his father had said, then realized it was in reference to his turning into a beast and back. *That looked like it hurt.*

"It does." Trying not to stagger from fatigue, Gryphon retreated to the back of the grotto where he'd left his clothes neatly piled. They were still there, undisturbed, save for a few droplets of blood that had sprayed back this far. He pulled on his trousers slowly, leaning back into the wall so he didn't keel over as he stepped from one foot to the other. He grabbed his shirt next but left the rest piled on the floor, too tired to dress completely.

"So why do it, then?"

Gryphon blinked again as he came forward, shrugging into his shirt. "Do what?" He winced as his sleeve slid over a couple of shallow gashes in his right arm. One of the assassins had gotten a few lucky nicks in with her blade before he'd torn out her throat with his teeth. The cuts weren't deep, but he would need to bind them to keep his clothes from rubbing over the wounds while they healed.

"Why turn into that beast," his father clarified. "Now that you control it, I mean."

Gryphon looked at the king. Now that he'd accomplished the task of dressing—mostly—he could focus his full attention on his father. King Victor seemed remarkably composed considering what he had just witnessed. His son turning into a beast that had ripped four—possibly five—people to shreds in a matter of minutes. He also seemed undisturbed by the remains of that massacre, by the bodies on the floor, by the blood sprayed over the walls. But then, the king hailed from the same warlike people Gryphon's mother did, and had been raised by a father even more single-minded and ruthless than he was.

But Gryphon didn't understand what his father was getting at. Why did he turn into the beast? The obvious answer lay before them. He gestured half-heartedly at the assassins' mangled corpses. "That's why."

King Victor still seemed perplexed, as perplexed as Gryphon was by this line of questioning. "Yes, but—you didn't have to—" He broke off without finishing his thought.

Gryphon studied his father. "If I hadn't," he said shortly, "we'd both be dead." That was the truth, plain and simple. But he thought he understood what his father was thinking. What he was wondering.

If it had only been the king's life at risk and not Gryphon's life as well...would he have done it? Changed into the beast, suffered through the pain of it, to save his father's life?

The answer was surprisingly easy. Yes, of course he would have. His life would not be any easier with his father dead. And turning into the beast, while still painful, was not the torment it had once been. In a way, it wasn't as painful as it used to be. Physically, yes, the snapping and reforming of his bones hurt as much as it always had. But having some measure of control over that pain—choosing it instead of being forced into it, day after day—that made a difference. Made it easier to bear.

And, Gryphon realized. As much as he resented his father. As hurt as he had been by him. He did not hate him. Nor did Garrett, who had always had a better relationship with Victor than Gryphon ever had. Garrett would mourn their father's death, and—if for his sake only—Gryphon didn't want his father dead. He didn't want to bring any grief to Garrett. The thought of his brother losing his eternally annoying cheeriness and optimism was strangely distressing. Not that he would ever tell Garrett that.

"Well." His father dropped his gaze. Looking over the slaughter they'd left in the grotto. If Gryphon wasn't mistaken, the king bore a glint of pride in his eyes. Gryphon had to stifle a snort at that. His father had held off *one* of the women with his sword while Gryphon dealt with the other four. Fairly quickly. Almost as soon as the fight began, Gryphon had realized he would have to be quick; the assassins were too skilled, and if more than one of them had gotten past him, they would have made short work of killing the king.

Instead, the beast had made short work of them.

Gryphon cleared his throat. "I hope there aren't more of them coming." He indicated the felled assassins. "It sounded like they shut the door to the crypt, which means they probably locked us in. But we should get up there to check it. Surely your guards will have realized something is wrong by now."

"Unless they're dead." Victor grimaced but nodded in assent, gesturing with his sword for Gryphon to lead the way. Gryphon did so, picking his way through the grotto, doing his best to navigate the corpses they left behind.

They made their way down the crypt's long corridor, the lantern-like fixtures on the walls casting overlapping pools of light across the paved stone floor. Gryphon moved slowly but tensely, half-expecting more assassins to appear at any moment, materializing from the shadows or leaping around the corner at the end of the corridor. But they rounded that corner safely, and when Gryphon peered up the long stone stairwell to the crypt's first level, there was no one awaiting them there. The stairs were empty.

His shoulders relaxing, Gryphon started up the stairs. It was a long climb, and even once they reached the top, there was no telling if they would be able to get through the heavy stone door the assassins had shut. Not if they had secured or blocked it somehow. Which meant they might have to wait a while before anyone found them. So Gryphon allowed himself to take the stairs slowly, easing his way up step by step.

Evidently, he was so slow that he aroused his father's concern. Or at least, his curiosity. "Were you injured?" the king asked, his voice drifting eerily up the dim stairwell.

"No," Gryphon answered, more curtly than he meant to. "It's just—tiring, sometimes. The change. Sorry."

"No matter." The king's tone turned wry. "I'm certainly not going to bother attending that state dinner after all of this, even if we do make it out on time. I think we've earned a night off."

"Hear, hear."

Silence fell between them again, but it did not last long. Only a few steps later, the king said, "Gryphon."

"Yes?"

But the king said nothing. Gryphon realized he couldn't hear his father's booted footsteps thudding up the stairs alongside his own softer, barefoot steps. He stopped climbing and turned around, placing a hand against the wall to steady himself.

King Victor had paused a few steps below him. He wasn't looking at Gryphon but frowning at his feet, as though preoccupied with something.

"What is it?" Gryphon asked wearily.

His father seemed to hesitate. Then he said abruptly, "I shouldn't have said what I did before. That you should be thanking me. That was thoughtless. You've obviously been through a lot, and...perhaps I should have realized. But whatever kind of life you live now, whatever happiness you've found for yourself—well, you've earned it." King Victor did not lift his gaze once as he spoke, and his voice turned gruffer with each word. "You may not want to be a prince anymore. But you deserve the title. You've proven that. So—though I'm sure you'll want to go as soon as this business with Princess Solena is done, or as soon as Garrett returns—you are welcome at this court. Whenever you like."

Gryphon listened to all of this in a sort of stunned fatigue. It felt a bit like a dream. Like perhaps he'd been knocked out while fighting down in the grotto and still lay down there, dreaming this all. But if he had dreamed this, his father would have spoken different words. Because what his father was saying to him now...

It wasn't what he wanted to hear. It wasn't *everything* he wanted to hear. When Gryphon had first returned to this castle, he would've said nothing less than a full apology could ever be enough. An admission from his father that he had done wrong in exiling Gryphon. That he should have chosen his son over court politics, over placating the Mariner king, over the very kingdom.

But as he stood here now, in this dark, cold stairwell, Gryphon found himself reaching for an anger that wasn't there anymore.

He had loosed it all upon his father already, down in the grotto before the assassins attacked. He had unleashed his fury, his bitterness, his pain. And now there was nothing left of it to spend.

He was just tired. So very tired. Physically, but emotionally as well. He was tired of holding on to past grudges. He was tired of living in childhood hurts. Strangely enough, his father was right. Gryphon had earned his happiness. He deserved it. And for all that he'd wanted more from his father, he wanted most of all to be done with this ugly thing between them.

Gryphon had wanted an apology. But he didn't think he was going to get one. Perhaps not ever. And that was all right. Gryphon had said his piece, and he realized now that all he'd needed was to be heard. And his father had said his piece, for all that it was not everything Gryphon had hoped to hear. But perhaps it was all Victor was capable of.

All Gryphon could think was how grateful he was that he himself had become a person who was capable of more.

It was not an apology, his father's words. But it was enough. Gryphon would allow it to be enough. Not for his father's sake. But for his own.

"Well." Gryphon swallowed. His throat felt incredibly dry. "You're right that I'll want to go. Back to my own life, I mean. But. Perhaps I could visit from time to time." After a pause, he added rather formally, "Thank you."

If his father was surprised or gratified, he hid it well. Gruffer than ever, his father said, "You're welcome."

Gryphon gave a crisp nod. Then he turned and started back up the stairs.

Again, the silence lasted for only a short moment before his father filled it, this time in a more casual tone. "Perhaps you could tell me a bit about it." Then, clarifying, "This life of yours, I mean."

"Oh. Well." As he continued up the stairs, Gryphon took a moment to consider this. Wondering what to share. "There's a girl who I love. Who I live with."

"Of course there is." There was a slightly resigned edge to his father's voice, but it was more amused-resigned than annoyed-resigned. As well it should be, Gryphon thought, since he and Victor both knew he was never seriously courting Princess Solena.

"Actually, I think you know her," Gryphon said. "She's Garrett's friend. Isabelle."

"Isabelle?" This time, Victor didn't bother to hide his surprise. It was evident in his voice. "You can't be serious."

"Why not?" Gryphon frowned, slowing even further to cast a disapproving glance down at his father. If Victor said anything to imply Isabelle wasn't good enough…

But the king said, "It's just—well. I rather like Isabelle. That is, she's a very sensible young lady, and, er…"

The retort Gryphon had begun to form, defending Isabelle, died on his tongue. "You don't think *I'm* good enough for *her?*"

"No, not at all," came his father's hasty reply. "It's just—you seem an odd pair, I suppose. She's quite the scholar, isn't she?"

Gryphon rolled his shoulders back. "She reads. I draw or paint. It works out well."

His father grunted. "Sounds peaceful."

"I suppose it is." Of course, they also ran the woods and hunted together in the middle of the night, and that was less peaceful. But Gryphon didn't feel like sharing that with his father. A deep sigh rumbled through him, in part fueled by fatigue, in part fueled by a sudden homesickness. "I am ready to go back to that life," he said softly. More to himself than to his father. "So Garrett had better hurry up and return."

"He'll have a lot to answer for."

Gryphon barked a laugh, then winced, placing a hand over his tender ribcage. "On that, we agree."

"We should greet him together upon his return. Let him know just exactly what we think of being manipulated."

"I'm in for that." Gryphon added, "Of course, he'll likely just be pleased you and I are in agreement for once. He won't even care that we're angry with him. All he'll see is that his mad plan succeeded."

"You're probably right." Victor sounded as though he'd bitten into a sour grape. "Nothing ever gets him down."

"He is an odd one."

"Hmm." His father paused. "He'll make a good king though."

"Yes," Gryphon agreed.

"Unless he gets eaten by a troll first."

"There's no such thing as a troll. According to Garrett, anyway."

"Really? I could have sworn he went off hunting one last year—"

"Probably an ogre. Those are real."

"That must have been it..."

They continued plodding up the long stone stairwell, the echo of their voices following them all the way.

DEPARTED

GEMMA SURVEYED THE EMPTYING bedchamber here in Princess Solena's quarters. The wardrobe stood open with only bare hangers inside, while several trunks lay strewn about in various states of packing, some full to bursting with neatly arranged belongings, others overflowing with garments waiting to be folded. "You know," Gemma remarked with thinly veiled amusement, "for a princess, you certainly pack light."

From across the room, Solena cast her a familiar look of disdain. "I didn't pack. Silly little Lena did. Well, she oversaw the packing. Princesses *don't* do menial tasks like packing."

"Is that why you're lounging about while everyone else does the work?"

"Of course. I am the princess now. For all intents and purposes."

She was right about that, Gemma supposed. It seemed the real Princess Solena—the entirely human Princess Solena—died nearly ten years ago in her childhood, of the same dreadful plague that took all the other heirs to the Desert Kingdom. It was for that reason that King Victor had consented to *this* "Princess Solena" returning to her kingdom—on a few conditions, of course. One of those conditions being that she cut her visit short and leave at once.

Understandably, the king didn't want a ghoul hanging around his court. Even one who had, he grudgingly admitted, helped save his life. By taking down the other ghoul who'd been trying to kill and replace him.

Gemma would have thought Solena relieved to return home after everything had gone so wrong here, but she seemed rather glum about it. Even now she pouted where she sat slouching in her cushy chair, her legs dangling over one arm in a rather unladylike pose. "Of course, if my visit had gone according to plan," she groused, "I should have been betrothed to the crown prince, and all my trunks overflowing with the many gifts I should have received. At the very least, I should have had time to go shopping. But I didn't even get to go into the city. Not once."

Gemma rolled her eyes. "You were never going to be betrothed to anyone. I told you, Prince Garrett and Gryphon both love other people. And neither of them are to be dissuaded."

"I could have dissuaded them." Solena smirked. "If I'd had more time."

"You're awfully sure of yourself."

"Of course. I'm a princess."

"Somehow, I get the feeling that's just you." Gemma unclasped her hands from behind her back and crossed her arms over her chest. "And not the princess."

Solena cast her a mysterious look from her dark, hooded eyes. "But Gemma," she said, "without these bones, I'm not *me*. Without these bones, I am nothing."

That's what she claimed, but Gemma had to wonder how true that was. From what she'd heard, Lena—the ghoul who'd been the princess before *this* iteration of Solena—had been a much different girl. Meek, uncertain of herself, uncomfortable in her role of power. Quite unlike the Solena before her now. It seemed to Gemma that even without a human body, there was some core to a ghoul's identity that carried through no matter whose bones they wore.

But according to Solena, they relied entirely on those bones for every part of their identity. They didn't even have their own names. When Gemma had asked after Solena's "real" name, Solena had dispassionately informed her she had none. When Gemma had asked what her first name had been, Solena claimed she couldn't remember. When she'd asked what Solena's last name had been—back when she was still a lady-in-waiting—Solena said it didn't matter. That name was dead, and only Solena, her present name, mattered now. It seemed a bizarre practice to Gemma, not to mention confusing. Whenever they spoke of the ghoul who'd wanted to kill the king, Solena's superior, it was always "Pila" now, and yet she had only been Pila for a few days, and before that, Pila had been her own person, a friendly, somewhat hapless handmaiden. It felt wrong to sully the poor girl's name with the actions of a gluttonous ghoul.

Solena had also provided some clarity on another matter: why Gryphon had never caught that rot-like scent around her, even though she was the one who'd left it that night in the king's apartments. Just like Pila had explained, when a ghoul traveled through shadow, what they were really doing was somehow vacating their human bones, melting back into that liminal space between this world and the next. Gemma still didn't quite understand how that worked—where did their human bodies go when they did that, and how did they step back into them?—but it made sense that a ghoul would only leave that particular stench while employing that trick. Outside of the shadows, Solena said, they should smell like any ordinary human.

They fell into silence for the next few minutes as servants whisked in and out of the bedchamber, packing more of Solena's belongings away. Gemma watched all the activity without really seeing it, and Solena lounged in her chair, looking petulant.

Then Solena said abruptly, "So, will you be one of them?"

"One of who?"

"The guards accompanying us home, of course." Solena's eyes were fixed on her fingers, running over a strand of her own hair, and her tone was as careless as ever. Yet Gemma sensed a weight to the query, one that belied Solena's casual pose. "Are you going to be one of them?"

That was another of King Victor's conditions on the princess. A score of his own guards would accompany her party home all the way back to the Desert Kingdom, though it was a long journey. At least six weeks, according to Solena, and then another six weeks back. The king didn't feel right sending a ghoul to one day rule the Desert Kingdom, even though Solena had assured him she had the kingdom's best interest at heart, and even though, she'd pointed out, there was no good alternative. Still, the king wanted to send Solena back with some supervision, just to ensure she wouldn't get up to any mischief.

So a score of Glen soldiers would accompany Princess Solena home, and they weren't the only ones—the king's supernatural investigators, Sabine and Demetri, were joining their party as well. Once they'd arrived in the Desert Kingdom, they would stay long enough to ensure everything was running smoothly there. Sabine and Demetri, of course, were meant to use their expertise to investigate anything potentially troublesome. But if all went well, they would leave Solena to rule her kingdom and return home later this summer.

"Well?" Solena demanded in a peevish tone. "Are you going to come with us?"

"I don't know," Gemma admitted. Honestly. The choice wasn't fully hers to make, though she could always put her name forward. And King Victor would probably like her to go, given her experience with Solena already. But...

But she wasn't sure how much longer she was going to *be* a guard. She wasn't sure it was what she wanted to do anymore.

"Well, you should." Solena spoke decisively, as if her opinion decided the matter. "Come with us, I mean. As a guard...or just as yourself."

Gemma turned a nonplussed look on the princess. "And what would I do in the Desert Kingdom? As myself?"

"Help me, of course," Solena said with all the puffed-up self-importance of a princess. "I'm the only ghoul left of our original cabal, but no telling how long that will last. None of the ladies died by those special bullets of yours like Pila did, which means they'll be back eventually. Maybe not for another hundred years...or maybe only in another few months."

"What's your point?" Gemma asked.

"I could use an ally. Especially an ally who can see a ghoul when they don't want to be seen. If the ladies ever come clawing back and try to take my throne—which I'm sure they will," Solena added acidly. "Knowing them. Oh, Kova will definitely want revenge, the little bootlicker..."

"Well. I'd be happy to kill Kova again."

"*You* didn't kill her at all. I did."

"With my help."

Solena laughed. "Exactly my point! So you'll come then?"

"Maybe," Gemma mused. "Maybe I will."

⸺◆⸺

The blade whistled through the air as it left Gemma's hand, spinning away to embed itself in the practice target. She was alone out on the training grounds in the barracks, and no wonder, for there was little daylight left. Though the weather was finally turning warmer, it had been a dreary day, the sky sunless and overcast. Now the gloom of twilight falling around Gemma was just as gray and dreary, bleaching her surroundings of color. She'd need to head inside soon, but for now, she let another blade fly.

The faint sound of footsteps alerted her to another presence coming to join her on the grounds. She didn't turn to see who it was. And she didn't flinch when someone leaned in close to her, whispered words ghosting over the back of her neck as she took aim. "So it wasn't just a fluke."

Gemma's blade left her hand and hurtled through the air. It buried itself to the far left of the target's center. Gemma decided to blame that on the distraction that had come up behind her.

Coolly, Gemma turned to face that distraction. "What wasn't?"

Klaus—standing so close she could have kissed him—let out a quiet laugh. "Your shot, of course. In the graveyard, when you took down Pila." He nodded, indicating the targets over her shoulder. "It wasn't a fluke."

"Well. It's not quite the same." Gemma cast a self-deprecating glance over her shoulder towards the practice targets. "As you can see." She wanted to get better with knives. A certain ghoulish princess had inspired her.

"Still. It wasn't a fluke. Was it?"

Gemma sighed. "No. It wasn't." She retreated from him, running a hand down her braid. She could tell him anything, she reminded herself, so she told him the one thing she hadn't yet confided in him. "My sight's been getting better for a while now. According to the physicians, it's been fully healed for a few weeks. At least, so far as they can tell from my physical exams."

There was no judgment on Klaus's face, nor any exasperation. "Why didn't you say anything?"

"Because I didn't trust it. Truthfully, I still don't. Not completely."

And she told him. She told him what Jesine had told her, that her sight might be forever compromised, thanks to the witch's dark magic. She told him how she'd begun to hallucinate, just as Jesine had predicted. Then she told him what Harper had explained, that her visions weren't hallucinations but a special kind of seeing.

As useful as that ability might be, Gemma still felt like she couldn't trust her eyes. Maybe she never would. But she also remembered what Sabine told her. That she needed to find someone she could trust. Someone who could always be there to tell her what was real.

She was hoping she'd found that person.

When she was done talking, Klaus lifted his head to gaze out at the grounds, growing darker and hazier every second. "I wish you'd told me."

Gemma made a rueful face. She turned, shrugging a shoulder, inviting him to join her as she crossed the grounds to retrieve her blades from the practice targets. "I should have," she admitted. She stopped at the first target and braced a hand against it to pull her knife free. "And I should have picked up a rifle weeks ago when the physicians first cleared me. Then I wouldn't have spent all this time being afraid."

Klaus mirrored her, pulling one of her knives from the second target. "Afraid that you still wouldn't be able to shoot, you mean?"

"No. Afraid that I *could* shoot."

Klaus pulled another blade free and turned to face her, his astonishment plain on his face. "Why would you be afraid of that?"

"Because..." Gemma dropped her arm to her side, a knife dangling from her fingers. "Because what if that's all I was?"

Klaus looked baffled.

Gemma began to twirl the blade in her fingers back and forth, thinking through her thoughts as she spoke then. "When I first woke up in Jesine's cabin after she healed me—when she and Sabine told me my sight had been damaged, maybe forever—I can't explain what that was like. How empty and hopeless it felt. Because I thought I was meant to be here, to do this. To serve the royal family as a sharpshooter and tracker. And if I couldn't do that, then what was I? What use could I possibly be?"

Klaus looked incredulous. "Gemma, you're worth a lot more than just those things. I told you before—"

"I know," she interrupted him. "I know that now. But I didn't before. And I started to accept it, you know, accept that I would have to be something else. And that was terrifying. But also freeing." She shook her head. "So when the physicians told me I was fine, that I could go back to being a sharpshooter...I don't know. It felt like a trap."

"Because you didn't want to get your hopes up?" There was a knowing gleam in Klaus's eyes. "Or because you would *be* trapped in a sharpshooter's life?"

"Both. I think."

Klaus nodded slowly. Then he turned to pull another of her blades from the next practice target. "So is that why you're leaving? Leaving the guard, I mean?"

"Oh. I was going to talk to you about that."

"Well, that's kind of you."

"I am leaving." It was official. She'd given her notice of resignation first thing this morning after taking the night to think about it. Truly, she'd been thinking about it ever since she'd first decided to quit in a fit of despair.

Her reasons had changed. She wasn't leaving the guard because she thought she couldn't be a soldier anymore, or because she thought she was a liability. She was leaving for herself. Because she wanted to see what else she could be.

"I'm going with Princess Solena to the Desert Kingdom," she told Klaus. She wished he would turn to look at her, but he just kept on down the line of practice targets, pulling her blades free, tossing them into a little pile near his feet. There was still a smidge of gray daylight on the horizon, but it had grown dark enough that she couldn't make out his expression.

"I don't know how long I'll stay with her," she added, raising her voice, "but, well, I'd thought. If you went as one of the guards in King Victor's contingent, then we could—I mean, we'd still be…"

Gemma let her words trail off as Klaus pulled the last knife from the furthest target, then turned to make his way back to her. She felt strangely vulnerable, standing there in the darkening dusk, in the cold of the oncoming night. Waiting to see how he would react. Waiting to see if he understood.

Waiting to see if he wanted the same thing she did.

The wait was interminable. Klaus was silent as he tramped back to her through the thin layer of fog settling in the air, as he bent, halfway, to pick up the little pile of knives he'd accumulated, cupping them in the circle of his arms. And when he came close enough to drop that pile at her feet, his scarred face was unreadable, his eyes solemn and his mouth drawn.

"I mean, I could do that," he said, and Gemma could tell by his blunt tone that it was not what he wanted to do. She fought to keep her own expression impassive, even as her heart sank. She opened her mouth to say it was all right, to assure him it didn't matter, that she understood—but before she could, he went on, "Or I could just quit the guard too. And come with you on my own. That way, however long you stay there—or wherever you go next—I'll be with you."

Gemma was so stunned that she said rather stupidly, "You can't quit the guard."

Klaus snorted. "Why not? You did. And you've always been much more dedicated to it than I ever was. I was only ever trying to escape Gryphon, and as it turns out, I couldn't even do that. He turned up here anyway."

Gemma realized she was fiddling with the knife in her hand again and forced herself to stop, letting it drop to the ground with the rest of the blades. "So this is you running away from him again? Because I thought you had more or less resolved your differences—"

"Gemma," Klaus broke in, and though his tone was exasperated, his dark eyes were soft like the mist enveloping them. "This is me saying I want to be with you. For always. No matter where you go or what you do...I want to be there too."

Gemma felt as though her heart was going to beat right out of her chest. She swallowed, trying to dispel the lump in her throat. "Well," she said when she found her voice, "Solena will be glad you're coming. Since you're her favorite guard."

Klaus stepped forward, glancing down to make sure he didn't trip over the pile of knives between them. A smile twisted his lips. "Oh, Solena will be glad, will she?"

"And I'm glad." Gemma reached up to slide one hand behind Klaus's neck. The other she laid over his heart. "You were never much of a guard. But you're my favorite too."

Klaus leaned down, resting his forehead against hers. "I love you," he breathed, and then he pressed his lips to hers, sealing them with a kiss. As he wrapped his arms around her, enclosing her within a warm embrace, Gemma heard his words in her head. *No matter where you go, I want to be there too.*

That's all I need, Gemma thought. He was all she needed. Someone to trust. Someone to love.

She could figure out the rest. What to do, what to be. Who she was without the guard.

She had all the time in the world.

Don't Miss the Next Book in the Series!

THE WRAITH QUEEN

While snowed in at the forbidding castle in the Mountain Kingdom, Kinsley and the witch Castel discover a ghostly presence haunting the castle. And when that presence lures Kinsley out into the frozen landscape, Castel is the only one who can find him and bring him back...

Turn the page for a sneak peek!

Kinsley woke in warmth and light, but inside, he felt cold. Voices and images swam inside his head, dreams or memories, he could not tell. Some of the voices were worried, muffled, words lost to wind and snow. The images were blurry, hazed in dark clouds and a blinding white sheet, images of faces he knew. Brows furrowed in concern, mouths shaping his name.

One image stood out more starkly than the rest: a forbidding hunk of dark stone topped with pointed spires as sharp as lances. The tallest of them vanished into the gloomy sky overhead, swallowed up by those dark clouds. The grim structure was dotted with red-orange lights, like a million little eyes in the face of some hideous eldritch monster.

The castle. In the Mountain Kingdom. Briar's castle.

Slowly, Kinsley opened his eyes.

He lay in a bed. A large, soft bed, much nicer than the one he was used to back home in the barracks of Glen Castle. And the room around the bed was large too, and warm and cozily lit and filled with rich furnishings. It was all very nice—an innately comforting place to wake up in—but it was completely unfamiliar to Kinsley.

Then the young woman sitting at his bedside swam into focus, and a rush of relief sank into Kinsley. Because her face *was* familiar.

"Princess," he croaked in greeting.

Princess Briar had been frowning down at a few sheets of paper in her hands, but at the sound of Kinsley's voice, she snapped her head up. "Kinsley!" Setting her papers aside, she stood, her frown deepening as she leaned over him. "Thank the stars. I was prepared to sleep in here, you know, if you didn't wake up. I wasn't going to leave your side."

Kinsley felt his lips form a weak little smile. "Hardly appropriate behavior for a princess."

"Yes, well, we both know how appropriate I can be." Briar smiled back at him. "*I* know my virtue and I would be perfectly safe with you, and that's all that matters. Now." Her smile vanished, her forehead creasing in concern again. "How are you feeling?"

Cold, was Kinsley's first thought, but he didn't say that. It was his job to worry over Briar, not the other way around. "I'm perfectly fine, Your Highness." He tried to sit up, pushing back against the plush pillow behind his head, but Briar pushed him back down, rather unceremoniously.

"You need to rest," she told him. She put a hand to his forehead, which only made Kinsley feel even more ridiculous. Being ministered to by his own royal charge.

"I'm fine," he insisted again. "Except—" Except. Except when he tried to remember how he'd gotten here, he couldn't. "What happened?"

"What do you remember?"

Not much, Kinsley thought. He cast his mind back. He'd been traveling here to the Mountain Kingdom over the last week, along with a few other guards. Princess Briar had sent a telegram asking them to join her here, in her old castle. They'd been making their way up this mountain when a blizzard struck, Kinsley suddenly recalled. It had been hard-going, but they were nearly at the mountain's peak. And then—

"You collapsed," Briar informed him. "Fell from your horse. The physician's been to see you, and he said you hadn't a fever. Only a case of over-exhaustion and mild hypothermia."

"Mild what?"

"It means you got too cold."

"Oh. I could have told you that."

Briar smiled again, though it didn't reach her eyes enough to erase the look of critical worry there. Still, she stepped back, lowering herself into her seat. It was only then, as she wrapped the folds of a voluminous velvet dressing gown tightly about her, that he realized how dressed down she was. Her sheet of white-blond hair, usually done up or held back from her face, lay around her shoulders, slightly rumpled.

"I've taken you from your bed," he said, chagrined.

"Well, in a manner of speaking." Briar looked puzzled. "I told you, I was going to sleep here. I didn't want to leave you until I saw for myself you were all right."

"No, I meant—" He gestured towards her, noticing his own arm was encased in the sleeve of a pajama top he did not own. A rather nicer pajama top than he *would* own, the brushed wool unbearably soft. "Where are we?" he asked, staring at his arm a moment longer before looking around the room. "Is this—"

"My castle." Briar nodded. "Well. Technically, it's my cousin Laurel's castle now. Since I abdicated to her and all that. But, yes. You're back." She grimaced. "Back in this haunted old ruin."

Something about the word *haunted* prickled at Kinsley in a most disquieting way, but he shrugged the feeling away and said, "It doesn't look much like a ruin."

It was true. The room he found himself in was covered in plush, clean rugs and littered with gleaming mahogany furniture, from the nightstand beside him to the ornate wardrobe, chest of drawers, and small writing desk in the corner. There were no windows, but the walls were paneled in wood, save for the one opposite him, which was covered in a tastefully patterned wallpaper.

"Yes, well." Briar leaned back in her chair, a deep, cushy armchair big enough for two people—three, if they were small. "Laurel has worked hard to improve the place over the last eighteen months. And trust me, there are still plenty of rooms in this castle that would give you nightmares, or at least, allergies—all the dust and mold, you know." She waved a negligent hand. "But I made sure you were afforded one of the nicer, recently renovated rooms."

At least she had said *room*, Kinsley thought with some dismay, and not *apartment*. Or worse yet, *suite*. "Princess," he said, trying to sound grateful, "this room is far too nice for me. I should stay in the barracks or wherever the rest of the soldiers are sleeping—"

"First of all, I would *not* consign you to a barracks while you are recovering from hypothermia, Kinsley." Briar straightened in her chair, looking indignant. "You are ill, and I won't have you sleeping in some musty old dormitory. And secondly, the rest of the soldiers are staying in this same wing of the castle, in the rooms right down the corridor. Granted, most of them are doubling up, but like I said, you're *ill*. And you're an officer and the head of my guard, so you deserve your own room. Understand?"

Kinsley smiled more genuinely this time as he took in the familiar, steely glint in the princess's gray eyes. He had missed Briar, he realized. In that moment, he realized how much he had missed her, and how right it felt to be back by her side. He had not been thrilled when he'd learned she wanted him to join her at this castle here in the Mountain Kingdom, but no matter where he was, it was good to be with her. She *was* his charge, but somehow, she was also like a sister to him.

"I understand," he promised, "but I'm not ill, Briar. I'm just tired."

Briar looked unconvinced. "Well. Get a good night's sleep, and we'll talk more in the morning. All right?"

And Kinsley did not try to argue with her, because truthfully, he was beginning to feel that exhaustion the physician had diagnosed him with. So Briar bid him goodnight and departed. Leaving him quite alone.

Kinsley glanced around the room and shivered. Partly from the cold festering like an open wound inside him, and partly from…well, the room. The quiet of it. The emptiness, now Briar was gone. Kinsley was the sort of person who could stand quite a bit of time on his own, but though this room *was* nicely furnished and more than comfortable, it was somehow…too big, too much. Making him feel his alone-ness quite keenly.

He wasn't just alone. He was lonely.

The thought was a *pang* in his chest, a physical, peculiar kind of pain, like something tugging at his heart, straining the muscles holding it in place. Kinsley had felt lonely for much of his life, though for many years, he almost hadn't noticed the feeling, hadn't been able to name it. It was so much a part of him that it just *was*.

That was life for an orphan.

But then he'd joined the ranks of Prince Garrett's personal company. He found someone to serve, someone he was proud to give his loyalty to. And he'd found friends among the rest of the guard, friends who'd lived lives like his own, or who didn't care what his life had been before joining the guard. Friends who were as loyal to him as he was to Prince Garrett and now Princess Briar.

And then...he'd found someone to love. Someone he'd thought he could trust his heart to.

Castel.

Kinsley's chest tightened at the thought of Castel. He had been wrong to trust himself to Castel, and yet, in that moment, he didn't care. In that moment, he would have given anything to see his face.

He'd decided months ago that he didn't need to trust Castel. He wanted him anyway.

But Castel was not here, so far north, up at the top of the snow-laden mountain, and he wasn't likely to be anytime soon. Not because he couldn't find a way to get here. Isolated though this castle was, treacherous though the way was, Castel could get here if he wanted to. He was a witch. A little blizzard wouldn't stop him. The cold, however, probably would. Kinsley vaguely recalled Castel mentioning how much he hated the cold. As he recalled, he'd grown up in the more temperate Mariner Kingdom and spent much of his long-lived life there.

Kinsley himself would have given anything to be in that more temperate kingdom now. Summer wasn't long off for the Mariner Kingdom, though that was hard to believe, given where he was now. And given how *cold* he was now. His extremities were still numb with cold, his fingers, his face, and even his toes, despite being stuffed into two pairs of thick woolen socks.

Luckily, he discovered that the connected washroom in this chamber was a full bathroom, complete with a large copper tub and pipes pumping in heated water. Kinsley was impressed at that; Queen Laurel really had been busy, he thought, if she'd had modern plumbing installed in the castle. Though he suspected only some of the rooms boasted this amenity.

It seemed a luxury, but, given how cold Kinsley was, he didn't care. He quickly undressed and turned the knob on the bath as far as he could, making the water so hot, it nearly scalded his skin when he climbed in. The tub wasn't even half full when he got into it, but he reclined, leaning his head back beside the rushing tap, the stream of hot water spilling over his shoulder and onto his chest. The room quickly began to fill with steam, spiraling up out of the tub and fogging up the large mirror on the wall. Kinsley closed his eyes as the water level rose, covering his arms above the elbow and most of his chest.

He didn't stay in the tub long after shutting off the water. No matter how good the water felt, finally warming him all the way through, the heat was so intense that it was making him sweat, not to mention increasing his exhaustion tenfold. He didn't want to fall asleep in the bath, and he really thought he might, if he stayed in much longer. So, with a slightly regretful sigh, he stood, rising up out of the warm water and reaching for the fluffy towel he'd left on the stool beside him.

Wrapping the towel around himself, he turned to climb out of the tub.

And froze. Staring at the opposite wall.

Where there were two perfectly formed handprints drawn through the layer of fog covering the mirror.

All the heat that had seeped into Kinsley's body rushed out of him, a preternatural chill taking hold of his insides. He suddenly felt the cold acutely, back in his fingertips, in his toes, whispering over his bare skin, creating gooseflesh along his arms and behind his neck.

Shivering, he stepped out of the tub, so quickly he nearly slipped and fell. He caught himself at the last minute, looking left and right. His heart pounded inside his chest as he took in the rest of the empty bathroom on one side—it was not a large room—and the open door on the other. Leading back into his bedroom.

Taking a deep breath, Kinsley crossed the bathroom quickly, sticking his head out the door. But a quick, searching glance showed the room was still empty; there was no one else there. Even so, he called out, "Hello? Briar?"

But there was no answer.

Shaking his head, Kinsley stepped back into the bathroom. He was trembling from head to toe and not entirely from the cold. Briar could be puckish at times; he was sure she would not shy from pulling a prank on him—she *had* pulled pranks on him in the past—but even she would not be so improper as to sneak in on him while he was naked in his bath. Though, he had seen *her* nearly naked, fresh out of a bath once, but that had been entirely different. It had been an emergency. Her fingers had fallen off, and she'd needed help finding them.

He turned back to the mirror and found the handprints still there. Clear as ever.

Fear washed over him anew. He hadn't realized he'd been trying to convince himself he'd imagined them until his gaze fell upon them again. Rigid, hardly daring to breathe, Kinsley inched towards the mirror, gazing at the handprints. They were sized for an adult, he thought, trying to be clinical as he observed them, trying to adopt a professional demeanor. Just a soldier, investigating strange phenomena. Sized for an adult, but the fingers were long and slender, almost absurdly so.

Eerily so.

Kinsley stepped even closer to the mirror, peering into it. In the space between the handprints, the mirror was beginning to clear, a spot of condensation dripping down the glass, leaving something like a tear track in its wake. As though the mirror was weeping.

Kinsley gazed into the mirror. Into that spot between the handprints.

And a figure materialized through the fog, staring back at him. But it wasn't his own face. It wasn't his reflection.

It was a woman, her visage an utter horror.

Fear gripped Kinsley tight, squeezing his heart inside his chest and trapping the air inside his lungs. It was a swift, instantaneous fear, driving out everything else inside his head. Kinsley had faced horrors before. He worked for Prince Garrett, a monster-hunting, horror-seeking madman, and even before that, his life had hardly been a picnic. Kinsley had seen terrible, grisly things, both in his time serving Prince Garrett and before it.

But never before had anything struck him with such abject terror as the sight of this woman in the mirror.

She was barely a woman. Her eyes were black pits in her lifeless face. Her face was gray and pitted, her flesh like thin scraps of cloth loosely woven together, gaping open over her cheeks and jaw, revealing only darkness beneath. The garments that hung on her emaciated frame seemed spun from shadow—save for the shawl she wore, wrapped around her head and draping her shoulders. That was a grimy white, the cloth wrinkled and tattered, barely holding together.

With a strangled cry, Kinsley recoiled from the mirror, stumbling as he threw himself backwards. He turned his back on the mirror, on the grotesque visage concealed within it. But there he stood, rooted to the spot. He should run from the room, slam the door shut behind him. But he couldn't move. He was frozen.

"Kinsley? Kinsley, are you in here? I dearly hope so, because if I've got the wrong room, this is going to be incredibly awkward."

Kinsley whipped his head, looking around in shock.

A figure appeared in the doorway to the bathroom. Not the spectral figure of that hideous woman in the mirror. No, this figure was much more solid, much more familiar, and frankly, much nicer to look at.

But just as shocking.

Because standing before him, here in this room in the castle of the Mountain Kingdom, was Castel.

Castel was not in a great mood. He'd spent the day hiking up the bloody mountain on his own, in the middle of a blizzard, which would have been bad enough. But a couple of mistakes had made it even worse. First, he had not set out until nearly noon, owing to his staying up a *tad* too late the night before, drinking at a pub in town. Well, he was heading up the bloody mountain to a remote castle; who knew when he might get another good drink?

But setting out so late meant he had little daylight to travel in, and the blizzard caught him early. To make matters even worse, he was sure now that he had been given faulty information about the best route to take up the mountain. He'd gone up the backside, which had proved a treacherous route even without the snowfall making it near impassible.

Granted, he was a witch. He had magic to use, which was probably the only reason he hadn't died coming up that forsaken mountain. But magic wasn't an unlimited resource, especially these days, which meant he had to be frugal in his use of it. He couldn't, say, sustain a warming spell the entire time he traveled, all the way up here. Which meant that now—even though he was finally inside the rotten Mountain Kingdom castle—he was cold, and tired, and *wet*. And cranky.

Still, some of that crankiness bled away when he finally tracked down Kinsley's room and found the guard standing in a warm, steamy bathroom. Clad in only a towel.

"Thank the stars," Castel said, slouching against the bathroom doorframe. The new wave of fatigue that washed over him was staggering, as though his body and mind had been holding it back until he found Kinsley. "I'm *so* glad you aren't some other random Glen soldier. Or worse, a corpse creature. I had nothing."

Kinsley looked shell-shocked, staring at Castel as though *he* was a corpse creature. Castel allowed himself to enjoy that for a moment. He did love shocking Kinsley. It was surprisingly hard to do.

"Nothing?" Kinsley echoed dumbly. Clearly confused.

"No cover story, I mean." Castel removed his fur-lined hat from his head and ruffled a hand through his hair, shaking it out. Despite the hat, it was damp from the snow. "No way to explain my presence here."

Kinsley blinked at him. Once. Twice. He didn't just looked shocked, Castel thought, but almost...shaken. His face was even paler than usual, absolutely bloodless.

Castel frowned. He'd expected Kinsley to be surprised, yes, but he'd hardly been looking to inspire fear. He went on alert, casting a sweeping gaze around the foggy bathroom, wondering what might be wrong. But there was nothing; everything looked perfectly normal.

His gaze snagged on the full tub, and he smiled, flashing a wicked glance Kinsley's way. "You should have waited for me. Too bad. I could use a hot bath."

The shock was fading from Kinsley's face, to be replaced by a very closed expression. "Well, I might have waited," Kinsley said, "if I'd known you were coming. *Here.*"

Castel blinked. There was an edge to Kinsley's usually placid tone, and that wasn't good. "That would have spoiled the surprise," he said breezily.

"Right." Crossing his arms over his chest—pity—Kinsley turned to face him head-on. "What was that you said about not being able to explain your presence here? Because I think you should try to explain it. To me."

"I'm not sure what there is to explain."

"Was that you before?" Kinsley demanded. He pointed a finger over his shoulder without turning away. "With the mirror? Was that meant to be some kind of joke?"

"The mirror?" Castel frowned again, flicking a puzzled glance over Kinsley's shoulder. "What do you mean?"

"I mean, how long have you been in here? Were you the one that—" Kinsley broke off as he spun around towards the mirror. When he remained silent, staring into it for several long seconds, Castel stepped up behind him, gazing into the reflective glass as well. It was a bit foggy from the hot bath, though the steam was already clearing, droplets of water dripping down it. Aside from that, it looked perfectly normal.

"There was—" Kinsley sounded strained.

"What?" Castel asked sharply. He was still confused, but something was going on here. Kinsley wouldn't start acting like a nutter for no reason. He was too steady for that. Nor would he behave this way to mess with Castel or make him angry. He was too honest for that.

Kinsley rounded on him again. "How long have you been in here?"

"I just came in." Something was going on, Castel thought, something that had nothing to do with him, but he couldn't help but bristle at Kinsley's accusatory tone. "About two minutes ago. You heard me come in."

"And that explanation?" Kinsley made a pointed side-step around Castel, exiting through the bathroom door and moving out into the adjoining room. His tone was clipped, even brusque. "I still haven't heard it."

Castel was becoming annoyed now. Following Kinsley out into the bedroom, he said, "Like I said. I'm not sure what there is to explain."

"What you're doing here, for one thing." Kinsley started pulling open drawers in the dresser, seemingly at random. Castel wondered if he even knew what he was looking for. "No. Not what." He straightened from the drawers. "*How* are you here, Castel? How did you even know I was going to be here?"

"Well." Castel shifted from one foot to the other, wiping his expression clean. *That* was a very specific question he'd been hoping to avoid. "I'm a witch, love."

"How fascinating that I never knew that about you." Kinsley's blue eyes were like ice. "But it's not an answer. What, have you made me some kind of beacon you can always find? Have you cast some...magical tracking spell on me?" He pinched the bridge of his nose between two fingers. "Or did you just follow me here?"

"Well." Castel coughed. He perched on the edge of an armchair and clasped his hands before him. "I mean. One of those things might be true." It all sounded very disturbing and stalker-like when Kinsley said it like *that*. And Castel would never stoop to such low behavior for a man.

Unless, perhaps, that man was Kinsley. Castel had been alive for many, many decades. He'd had all that time to build up a lot of rules about things like trysts and feelings. Namely, that the two shouldn't mix.

But he had broken all his rules for Kinsley.

"You followed me," Kinsley said flatly. He strode swiftly from the dresser drawers to the wardrobe, yanking it open. Taking out a black dressing robe hanging inside, he pulled the robe on, not allowing his towel to drop until the robe was firmly tied about his waist. "For how *long* have you been following me?"

"I'm not sure that's really relevant." Castel's reply was waspish. He hadn't the best time of it, after all, climbing that bloody mountain. For *him*, for Kinsley, who didn't seem pleased to see him at all. Now he sat here in his cold, wet clothing, which he'd rather hoped to be out of by now. "And I don't understand why you're so upset." After all, they had been meeting in secret like this for nearly three months now.

"Because you're here, Castel!" Kinsley blew up. Kinsley *never* blew up. Even when he was angry, Kinsley was the type to get quieter and quieter, his anger a cool, even thing. He was never explosive. "*Here* in this castle, in the Mountain Kingdom. In *Briar's* kingdom. You do know Briar is here, don't you?"

"Well, I assumed that was why you are here," Castel said coldly, "so, yes." Blasted Princess Briar. It *always* came back to her.

"And you do remember that Briar doesn't like you very much, don't you?"

"And? She's been in Glen City these past few months, hasn't she, when we've been meeting there?"

"She's been in Glen *Castle*," Kinsley corrected him, "while we've met on my off-duty time out in the city. Or sometimes even outside the city. Not under the same roof as her, while I'm working!"

"I'm sorry," Castel retorted. "I didn't realize you were on duty at this very moment. The princess ordered you to take a bath, is that right?"

Kinsley took in a deep breath, though by the tense set of his shoulders and the awful look on his face—part-exasperated, part-exhausted—it didn't do much to calm him. But when he spoke again, it was with that more Kinsley-like, quiet anger. "You can't be here, Castel."

The words hurt more than they should have. More than Castel liked. Stones, that they hurt at all was a catastrophe.

Still, he would die before he let Kinsley see how much he was hurting. "Well, I'm not staying in that dingy little village."

"Then find another room," Kinsley said, "because you're not staying here."

Now Castel's annoyance blossomed into his own anger. It was a quiet anger too, only his ran hot instead of cold, like molten lava bubbling beneath the cracked surface of the earth. "So we're doing this again? Only, I thought we'd played out this game."

"What game? What are you talking about?"

Castel pushed himself to his feet and wove his way through the room, past the ornate coffee table and the dresser, to stand before Kinsley. To face him fully. He shoved his hands into his coat pockets so Kinsley wouldn't see them clenched in anger. "When I came to you three months ago. After the holidays, after—" After. After he had helped Prince Garrett and his friends out in the southern Glen woods, after he'd turned against his own kind to help them. Not that he had much love for his own kind, especially the witches he'd been working with, but still. He'd taken risks.

The look on Kinsley's face said he knew exactly what he meant, but instead he said in a tight voice, "After you'd been dogging me for weeks, you mean?"

Well, that wasn't true. Yes, Castel had appealed to Kinsley before that day three months ago. Twice, he had appealed to him. But only twice, and long before that last, and final, time. "When I came to you three months ago," Castel repeated, "I told you I would never bother you again. I told you if you turned me away, I would never come back." He was appalled to find he had to fight to keep his voice steady. "*You're* the one who said yes. You're the one who told me *not* to go. So. Have you changed your mind?"

Kinsley closed his eyes. Castel could see by the pained look on his face that he had not changed his mind. And he, Castel, didn't know how to feel about that. Triumphant, relieved. Bitter, dismayed.

He thought maybe he loathed himself a little bit. That he felt even a little *relieved* to see Kinsley in pain. To know that he, in some way, was causing that pain.

He didn't want it to be this way.

"No, I haven't." Kinsley spoke without opening his eyes. "I haven't changed my mind. But I'm tired, Castel. It's been a long day, and I don't—I just want to sleep."

The words were out of Castel's mouth before he could stop. "We can just sleep."

Kinsley's eyes flew open. "No." The sharp snap of the word cut Castel to the quick. "We don't do that. You know that. There are rules, Castel. No attachments, no promises."

The rest of it went unspoken. *No feelings. No love.* "Right." They were not Castel's rules. Not anymore, anyway. He'd given up trying to control his feelings for Kinsley a long time ago, long before Kinsley had agreed to see him again.

But it was the only way. The only way Castel could have him. And pathetic as it made him, he would take what he could get.

"Right," Castel said again. He quickly fastened the buttons on his coat, even though it was plenty warm in here. It was not so warm in the rest of the castle, and it seemed that was where he would be spending the night. In some other, darker, colder place. "Fine. I'll go. But I'm not going far."

"Go where you want." Kinsley half-turned from him, bowing his head and rubbing at his forehead. "It doesn't matter."

Well. That was that, then. Castel swept from the room, pausing only long enough to be sure the corridor outside was clear before he went. He wasn't going to stay any longer, *beg* any longer. He had humiliated himself enough as it was.

It wasn't really all that late. Nine o'clock perhaps, perhaps a bit later. But the castle was quiet and dimly lit even so. Quieter and dimmer still the deeper Castel went, traversing narrow side corridors and back stairwells to stay out of sight. Colder, too. The room Kinsley had been allotted had clearly been renovated, but there were parts of the castle that hadn't been, parts where cobwebs still gathered in dark corners, parts where dust layered the stone floor and grime caked the bare walls.

Parts where ghosts still lingered in the shadows.

This castle was full of ghosts. Figuratively, yes, but also literally. As a witch, Castel was sensitive to their vibrations, and this castle positively reeked with spectral energy. As he made his way through the dilapidated castle, he moved through pockets of air humming with ghostly auras, cold spots and patches of unnatural darkness. None of it bothered him much. One grew used to that sort of thing, as a witch who'd lived as long as he had. And who was as sensitive as he was. Not all witches could see ghosts, but Castel had a penchant for it.

He turned a corner from one narrow corridor into the next and stopped. A low stairwell lay at the opposite end of this corridor, and a modern sconce set with a gear-bulb fixture hung over it. The light fixture was a good sign; it meant he was moving into a slightly more refurbished part of the castle. He wanted to stay somewhere out of the way, someplace he wouldn't be found, but he wouldn't sleep in *complete* ruin and disarray.

Still, he stopped at the sight of the fixture. Because the gear bulb was flickering, giving off a low *buzz-buzz-buzz*.

That wasn't completely out of the ordinary. A gear bulb might flicker like that if its winding mechanism was loose, or if the device was very old and draining its stores of elarium.

But this bulb was flickering for neither of those reasons.

"I'm a witch, darling," Castel said aloud to the seemingly empty corridor. "I've probably been alive for longer than you've been dead. I'm not afraid of any ghost."

For a moment, the gear bulb's flickering seemed to intensify, flashing back and forth, the *buzzing* growing louder. Castel sighed. Most ghosts meant no harm; most of the time, they weren't even all that aware of their own existence. But some of them liked to cause trouble.

Some of them were outright violent. Capable of causing actual injury. Castel wouldn't be surprised if this castle housed at least a few of those. Given its history.

Still, he could tell this particular spirit was not one of those. This one was of the troublemaker variety. With a sigh, Castel strode forward down the corridor, hands in his pockets, completely unconcerned.

When he mounted the first step at the end of the corridor, a dark, grayish figure suddenly appeared, flickering into sight on the landing before him.

Unafraid though he was, Castel had to fight the urge to flinch. It was instinctual, even when he knew it was coming. The figure before him made a nasty sight; it was a woman, fairly young, with a face as white as a sheet and bloodshot eyes. Her dark hair was matted on the left side where her skull was split open and sticky with congealed blood. Interestingly enough, she did not look like a corpse creature. Perhaps she *had* died before Castel was born.

It didn't matter. Castel didn't stop, didn't hesitate. He climbed the three steps that separated her from him, then walked right through her, turning left to ascend another staircase. A slick, disturbingly cold feeling sluiced through him as he passed through her, but that was all. She did him no harm, and Castel continued on in search of a place to spend the night.

Still. He could not help feeling vaguely...unsettled...as he moved through the castle, mounting staircase after staircase, climbing higher and higher. He couldn't quite pinpoint why until he finally found a suite of rooms to occupy in a secluded wing near the back of the castle. The rooms obviously hadn't been used in quite some time, though they were lush and spacious, likely once belonging to someone important in the royal family. There weren't any pipes to pump in water, nor gear-bulb fixtures, but there were plenty of unused candles and a couple of old oil lamps, as well as a fine porcelain tub. Hot water wasn't a problem; he could provide that himself.

Still, he hesitated after he scoped out the suite, lingering by the single window in the bedroom. He glanced out into the darkness, but that was all he could see: darkness, the veiled starlight too faint to give form to the vague shapes on the grounds far below him. He sensed no spectral energies in this suite, but he still felt vaguely uneasy for reasons he couldn't identify.

Then he realized. The ghost he'd seen back on that stairwell.

She hadn't dissipated after he'd walked through her.

At least, he didn't *think* she had. He hadn't looked back, exactly, but he had a notion that she'd still been there, just visible out of the corner of his eye. And she should have dissipated. The power Castel carried inside him, the magic he stored, should have suppressed her energy, dampened the strength of her enough to make her vanish. He hadn't done any spell; he didn't need to. It was a bit like...the one power cancelled the other out. The magic, and the ghost.

That this one hadn't been dispelled by his touch suggested an unusual strength to the spirit's energy. A very unusual strength.

And that was why Castel felt so unsettled.

There was something very wrong in this castle.

In this Rapunzel-inspired novella, Demetri and Sabine get more than they bargained for when they investigate a ghost story in a dark forest. Sign up for the author's newsletter and download your copy of *Don't Go Into the Woods* for FREE!

WWW.ELIZABETHKKING.COM

Scan the QR code to sign up now:

Acknowledgements

Ghoul Girl was the first book I wrote after a two-year hiatus from writing, most of which fell during the pandemic. Needless to say, coming back to writing was something of a recovery process, one that took another few years. As such, I must give my many thanks to Emilie, who continues to provide the most amazing feedback. This story needed quite a bit of work and improvement, even after several drafts and rounds of edits, and without that amazing feedback, I could not have gotten this story into the final version you read here now.

I also must thank my wonderful family who provided much needed support and love throughout the difficult process of working on this book. Thank you for listening to my sometimes unintelligible musings on my problems with this story, and thank you for your words of encouragement.

I also want to thank the entire team at Miblart for the book's beautiful cover. Each cover is more stunning than the last. Thank you. Thank you also to Saumya Singh, who created the wonderful map for this book.

And lastly, to all you wonderful readers. Your continued support of my stories means more to me than you could ever know. Thank you.

GLOSSARY OF TERMS

THE FIVE KINGDOMS

The Mountain Kingdom

Princess Briar's home kingdom. Currently ruled by Briar's cousin.

The Glen Kingdom

Originally ruled by Demetri's family, the Georgas, until their fall. Currently ruled by King Victor and his son, Prince Garrett.

The Mariner Kingdom

Princess Snow's kingdom. Currently ruled by a council of lords.

The Forest Kingdom

A fallen kingdom. The last king vacated the throne 150 years ago.

The Desert Kingdom

Located far to the south. Little is known about this kingdom.

―――◄O►―――

MAGICAL ELEMENTS

Fairies

These woodland creatures have green skin, black eyes, and large wings. Though at peace with humans, they retain the ability to curse them. They are forbidden to kill humans, and humans cannot kill fairies without dire consequences.

Djinn

Mortal enemies of the fairies, the djinn are confined to a shadow world. Theirs is the ability to grant wishes. They gain freedom from their confinement by feeding off the life force of descendants of the royal families. They can be identified by the blue markings on their faces; however, they can shapeshift into other forms.

Witches

Witches can only access magic through fairies, usually by spilling and consuming fairy blood. Witches also must make a deal with dark forces to access magic. This deal grants them long life, but guarantees an eternity of torment once they die.

Were-wolves

The were-wolves were created when a witch cursed the last king of the Forest Kingdom to become a beast. The curse is tied to the moon and continues to affect the descendants of the last Forest king. While in some cases, the bite of a were-wolf can pass along the curse, most who are bitten go mad and die.

Naiads

Also known as mermaids, the naiads once had to hunt and eat humans to survive. Now free of that curse, they live in the sea but can assume a human form when they wish to.

Demons

Little is known about these terrifying creatures, other than they kill quite gruesomely. They are believed to hail from a dark realm and can only appear in the world when summoned by a witch.

The Gift

This term commonly refers to the pact that ended the ancient war between fairies and humans. Specifically, the Gift was a gift of fairy blood, bestowed upon the five original royal families.

Elarium

A mineral unique to the Five Kingdoms, which is capable of powering various devices, including bulbs, mechanical devices, vehicle engines, and more.

CAST OF CHARACTERS

MEMBERS OF THE ROYAL FAMILIES

Princess Briar – a princess of the Mountain Kingdom. Abdicated her throne and currently lives in the Glen Kingdom. A "corpse creature," blessed with supernatural strength and speed.

Prince Garrett – crown prince of the Glen Kingdom and heir to the throne. Romantically involved with Princess Briar.

Demetri *(formerly prince)* – Was crown prince of the Glen Kingdom until his family was deposed. Now works as a monster hunter for the current Glen royals.

King Victor – the king of the Glen Kingdom and Prince Garrett's father.

Princess Snow – a princess of the Mariner Kingdom. Once betrothed to Prince Garrett. Hexed and killed by her evil stepmother, the witch Delphine.

Queen Laurel – the queen of the Mountain Kingdom and Briar's cousin.

Gryphon *(formerly prince)* – older half-brother of Prince Garrett. Was the crown prince of the Glen Kingdom until his exile. Also a descendant of the last Forest king.

Queen Alivia – the late queen of the Glen Kingdom and mother to Gryphon. Died of illness when Gryphon was a child.

Princess Solena – the last surviving heir to the Desert Kingdom.

PRINCESS SOLENA'S RETINUE

Tashi – handmaiden to Princess Solena.
Pila – handmaiden to Princess Solena.
Lady Kova – Princess Solena's first lady-in-waiting.
Lady Ilana – Princess Solena's lady-in-waiting. Flirtatious.
Lady Marisel – Princess Solena's lady-in-waiting.
Lady Danya – Princess Solena's lady-in-waiting.

WITCHES

Jesine – a good witch from a long line of good witches. The most powerful known witch in the world. Healed Gemma and saved her life.

Adela – a bad witch hunted by Ansel. Assisted in an attempt to control and kill Prince Garrett's brother, Gryphon. Injured Gemma and damaged her sight. Killed by Jesine.

Castel – a bad witch who likes to play both sides. Used to work for the sea witch, Sohalia.

Malina – an ancient bad witch with a mysterious background.

Harper – a bad witch who has a history with Jesine and Ansel. Currently imprisoned in Glen Castle.

GLEN KINGDOM SOLDIERS

Gemma – a tracker and sharpshooter. Accompanied Prince Garrett to the Forest Kingdom when they encountered Garrett's brother Gryphon.

Klaus – a tracker, new to Prince Garrett's company. Served Garrett's exiled brother, Gryphon, until they had a falling-out.

Sabine – served as a guard for Princess Briar. Left her service to work with Demetri as a monster hunter.

Kinsley – personal bodyguard to Princess Briar. Was once romantically involved with the witch Castel.

Roy – an archer and sometimes Prince Garrett's medic. Accompanied Prince Garrett to the Forest Kingdom when they encountered Garrett's brother Gryphon.

Spencer – a soldier in Prince Garrett's company. Accompanied Prince Garrett to the Forest Kingdom when they encountered Garrett's brother Gryphon.

Gallia – a new soldier, usually serves in Princess Briar's personal guard.

Beckett – a veteran soldier in Prince Garrett's company.

Falcon – an archer who served Prince Garrett. Killed by the were-wolf Viveca in the Forest Kingdom.

Evans – a solder in Prince Garrett's company. Killed by a were-wolf bite in the Forest Kingdom.

OTHER FAIRYTALE CHARACTERS

Ansel – a witch hunter and brother to Isabelle. Killed a cannibalistic witch with Isabelle when they were kids.

Isabelle – sister to Ansel and romantically involved with Gryphon. Was turned into a beta were-wolf when bitten by Gryphon.

The Dark Fairy *(full name: Tenalabralilah)* – the fairy who cursed Princess Briar and her kingdom to sleep and rot for a hundred years. Killed when Briar took her wings and made her mortal.

Perpetua – a naiad who lived in the Mariner Kingdom. Was romantically involved with Demetri. Sacrificed her life to save the rest of the naiads.

Viveca – a power-hungry were-wolf and descendant of the last Forest king. Attempted to use Gryphon in a plot to create more powerful were-wolves. Killed Falcon and tried to kill Klaus. Former paramour of Klaus.

ABOUT THE AUTHOR

ELIZABETH K. KING is a fantasy and horror writer. Over the years, she has nurtured her love of monsters through TV shows like *Buffy the Vampire Slayer*, *Supernatural*, and *Grimm*. She spends her time writing in her gothic study and roaming the Shire (her backyard) with her cocker spaniel, Blue. She lives in Houston, Texas.

You can find Elizabeth online at www.elizabethkking.com, on Instagram @elizabeth_k_king, and on her Facebook page, Elizabeth K. King, Author.